BORING GIRLS

A NOVEL
SARA TAYLOR

eCw

For Lance Webber, my friend —
and the blue sky over Griffith Park

It seems like everyone I talk to wants to know two things. One is whether I'm a serial killer or a mass murderer. The way I understand it, a serial killer kills people over a length of time and doesn't get caught for a while. A mass murderer does it all in one go and gets caught in the act. I'm going to have to leave it up to them to decide, because Fern and I did both, and I'm really not an expert.

People like to label things. The news people need to know what to call us in the headlines. They need to figure out which names to list us beside when they're categorizing killers. I've even heard the word "massacre" used to describe everything that happened at the end. We wanted it to be dramatic, but not because we wanted to make a big scene. It had to be dramatic so that no one would figure out what was happening until we were finished with it. We needed to have time. And we had definitely been thinking about it for ages, so I guess you could call it "premeditated."

The other thing they want to figure out is *why*. And I keep telling them and telling them. I'm always telling them the same thing. But they don't believe me. My answer isn't good enough. They want more. They want to be able to blame something else, and other people, and have a long, complicated chain of events that add up to who Fern and I ended up being so that they can reassure themselves it can't happen to just anyone.

Not just anyone can become a killer. That's what they want to think. It takes special circumstances. Two young ladies from good homes cannot commit a *massacre* without something very evil and unusual happening, the fates aligning to produce this sort of thing.

Well, they're right, but it has nothing to do with my family. They keep asking me about my parents. Did my father hit me? Did my mother verbally abuse me? Did I have a creepy uncle who touched me? Did my *father and mother* touch me? No, I tell them. Over and over. And I'll tell you now: my parents raised me well. I love them very much. And even though they aren't too interested in talking to me right now, which I understand, I will always love them. They were always good to me and my sister. I had a nice childhood. And from what I know of Fern, she did too. And I keep telling them that, and they act like I didn't answer the question. They always ask again.

What about the music I listened to? The music I played? Hasn't it always been easy to point the finger at that sort of thing? The music, the video games? Setting young people out of their minds onto killing rampages? The parents wringing their hands and blaming the vicious rock stars for warping the innocent? Running through their schools with semi-automatic weapons, gunning down *nice* people who listened to *nice* music?

If you want to blame the music, it wouldn't be hard. Fern

6

and I like death metal. Dark, heavy, disgusting death metal. Filled with lyrics that a lot of people don't like. Most of the people in these bands are guys. Angry-looking guys. And I mean, these bands have names that seem tailor-made to be blamed for a *massacre*: Deathbloat? Bloodvomit? Torn Bowel? And, of course, Die Every Death. I can't leave them off the list. Lest we forget.

So how easy is it to point at me and Fern and then slide that pointing finger to our CD collections? Really easy. I mean, let's be real. Torn Bowel? I totally get why somebody's mother wouldn't like the sound of that. Too bad. They're some of the nicest guys I know, and I'm sure they've been hounded by the press about me and Fern, and I feel bad about it. They didn't kill anybody. As much as they might have written songs about murder, they never did it. I'm sure they're facing a lot of questions now, simply because they're our friends. They'll have to explain the music to outraged activists and families and journalists and church folks and talk-show hosts. A lot of bands will. Ones we were friends with, ones we weren't. I'm sad for that. It wasn't their fault.

I'm sure there are murderers in the world who listen to nice acoustic folk music or play the harp or something. Killing people isn't exclusive to those of us who listen to Torn Bowel. People were murderers before there was recorded music. Before radios. Before running water. The whole thing is silly.

You can't blame music. You can blame me.

And you can damn well blame the people who gave me the reason to do it.

I tell them over and over again why we did it. It's very simple. Maybe we should have dealt with it differently. Maybe we should have exercised forgiveness. But in my opinion, some things cannot be forgiven. Some people cannot be looked at with compassion. It's kind of ironic, because the people judging me believe that I should have been compassionate, but they aren't looking at me with any. Everyone is a hypocrite. Everyone, deep within themselves, whether they want to acknowledge it or not, knows that there are things that they would not be able to forgive.

Fern and I could not forgive. And the reason we murdered these people was very simple.

It was for revenge.

BORING
GIRLS

ONE

I have always lived in the same house in Keeleford. My family never moved, I never had to start all over again in a new school. I had that sort of idyllic childhood, growing up on a street with neighbours we knew. A nice community, you know. A normal youth. A good family.

My parents didn't have a ton of money. We have a small bungalow, with three bedrooms, on Shade Street. Next door was Mrs. Collins, who lived alone after her husband died. Across the street was an elderly couple. On the corner lived a family with a few kids younger than me and a dog that always chased us along its side of the backyard fence when we'd walk by. When I was five, my sister, Melissa, was born. There was a little store where Dad would take us to buy candies: red jelly feet, cinnamon-flavoured lips, black licorice sticks. There was a park nearby. Our schools were in walking distance.

My father was a high school teacher, but he worked at a school in a neighbouring town, so luckily Melissa and I would never have to face the social awkwardness of having our dad in our high school. We did, however, have to face the awkwardness of having a father who taught English and always liked to hit us up with word games.

He would sit at the dining room table, marking his papers, and I believe he liked to compare the intellect of his students with the intellect of his daughters, always raging to Mom about our superiority, of course.

"Rachel," he once said to me, "can you think of a word that rhymes with orange?"

I thought for a minute, because when I was younger, I liked these games. I liked that my dad, a teacher, would come to me for my ideas. I liked thinking that I was smarter than the older kids in his classes.

To this particular question, I answered "porridge."

"Okay," Dad said. "Now make a 'roses are red' poem with orange and porridge."

I thought for a few more minutes and then announced,

> *Roses are red,*
> *Violets are orange.*
> *Goldilocks ate*
> *The three bears' porridge.*

"I love it!" my father said, beaming at me. "Creative. I've got fifteen-year-old kids in this class who couldn't think of that. Marilyn," he said to my mother, "your ten-year-old daughter is writing better poetry than my class is."

Melissa got into it as well:

Roses are red,
Violets are orange.
When it rained,
It was a storm.

"Brilliant!" My father applauded. I knew that mine was better. Of course, Melissa was only five, I could concede that. But I believed that my father thought me to be a genius, and it inspired me to start writing poems and stories. I kept many journals, which I never showed my parents despite my desire for their praise. I believed my diaries to be full of secrets that were mine alone, regardless of the irrelevance of the events they recorded.

But I always wrote them with the idea that someone would read them. I remember being in fifth grade and receiving my first diary as a birthday gift. It had a little lock on the outside that you could easily pick. I wanted to make a good impression on my phantom audience. I wanted my future readers to be intrigued by me, to marvel at how exciting a life I was leading, to be impressed by my intellect. If my family ever snooped, I wanted them to be surprised.

So I started making things up. Spicing up my existence. I would casually mention how a police officer had asked for my help to solve a crime and how he had admired my detective skills. I would write about how I had fought off a kidnapper who was attempting to abduct a little kid and how the kid's parents offered me a reward that I graciously declined. My diary overflowed with so much fantasy, which was more interesting to me than the dull normality I actually existed in.

My mother worked as a receptionist in a dental clinic, and she also loved art. When me and Melissa were babies, she created paintings for our rooms: watercolour scenes, flowers, portraits of us. Her stuff was all around the house, really. And her shelves were packed with books on art history. Big heavy books with thick glossy pages filled with paintings. Those books were really something special to me, almost magical.

I remember looking through the books with her, always focusing on the art with children. She'd talk to me about the paintings and the artists, pointing out the colours they used and why they worked well together, complementary colours — you could make blue look brighter by putting orange next to it, things like that. I didn't really absorb much colour theory, but it was fun that Mom would do crayon drawings with us and let us use her fancy grown-up paints too. I didn't know any other kids with moms who would do that.

Some of the pictures in the art books were pretty frightening to me when I was little. She'd skip by sections of the book to avoid them, but I'd see quick flashes: Christ being crucified, his haunted eyes and bloody hands. I didn't like that.

One afternoon when I was about twelve, I was looking through one of her books by myself and I flipped to a page and froze.

The painting was of two women. One wore a blue dress and one wore a red dress. They had pinned a very large man down on a mattress and were obviously struggling with him, and winning. The woman in blue was cutting the man's neck with a sword, and blood was spilling onto the bed.

I was transfixed. The women looked so calm, so focused. They were working together on this. The title of the painting was *Judith Slaying Holofernes*. I called my mother into the room.

"Mom, what's this painting about?"

She looked at it thoughtfully. "I believe Holofernes was a cruel war captain, and Judith is the woman who was sent to kill him to save her village. You know, the artist of this painting is a woman. She's remembered as sort of a feminist artist who did some very important things for women in her time."

"Who's the other girl?"

"Judith's maid, I think." My mother turned the page, and there was another painting, where Judith and her maid carried a suspiciously shaped bag. "Yes, it says here, *Judith and her Maidservant.*"

"They have his head in that bag," I said.

"You know, Rachel, I don't really like these paintings," my mother said. "Don't you think that they're very violent?"

"But the girls are friends. And they killed him for a good reason."

"Yes, they did," my mother said. "But I think it would be nice for you to look at some other paintings in this book. That picture is very sad, and I think it's nice to look at good things to make ourselves happier. It's more inspiring."

In bed that night, I kept thinking about Judith and her friend killing the war captain, against all odds. I didn't see how my mother couldn't find that inspiring. I wanted a friend like that. I wanted an ally, someone to have a secret with, someone I knew I could rely on, someone I could trust with my very life if I needed to.

XXX

So with our father praising our intellect and my mother encouraging creativity, Melissa and I really did grow up happily. I got good marks in school, especially in art and writing classes, and I had a few good friends.

I was not overtly social. I preferred to read or draw or write in my free time, but I went to the birthday parties and was in the school play in some minor role. I enjoyed all those things, but what I really wanted to do was be creative on my own. And my parents always supported that.

15

Once I reached high school, like pretty much every human being on the face of the earth, I stopped caring so much about what my family thought of me. My dad's cute word games became annoying, but Melissa still played with him, so I was luckily exempt. I didn't care so much for my mother's paintings, seeing as how I can only get so excited over a watercolour sparrow. And then I discovered metal.

TWO

I had never been popular, and right around the time I turned thirteen, I started realizing that most of my "peers" were annoying as hell. I watched good friends reprioritize their whole lives: instead of wanting to make up stories or read, they wanted to wear lip gloss and have all the expensive name-brand clothes and giggle whenever a boy said *anything*. Don't get me wrong, I wanted a boyfriend too, but for some reason I wasn't willing to laugh at bad jokes or present myself as some sort of airhead to impress someone. And my unwillingness to do these things ostracized me when I began high school.

But I was fine being a loner. I didn't mind that there were no party invitations. I preferred going home, shutting myself in my room, and working on stories or my journal or my (in retrospect embarrassing) poetry. I didn't want to hang out with my parents and Melissa; I enjoyed being by myself.

What I wasn't fine with was the abuse that came with it. It

wasn't enough that I had no friends. I had to be mocked as well, apparently. I didn't have it as bad as some kids, because I wasn't chubby or pimply or smelly or poor. But I was "weird."

Some kids who got picked on desperately tried to fit in with those assholes. Which I found pathetic. They'd make fun of a kid for having stupid hair and the kid would show up the next day with a new haircut and a hopeful look on their face, which always resulted in more ridicule. They'd tease a kid for having cheap shoes, and the kid would show up with a rip-off of the expensive brand, and they'd just get destroyed for it. But they'd always scramble around, trying to please. Whether it was to actually fit in and be accepted or whether it was just to make the bullshit stop, I have no idea. But I couldn't respect it. Which made me hate the outcast group too.

The thing with me was, they victimized me but it didn't have the effect they wanted it to.

One day in ninth grade, I was sitting by myself in the hallway eating an apple. I was wearing a dress I liked, green with a purple paisley pattern. One of the biggest wastes of the earth's resources I have ever encountered, Brandi Stone, came and stood in front of me, arms folded, flanked by two of her idiot friends.

"That," she said to me, "is the ugliest dress I have ever seen."

Brandi was one of the school's beloved, celebrated and gorgeous. She was in my grade but partied with the older kids. I had seen many a nerd attempt to take her cruel fashion advice, only to set themselves up for more abuse.

"This dress?"

"Yes. That dress. It is the ugliest dress I have ever seen," she said, smiling at me. Her friends giggled and all of them awaited my response.

I had no idea what to say. I couldn't believe their ignorance. Hadn't they seen the teen movies? Couldn't they tell that they were parodies? Didn't they know that they are the sort of bitches that everyone is supposed to hate?

I puzzled this over while we looked at each other. I guess I was supposed to cry.

"I said, *that is the ugliest dress I have ever seen,*" she repeated. "Are you retarded?"

I didn't say a word. I was so stupefied by their ignorance of themselves, of who they were.

"*Retard,*" one of her friends sneered.

I sat like a statue. They stared at me. I'm sure they started feeling kind of stupid. I was supposed to weakly defend myself. I was supposed to snivel, *Leave me alone.*

"Stupid bitch. Stupid weirdo," Brandi yelled at me, and they traipsed off down the hall, where they joined some older boys by their lockers and started giggling.

So that was it. I was a stupid bitch and a stupid weirdo, a fact that they never failed to remind me of for the rest of that year. And not just Brandi and her friends; apparently they felt that my failings needed to be communicated amongst their entire social circle. Kids in the older grades who I didn't even know shouted stuff at me as I walked to my classes. And I started feeling like shit about it after a while.

See, it wasn't being alone or disliked that I minded. It's that I couldn't understand where the hell the other people like me were. I didn't just want a friend. I wanted an ally. I wanted a partner. Someone else who would get it. Someone who understood what it was like to not have the desire to be accepted by these people. I started feeling very lonely, which pissed me off in principle. I liked being alone, but I was starting to think maybe I was insane or something, because all I saw, all day at school, were assholes and people trying to kiss up to them. It disgusted me that it was making me question myself.

Brandi seemed to develop an intense personal dislike for

me, which I found baffling, as I had barely said a single word to her and she knew absolutely nothing about me. And yet she would literally go out of her way to call me names, to verbally assault and mock me. Teachers let her get away with things, boys adored her, the nerds worshipped and feared her. I couldn't understand her. I hated that I was even wasting energy on trying to, but it became a daily thing that year. I hate to say it affected me as much as it did, but at least I always kept my head high and pretty much ignored what they said to me.

It was towards the end of my grade nine year, which I had spent friendless and tormented, that something changed me. I had not gone out once, I had spent all my time in my room, but I was proud of myself. I'd done well in my classes and I had focused so much on my poetry and writing. My parents were fine with me. Sure, my mother would occasionally ask me if I'd met any new friends, but I wasn't getting into any trouble. I was a good kid. There was no reason to really worry.

It happened at the end of that school year. All that was left were exams, then a few months away from the assholes. The school was pretty empty that day, just a bunch of exam-stragglers kicking around, and I was heading out after writing a geography exam. It was very hot outside, and as I opened the back doors of the school, a rush of heat swept over me, contrasting the air-conditioned cool of inside.

I saw Brandi leaning against the wall. Her eyes narrowed when she saw me. I was confused. She wasn't a bully who would wait for their victim out back. I began to walk past her.

"Hey, bitch," she called.

Of course I ignored her.

"I said, 'hey, bitch.' You should listen to me when I'm saying something to you," she hissed and grabbed my shoulder from behind, turning me roughly around to face her.

I was absolutely, completely stunned. Not only had I never

had any sort of violent confrontation before in my life, but I had never been so physically close to Brandi. I could see light freckles on her nose. I could smell her coconut perfume. It was too intimate and I felt overwhelmed and sick.

She leaned in close, with that familiar smirk on her face, and I recoiled. I was afraid she was going to hit me — I knew I couldn't fight, and I didn't know what was going to happen.

"Yeah, that's what I thought," Brandi sneered. I knew she could see the fear on my face, and I hated that. I hated it so much that my eyes welled with burning hot tears.

She laughed. "Are you going to cry now?"

I felt the strength that I'd tried to bolster myself with over the school year collapse. My reserve of proud nonchalance was destroyed. I'd tried to be so arrogantly numb to people like Brandi, almost amused by their stupidity, and here it was: in the moment it counted the most, I succumbed. I wilted. I felt tears roll down my cheeks.

"Fucking retard." Brandi seemed to lighten up, giving me a pretty smile. "You want to know what? Next year, I'm going to fucking *get you*. Do you understand? I fucking *hate* you, you ugly bitch."

Then she pushed me, hard. I stumbled backwards and fell on my ass. Instinctively I curled up, hunching my shoulders and moving my arms to protect my face in preparation for her attack. But there was none, and when I looked up at her, she was laughing.

"Ugly bitch," she repeated, and then walked back into the school.

I got to my feet and walked quickly across the schoolyard towards the back gate and the sidewalk that would lead me home. I wanted to run, but part of me feared that Brandi was watching me from the back door and would get such a laugh out of that. Watching the stupid, ugly bitch run home.

As I walked down the streets that I had walked so many times before, I tried to calm myself down. I could worry about next year at school later. If Brandi planned to *get me*, whatever that meant, I'd have to deal with it then. I had time to figure something out.

I hated myself for showing her weakness. If only I hadn't cried. If only I had stood up for myself. Slugged her right in her smiling pink mouth. Made *her* cry. Made *her* afraid of *me*. I clenched my fists so hard that my nails dug into my palms. I was absolutely furious at how weak I had been. She'd won. I'd had the power to change the outcome, and I had collapsed.

A car pulled up to the intersection beside me and paused at the stop sign, and my ears filled with a sound that made me stop in my simpering, faltering step.

It was music that I had never heard before. It sounded *pissed*. The drums were fast, the guitars were manic, and the voice that rumbled along with it sounded evil. Absolutely furious and evil. It barely sounded human, it was so deep and guttural — like a fucking monster. The sort of monster that would terrify Brandi and her ilk. It sounded like how I felt inside in that moment. It sounded like what I wanted to unleash on Brandi.

I looked at the car as it drove off, desperate to know what band was playing. The car's bumper was plastered with stickers. Many of them were written in a font I could not decipher, spidery and electrified. I knew I was looking at band stickers, but I could not read a single one of them except for one: "DED."

I decided to go to the music store and see if there was a band called DED. I wanted to hear that music again. I detoured and headed downtown, already feeling better. I almost felt light-headed.

I got to Bee Music and immediately went to the alpha-
betically organized racks. There was no DED. Now, I have
always had a problem with shopping in that I tend to want
to hit the salespeople over the head or avoid them at all costs.
I dislike their tendency to either be overly enthusiastic to
encourage you to buy something, or to stare at you as though
you are too filthy and uncool to *possibly* belong in *their* store.
I was going to have to ask the guy at the counter about DED,
and as I approached him, I started to doubt myself. What if
they weren't a band at all? What if the sticker was in reference
to something else? How would I ask the guy about the music
I'd heard? *Pardon me, could you refer me to the pissed-off monster-
guy section?*

The guy was long haired and covered in tattoos, and I
was definitely going to look like an idiot. But nothing could
be worse than what had happened with stupid Brandi, and I
needed to know about that band.

"Hi," I said to the guy. He looked up from his magazine with
the disapproval that I'd expected. Nevertheless, I continued.
"I'm looking for a band called DED."

The guy nodded, his expression turning into one of interest.
"Oh yeah. We've got 'em. In the back, in the metal section."

I nodded and went to the back of the store. This place
obviously kept their "specialty" stuff in separate places from
the regular racks, a fact I did not know because I had never
really listened to music other than what was on the radio, and
I barely listened to that.

And there they were. DED. I picked up the CD. Like Every
Death was the full band name, and I shivered with excitement.
The album was called *Punish and Kill*.

There were plenty of other bands, plenty of other CDs with
that unreadable electric font, tucked in the back of the store. I
felt like I'd uncovered a secret world.

23

The guy from the front counter had wandered back to join me. "That's a great record," he said, referring to *Punish and Kill*. "They're awesome."

"Yeah, they are," I agreed. "I've only heard a little bit, but I really like it."

"Oh man, you have to check out track six. 'Stomp Your Skull.' It's completely killer. The whole record is."

"I totally will," I said. "Awesome."

When I arrived back at my house, Mom and Dad were sitting at the kitchen table. Dad was marking a pile of papers and was in the middle of a rant about the idiocy of his students when I burst in through the side door, desperate to listen to my new CD.

"Well, Rachel, how was the exam?" my mother asked.

"Fine. Good," I said.

"What's in the bag?" my father asked. "You bought a CD?"

I knew that they would not approve. But I had never been the sort to lie to my parents. I isolated myself in my room, but I did not hide things from them.

"I did."

"Well, let's see what you bought!" Mom said cheerfully. I placed it on the table in front of them. Dad picked it up.

"DED. Die Every Death," he read, pushing his glasses up on his nose. "*Punish and Kill*."

"*Punish and Kill*?" repeated my mother.

"It's really good," I said. "I really like what I've heard of it."

My parents looked at each other across the table, and for the first time I felt a line slowly etch itself between me and them. Then they looked at me.

"Where did you hear about this band?" Dad asked, handing the album to my mother.

"Oh, Rachel, it looks like very upsetting music," Mom said. "Look at these song titles. 'Cut Gut'? 'I Ignore Your Screams'?"

"You just don't understand it," I said crossly.

"Honey, it's not that. It's that I don't think we *want* to understand it," Dad said. "You're a bright girl. You don't want to listen to music like this."

"Well, maybe I do want to listen to it." My voice was rising. "You don't know the sort of things that I like. You don't get who I am."

My parents exchanged another seemingly telepathic look, which infuriated me.

"Just be careful," Mom said. "Make sure you listen to all types of music until you find something you really like that speaks to you. You shouldn't surround yourself with just one kind of influence. There are many perspectives in the world —"

"Oh, it's just a stupid CD!" I interrupted. "It doesn't mean anything. And I like it. So I am going to listen to it."

I grabbed the CD from my mother's hands and stormed out of the kitchen towards my bedroom. Melissa stuck her head out of her bedroom, a look of bewilderment on her face. Our family did not tend to argue.

I shut my door firmly, not allowing myself to slam it. I sat down on my bed and unwrapped the CD. I opened the jacket and was presented with the members of DED: five tall men in black, with long hair. To their waists. They were gloomily lit and silhouetted against a purple-skied wasteland. Their faces were in shadow.

I could hear them talking in low voices in the kitchen. When I muttered a reply to the knock, Melissa came in quietly and closed the door behind her.

"What happened?"

I sighed. "I bought a CD and Mom and Dad don't like it."

"Let me see!"

I showed her the album. Melissa opened the booklet. "They look like Dracula. But with long hair, like girls. Why do they have long hair like that?"

"Because it looks awesome." I didn't want to get frustrated with a nine-year-old.

"I don't know any boys with hair like that," Melissa said, studying the picture.

"That's because you're a kid."

"I wish mine was that long," she said, absently tugging on her short brown hair. "Can we hear the music?"

"Yes we can." I put the disc in my stereo and pressed play. The first track was "Cut Gut."

Immediately the guitars began to grind, fast and menacing. The drums sped. I couldn't imagine a drummer playing that fast. The bass line was menacing and creepy. And then the voice came in. It was indecipherable. I could not understand a word he said, and there was no melody to it, but it dripped with an absolutely poisonous, cruel sound. I was transfixed.

Melissa pulled me out of my concentration. "I don't like it," she said, covering her ears. "He sounds like a monster. It sounds bad, Rachel. I don't like it!" She shook her head. "Please turn it off."

As the music stopped, my mother came in. She hadn't even knocked.

"Melissa, go to your room for a little while, please," she said. "I would like to talk to Rachel."

My sister left immediately, and Mom closed the door behind her. "I want you to listen to me very carefully. I understand you're upset."

"Okay," I replied.

"I understand that you're going through something and you're exploring different things, and your father and I are

26

going to support you as long as we feel it's healthy for you and that you're expanding yourself. But I really must insist that you not . . . expose your sister to this kind of music. She's too little to understand." She sat down on the edge of my bed. "She gets nightmares. Please try to respect that what you find appealing might not be appropriate for someone who's still little."

"Yeah, I get that," I said. "Sorry. I won't show it to her again."

"Thank you for understanding that, honey." She paused. "Now, I guess I have a question for you. Did something happen? Anything you want to talk to me about? I have to admit I'm having a bit of difficulty understanding you right now."

Part of me wanted to tell her about Brandi, about the confrontation, about how stupid and helpless I had felt. That would make her feel better. That would give her an explanation. It might even have made me feel better too. "No. Nothing happened."

"It's just that all year you wanted to write, be alone in your room, which is fine. I would have liked it if you'd met a friend or two, but we didn't let it worry us because you've always just been so happy doing your own creative thing. We support that. But . . . I guess I'm just trying to say that if you want to talk about anything with me, or with your dad, you can."

"Mom. It's just a CD. Please don't worry." I appreciated that my mother was concerned. I wanted to reassure her that everything was fine. Because everything *was* fine. In fact, I had hope that everything was going to be much better than before.

THREE

I spent that summer in transition. I devoured that Die Every Death CD and investigated other bands, getting into Bloodvomit and Goreceps next. I didn't hide my purchases from my parents, and they tried to be good natured about it. When I brought home the Goreceps album *Excrement from Birth*, my dad even tried to have a laugh about it.

"Goreceps? That's like 'forceps,' right? That's sort of clever," he said. My mother said nothing. I knew she was disgusted. But to me, it was funny. It didn't speak to them on any level other than how scary and inappropriate it was. But to me, it was power. It was anger. It was creative. And it was tongue-in-cheek in some ways. I mean, you can't name your band *Goreceps* without acknowledging it's kind of a funny name.

I started really focusing on the lyrics of the songs, which thankfully were included in the CD jackets. I was grateful that you could rarely make out what the vocalists sang; my parents definitely didn't need to know.

One of the DED songs really stood out to me. "I Ignore Your Screams" painted a picture of where I wanted to be.

> *Standing on your face*
> *Crushing all your dreams*
> *Put you in your place*
> *I ignore your screams*
>
> *Who's the big shot now*
> *On the winning team?*
> *You fucking little cow*
> *I ignore your screams*
>
> *Beg, beg, beg*
> *I show no mercy for the wicked*
> *I am the cruellest of them all*

Is it bad that I'd listen to that song and imagine another confrontation with Brandi? Of course, I would never carry out anything violent. And neither would the vocalist from DED, Balthazar Seizure. He understood what it was: a fantasy. It wasn't madness and blood lust and something for parents to worry about. It was empowering. It was going to make me stronger. And it sure made me feel very pleased to picture myself standing on Brandi's stupid face.

Most of DED's lyrics were about vengeance against some from tormenting and eventually erasing bullshit people from your life. Another song I liked the lyrics to was "Moon" from the band Bloodvomit.

We will ride through a sky
That is black with your pain
We will howl at the moon
Red with bloodstains

Together we pull you apart
Piece by fucking piece
Your suffering death
Is my only release

I liked the directness to the lyrics. They weren't trying to be fancy or poetic, they just conveyed their message. They weren't great artists who would be held up for public acclaim or approval. They just knew how full of bullshit most people are, like I did, and they were creating music based on pure emotion. I admired it.

I started buying metal magazines, which talked not only about other bands I wanted to check out, but also about the members of the ones I already liked. DED was my favourite; they had been my initiation into this secret world, and I wanted to know who they were as people. But aside from accumulating photos of them, it was hard to learn much about them from these magazines other than their names: Balthazar, the singer; Ed and Sid, the guitarists; Victor on bass; and the drummer, Chaos.

Because I could find little information about them, I could make up my own story for them. I imagined them to be very much like myself, isolated and angry. They'd been lonely, until they found each other and formed their alliance. In a way it was better to be able to fantasize about who they were, and that they would like and accept me, rather than learning potentially disappointing facts about them. I was free to write in my journal and speculate to my heart's content.

"Rachel, I know you're listening to more than one band in there," Dad said to me one night that summer as we ate dinner together. "But I can't tell them apart. It all sounds the same to me."

"Oh, there are differences," I said cheerfully. "You just have to listen closely. None of them sound exactly the same."

"I think I'll leave that to you," he said.

"I can't even tell the songs apart," my mother said. "It really does all sound the same."

"It sounds like Dracula," my sister mumbled into her casserole.

I was very happy that summer and I think that's why Mom and Dad didn't complain or try to wrestle the CDs away from me. It was totally expected that they wouldn't understand the finer nuances of the music. They weren't supposed to. But I was able to. And I knew there were other people out there who would understand it as well. I just had to find them.

XXX

There were two things I was preparing myself for that summer. One of them was Brandi and another year of shit from her that I worried would be more violent. I never wanted to be as weak as I had been after that exam. The other thing was to express how I felt on the outside. I didn't fit in with Brandi and her people, and I wanted to show that as strongly as I could, for them to know just by looking at me that I rejected them and everything they stood for. And, if I was able to express how I felt by looking a certain way, maybe I would finally attract another soul like myself and start meeting more people who felt like I did.

31

I hoarded black clothes and started brushing my hair, which only fell to my shoulders, so that it covered half my face. I bought some black eyeliner, which Mom very reluctantly agreed I could wear in *small amounts*. I dug up a pair of black winter boots that had buckles on them and could pass as kind of cool. I needed to change how I looked, but I knew my parents would freak out if I demanded a new wardrobe. So I adapted what I had. I wanted to be ready for when school started. I wanted Brandi to know she wasn't going to be able to get *me*.

FOUR

That fall I went back to school steeled. Ready.

When I saw Brandi in the hallway, she gave me a once over and laughed, walking past me with her little group of friends. It was so anticlimactic. I actually felt *disappointed*. And then I got pissed off with myself for being disappointed. I sat through my first class that day, my head pounding with rage. The teacher was outlining what the year would bring for us, ancient civilizations—wise, but I barely heard a word. I was too consumed with trying to figure out *why* I was so irritated by Brandi's nonchalant reaction to me. I hadn't changed myself for her, had I? The snide, the impression on her? Her laughter was a given. Had I wanted her to attack me? What had I been expecting?

My second class was art, which is a subject I always did well in, but when I walked into the classroom I was faced with my usual dilemma of where exactly I was going to sit. See, when you're a loner, it's easy to find a seat in a normal class with individual desks. You just plunk yourself down as far away from the "cool kid desks" as possible. But in an art classroom, there aren't any desks. It's all tables where four kids can sit and you end up sharing your space with them. Last year hadn't been bad; I had shared with three girls who were friends with each other, but who weren't shitty people either. They had ignored me all year and talked amongst themselves, and I had half-heartedly eavesdropped on their conversations and worked on my stuff. The teacher liked me, and I did well in the class, even though it was boring to me. It was the same stuff I had done with my mother: paint an apple. Draw a leaf. I was doing that shit when I was five. This year, art was an elective, so I was hopeful there would be fewer assholes. I chose an empty table in the far corner at the back next to the window.

The class filled up, and no one sat at my table. Fewer kids this year, I happily noted, even though there was a table with a bunch of guys I could have done without. Some of the Brandi bunch, who greeted each other with stupid handshakes and high-fives, as though they were some exclusive society. Which I guess they sort of were. It's always been a mystery to me how people who are so horrible end up finding each other and don't seem to mind being cruel to everyone else.

The teacher, same as last year, Mr. Lee, saw me sitting by myself. I guess he felt bad for me, because he made a point of saying, "Rachel, I love the new look."

I knew that he was trying to make me feel special, because he probably thought I felt upset at having to sit by myself, you know, *make the poor girl feel good about herself*, but I fucking hated that because all it did was draw attention to me, and I was trying to be unnoticed and left alone.

Of course, Mr. Lee's comment drew a few guffaws from Brandi's buddies. Fine by me. Nothing new. At least this year, I

34

would have a whole table to myself and I could look out the window.

Just before class began, a light-haired girl came into the room, looking flustered. She scanned the room, presumably for a seat, and then hurried to my table, sitting in the chair kitty-corner from me. She didn't look like one of the assholes, or like she knew anyone in the class. I hadn't seen her last year, and she was just wearing a boring old smock dress. Sure, I'd share a table.

Mr. Lee began to talk about what the year would cover. Colour theory and different mediums that we would use for our projects. This year would be more technical, apparently, which was fine by me. I already knew most of this stuff. At least this class would go well.

When the bell rang, I started gathering up my notes. Next up was math. I wondered who'd be in that class. See, this is what really sucks about the first day of school. It's a whole new year, with new classes, and you get to see who you're going to have to deal with for the rest of it, who's going to make fun of you when you walk in and out, who's going to snicker every time you're called on to answer a question. And who you're likely to end up with at the dreaded moment when the teacher says, inevitably, *"Partner up!"* I was always one of the people who would have to raise their hand when the teacher asked who didn't have a partner. I would end up working with some nerd, but I never minded that part of it. Nerds are smart, and I'm pretty smart too, and we'd get a good mark on whatever the assignment was, and there was no chit-chat bullshit. What bothered me was that moment of having to raise your hand and declare to the class that you are a loser with no friends. I don't understand why teachers do that. It's so damn *segregating*. They may as well just say, *"Raise your hand if you have no friends and no one here likes you."*

I was mulling this over when I noticed that the girl I'd

35

been sitting with was staring at me expectantly. I realized she must've said something, but I'd been so lost in thought I hadn't heard it. I cleared my throat like some nervous public speaker. "Uh, pardon?"

"Oh, I just said, 'See you tomorrow,'" she repeated, and smiled. I sat there as she gathered her things and walked out of the classroom.

As I left the room a few moments later, I kicked myself for not having smiled back or replied in some pleasant way.

xXx

The rest of the classes were the usual. The only class I shared with Brandi was math, a blessing because math is not a "social" class. It's dead quiet with a serious teacher, usually. And she didn't even bother making fun of me when she saw me, because she was trying to leech on to some guy she thought was hot.

Leaving school at the end of that first day, I noticed a guy in the hallway. I hadn't seen him last year. He looked a couple of grades older and was by himself. His hair was long, light brown, almost to his waist. And he was wearing a Bloodvomit shirt. I hadn't seen a scowl like his other than on Balthazar Seizure's face. I'd have to find out his name somehow.

xXx

I got to know the girl who'd talked to me that first day as the school year got underway. When we were left to work for the rest of the period on our colour wheels, she struck up a conversation.

"So my name's Josephine," she said casually, after Mr. Lee had handed out the paintbrushes.

"I'm Rachel." I hoped I sounded as casual as she did. It's so stupid: I am not an awkward person. I can communicate. I'm not stunted. But in school, I was just so damn uncertain and at that point, I was so used to being by myself, and I guess part of me really did want a friend.

"I just transferred here from Our Lady of Heaven. My family moved and it was too far to go there. Do you know anyone from there?"

I certainly didn't know anyone from the Catholic high school. I mean, I didn't even know anyone from *this* school. "Nope."

"I still have a bunch of friends there, but I'm glad I'm not there anymore. All the religious stuff, it was just stupid."

I nodded, dipping my brush into the red paint.

"My family isn't that religious or anything," Josephine continued. "We don't go to church. It's just that Our Lady was in our district. You wouldn't believe how much they talk about God and stuff at that school. Every morning you pray first thing. And you have to take religion, it's not an elective. They treat it like it's as important as science and English. You have to go to Mass. I sure won't miss that. And it's also nice not having to wear that stupid uniform."

"Yeah," I mumbled, staring at my work. I had no idea what to say.

But Josephine carried on, apparently oblivious to my awkwardness. "It's going to suck only seeing my friends on the weekends, but whatever. I don't really know anyone at this school at all. Are people nice here?"

"Nope."

Josephine laughed, to my surprise. "Yeah, that's what I've heard about this place. Glen Park's full of assholes. John Hespeler is the stoner school, Queen Liz has all the rich kids, and Glen Park's got the assholes."

"My dad's a teacher at John Hespeler," I offered helpfully.

"Oh yeah? Does he smoke a lot of pot?"

We laughed. I started feeling more comfortable. "Fuck no.

37

What are the kids at Our Lady like?"

"Really cool. It's probably because most of them grew up with religion and stuff and their families are real strict. So they get pretty crazy. But there's assholes there too."

For the rest of that period we talked. And we ended up having lunch together too. And every day after that.

FIVE

Mom was relieved that I'd found a friend. When I'd hole up in my room and listen to music and do my homework, she never complained about the bands or anything. She didn't say a word about how I was dressing or wearing my hair. Neither did Dad. I think they were really happy that I was doing well that first term, that I'd talk about Josephine, and that my grades were good. I was pretty happy too. Sure, Josephine didn't listen to any of the bands I liked, but that was okay. She didn't make fun of me for it either.

We'd go shopping downtown sometimes on Saturdays, mostly looking for clothes and stuff in thrift stores. Neither one of us had a big enough allowance to shop at the trendy stores, but that was fine because neither one of us was interested in that crap. I was always looking for black stuff, or dark plaid, and old, tough-looking boots. She had more of a hippie thing going on and would look for long dresses and sweaters. We never had to compete when we'd find something cool, and we never judged each other on any of it. It was a beautiful autumn. As the leaves changed, I spent many afternoons with Josephine, chatting as we made our way downtown. I felt important because I was with a *friend*. I learned to relax with her and be myself, talking openly about how the kids at school made me sick. She'd encountered Brandi by this point, but Brandi had treated her like wallpaper, preferring to abuse kids who offended her in some way that Josephine didn't.

She started inviting me to go to parties with her friends from Our Lady. They'd have them every few weeks. "They're really nice people, you'll like them," she insisted. But I never went. The thought of going to a party was uncomfortable. Just because Josephine liked me and accepted me didn't mean that her friends would. I imagined walking into a room filled with strangers who would totally reject me. The only person I would know there would be Josephine, and she'd abandon me to catch up with her *real* friends, and I'd be left sitting by myself surrounded by people having a great time with each other and totally ignoring me. It's one thing when that happens at school; it's quite another when you've *chosen* to be in that situation. I even worried that once Josephine's friends rejected me, *she* would reject me. She'd realize that I was a total fucking loser.

On one of those Saturday afternoon shopping trips, I'd picked up a Gurgol CD, *Tear Off the Scab*. It became one of my fixtures that fall, as well as DED's ever-present *Punish and Kill*. The thing I liked about Gurgol was that there was a girl in the band. She played bass. Her name was Marie-Lise, which sounded very exotic, and her hair was done in bleached white dreadlocks. In the band photo with three tall dark-haired guys, she stood out but didn't look out of place at all. The guys glowered and frowned, and she glowed, while still looking

40

pissed and tough. In all my research of metal bands so far, I hadn't seen a woman in one. When Josephine and I shopped, I have to admit I kept an eye out for stuff that Marie-Lise would wear. She always looked so awesome in their pictures, wearing ruffled black dresses and coloured tights and leather skirts. And I loved how she fit in with those guys. I wanted to be tough like her, surrounded by furious guys; everyone would look at us and be terrified.

Of course, Marie-Lise wore a hell of a lot more makeup than I could get away with. She wore dark lipstick, powdered her face completely white, ringed her eyes with tons of liner. She looked absolutely sinister and, to me, beautiful. Even Melissa, who was scared of everything to do with the music I liked, admired the pictures of Marie-Lise. We both agreed she looked like a beautiful vampire doll or something. Well, Melissa said that. I said that was childish, but secretly agreed.

Instead of just writing poetry and short stories, I started to write stuff that would be more in sync with the music I was into. I don't want to say they were lyrics, but I guess they sort of were. They were terrible, these early attempts. But I felt a strong creative pull in that direction.

I was very happy that fall, but I didn't have to be furious and full of rage to enjoy the music or its messages. That whole time, after all, despite Josephine, despite shopping and enjoying school, all of that was still inside me. Just because Brandi hadn't bothered with me in a while didn't mean that I was over wanting to splinter her nose with my fist. It didn't mean that I hated the assholes in my classes any less. It just meant that I wasn't alone anymore.

Now that I had Josephine, I ate lunch in the cafeteria rather than sitting on the floor by my locker, so when we would take our lunches to a table, I would always nonchalantly keep an eye out for the guy I'd seen in the hallway with the band shirt. He always ate in the cafeteria too, with a couple of his friends, and as me and Josephine chatted and ate, I would steal very discreet glances at him.

At least I thought they were discreet. One day Josephine totally busted me on it.

"Okay, so who is that guy?" she asked me.

"What guy?"

"The one you're always looking at. The long-haired guy with the Vomiting Blood shirt."

"It's actually Bloodvomit."

"Whatever. You realize he wears that shirt, like, three times a week, right? I bet he doesn't wash it." She glanced over her shoulder to where he sat a few tables over. "You like him?"

I blushed and looked down at my tapioca. "Yeah, he's cute."

"He's got nice hair. You guys would make a good couple. What's his name?"

"I have no idea."

So Josephine made it her personal project to get very involved in my nonexistent relationship with the Guy. She'd set up little experiments, like telling me to walk past his table while he ate lunch and she'd watch to see if he looked at me. Which, apparently, he *totally did*.

"You have to talk to him," she said. "He likes you. He checked you out."

"But what would I say to him? He's in eleventh grade. He doesn't want to bother with me."

"So what? You're only a year younger. That's fine. And you like the same bands, obviously. You should talk to him. Ask him about his vomit shirt. That's a good icebreaker."

XXX

42

I nervously considered all of this for a few weeks, feeling sweaty excitement every time I saw him. One morning when I was getting ready for school, I looked out the window and saw that overnight there had been a light snowfall, dusting all the trees and shrubs in my backyard with white. It looked beautiful. I felt refreshed. And I decided that this would be the day I would approach the Guy.

I got my chance sooner than I expected. I had to go to the bathroom during my first class, history, and when I walked out into the quiet hallway, there he was, at the other end of it, at his locker. The bathroom was right near his locker row, and I walked towards it and him, relishing the tension of the two of us, alone, in the hallway. As I neared him, I started feeling sick, my palms began to sweat, and I gave up on the idea. I went into the bathroom. Then for a few minutes I proceeded to kick myself for not having said anything and blowing my only chance. I'd never be alone anywhere with him again. I had no fucking gumption. I cursed myself as I washed my hands, glaring at my stupid reflection in the mirror. When I left the bathroom, he was *still there*. It was now or never. If I so much as stopped walking, he'd know I wanted to talk to him, and then I would be forced to. It was as easy as just stopping. And I did.

The Guy looked at me. His eyes were so *blue*. My stomach went through the floor. He was cute. He was *handsome*. He looked like Balthazar Seizure. Sure, a high school version . . . but he did. His hair was shiny. He wore all black. And he was looking at me.

"Yes?" he asked. His voice was *deep*! I almost gasped.

"Sorry to bother you," I said, hoping I sounded confident and relaxed. "I like your shirt."

He stared at me. "Bloodvomit? What do you know about them?"

"I like them," I said. "I'm also really into Gurgol and DED.

43

Do you know them?" I was impressed with myself, listing off other bands so casually, proving my knowledge, fitting in.

"Yeah, I *know* them," he said irritably. "How the fuck do *you* know them?"

I could not think of a single cool-sounding answer to that question, and I was starting to lose my confidence. I don't know exactly *what* I had expected, but it wasn't this. And in no way, shape, or form was it cool that I had found out about the bands from a bumper sticker. I'd keep that little tidbit to myself.

"Oh, you know, through the grapevine," I said stupidly, and froze. I could not have sounded more idiotic.

"Through the *grapevine*?" he repeated with disgust. "What *grapevine*? What the fuck are you talking about? Who the fuck do *you* know in the scene?"

Absolutely no one.

"I didn't know there was a scene," I said falteringly, feeling a collapse within myself. Feeling my strength just drain, standing there like a moron.

He stared at me for another moment, and then turned back to his locker. "Get the fuck out of here."

So I was left with the horror of having to silently acknowledge my uselessness to his hemisphere, turn, and walk back up the hall away from him, back to class. I was reminded of my moment with Brandi, of fearing she was watching me run home across the schoolyard. Even though I knew he wouldn't bother watching me walk away, I felt so dowdy in my stupid plaid skirt and tights, still wearing my pathetic winter boots, which I wore every stupid day, because they vaguely resembled the "cool" style I didn't own. Blood pounded in my head. Even my own kind weren't going to accept me.

The grapevine.

What a fucking idiot.

SIX

When I got home, I could barely look at my DED poster.
Balthazar looked too much like the Guy, with his long hair
and his high cheekbones, that slim, strong body, the tight
black pants. I was confused. Part of my fantasy, part of my
empowerment, was that Balthazar and his band and the others
who were a part of that music world would accept me, and I
would belong, standing like Marie-Lise next to someone like
the Guy, allied, ready to beat the shit out of the assholes and
prove our superiority, together. If the Guy thought I was an
idiot, would Balthazar too?

But, in the end, metal was still mine. Just because the Guy
liked it too and he was an asshole didn't mean that I was going
to allow him to ruin it for me. Fuck him. He could look at me
like I was an idiot. It didn't matter.

However, I couldn't face DED right then, so Gurgol it was.
I blasted my favourite song of theirs.

Your face is like a mask and I want to break it.
Your life is in my hands and I'm going to take it.
What did you say to me?
You turn your back on me?
I put my knife in you.

Your life is such a joke that it makes me laugh.
You just can't seem to see that you're made of crap.
Soon you'll understand.
When your blood is on my hands.

I bet Marie-Lise encountered guys, even in the metal scene, who'd try to make her into a joke. She was better than letting some asshole ruin how she felt. If anything, I bet it made her stronger. It gave her more hate, which would make her more creative. Sure, it was a guy singing, but her bass was there. She felt this song. She felt every word that the singer was feeling.

If anything, the Guy was just an asshole in disguise. He'd missed the true meaning of metal music, which was so obvious to me: hating assholes and empowering yourself against them. I started to feel elated. *He* didn't get it. I had won. I understood it and, despite his obvious disinterest in how little I knew, I was more metal than him. Maybe he knew something about a *scene*, but what I knew was more important. I decided to try to write something. Inspired by the Guy.

Did you pay, what, a dime for that disguise?
You suck and fail, that's no surprise.
Others like me hear my call.
We orchestrate it when you fall.

First I tear out your blue, blind eyes.
Such a sexy voice, such tortured cries.
And blood will fill this hollow hall,
Cause I'm the wickedest witch of all.

It was one of the best things I had ever written.

In fact, I submitted it as a poem in my English class. The teacher, Ms. Voree, returned it with a good mark, but with some comments in red ink. *Disturbing. Have you been watching horror movies?* With a smiley-face beside it. She also mentioned that the word "suck" was a bit too much slang for the assignment. I didn't care. I knew I was a good writer. And I was extremely proud of what I had written. It might not have been the perfect fit for my stupid school, but fuck it, neither was I.

Whenever I saw the Guy in the halls or in the cafeteria, I ignored him. Seeing him made me feel a bit stupid, but then I would just repeat to myself *I'm the wickedest witch of all*, and I'd feel better. Picturing myself pulling out the eyes of that faker made me feel great too.

Of course I told Josephine what had happened, and after wincing over my moronic use of the word "grapevine," she tried to help me rally.

"Fuck him. He doesn't do laundry anyway, you can tell. I bet his hair reeks too. He probably doesn't shower. Fucking looer." But her insults, while appreciated, were insignificant to the reassurance I got from just knowing I was better than him. And the good feelings I got thinking about pushing him down the stairs and watching his teeth shatter against the tile floor. Josephine didn't understand that. I showed her my poem and explained to her that it was about him, and she laughed, but she didn't *get it*.

47

Josephine and I were good friends by that winter, and I liked her very much. School was pretty tolerable. I was surprised. Things had gotten better with the assholes. They'd still jeer and make fun of me from time to time, but it didn't seem as often as the year before. Maybe it was because I was with Josephine a lot, and they didn't see me as such an easy target. Maybe they had just finally gotten sick of picking on someone who didn't respond, unlike some of their other targets. And Brandi had a boyfriend. That couple was truly a stain on the school, but at least she was distracted with her new project and left me pretty much alone.

Writing became very good therapy for me, but I still had to deal with assholes. Ms. Voree, for example, developed a problem with the work I submitted as part of our "creative writing" assignments. I'd submit really fucking good poems, and she'd hand them back, scrawled on with red marker.

Rachel, this is well written,
but I'd like to see some lighter subject matter.

Rachel, you're a happy girl!
I'd like to see some of that in your writing!

Rachel, you are very talented.
Please explore different subjects as your talent grows.

Well, it wasn't my fault that she didn't like my stuff. She couldn't argue that it wasn't good writing, though, so she had to give me good marks, but I didn't appreciate that she was critical of what made me passionate.

So I submitted a poem that I wrote with Ms. Voree in mind.

Lady in your proper dress,
Telling me my brain's a mess.
Listen now and I'll grade you
For judging me on speaking truths.

You fail at smarts,
You fail just fine.
You'll fail at living
When I snap your spine.

I didn't think Ms. Voree would take it so personally. In retrospect, I can see that she would obviously apply it to herself, but at the time, I was pretty wound up and I was writing some good stuff and I figured I was clever enough to get away with ironically giving her a poem about herself. When she returned the poem to me, the red marker ordered *See me after school.*

And when I went to her classroom at the end of that school day, not only was she sitting there, but the principal of the school, Ms. Coates, was there too. I had never had a run-in with Ms. Coates before, and Ms. Voree looked pretty upset. I knew I was in for it.

"Rachel, please sit down," Ms. Coates said, gesturing to a desk. As I did, my mind raced with ways to get myself out of trouble. "Ms. Voree, please explain the problem once again, now that Rachel has joined us."

Ms. Voree wouldn't look at me. "Rachel is a talented writer, and she has been very consistent this year, handing in great poems for our creative writing unit. But I have become dismayed by her choice of subject matter." She gestured to a short pile of papers on the desk beside Ms. Coates, presumably my poems. "As you can see, the subject matter worsened throughout the semester, leaning more and more towards violent imagery."

Ms. Coates interjected. "Yes. Rachel, would you agree?"

"Yes," I said, hoping I looked attentive and concerned.

"Please go on, Ms. Voree."

My teacher cleared her throat. "In my comments on her work, I have suggested multiple times that she explore different themes and feelings in her writing. I've encouraged her to expand. I really believe she is the best writer in her class, but the drawback is always the imagery she chooses to write about."

"Having read the poems, I can see that," Ms. Coates agreed. "Please go on."

"The problem right now is this most recent submission. It's on the top of the pile," Ms. Voree gestured at the poems. "I couldn't help but feel that Rachel is now directing this violent focus onto me."

Ms. Coates sighed and addressed me. "Rachel, having read this poem, I can see how Ms. Voree would take your wording very personally. And as you know, here at Glen Park Secondary, we don't want anyone to feel their work environment is threatening or harassing in any way, be it teacher or student."

"I understand that," I said, nodding.

"Ms. Voree is concerned, after reading your poem. But she's also stressed to me that you are a good student, a pleasant personality, so she is having a dilemma in reconciling your viewpoint in this particular poem to your personality as a student, as delinquent behaviour is not typical of you. I've certainly never had any run-ins with you, and I tend to be able to learn who the bad seeds are pretty early on in their scholastic careers here at Glen Park." She chuckled. I chuckled too, and so did Ms. Voree. We all fucking chuckled, even though it wasn't funny.

"Ms. Coates, if I may take it from here," my teacher said. "I'd like to express to you, Rachel, that I give you credit as a writer and I hope I am wrong in my reaction to this poem. I'd like to give you the opportunity to explain it to us, if perhaps we are misunderstanding your meaning."

Both of them looked to me expectantly.

"Well, yes," I said. "I think it's a misunderstanding. I mean one of the things I'm learning about in English class is the use of metaphors. And so I've been trying to use metaphors in my poems. I mean, that first line, about the lady in the dress, that isn't supposed to be Ms. Voree. It's supposed to be, like, a metaphor for 'education,' you know?"

I cleared my throat and continued. "Like, the school system. I guess I had this idea about education, you know, maybe if it was corrupt. A corrupted school system teaching kids the wrong things." They watched me, and I wiped my palms on my skirt. "Sort of wanting to rebel against the system or something. You know? Like the school system being a symbol of something evil. But it's all metaphors. It wasn't about Ms. Voree."

They absorbed this, and Ms. Coates thoughtfully looked over the poem. "What about this part, about 'snapping your spine'?"

"It isn't *literal*. It's just another way of saying, like, 'stopping' it. The whole thing is about being unfairly judged and turning the table on people judging you. 'Grading' means 'judging.' Just sort of fighting back against things that are unfair, and I used the whole school thing as a metaphor."

Ms. Coates nodded and looked to Ms. Voree. She was also nodding.

"You're very creative, Rachel," Ms. Voree said, "and I appreciate that you employ these sorts of concepts in your work. Clearly, you are capable of some very interesting ideas. I can accept that explanation.

Ms. Coates agreed. "I'm glad that this matter seems as though it can resolve itself. Both of us had hoped for just such a clear resolution from you. You're a very bright girl. But please do try to take a lighter note in your work from now on, as Ms. Voree has suggested. These violent metaphors are present in most of your assignments here, and I agree it would be nice to see some other ideas from you."

Everything was pleasantly wrapped up and I was able to leave, boiling with fury. I was relieved that I wasn't in trouble, but I felt incredibly wronged and patronized. My teacher wanted me to write about things I didn't believe in and didn't feel. Shouldn't a good teacher approve of, and encourage, strength and inspired emotion? It was a *creative* writing unit, not a *let's make the teacher think happy thoughts* unit. Shouldn't she want to bring out the best in me? Sure, the poem had been about her, but I wasn't actually going to walk into the class and break her neck. How naïve was she? She had been one of the teachers I actually kind of *liked*.

As I walked home through the snow, I got some more ideas for poems. How bright blood would look spilled across a blanket of white snow. Ms. Voree's and Ms. Coates's blood. Of course, I wouldn't be able to submit that poem to her class. I'd have to write something stupid, like *how the snow sparkled, glittering, as the afternoon sun slanted across it.* Whatever.

> *The two of you are one of a kind.*
> *Fucking brain-dead. Fucking blind.*
> *School's out now. It's time to go.*
> *Scarlet blood on ivory snow.*

SEVEN

The school year crept along. One of our art assignments was to choose a favourite piece and recreate it using a different media. You know, take the statue of David and paint a picture of it. Or make a sculpture of the *Mona Lisa*. Something like that.

Josephine was really into Jackson Pollock, so she decided to take one of his abstract paintings and recreate it using collage. I've never liked his stuff. Looks like a bunch of random paint splatters to me. It doesn't have any mystery to it, it doesn't tell a story, there's no atmosphere. But Josephine loved his work. She said she can feel excitement and movement in it. Josephine was also into straw sunhats and floral print. But, hey, different strokes, right?

I was feeling pretty damned good that day. Most of the kids in the class didn't know much about art history, so a bunch of them were crowded around Mr. Lee's collection of books, turning pages. Mr. Lee found that depressing, and he was barking at them about how *true* artists would at least know *one* work of art from that book before they even walked into his class. Not a problem for me, of course. I'd grown up with those books. I knew who Vermeer was when I was a toddler.

And there was no question as to which painting I was going to recreate.

"That's a pretty creepy painting," Josephine said when I showed her my colour photocopy of *Judith Slaying Holofernes*.

"It's so fucking cool. The girl in blue is Judith, and the girl in red is her maidservant," I explained. "The guy on the bed is Holofernes. He was this war general guy who was destroying Judith's town, really brutal. He had to be stopped, right? So Judith and her friend sneak into his camp. Some of his guards stop them at first, but these are just a couple of girls, right? What could they possibly do? So Judith and her friend hang out with Holofernes and get him drunk, and then when he's passed out, they attack him."

"It looks like she's cutting his throat," Josephine said.

"She's actually decapitating him. Judith cuts off his head, and then they put it in a bag and take it back to their village and show everyone. They totally saved their own village and became heroes for it." I grinned. "I love this painting. Look at them, they're so beautiful. Look at the way the maidservant is struggling with Holofernes, holding him down. You can see how strong she is. Judith is totally into it, cutting into his neck. And the look on his face, like he can't believe that these silly, weak women are going to decapitate him and stop all his evil bullshit. He can't believe that he isn't as strong as they are, and that they were able to get close enough to kill him."

Josephine gazed at me quizzically. "You're really into this, aren't you?"

"Oh, yeah. I remember when I first saw this painting when I was a kid. I thought it was so beautiful, the way the blood is

54

just streaming out onto the bed. You know, a woman painted this. I love how she also showed what great friends Judith and the other girl are. You can see how much they trust each other."

"All I see is some guy getting killed," Josephine said. "You're thinking about it too much."

I didn't agree, and shrugged. We got to work on our projects. Mr. Lee was still at it with the other clowns, so I tuned them out and focused on recreating the painting in oil pastels.

Mr. Lee came by after a while to observe, moving from table to table. "Josephine, I love what you're doing with those small bits of paper. You're really capturing the movement of the Pollock." Looking at mine, he said, "Rachel, I am absolutely in love with the fact that you know Artimesia Gentileschi. And I love that painting myself. But I wonder if you'd reconsider your choice of oil pastels. I'd like to see a completely different take on the work, perhaps sculpture or even watercolour. The painting is so dark as it is, and a lighter, softer perspective could be more interesting. Think about it." He moved on to the next table.

But that was exactly why I had chosen the pastels. The colours were dark and bold. Mr. Lee didn't understand that I was going to make my version of the painting even darker than it already was. If all Josephine could see was a guy getting killed, if that's all everyone else saw when they looked at this painting, I wanted them to see the rage and passion and intensity.

I copied the scene, but I twisted Holofernes's expression, highlighting his agony and confusion. The blood spilled from his jugular onto the bed, as in the painting, but I took it further, pooling it on the floor. I emphasized the wound on his neck, giving it dimension, hinting at the rupturing, severing veins. Judith's maidservant pinned him to the bed, her face a mixture of determination and amusement, her muscles tensing, her fingers digging into his sweating skin. And Judith, so focused, but also with a hint of a smile on her face. Brandishing the blade fiercely. I added blood to her hands, almost feeling its warmth as it flowed from the cut. I imagined she would relish the feeling of that blood enveloping her fingers. I decided to add some blood to the maidservant's hands as well, picturing that they would both get satisfaction from feeling their enemy's life drain away over their skin.

The background, which in the painting implied a candlelit, shadowy bedchamber, I got creative with. I added in some words from a poem I had written, garishly like the metal band fonts I could barely decipher. I made them crackle like spiderwebs, scrawled across the wall. *He will die and we will laugh. You, my love, my other half.*

My fingers were covered with oil pastel for three days, even after I washed them. The shadows of it would remain there, but I was so excited for art class those days, I felt like I was buzzing just thinking about it. I barely even noticed Josephine beside me as she snipped out her pieces of paper. What the hell did a stupid Jackson Pollock painting have to do with anything? God love her, but she didn't understand passion and feeling either.

When I was finished, I was so proud. I'd worked hard. It had taken me three classes, while some of the morons were only getting started. Too bad for them that they weren't inspired by anything. Too bad for them that they didn't believe in anything, couldn't express anything.

I sat back in my chair and gazed down on my completed *Judith* replica. It was dark, it was passionate, it flowed with hate and accomplishment and beauty. And the words on the wall behind them felt like my own little secret.

"Holy shit," Josephine said. "That's really . . . really fucking scary, Rachel. It's gory as hell."

"Do you like it?" I asked.

"It reminds me of you." She grinned.

Mr. Lee noticed that we were talking and wandered back

through the class. "Are you finished with yours, Rachel?"

"I am."

"I can't wait to see your interpretation of my favourite Gentileschi painting," he said, smiling as he arrived at our table.

He gazed down at the pastel drawing and was silent. "Are those words on the wall behind the scene?"

"Yes."

"What do they say?"

"Er, '*He will die and we will laugh. You, my love, my other half,*'" I recited, feeling stupid. Josephine was listening. I didn't like having to talk about my work in front of her and her little cut 'n' paste project.

"Did you write those words yourself?" Mr. Lee asked.

"Yes, I did."

"Well, the rest of the class is *hard at work*," he said, raising his voice to quiet some assholes who were guffawing about some dumb shit. "So why don't you come up to my desk, and we'll have a chat about what you've created? Keep that up, Josephine, I'm loving it so far." We walked up to his desk, him carrying my drawing.

Great. Maybe we could have Ms. Voree in here too and have a round-table discussion on *lighter themes*.

"This is a wonderful drawing," he said quietly, allowing the class to continue to work and not overhear our conversation. "Tell me about it."

"Well, it's always been my favourite painting," I said. "*Judith Slaying Holofernes.*"

"Do you know the story behind it?"

"Yes, my mother told me when I was little. About who Judith was and why it was very important that she kill Holofernes."

"What emotions did you feel while you were drawing this?"

"I was very excited because I love the painting. I wanted to try and express the scene with as much emotion as I could."

57

"And this resulted in emphasizing the violence and pain," he said, gesturing, "but also focusing on the strength of the women."

I nodded. "Yes, that was an important part of it for me. I've always sort of admired Judith and her friend for being strong women."

"Artimesia Gentileschi was pretty strong herself," Mr. Lee said.

"I know. My mom's really into art, she taught me a lot about it."

"Well, Rachel," he sat back, "I love it. I love that you incorporated creative words into it. It's obvious to me that you have a great passion for the painting. And I like that you took a dark approach to the dark subject matter. I didn't expect it."

"I wanted to make it darker," I said.

"Well done. We're going to be doing this project for the rest of the week, and since you've finished early, you can work in your sketchbook for a while." As part of the class, we were to hand in a sketchbook at the end of the year for bonus marks.

I took my seat, careful not to rustle any of Josephine's stupid paper scraps.

xXx

I ended up hanging that drawing on my wall, next to the pictures of Marie-Lise and DED. It made me feel good, looking at that wall. Empowered. I could tell Mom and Dad hated it, naturally, but how could they complain? I was doing well at school, I had a friend, and I was still being creative, which they approved of. I didn't get any more lectures that winter from anyone. Not from Mom and Dad, and not from Ms. Voree. Of course, that was because I *lightened up* the things that I wrote for her class. She totally approved of nature and snowflakes and the moon and soft deer in the snow and all that shit. In

Mr. Lee's class, I knew I could create whatever I wanted and he would approve. I could express myself at school through art, and I could express myself at home through writing in my journals, which were quite rapidly turning into page after page of what can only be described as lyrics.

Even Ms. Voree had been forced to concede: I was a good writer, a creative person. And I knew it myself. I might only have had one friend, and she didn't understand me, and the cutest boy in school thought I was a loser, but I was still better than the other kids. My dad had been right. I was smarter than them. I *got* it. I understood real feelings and I knew how to convey them. And I had my *music*. Fuck, it was such a comfort to me. I kind of liked that no one else I knew would ever be able to understand it. It was *mine*. To quote DED's song "This Sad Earth":

> *Me and myself*
> *That's all I need*
> *To destroy this earth*
> *To make it bleed*
>
> *And if I'm alone*
> *I feel no pain*
> *Because the blood will purge*
> *This sad earth again*

That's the stuff that carried me through the winter. And I felt just fine.

EIGHT

Even just saying her name today, I feel amazing. Something flows through my veins that I can't describe. Like fire, like comfort. Like bliss. I don't even know.

Fern.

I met Fern that spring. I'd enjoyed the winter: the days ending early, the long darkness. It was the perfect environment for me to write and fantasize about the bands on my wall who felt like a group of friends to me. I spent time with Josephine, and while I truly appreciated her, now that I was comfortable with the idea of making friends and having fun and going shopping and all that crap, I wanted something more. Josephine was wonderful, but we weren't connected. We didn't share a common view. There was no passion in it.

And before anyone gets carried away, I'm not talking about sex. I wasn't looking to Josephine to satisfy any sort of romantic need, or lust. What I wanted was more important than that. Sex is stupid, and it could not have been any less important to what I needed. To describe it in a romantic way would be to cheapen and trivialize my feelings. I wanted a bond. I wanted to truly feel close to someone.

Still, I continued through the school year with Josephine by my side, hemp shoulder bag and all. There was some boy she liked, and we did all the same things that we'd done with the Guy: she walked by him, I dutifully watched to see if he turned his head. I did my halfhearted best to find out his name for her. But it was all so silly. Having a boyfriend seemed completely insignificant next to the more important goals I had: to write. To be creative. But I humoured her.

And I have to admit that whenever I saw the Guy, I still felt stupid. Even after months had passed. I'd tell myself, *Fuck him if he doesn't understand the world*. Let him live in his little box. How pathetic, to wear a Bloodvomit shirt and not even understand the message. It was almost comical. Not comical enough, mind you, that I was able to erase from my mind the memory of my voice croaking, "*Oh, through the grapevine.*"

When the snow began to melt and the little buds on the trees were providing me with plenty of fodder for Ms. Voree's class, Josephine invited me to yet another party. She was still close to her Our Lady friends and would natter about them from time to time.

I don't know what it was this time that made me agree to go. She was surprised, but it was all set. The party was on Friday night, and we'd meet in the park and head over. Which left me with a couple of days to regret my decision.

There was so much to worry about. My fear of her friends disliking me and being forced to either endure the awkwardness or think up some lame excuse so I could leave; of Josephine ditching me and realizing how pointless I was; and, obviously, of the *normal* institutions of drinking and drugs. I hadn't had a drink before, and I certainly hadn't smoked weed, but Josephine had, and when she'd brought it up, I'd implied that I had also. Well, not so much as implied as I definitely let her know that I had. I mean, I was *cool*, right? So now I would likely be faced with a situation where my *extensive coolness* would be put to the test. I'd have to act like I knew what I was doing. And I fucking didn't even want to drink or smoke weed. So how the fuck was I going to fit in at this *badass* party?

Friday evening I let my parents know I was going to go to a party. It was the first time I had ever gone to a party, or gone out at all for that matter, on a Friday night. I approached them after dinner; Mom was in a good mood having just finished a painting.

"With who?"

"Josephine," I said, and immediately they both visibly relaxed. I guess they were pretty worried that one of these days I was going to fall in with the *satanic criminal* crowd.

"Oh, that's good," Mom said. "Whose party is it?"

"I don't know. Some friend of hers."

"What friend?" Dad said.

"I don't know. Some girl from Our Lady of Heaven."

"Okay," Mom said. "This is exciting! You're going to a party. Is it a birthday party?"

"No, Mom, it's just a regular party," I said, which silenced them both again. I began to feel the familiar skin-crawling sensation of annoyance creep up my body. I wanted to go to my room.

"Will there be alcohol involved?" Dad asked slowly.

"No, Dad. They aren't like that. It's just to hang out."

Dad frowned. "Rachel, don't forget: I'm a *teacher*. I deal with kids your age every day, and I know what goes on at these *parties*."

"Oh, Rachel, I don't want you drinking," my mother said.

"Or doing drugs either. Smoking pot, causing trouble." My dad was getting into preach mode, and it was all I could do not to roll my eyes. "Doing acid. I know what goes on. It's dangerous. You're a smart girl, you don't want to start making bad decisions. You have to be very careful."

"Guys, it's fine. Don't worry about me."

"Be home by nine," my mother said.

"But it's *eight o'clock*! I'm not even meeting Josephine until nine!"

"Oh, right. Well . . . be home by midnight."

"And if you need a ride home, call us. Don't get into a car with anyone who's been drinking," Dad said. "We want to keep the doors of communication open. Don't be afraid to come to us to talk about drugs, drinking, sex, whatever you need advice with."

"I get it, all right? I'm going to go get dressed."

I put on one of my best outfits, a dark blue plaid jumper with a black puff-sleeved blouse underneath. Black tights, and my trusty old winter boots. I put on a bit more makeup than normal, trying to channel a hint of Marie-Lise despite my boring brown hair and protective parents, and after insisting to my mother that what I was wearing was *fine* for a party, I left for the park.

Josephine was waiting there for me. We headed off across the neighbourhood. She babbled away about which of her friends would be there tonight, about some cute guy who was supposed to go also, and about who was going to bring the beer. I was nervous. I wished I'd brought my Discman along so I could have one ear in while she talked, listening to something that would make me feel stronger. Fuck, it was so frustrating dreading these social situations. Josephine knew I was nervous

63

and reassured me that everyone would be really cool. "Once you've had a few beers, you'll be fine."

Yeah, great.

XXX

After a bit of a walk into a neighbourhood I'd never been to before, we walked up to a house with loud music playing and people hanging out on the driveway.

"Oh, I don't know about this," I said, stopping at the bottom of the walkway leading up to the house. I felt shaky, and my stomach was upset. My stupid palms sweated. "I'm nervous."

Josephine turned to me and touched my arm. "Rachel, you're wonderful. And I promise I will leave with you if you want to go. Just give it a chance."

She smiled, and I appreciated her so much in that moment. "You promise?"

"I won't abandon you," she said.

We smiled at each other and then walked up to the door. She flung it open and strolled in as if she owned the place.

I knew immediately it was a bad idea that I had come. The music was fucking annoying, too loud and it was some kind of bullshit you'd hear on the radio. There were people everywhere. Just hanging out and laughing it up, all of them holding beer bottles or drinks, smoking cigarettes, and all of them looked like assholes. I expected to see Brandi. A bunch of people looked over as they noticed us walk in. Mostly they just went back to their conversations, but two girls came running over.

Squealing, they embraced Josephine and launched into immediate chatting bullshit. I squeezed in behind her so I could close the front door, trapping us in that awkward living room.

"This is my friend Rachel," Josephine said, gesturing to me. "Rachel, these are my friends Erica and Heather."

"Hi," I said.

64

"Hey, Josie's told us all about you," Erica said. "Nice to meet you."

"This is my house, just so you know," Heather said. "So you can grab a drink from the kitchen, whatever you want. It's nice to meet you."

They were both really nice, but I couldn't help but feel how superficial it was. They were only interested in hanging out with Josephine, of course. The three of them lapsed back into familiar conversation as we moved further into the room. And there it was. The moment I knew would happen. Josephine talking to her friends, and a room full of disinterested morons jabbering away, and me, standing there like a fucking outcast, pretending like I was fine with it.

I stood close to the three of them so it would at least look like I was included, and finally Heather said, "Rachel, why don't you go get yourself a drink?"

Nice. I hadn't noticed that the two girls had brought Josephine a drink when we came in, so the three of them all had beer bottles.

"Uh, sure, thanks," I said. At least going to the kitchen would give me something to do; it would look like I was either on my way to a conversation or coming from one. I weaved around the people, none of whom noticed me, into the kitchen. It was also filled with people, some of them sitting on the kitchen counter, some of them sitting around the table, which had bowls filled with chips and stuff on it. The music was loud in here too, and everyone was just blabbering away about god-knows-what, and I couldn't see drinks anywhere. I guessed the fridge would be a good place to start.

I squeezed through the people and opened it. There was a lot of beer in there. I didn't want one, but I figured I'd try it anyway.

"Yo, grab me one too," some guy said, pushing up behind me. "There's too many people in here."

"Uh, sure," I said, taking two bottles out and handing one to him.

"Thanks. Let me open that for you." Using a bottle opener he had on his keychain, the guy opened them. "Hey, cheers," he said and took a swig.

Gamely, I took a swig too. It tasted like filthy shit, absolutely horrible. I couldn't keep the wince from my face, and the guy laughed.

"Yeah, this beer sucks. Hey, my name's Mark," he said, holding out his hand. "I'm Robbie's friend."

I shook it, still marvelling at how foul the beer tasted. "I'm Rachel. I'm here with Josephine."

"I don't know who that is." He gulped down some more beer. "So what school do you go to?"

"Glen Park."

"Ah, fuck! Do you know Danny Bastin?"

"Nope."

"Oh. Well, he's my buddy. I go to Our Lady. It fucking sucks."

I nodded amiably. He and I stood there awkwardly for a minute, and then he noticed someone on the other side of the room he wanted to talk to. Or maybe he didn't, and it was his way of making an excuse to get away from me. "Well, hey, it was nice meeting you, Rachel."

"Yeah, you too," I said, and he disappeared into the kitchen-herd, and I was left standing alone again, now with a disgusting drink in my hand. I didn't want to go back to the living room and stand awkwardly with Josephine and her friends. Walking to the kitchen had made me feel more comfortable, so I decided to take a stroll around the house. It seemed like a better idea to walk around alone than to *stand* alone.

I moved through the kitchen and dining room. Everyone at that party looked like an asshole. From across the room I noticed Josephine chatting with her friends; she raised her eyebrows at me. *You okay?* I nodded. She raised her beer bottle at me questioningly. *Did you get a drink?* I held mine up so she could see it and tried to smile at her. She smiled back and resumed her conversation. I was fine. I was *just fine.*

I wandered down a hallway, past a couple of people making out, and saw the back door to the house was open. I wanted to go outside. Maybe I could even find a place to discretely dump out half my beer so it would look like I'd been drinking it.

When I stepped onto the back deck, it seemed like the night stopped.

There wasn't too much snow left, and people were sitting on patio furniture, yapping away. Coloured lanterns and strings of lights hung across the deck and railings, so it looked very pretty. Beyond the deck, in the yard, a few people sat at a picnic table smoking cigarettes.

One of them was wearing a black blouse and tight jeans. She had long blonde hair past her shoulders, but it wasn't bitch-blonde. Something about her made me stop and stare. She wasn't notably gorgeous, but I could not take my eyes off her.

Of course she caught me looking at her, which made me freeze with horror. But immediately she smiled and waved at me.

I waved back and she gestured at me to join them.

I made my way across the deck and down the steps, then sat down. The girl was sitting with a guy and girl that I barely noticed.

"Hey, I'm Fern," she said, warm and friendly. She introduced her two friends, but I didn't hear their names.

Fern.

NINE

The four of us sat and talked. Fern and her two friends, Edgar and Yvonne, both went to school at Our Lady and were in my grade. I confirmed their suspicion that Glen Park was the "school of assholes" — its reputation, apparently. I took more sips of beer, trying to control my reactions of disgust. Edgar and Yvonne soon went back inside the house, leaving me with Fern.

"So, can I ask you a question?" I said.

"Sure."

"When I came out back, why did you wave to me?"

She shrugged. "I don't know. I guess you looked familiar to me, or something."

"We've totally never met before."

"Yeah, I know." She took a sip of her own beer. "So who do you know here?"

"I came with my friend Josephine. She's in our grade."

Fern nodded. "She was in a couple of my classes last year.

I'm not, like, friends with her or anything, but she's a nice chick."

"Yeah she is."

Fern lit a cigarette, offering me the pack. I declined. The beer was disgusting enough, I didn't think I could handle that on top of it. "No thanks."

She grinned. "The only reason I smoke is to get the taste of the beer out of my mouth. Then the smoke tastes so bad, I have to drink the beer to get rid of *that* taste. It's stupid."

"Why drink beer at all if you don't like it?"

"I don't know. Probably because everyone else here drinks it." She inhaled and then blew a plume of smoke across the picnic table, politely directing it away from me. A burst of obnoxious laughter came from inside, and she rolled her eyes at me. "Lots of assholes here."

"Yeah."

"I really like your dress," she said. "It's pretty cool."

"Thanks! I got it at one of those thrift places downtown," I said.

"Oh, I *love* going there. You find such cool stuff," she said. "You and me should go sometime."

"Yeah, we should," I said. Was it really this easy to make a new friend?

"What else do you do for fun?" Fern asked.

"Not much, really. I kinda just like to stay home. I really like writing. I'm pretty into poetry and art," I said.

"That's cool. I'm trying to learn how to play guitar — it's really fun. I'm not good at it, but I want to make my own music one day."

"What bands do you like?"

"I'm into a band called DED," she replied. "It's, like, heavy music. They're not on the radio or anything."

I felt my stomach clench with excitement. "Oh, totally. Do

you like Gurgol? They're amazing too."

"Oh, yeah!" Fern brightened. "Marie-Lise, their bass player? She's *amazing*. I'm not too into Josh Galligan's singing, though. Have you ever heard Surgical Carnage?"

And so we began to talk very animatedly. I was so fucking excited. I'm sure by this point the beer I had been gagging down was doing something to me, but I can't use that as an excuse for my giddiness.

"I don't know anyone else who likes metal," I said. "I guess I don't really have many friends." *Ugh*. Yes, the beer was getting to me. No reason to let this girl know how much of a loser I was.

"That's because you're smart," Fern replied. "Most people aren't worth knowing."

"That's what I think too," I said.

"I know a few cool people but, yeah, nobody in this city is into anything good. If you want to meet other people in the scene, you have to go to one of the bigger cities. You know, Surgical Carnage is doing a show in St. Charles next weekend. It's all ages. You want to go?"

St. Charles was about two hours away. My mind spun as I tried to work it out. Would my parents let me go? I had enough allowance money if the tickets weren't too expensive.

"How would we get there?"

"My buddy Craig can drive. There'll be room in the car. And we'd come back the same night. Pretty late, though."

"How much are the tickets?"

"Fifteen bucks. Surgical Carnage isn't that big. When I saw DED last summer, the tickets were forty." Fern lit another cigarette. "I can get you a ticket. You wanna come?"

"Yeah, sure." I'd deal with Mom and Dad later. Part of me was pretty sure they'd be okay with it. They always encouraged me to hang out with Josephine and go shopping and make friends and all that crap. Of course, driving two hours to a concert and coming home late was a different story than Saturday shopping downtown, but I was fifteen. Definitely old enough to start doing some cool stuff.

"Let me grab your phone number," Fern said, reaching into her bag for a pen.

While she was writing it down, Josephine came into the backyard. As she walked towards the picnic table, I felt a pang of embarrassment at her long green hippie skirt and brown sweater.

"What's up, guys?" she said, sitting down across from us. "How are you doing, Fern?"

"Fine," Fern said. "How are things? You miss Our Lady?"

"Yeah, Glen Park sucks. But I don't miss Mass."

I hoped that Fern didn't mention the concert to Josephine. I didn't want Josephine tagging along. It made me feel sort of bad; Josephine had never been anything but a good friend to me, but I felt panicked at the thought of her hanging out with us. I knew she just wouldn't fit in, and maybe this was going to be my chance to meet some more of my own kind of people. How was I supposed to make new friends if Josephine was there?

"Are you having an okay time, Rachel?" Josephine said.

"Yeah, for sure," I said. "I'm fine."

She sat there for another minute, and I realized I was waiting for her to leave so that Fern and I could talk some more. No one said anything, and Josephine stood up just as it began to get cooler. "Okay, great," she said. "I'm just going to be inside. Let me know if you want to get going."

"I will," I said.

"Okay, see you guys in a bit." Josephine glanced at Fern and then back at me and smiled, and made her way back across the yard.

71

"Josephine's really nice," I said to Fern. I didn't like how I felt. Like I had snubbed Josephine, who truly was my only friend. I mean, as cool as Fern was, I didn't know her. I knew Josephine, and I had been a shitty friend just now. At the same time, I could have gone inside with her, and I didn't.

"Did you want me to invite her to the concert?" Fern said, glancing at me sideways.

"No," I said. "It's not really her thing."

"I didn't think she'd want to go anyway. I know she isn't into the same things we are."

We smiled at each other.

A while later, Fern and I decided to leave the party. She said her goodbyes to Edgar and Yvonne, and I went to seek out Josephine. The party inside was truly in full swing: everybody was drunk and noisy, and the cigarette smoke was thick and stifling. It seemed like the shitty music had gotten even louder, and everyone was yelling and howling with laughter. I slipped unnoticed through the people, looking for Josephine. I found her, sitting on the couch in between Heather and Erica from earlier.

"Hey, Rachel!" Josephine said loudly as I approached. She was obviously drunk. "You were out there a long time."

"Have another drink," Erica said. "Sit down here with us. We want to get to know Jo's new friend better."

"No thanks," I said. "I think I'm going to head out."

"Oh," Josephine said, "I'll go with you."

"No, it's fine, stay," I said. "I have to get home anyway."

"It's only 11. You still have an hour before your mom wants you home. Why don't you stay?" Josephine continued. "Come on. I'd really like you to get to know Heather and Erica. You guys are all my best friends."

"Yeah, Rachel! Come on. You can tell us all about Jo's *boyfriend*! She won't tell us anything." Heather laughed, sliding over on the couch to make room for me. "Sit here."

I almost said that Josephine didn't have a boyfriend, then vaguely recalled something about whichever guy she thought was cute that week. The three girls smiled up at me, and I thought about sitting down with them. But then I saw Fern walk into the room, giving me the *ready* nod, and I shook my head at Josephine. "Sorry, I have to go. It was nice meeting you, thanks for the party. I'll see you on Monday, Josephine."

I turned my back on her disappointed look, and together with Fern, walked out the front door.

"Let me walk home with you," Fern said, and I told her where I lived. "I'm not too far away from there, it'll be fine." So we walked and chatted. It felt amazing, wandering through the night with her, feeling fearless, the two of us, talking like we'd known each other for a long time. I was totally comfortable telling her about my lyrics, and she talked more about how she was trying to learn guitar. "We should start a band," she joked, and we both laughed, but secretly I thought that was a pretty cool idea.

When we got to my house, we paused on the driveway. All the windows were dark.

"My parents are probably asleep by now," I said. "Do you want to hang out here for a bit?" We sat down on the curb out front. "Er you ran get me a ticket for the concert?"

"Sure," she said. "I'll have to go down to the record shop next week. Why don't you come with me? We can do some shopping too. Try to find something cool to wear to the show."

"Sure," I said. "And your friend will have room in the car?"

"Definitely. It's just going to be me, that girl Yvonne, Craig,

73

and maybe one of his friends. There'll be room. You're going to love Surgical Carnage, they're amazing."

"Sounds really cool," I said. "My parents will let me go for sure. They're pretty laid back."

"I'm going to bleach my hair this week."

I looked at her long pale hair. "It's pretty light already."

"Yeah, but I want it to be white." She giggled self-consciously. "Like Marie-Lise, I guess."

I giggled too. "That'll look awesome."

She lit a cigarette. "You should dye your hair too."

"Yeah," I said, inspired. "I'd like to dye it black."

"Well, after we go shopping, why don't you come back to my house? We can help each other do our hair," she suggested. "I don't think I can do a good job on mine by myself. My hair's too long."

"That's great, totally," I said. Going shopping, dying hair, going to a concert, with Fern, my new friend. It was like a whole bunch of opportunities were opening up in front of me. Black hair! A metal concert! Things were definitely looking up.

As we continued talking, I was horrified to hear the side door of my house open and close. I looked up the driveway and saw Mom, wrapped in a sweater, her feet shoved into sneakers, approaching us.

"Er, I thought I heard voices," she said.

"Hello!" Fern said and, in one fluid motion, quickly discarded her cigarette by the curb and stood up.

"This is Fern," I said. "Fern, this is my mom."

My mother smiled politely at Fern. "Nice to meet you. Rachel, it's after midnight. It's quarter past."

"Sorry," I said. "We were just walking home and we stopped to talk for a few minutes. I was about to come in."

"Fern, do you need a ride home? I could go get Rachel's dad and he'd be happy to drive you."

"Oh, no thank you. I don't live far, and I can walk from here. That's okay."

"Don't you have a curfew as well?" Mom said.

"Yes, one o'clock. So I should probably get going. It was nice to meet you," she said to my mother, and to me, she said, "I'll call you tomorrow."

"Bye," I said, feeling stupid that my mother had come shuffling out of the house and ruined our talk.

I watched as Fern proceeded back the way we'd walked. I wanted to watch her until she disappeared into the darkness, but my stupid mother was right there and completely ruined the moment.

"Rachel, come inside right now," my mother said.

I followed her up the driveway and inside, where I saw my dad sitting at the kitchen table in his pyjamas.

"Were you guys waiting up for me?" I asked, incredulous. "I was hardly late. And technically I was *home*. I was right outside the house."

"You've never gone to a party before or stayed out late," Dad said. "Of course we waited up for you."

"Well, I'm *fine*. I'm *here*. Everything is okay."

"You smell like cigarette smoke," Dad said.

"She was outside with a girl who was smoking," Mom informed him.

"Oh, Rachel."

"Listen," I said irritably. "At the party, a lot of people were smoking. And yeah, so what? Fern had a cigarette outside."

"_____," I had asked.

"Fern's a friend of mine. But *I* didn't smoke. I didn't drink. Everything is fine. I'd like to just go to bed now, if that's okay with you."

My dad started in with another of his teacher speeches and began to list off the dangers of smoking, of drinking, reminding

75

me that I was only fifteen years old. He warned me about hanging out with a bad crowd, and started talking about how marijuana is a *gateway drug*, even though there hadn't been any marijuana involved in the evening. As he rambled, I wanted to scream. I wanted to slam my fists on the table, and I imagined that would scare him and Mom pretty good. I pictured myself opening my mouth and just *screaming* into his face. He didn't understand at all. Neither one of them did. I wasn't drunk. I hadn't smoked. I had been home on time, as far as I was concerned. But they couldn't see that everything was fine. They thought I was stupid. Mom had to come outside and embarrass me, and now Dad was treating me like I was an idiot. Both of them staring at me with wide, concerned eyes, like stupid cows. I wanted to shriek at them and scare them and shut them *right up*. I would scream so hard that my eyes would bulge out of their sockets. My fists clenched as I fought this urge, as I tried to swallow the anger building rapidly inside of me.

Because common sense must always prevail. If I started screaming at them, they would punish me. And I was on the verge of some really cool stuff. They'd ground me, and I wouldn't get to hang out with Fern next week and go shopping. They certainly wouldn't let me go to the concert. I couldn't risk any of that happening. And so, I bore my father's stupid lecture like a champion. I kept my mouth shut and nodded at all the right times, agreeing with him. Pretending I was stupid like they were. I would have to play nice and wait for the dust to settle a bit, and then let them know about the concert. If they couldn't see that I was smart enough to make the right decisions, well, that was their fault. In the end, they were only discrediting themselves as parents. Didn't they understand that I knew right from wrong? That they had taught me that from when I was a little kid? How insecure of them to doubt themselves. Didn't they think they'd done a good enough job as parents? And if they didn't think so, why punish me for their own weakness? It was almost comical.

In the end, they conceded that I had technically been "home" at my curfew, but next time I should actually be in the door. I agreed. They said that smoking and drinking are not good ideas, and I agreed. I agreed and agreed, nodding so much that I started feeling dizzy.

TEN

On Monday in art class, Josephine was quiet. I knew why, but for some reason I decided to play dumb. She was hurt by the way I had acted at the party. She had asked me for months to go with her, and I always said no, and the time I did accept, I ignored her the whole time. And this was after she'd assured me that she'd look after me. She was a good friend, and I did feel bad. Which sucked. I should have been on top of the world, excited about the week ahead, planning ways to ask my parents about the concert, but no. All because Josephine was making me feel guilty, sitting next to me quietly, with only a cold little "Hi." It was irritating. I didn't want to talk to her about it, because I didn't want to have to apologize for it. It wasn't my fault that I'd met someone I had more in common with than her.

After working for quite a while in silence, she finally said, "Aren't you going to ask me what's wrong?"

I straightened up and looked at her. "Yeah, of course. Are you okay?"

"Well, not really," she said, clearing her throat. "I mean, you took off from that party, and it made me feel like you didn't want to hang out with me."

Gee, don't hold anything back. "That isn't true," I said.

"Yes it is. I was really excited for you to meet Heather and Erica, and you didn't even spend any time with me at all, or give a shit about my friends. All you did all night was hang out with *Fern.*"

"Girls," Mr. Lee said from the front of the class. "Down a few notches."

Josephine continued in a whisper. "I'm really pissed off about it, Rachel. You made me feel like crap."

"How do you think you're making *me* feel?" I whispered back. "You know I was scared to go to the party. And when I make a new friend, it's like you're *jealous* or something!"

"I am not *jealous!*"

"Yes, you are. You're not my boss, you know. You can't tell me what to do, at *all.* Just because you wanted me to hang out with your friends doesn't mean I'm going to like them. It doesn't mean they're going to be the type of people I'd get along with."

"No, but you didn't even give them a *chance.*" Josephine's face was turning red.

"Sometimes you don't have to give people a chance," I said, scowling. "If you're going to be pissed off at me for the simple fact of me talking to someone at a party who isn't you, fine then. I think you're jealous, and it's really *pathetic.*"

I turned back to my work and realized my face was probably just as red as hers was. I can't really explain the emotions I felt. One part of me was glad I had hurt Josephine, but I couldn't really figure out what she had done to me. The other was really

79

damn upset and wanted to apologize. But I knew I wasn't going to. It really bothered me that I wanted Josephine to be upset. I was not a callous person. She was my friend. My first real friend. Why did I want to turn this on her?

After a while she spoke again. "Listen, I'm sorry," she said softly, keeping her eyes on her work. "I just felt hurt, that's all. It was stupid of me. Of course I'm totally fine with you making new friends."

She paused, and I knew that it was my turn to apologize. "I'm sorry too, Josephine. I guess I just got caught up talking to that girl, because we like a lot of the same bands."

We worked quietly for a while, and Josephine suddenly said, "You should be careful with Fern."

"Why's that?"

"She's weird."

"Oh, we're all weird," I said.

"No, I mean *really* weird." Josephine lowered her voice conspiratorially. "When I went to Our Lady, I knew her. She was in a bunch of my classes. Everyone used to say stuff about her."

"What stuff?"

"Like, she's into Satanism and shit like that. Do you re-member in the newspapers a year ago, last winter, about those peacocks in the petting zoo at Bingeman Park? How someone broke in there at night and killed a bunch of them?"

"Yeah, my dad was talking about that."

"Yeah, well they say Fern was one of the people who killed them. That it was like a sacrifice to the devil, something like that. And it gets worse."

I stared at her, waiting.

"I guess her family had a dog and she killed the dog too. Sacrificed him to the devil. And she has an older brother. They say she has sex with him, that he's a devil worshipper too, and

80

they have, like, *orgies* with the other devil worshippers in their *coven*, or whatever."

"Witches have covens, not devil worshippers," I said.

"Whatever. It's all the same shit."

"Josephine, I don't believe any of that. It's just stupid gossip."

"Maybe." She shrugged. "But I know Fern better than you do, and I know she's weird."

"People just like to pick on people who are different," I said. "Fern listens to music and dresses different from most of the people at school. So they have to go make up rumours about her. This is exactly the same kind of stuff an asshole like Brandi would start about *me*. I mean, how would anyone know what happened to her *dog*?"

"I don't know," Josephine said. "You're right, it could just be gossip, I guess. But what I'm telling you is to be careful. I don't know *anyone* who likes her."

"Well, now you do," I said.

I felt exhausted for the rest of that day over the argument we'd had. All that crap about Fern was so obviously just stupid gossip, churned out by the assholes. Incest and killing animals? It was completely ridiculous, and how weak of Josephine to buy into it. How lame of her to tell *me*! All it did was prove my point, that she was jealous about me and Fern developing a friendship, and she wanted to try to ruin things. I mean, it didn't even make sense. Orgies? How had that managed to leak out into the world of gossip Josephine? Had someone seen her kill her family's dog, or *caught* her having sex with her brother?

The worst part of it all was that I was now thinking about what Josephine had said. Of course I knew it was garbage; none of it was true and Josephine should be fucking ashamed of herself for perpetuating it. On the other hand, I couldn't help but be a tiny bit interested in the potential shred of truth in all of it. Was Fern *really* into devil worship? Killing her dog and sleeping with her brother were revolting concepts, but I couldn't help but feel scandalized in a very fascinated way.

That evening I planned to talk to my parents about the concert. I already knew that there was no way they would let me dye my hair, so there was absolutely no point in asking about that. That was something I'd deal with later. But I knew as we sat down to dinner that they were still irked about the party, and I hoped that all my patience and tolerance for listening to their crap that night would pay off.

Mom, Dad, and Melissa were talking about something mundane, and when they paused in their conversation, I decided to speak up.

"A few friends of mine are going to St. Charles next weekend," I said.

"You have friends who drive?" my dad asked, raising an eyebrow.

"It's actually the older brother of one of my friends," I said, thinking I had lied quite smoothly.

"What friend?" Mom asked.

"That girl Fern you met," I said.

Mom put down her fork. "I don't know, Rachel. What about Josephine? I thought she was your best friend. Why don't you spend time with her anymore?"

"Fern's a pretty name," Melissa said.

"I *do*," I insisted. "Josephine's going too."

"Oh," Mom said, and hesitated. "So, why do you have to drive all the way to St. Charles? Do you want to go shopping?"

"No, it's actually for a concert," I said, as casually as possible.

"What concert?" Dad asked.

82

"They're called Surgical Carnage."

No one said anything. Melissa looked back and forth at them, and I stared at my pork chop.

"Is Rachel *rebelling*?" Melissa asked. "'Cause the book we're reading in class talks about how the older sister in the family is a teenager, and she gets in a fight with the mother because she wants to go to some dance at her school, and the mother says she's *rebelling*."

My parents chuckled. Dad said, "Do you think you're rebelling, Rachel?"

"I don't think there's anything rebellious about wanting to go to a concert with my friends," I said. "I'm fifteen years old. You guys have always wanted me to make friends and do things."

"It's just that St. Charles is so far away," my mother said. "And, I mean, that *music . . .*"

"You can hate that music all you want, but I don't see why you think it's a bad influence," I asserted. "Have my grades fallen? No. Am I on drugs? No."

"But your friend was smoking . . ."

"Do you think people who listen to my music are the only people who smoke? No. A lot of people my age do. It has nothing to do with what bands they listen to."

Mom nodded slowly.

I sighed. "Why don't you guys wait until I mess up my life before you get all worried about what a bad influence it is? I have friends and I'm *fine*."

Dad shook his head. "Our job is to try to stop that from happening. Nip it in the bud. You're young. You don't know the warning signs."

"Being around someone who smoked a cigarette is not a warning sign," I shot back. "It wasn't *me* smoking. I know smoking is stupid. You guys raised me to know that." I allowed myself to smile smugly. "I think it's too bad that you guys doubt yourself so much about how well you raised me. It seems to me like you doubt yourselves more than you doubt me."

They both paused, staring at me. I could tell they didn't know what to say, and I congratulated myself for besting them. "Why don't you let me go to the concert and see how it goes? See if my grades drop or if I mess up somehow. See if I come home on drugs or drunk. Then panic over the choices I'm making."

"You don't make the rules around here," my mother said, but I had won. I could go to the concert. One condition was that we had to leave immediately after it was over and drive straight home, which I agreed to because how would they know? I had won myself a flexible night out, and I had out-thought my parents. I had lied to them about Josephine going along, but that was unimportant. What they didn't know wasn't going to hurt them. I recalled how drunk Josephine had been at the party and chuckled that my parents seemed to think that she was such a great influence.

Fern and I decided to meet downtown on Wednesday after school to go shopping for some stuff for the concert. Being a total loser has its benefits — I had a ton of allowance saved up. We met up outside one of the thrift stores. When she showed up, she looked tough and beautiful. I admired her dark purple eyeshadow and the amount of eyeliner and mascara she was wearing. I wasn't allowed to wear powder or anything, and I felt so plain with my usual getup of light eyeliner and ChapStick.

"I wish my mother would let me wear more makeup," I said.

"Why don't you just put it on when she isn't around? Do it at school in the morning or something," Fern said. "My mom's cool with the eye stuff, but she won't let me wear dark lipstick. I wait till I leave the house and then put it on."

Shopping with Josephine had never been competitive, and I worried that it might have been with me and Fern, but instead it was totally collaborative.

"Look at this," she said, pulling a crimson dress off one of the racks. "This will look amazing on you when your hair's black. With some red barrettes or a ribbon or something?"

I agreed. I usually looked for black clothes, and Fern was opening my eyes to a whole new level of ideas. I could wear pink, even, and make that look awesome. With lots of makeup and black hair . . .

"I need some shoes too," I said once we had both chosen a few pieces of clothing.

We looked at the shoe section, and I scanned the shelves in my size for a tough pair of boots. "See, there aren't any. I hate that." I scuffled my feet. "I always wear these, and they're my old winter boots."

Fern studied the shelves. "How about these?" She pulled down a pair of black boots in my size. They had a pointy toe and a very feminine high heel. "These are cute as hell."

They didn't have any buckles and I wasn't sure about the heel. "You think they're cool?"

"Just because they aren't masculine doesn't mean they aren't tough. These will work great with the clothes you have. Just do your hair awesome, wear tights, accessorize, and they'll look great."

They looked like witch boots. But was that so bad? I decided to get them. Even if I didn't think they were that metal, it would still be nice to have a change of shoes for once. And I did trust Fern's fashion sense.

At the drugstore, Fern picked out some makeup for me: foundation and powder, dark eyeshadows, and I chose a deep red lipstick. Then we went to the hair dye section. While Fern picked out a bleach, I scanned the boxes of black dye. One had a very pale girl with blood red lipstick. I chose that box based simply on how cool the girl looked. Well, that, and because it was relatively inexpensive.

We paid for the stuff and then, after grabbing a ticket for the concert at the record store, decided to head to Fern's place. My stomach simmered with excitement as we walked together, my hands full of shopping bags. I felt like I was about to undergo a transformation. I knew I could hide the makeup from my mother, but I wouldn't be able to hide my hair, and I was pretty confident that she would freak out when she saw it. But it would be too late by then for her to do anything about it.

Fern's mom was really nice. We promised to keep the black dye off the shower curtain and be very careful and lay down towels, and she was cool about it. Me and Fern headed to Fern's bedroom.

Her room was amazing. The walls were purple. She had a shelf of books and CDs, on top of which were several vases of dried flowers. Her bedspread was black satin, and her sheets were black. All of her furniture was painted black as well, and the room smelled vaguely of warm vanilla. A black electric guitar lay casually on the bed. There were candles on her nightstand and several posters and paintings on her walls. She had a vanity covered with cosmetics and perfume bottles and a string of small white Christmas lights around the mirror. I swallowed hard, picturing my own white-walled, mismatched bedroom with the old powder-blue comforter on the bed and the porcelain duck lamp I'd had since I was a baby. I wanted to make my room cooler before she saw it. This room had a dark, cozy mood to it. Perfect for holing up and writing.

"Your room is great," I said.

"Thanks. It took awhile to convince my mom to let me paint it this colour," she said.

We got started by bleaching Fern's hair in the bathroom. She sat on the toilet lid and I wore plastic gloves and tried to get as much of her hair covered with bleach as I could. It was a difficult job; not only because I had never done it before, but also because Fern's hair was so bloody long. She had roots growing in, which were dark brown, and she told me to do the roots first so they'd have longer to lighten than the ends, which were already pretty light. I was a bit nervous. I didn't want to totally ruin Fern's hair.

After inspecting herself in the bathroom mirror, she deemed my job thorough, and we went back into her bedroom to wait for the bleach to do its stuff.

"Play me something on your guitar," I suggested.

She giggled nervously and picked it up, sitting on her bed and resting the guitar across her lap. "I'm not very good," she warned. "I have a book I was trying to learn from."

Fern played a few chords and then launched into a sloweddown, faltering version of the opening guitar riff from "I Ignore Your Screams" by DED. Flawed as it was, it was totally recognizable, and I was thrilled.

"That's great!"

"Eventually I want to get an amp and some effects pedals," she said. "But I can't afford any of that right now. It sounds so stupid like this."

"Will your mom let you have an amp?"

"It won't be too loud. I can listen over headphones," she said. I was impressed at her knowledge of guitar gear.

"Can you write music?" I asked.

"I want to eventually, but I kinda want to get better at playing before I try," Fern replied. "I want to be in a band one day."

87

"I told you I'm starting to write lyrics," I said. "We should *totally* start a band someday."

"Yeah, we should. You'll have to show me some of the stuff you're writing. Can you sing?"

"I don't know," I said.

XXX

When Fern went back to the bathroom to rinse the bleach out of her hair in the shower, her mother invited me to have a cup of tea with her in the kitchen. Her mom was older than my parents were, with grey hair, but not old enough to be a grandmother type. She'd made some green tea, and I sat across from her at the table.

"I'm happy to see that Fern's made a friend," she said, sliding a plate of cookies across the table towards me. "Especially one she has things in common with."

"We like the same bands," I said, eating one of the cookies.

"You're dying your hair black?"

"Yes."

"Well, I think that will look very striking on you. You have a very light complexion, you'll look quite vampy."

The kitchen door opened and in skulked a tall dark-haired guy. His eyes flicked from me to his mother. "Hey."

"Frederick, this is Rachel, Fern's friend. Rachel, this is Fern's big brother, Frederick."

"Hi," I said, eyeing him. So this was the big brother that Fern apparently was having sex with, and that was also a member of the devil worshipping *coven*. He smiled politely at me and took a cookie from the plate. He didn't seem like a devil worshipper, even though he was wearing black clothes. Of course, how would I be able to recognize one? Should he be wearing a hooded robe, hands dripping with peacock blood?

"Do you guys have any pets?" I asked, realizing too late that it was a suspicious question.

Frederick and his mother looked at each other. "We used to have a dog," his mother said, "but she died last year."

"Yeah, she was hit by a car," Frederick said. "We still have a cat, though. She's lurking around here somewhere I guess." Abandoning the subject, he addressed his mother. "Can I use the car tonight?"

"Once your dad gets home and we've had dinner," his mother agreed. "Rachel, will you be joining us for dinner?"

"I think I should be getting home after my hair is done," I said. "But thank you."

Fern blow-dried her hair after she came out of the shower, and it definitely was closer to white than it had been before. The only problem was the roots, where the hair had been darker, had a slightly orangey hue to them. But Fern assured me that she could brush it to hide the orange parts, and that next time she bleached it, it would look more consistent. It did look really nice, and I was proud of myself. And it was my turn next.

The hair dye smelled awful and it sort of burned my scalp. It was also really messy. We were really paranoid of getting it on the bathroom walls or the rug, but we were as neat as possible. When I looked in the mirror after Fern had finished applying the dye, my head looked like it'd been dipped in grape jam. We waited the allotted time, and then I jumped in the shower to rinse it off. I scrubbed at my head and watched dark purple water splattering in the bathtub and running down the drain. *Vampy*, Fern's mother had said. I couldn't wait.

Fern blow-dried my hair, not letting me look in the mirror yet. "Ooooh, it looks really, really good," she cooed, and when I finally looked in the mirror, my mouth dropped open.

It was shiny and *black*. It made my skin look even paler and my blue eyes jumped right out. I could not believe the difference. My hair had always been mousy and brown, and my eyes and skin tone bland. Now I looked *pretty*. I couldn't believe it. I felt beautiful.

Mom was going to kill me.

"Let's do your makeup," Fern said, excited.

I sat down at her vanity and she hovered over me. Again, I wasn't allowed to look in the mirror. I'd never had anyone do my makeup before, and it was awkward. When she was putting on the eyeliner and mascara I kept blinking and squeezing my eyes shut and smudging her work. My eyes started running at one point, and Fern had to dab away the smeared makeup. After a few minutes she stepped back. "You put on the lipstick," she said. I unwrapped the dark red colour I'd chosen and stroked it onto my lips as accurately as I could without the aid of a mirror.

"Done," Fern said. "Check it out."

Once again I gasped at my reflection. I barely looked like myself. I looked like a wonderful, beautiful version of me. She'd powdered my skin, making it even paler, and used a dark grey eyeshadow and tons of black liner on my eyes. There was a hint of pink blush on my cheekbones, which prevented me from looking too washed-out pale, and my lips looked gorgeous with the lipstick. I looked *amazing*.

As we'd been doing makeup, the smell of cooking from the kitchen had begun to permeate the bedroom. I knew it was time for me to head home. I hated to wash the makeup off, but there was no way I could go home done up like that. It was going to be hard enough with my new black hair. Sadly, I wiped off the lipstick and scrubbed my face with soap and water.

I said goodbye to Fern's mother and brother, stupidly trying to pay close attention to their interaction for traces of incest. Finding none, I kicked myself. Fern and I walked outside onto the front porch. The sun had gone down, but it was still early enough in the evening that my parents shouldn't freak out too bad that I'd stayed out after school.

"You look amazing," Fern said. "I'll call you Friday and I'll let you know what time we'll come by on Saturday to pick you up. And we'll figure out what to wear too," she grinned. "I swear that red dress will look *awesome* with your new hair."

I clutched my shopping bags and smiled. "Thanks for today, Fern."

"Thank *you*," she said. "You know, I'm really glad we met."

"Me too."

ELEVEN

When I got home, my parents and Melissa were eating dinner at the kitchen table. I walked in and immediately my mother's fork clattered to her plate.

"Rachel, what have you *done*?"

"I dyed my hair," I said, raising my chin confidently.

Mom, Dad, and Melissa all stared at me. I fearlessly made eye contact with all of them.

"I think it looks pretty," Melissa said.

"Thank you," I said, smiling at her.

"What was wrong with your nice brown hair?" Mom asked unhappily. "You looked so pretty before."

"I think I look pretty *now*," I retorted.

"Okay, all right," my dad stumbled. "I work with kids your age. There are goth kids in some of the classes I teach —"

"It's not goth!" I interrupted. "You don't get it."

I went to my room and slammed the door. I threw my

shopping bags on my ugly bed and sat down at my desk. Stupid bedroom. I looked at myself in my mirror. My hair looked awesome. And here I was, in my stupid room, with my stupid family who didn't understand. I thought of Fern, with her nice mother and her cool bedroom, and felt tears of jealousy prickle my eyes. I lay down on my bed next to the shopping bags and pressed my face into the stupid flowered pillowcase.

Shortly after, there was a knock on my door. I didn't want anyone to see me crying, so I didn't respond, but my mother let herself in anyway. I sniffled and glared at her, but she came and sat down beside me.

"I didn't say you could come in."

She ignored me. "Rachel, we have to talk."

"I don't want to talk. I have nothing to say," I said, muffled through the pillow.

"Well then, just listen to me. You have to be able to understand that your dad and I are very confused when you come home with your hair dyed black and when you listen to that music."

"Just because you don't like it doesn't mean it's *wrong*."

"You're right. And I realize that you are trying to express yourself, and you're growing up. You have to be able to make some of your own decisions. Your father and I have to trust in you to do that." She paused, reached out, and stroked my leg. "We have to try to understand where you're coming from, and you have to try to understand where *we're* coming from. You were right the other night. Your father and I raised you with good values. You're fifteen, and you're going to start making your own decisions.

"Yeah," I said.

"The last thing I want to do here is make you feel as though you can't come to us, because you're afraid we're going to judge you."

"It's just some stupid hair dye."

Mom was quiet for a minute. "It just seems to us like things are happening very quickly. You're going to parties, making new friends, going to a concert, and now dying your hair. Can you see that these things are going to take some getting used to for your father and me?"

"I guess."

"And can you also understand that you're a part of this family, and that you have to communicate with us? Be home when you say you're going to, play by the rules?"

"Yeah."

"We just want you to be *careful*, Rachel. That's all. And as long as you're doing that, and keeping up your end of the bargain and not getting into any trouble or slipping at school, we're going to try to understand where you're coming from when you dye your hair and make new friends and get involved with things that we don't necessarily understand."

"Do you think maybe I could paint my bedroom a different colour?"

"*Paint*? I don't know about that. Do you want to change your room?"

"Yeah, kinda." I gestured to the duck lamp. "It feels babyish in here."

My mom frowned. "But you've always loved that lamp! Your grandma gave that to you when you were one."

"Exactly."

Mom thought for a second. "Let's talk about it with your dad. Maybe we can give you some extra chores around here and come up with a compromise about getting you some new things. A trade."

"That'd be great," I said, brightening up. "I'd do whatever."

"We'll see." Mom smiled and patted my leg. "Just remember, Rachel, we love you. We aren't monsters. We just have to work together, all of us, and communicate."

"I understand," I said, nodding.

She gazed at me fondly. "I never thought my little Rachel would dye her hair black," she said, smiling sadly. "You're growing up."

I fought the urge to roll my eyes.

Josephine asked me if I wanted to go shopping on Saturday. Saturday was the concert. Fern had said that she and her friend Craig would be by to pick me up in the late afternoon, and I was looking forward to taking my time getting ready, so I didn't see how I'd be able to go with Josephine and make it back in time.

Besides, I didn't really *want* to go shopping with her. I much preferred going with Fern. And I also couldn't tell Josephine about the concert, because I didn't want to hurt her feelings at not being invited.

"I have plans with my parents that day," I lied.

"What plans?"

"We're going out for dinner and stuff," I said. I wasn't even fooling myself.

Josephine studied me for a few moments. "Is everything okay?"

Angry at myself, both for lying and for not being able to do it convincingly, I snapped, "Everything's fine!"

She shrugged and didn't speak to me for the rest of the class. I was so pissed. If only Josephine fit in better with Fern. If only she liked something, *anything*, cool. I didn't like lying, but at the same time Josephine did suck in a lot of ways. I mean, perpetuating those rumours about Fern and the devil worshipping? About having sex with her brother? Josephine had alienated *herself* by buying into that stuff and trying to make me dislike Fern. It was shitty of her to have done that, and all because she was jealous!

Still, I felt bad, and tried to be as nice as possible to her. I could tell she didn't like my new hair, but she didn't say anything about it. I felt as though Josephine and I were growing apart. Whatever. She had her stupid friends, and I had Fern. At this point, I wouldn't have cared if I had to eat lunch alone. Aside from maintaining good grades, school was completely irrelevant to me.

XXX

Saturday arrived, and I did my best to doll up appropriately. I put on the red dress, black tights, and the high-heeled witchy boots. I put my hair up in pigtails and tried to emulate what Fern had done with my makeup the other day. In the end, I guess I probably caked on a little too much, but when I looked in the mirror, I liked it. I thought I looked good.

I watched Mom literally bite her lip to keep from saying something when I walked into the kitchen. "Those are nice boots," she finally said.

Dad did his best to nod enthusiastically. "It's nice to see you wearing some colour," he said, glancing at Mom.

"Thanks," I said. "Fern should be here soon."

"So you don't know what time the concert is over?"

"No."

"But you're to come straight back," Dad said. "I don't like the idea of you being out on the highway late at night. It's a long way."

"We'll come right home," I said. "You don't have to wait up."

"We probably will anyhow," Mom said. "I want you to promise us to be very careful."

"No alcohol," Dad insisted.

"Don't worry. None of us are old enough to buy drinks anyway," I said.

"I know all about false ID cards," Dad said. "I know how easily obtained they are. And I'm sure you know how dangerous drinking and driving is."

"Oh, Dad! No one's drinking and driving. We just want to watch the band!"

I felt nervous and excited. I couldn't wait for Fern to get here and to meet her friends. Mom had made some soup and sandwiches, but I was too fidgety to eat anything. Besides, I didn't want to ruin my makeup. Finally I had some soup at her insistence.

"You know," Mom said, watching me eat, "I was always taught that if you're going to do dramatic eye makeup, you should do a subdued lip, and vice versa. If you do heavy eyeliner and dark lipstick, it's a bit . . . *overwhelming*."

"Maybe I like *overwhelming*."

"The band *is* called Surgical Carnage," Dad joked. "That sounds a bit overwhelming. She'll fit right in."

We heard a car pull up outside. Mom peered out the kitchen window. "I guess your friends are here."

I jumped up from the table. "I'll see you guys later!"

"Rachel," my father said, "be careful. St. Charles is a big city. Stay together and keep your eyes open. Don't get into any trouble."

"Oh, Ken — you should see the boy who is driving," Mom croaked, peering out the window.

"And remember — *straight home* afterwards."

"Yes, I know. I'll be careful. See you later." I pulled open the kitchen door.

I tried not to skip as I walked down the driveway. The car was parked at the curb, and I saw Fern waving frantically at me from the backseat. I waved back, recognizing Yvonne from the party sitting in the passenger side. She smiled at me through the window.

Fern opened the back door for me. "Squeeze on back here with us," she said, sliding into the middle. Her friend Edgar was on the other side, and he gave me a friendly wave. "You remember Yvonne and Edgar from the other night," she said. "And this is my friend Craig."

Craig looked back from the driver's seat, and my heart sank as I recognized the long hair and blue eyes. It was *the Guy*.

He recognized me in the same instant, and I watched his eyes narrow. "Hi," he said coldly. "All right, let's get going."

He pulled away from the curb and turned up the music. As we drove off, Fern leaned in close to me so I could hear her over the music. "You look great," she said.

"So do you." Fern was wearing a silver slip dress. She'd brushed her hair over to hide the orangey roots. "What band is this?"

"Surgical Carnage," Fern replied. "To get us in the mood."

Yvonne turned around in the passenger seat. "Rachel," she said, "I really like your hair."

"Thanks."

"My mom won't let me dye mine," she said.

"Your mom's a *bitch*, that's why," Fern said, and Yvonne reached back to playfully slap her.

"So you're friends with Josephine?" Edgar asked me.

"Yeah, kinda," I replied.

"Good ol' Josephine," he said, and laughed.

"It's a shame, really," Yvonne agreed, and laughed with him.

"Shut up, guys," Fern ordered.

I had no idea what they were talking about. "What?"

Yvonne looked at me. "Didn't Josephine tell you why she transferred to Glen Park?" She chewed on her lower lip.

"No."

Fern slapped Yvonne's arm. "Shut up, seriously."

"Hey!" Yvonne smacked her back. "I'm just asking a question."

"Why did she transfer?"

Yvonne's eyes widened. "Her mother had this boyfriend. Her parents are divorced, right? So her mom's dating this young guy. And Josephine's *sleeping* with him. And one day the mom comes home and catches them. So she tries to kick the guy out, but it's his place, right? So the mom has to move out, across the city. It was a total scandal last year."

"It's all just gossip," Fern said.

"Maybe," Edgar said. "But everyone knew about it."

I had been to Josephine's apartment a few times. Her mom had always been at work, so I'd never met her. And there had never been mention of her mother having a boyfriend. Josephine had only mentioned that her parents divorced when she'd been really young.

"How old was the mom's boyfriend?" I said. "I mean, she was fourteen last year; wouldn't that make him a child molester?"

"Yeah, you'd think so," said Yvonne.

"Not if the chick wanted it," Craig said from the front seat.

Fern and I shrieked angrily at the same time. "Shut the fuck up, Craig. That's fucking horrible," Fern said. I wanted to back her up, but I didn't know these people very well, so I felt uncomfortable with the idea of yelling at the guy driving. Instead I raised my chin. Surprise! Craig was an asshole. It wasn't news to me.

"Let's talk about something else," Yvonne said. "Like the show. Remember those guys from last time?"

Edgar scoffed, "Yeah, I really really hope they show up tonight."

"I'd like to see them try something," Craig said.

"See, last time we went to a show in St. Charles, these skinhead guys were there," Yvonne said to me. "You know, really racist dudes."

"Oh," I said, nodding. I didn't know anything about skinheads.

99

Edgar laughed bitterly. "I guess they have a problem with black guys who are into metal."

Yvonne nodded. "They tried to start some shit with Edgar."

"That's stupid. The guitar player in Goreceps is black," I said.

"No shit. Some people are just fucking assholes," Edgar said.

"Anyway, they got all up in his face," Yvonne continued. "Talking some real shit. Like they were going to kick his ass."

"I'd like to see them try," Craig said. "If they show up tonight, we'll see."

We flew up the highway, music blasting. We chatted about bands. Every time Craig added something to the conversation, I ignored it. But I was having a great time. It felt amazing, sitting next to Fern, talking and laughing. We cruised past other cars, and sometimes Yvonne would make stupid faces at the passengers in them. We passed a car full of baseball cap–wearing jock guys, and Yvonne rolled down the window, shoved her upper body outside, and gave them the finger with both hands. We all howled with laughter and sped past them. It felt good. I felt like we were unstoppable.

I'd been to St. Charles a few times with my family on day trips over the years, and driving into the city always filled me with excitement. The skyscrapers and high-rises, the video billboards, and of course the Bay Tower looming over it all. Even the slow-moving traffic. It was that feeling of driving into the big city, with the sun glistening on Charles Bay, sailboats gliding over its surface. I'd looked out the window of my family's car when I was a little kid, loving the feeling of being here, knowing the day would be full of crowded streets, musicians performing for change, street vendors and, when the sun went down, neon lights and glowing fountains.

I had the same childish feeling of excitement now, but this was the first time I'd been here without my family, so it was heightened. I felt adult. Tonight would be a new experience for me. As we drove into the city the sun was setting, turning the water in the bay orange, sparkling.

TWELVE

Edgar was hungry and so was I, so we stopped at a hot dog vendor on the corner by the parking lot and the two of us bought a hot dog.

"I've never been to a concert before," I said, slathering ketchup and mustard on my hot dog. I didn't feel stupid telling him this, I felt completely comfortable.

"You're going to love it," he said.

We walked up the street and found ourselves at the end of a lineup for the concert. At the beginning of the line I could see the venue sign illuminated in neon: The Grey Room.

Craig waved to a few people he presumably knew who were ahead of us, and for a second I hoped he would go join them, but he stayed with us.

Most of the guys in the line had long hair, total heavy metal types, wearing band shirts. Pretty much everyone in line was dressed in black, and most of them had dyed hair. The girls all wore heavy makeup, and I noticed that some of the guys wore eyeliner too. I wondered if wearing a red dress made me look awkward, but then I realized that standing out was a good thing. People were looking at me too; I felt great, like I belonged, but at the same time, like I was slightly above it because I stood out. Wearing the red dress had been a good idea. Fern stood out too, gleaming in her silver outfit. Both of us were unique.

It was almost dreamlike that this many metal people existed. I sure hadn't seen any of them back home.

Edgar was on edge, worried about the skinhead guys from the last show. He kept looking up the line and back down it as it continued forming behind us. I looked around too. The whole idea of these racist guys confused me.

"So you think these guys will show up?" I asked Edgar.

"I don't know." He eyed a group of guys with shaved heads who walked past us towards the back of the line. These were skinheads, I could tell. They were wearing bomber jackets and had their jeans tucked into their boots. But they nodded to Edgar as if they knew him, and he nodded back as they passed us.

"That wasn't them?" I asked.

"Nah. I know those guys from around," he said. "They aren't dicks. Not all skinheads are all racist and shit," he informed me. "Only some. There are assholes in every crowd, right?"

I laughed and nodded, thinking of Craig. I glanced at him. He was gazing sourly towards the front of the line.

"So you guys both go to Glen Park, right?" Fern said, addressing me and him.

"Yep," Craig said, not looking at me.

I didn't say anything, just lifted my chin and looked away. Fern gave me a quizzical look, and I shrugged and rolled my eyes.

The line started moving, and before too long we were inside

the venue. I tried to play it cool, but I couldn't help grasping Fern's hand with excitement. She grinned at me.

It was a large room, with a bar along one side and couches along another. The stage took up one entire end of the room. Instruments were set up, but no one was onstage yet. It was pretty dark. There was a big, sparkling disco ball suspended from the ceiling and tea lights flickered on the small tables around the back. A few hundred people milled around. There was nowhere left to sit. Metal blasted from the speakers.

We secured ourselves a place in the crowd in front of the stage. "If we get separated," Yvonne said loudly, "we'll meet by the door after the show."

Fern went to the bathroom and I stood with the others. Yvonne and Craig started talking to some people beside us, but I couldn't make out what they were saying. I stood beside Edgar and soaked up the atmosphere in the room, waiting for the concert to get started.

"I've seen Surgical Carnage a few times," he said. "They're fucking great."

"I can't wait," I said.

"There's supposed to be an opening band too," he continued. "I've never heard of them."

Fern rejoined us, and right when she got back the overhead music stopped playing abruptly. A loud cheer came up from the crowd, and I joined in, raising my hands over my head.

Three guys with long hair came onto the stage. One took his place behind the drum set and the other two picked up a guitar and a bass. The bassist stepped up to the microphone.

"We're Catastrophic Enzyme," he growled. *"Fuck you!"*

The band launched into their first song, and the crowd started swelling and moving. It became a mass of pushing and flying hair as everyone whipped their heads around. Stunned, I almost lost my footing. Edgar grabbed my arm to help me regain my balance. I looked for Fern. She was right beside me, and when she saw me looking at her, she smiled.

A few songs in, the crowd lost its enthusiasm. The band wasn't very good, even I could tell. People still cheered and a few heads whipped long hair around, but things definitely quieted down. The singer from the band harassed the crowd between songs, which got a bit of reaction, but the songs all sounded the same. I couldn't make out any of the lyrics, and no one else seemed to know them either. I began to get bored.

After a while their set ended with the singer reminding us that Surgical Carnage was next, and the shrieked response from the crowd was deafening. All three members of Catastrophic Enzyme gave the crowd the finger as they left the stage.

A few guys came out and started taking away the band's gear, and the overhead music started playing again. I had to pee, so Fern and I went to the bathroom together.

We washed our hands in two side-by-side sinks. The counter was crowded with girls fixing their makeup and chatting, and we took out our lipsticks to reapply them as well.

"So what's up with you and Craig?" Fern asked.

"Honestly? He's an asshole. I know he's a friend of yours, but I can't stand him."

"How come?"

I shrugged. "I tried to say hi to him one time, and he totally blew me off. He was really rude."

Fern was quiet for a minute, dabbing powder onto her nose. "Yeah, he's a bit weird."

"I wouldn't say weird. I'd say *asshole*," I said. It sounded pretty arrogant, and I glanced sideways at Fern, hoping I hadn't offended her, but she was nodding.

"Well, fuck him if he was rude to you."

We went back out and found the others. More people had packed in front of the stage, and it was pretty much shoulder-to-shoulder. I could feel the impatience and anticipation coming from the crowd, and it made me jittery. I was annoyed that my view of the stage was blocked by people's stupid heads, but I was glad I'd worn the high heels. They raised me up a little bit, even though my feet were getting a little sore.

When Surgical Carnage took the stage, the crowd went insane. The singer didn't even bother making an introduction, and they launched into their set.

My face immediately smashed up against the sweaty back of the moron in front of me and I lost my footing, but the pressure from behind and front kept me upright. I lifted my face away, gagging at the stench of the guy's sweat, and opened my mouth to gasp for air. Immediately I got a mouthful of the guy's disgusting hair, and I choked. It was absolutely disgusting. I felt panic rise up my throat as I gagged, struggling to breathe.

I felt arms close around me and pull me back. Thank god for Edgar. "Are you okay?" he yelled into my face.

"Yeah."

Yvonne pressed her face towards me. "I'm moving to the back. I'll meet you guys after." With that, I watched her turn and disappear into the crowd.

With Edgar doing his best to shield me, I was able to catch glimpses of the stage through the bouncing, rioting crowd. The band looked great. They all threw their heads around in unison, and the singer bellowed and growled through a veil of hair. It was deafeningly loud. I turned to look at Fern. She had one arm braced against the guy in front of her to keep his sweaty back away, pushing him aggressively. Her other hand reached up in the air, fist clenched. Her mouth was wide open in a snarl. She looked amazing. Craig stood behind her in the same way Edgar was behind me, whipping his hair around. Sometimes it would hit Fern, but she didn't seem to mind it. I was grateful Edgar wasn't moving his head. He had long dreadlocks and I imagined that it would suck getting one in the eye.

By the second song, a mosh pit formed in the crowd ahead of us. I watched people move through it, smashing into each other. "Hey," I shouted, grabbing Fern's arm. "Want to go up there?"

She nodded, her eyes shining. We linked arms and pushed through the crowd. Edgar and Craig followed. It was strange, because to get through the crowd, we had to shove people hard and elbow them aggressively, and no one seemed to mind. It was a very powerful feeling.

"Fuck, Rachel, be careful," Edgar yelled into my ear, making me pull back at the volume of his voice.

"I'm fine," I said and threw myself into the mosh pit.

Mistake. I slammed into some huge guy immediately and almost fell over. Then as I rebounded off him, someone smashed into the back of my head and my vision went pure white, my eyes pricking with shock. I threw my arms up around my head and kept myself from stumbling. This had been a bad idea.

When I opened my eyes I saw a giant, long-haired monster careening towards me, his eyes frenzied. He didn't even know what he was doing, I realized. Everyone in this mosh pit was insane. As he stumbled into me, I shoved him as hard as I could. He reeled off in another direction. Okay, maybe I could figure this out. Glancing around, I saw a few other girls in the mosh pit as well, holding their own. Okay, I braced myself to absorb the impact of another guy, and then was sent crashing into Fern, who laughed hard. I realized if I just relaxed and went with the motion of getting smashed into, it wasn't as painful. And I had to push back. It started to feel surreal, with the constant motion and the deafening music in my ears. I didn't notice any pain. It was fun. A short girl slammed into me, and I shoved her hard. She stumbled backwards and I laughed, turning to the left to absorb the impact of another guy with my back.

I noticed Fern, who had been knocked away from me, her mouth hanging open in a shriek that I couldn't hear. Some tall guy's hand was on her chest. I looked up at his face. The guy was grinning. Nobody around them seemed to notice what was happening. Rage streamed through my veins, and I froze for a second, staring at Fern's terrified face and the pale, spidery hand crawling across the front of her dress.

I felt a hard push from behind me, but I was so furious that I remained planted where I was, sending whichever moron had slammed into me reeling back the way they'd come. The music pulsed in my head. I saw Craig and Edgar coming in from the other side towards Fern, but they were too far away.

I opened my mouth in a scream of rage and threw myself towards Fern. My boot slammed down hard on someone's foot, and they cried out painfully into my ear. I felt the high-heel snap off, giving me a lopsided gait as I shoved my way towards my friend. Some oblivious girl stumbled in front of me, and I grabbed her firmly by the shoulders and shoved her aside, barely breaking stride.

Fern's eyes were fixed on mine. I could see the panic in them as she struggled to break away from the asshole. I launched myself at him, pulling back my fist and slamming him right in the face as hard as I could.

I felt his nose crack and give in under my knuckles. His eyes widened in shock and blood exploded from his nostrils. The blood splattered onto Fern's hair and his arm loosened its grip around her shoulders. Craig and Edgar finally got to us, and I watched Craig grab Fern away from the guy. Edgar's hands began to close down on my shoulders, but I jerked myself away from him and hurled myself towards the guy once again. His hands were pressed to his nose, blood streaming. He backed away, scanning the people who still pushed and staggered around him to see which big, scary guy had punched him.

"It was me, you prick!" I screamed, even though I knew he couldn't hear me. I drew back my leg, laughing, and kicked him in the crotch as hard as I could with my pointy-toed boot. His hands flew away from his face and he doubled over. On his way down he saw me, finally registering that it had been me, a stupid little girl, who had done this to him.

Edgar grabbed me and dragged me away from the mosh pit. Everyone was still shoving and slamming into each other, and no one apparently had noticed what had transpired. As Edgar pulled me backwards I tried to catch another glimpse of the asshole, but he'd been swallowed by the crowd.

We proceeded towards the back of the venue, where Craig and Fern were with Yvonne. This was a safer place to watch the show, I could see why she'd escaped back here. Better view, fewer people. The music was still loud as hell, but it was easier to hear ourselves talk.

"What the *fuck* happened?" Yvonne shrieked, staring at the blood in Fern's hair.

"It was crazy. Some guy was grabbing Fern, and Rachel punched him right in the face," Craig said.

"Oh my god. Are you okay?" Yvonne squealed, grabbing Fern's arm.

She nodded, obviously trying to compose herself. "Yeah, I'll be fine," she said. "Holy shit, Rachel, that was crazy. You broke that guy's nose."

"That asshole deserved it." I felt electric. I could still feel the guy's nose crumbling under my fist.

"She kicked him in the balls," Craig said. "It was crazy."

"Asshole deserved it," I said.

109

"Let's all just calm down," Edgar said. "Fern, you're sure you're okay?" After she nodded her reply, he turned to me. "Are *you* okay, Rachel?"

"I'm fucking great," I trilled.

"You gotta be careful," Edgar warned. "There are some real psychos here. I'm glad me and Craig were there."

I had to stop myself from laughing. Craig and Edgar hadn't helped Fern. They had done nothing. Obviously I could take care of Fern and myself.

"You're fucking *tough*," Fern said to me, and I beamed. Craig nodded, and I looked away from him. I couldn't help it, though; I felt a surge of pride that even *he* had to admit I'd done good.

THIRTEEN

I was pissed that I'd broken off my heel and was now hobbling, but it was so worth it. I kept replaying what had happened as Fern, Yvonne, and I made our way through the crowd to the girls' bathroom. I kept an eye on the crowd, brazenly making eye contact, daring any of them to approach us.

In the bathroom, Fern wet some paper towels and tried to wipe the blood out of her hair.

"I can't believe it," Yvonne said. "Rachel, you're an animal. That's so cool. You beat that guy up!"

"It was amazing," Fern said. I soaked it all in, gazing into the mirror. My makeup was smudged, but it was everyone's. My hair frizzed and stuck out, but still looked good. My hand was starting to ache dully, and my knuckles were red. They'd probably bruise.

"Bam! *Fuck you!*" Yvonne punched the air in front of her,

imitating me. "Damn, I wish I was that tough. I'd probably have been too chickenshit to do anything."

"I wonder if we should get out of here," Fern said. "I wonder if that guy will try to find us later or something."

"Fuck that!" I said. "I'm not letting him ruin our night. What's he going to do? Obviously he's a fucking moron. I'd like to see him try anything with us." I grinned.

"I guess," Fern said, frowning. "You're probably right."

We watched the rest of Surgical Carnage's set from the back of the club. My lopsided heels bothered me so much that I'd had enough. I slammed my foot against the floor over and over until the other heel broke off too. Still felt awkward, but at least now I was reasonably balanced again.

When the concert was done, a huge swell of people made their way back out the door. The five of us joined the crowd, shuffling forward slowly.

As we reached the door, someone said, "There! There she is."

There was a burly security guy wearing an orange shirt by the exit door, and next to him stood the tall gangly asshole from the mosh pit. His face was covered with dried blood, and his eyes were wild with anger. He was flanked by a few of his friends, who looked somewhat amused and annoyed. The guy pointed at me. "That's her."

The security guy looked down at me in surprise. "Her?"

"Yeah! That little bitch broke my nose."

The security guard chuckled, and even the guy's friends cracked up. "Really?" the security guy said, grinning. "Sweetheart, did you beat this guy up?"

I smiled. "Nope. I have no idea what happened to him."

The bouncer turned his smile on the guy. "The little lady says no, my friend. And I'm inclined to believe her."

"Yeah right!" the guy said. "Why would I make this up?"

"Maybe because I wouldn't make out with you," I improvised, rolling my eyes at the bouncer.

The guy's friends howled, and interested onlookers started laughing too. The bouncer waved his hand at me dismissively. "Go on home," he said to me, and then turned to the guy. "Just 'cause you can't get lucky doesn't give you the right to try to get this girl in trouble." The guy started arguing like an idiot, flailing a pointed finger towards me, and I rolled my eyes again and turned my back on them. The five of us filed out of the building.

"Rachel, you are fucking *amazing*," Fern said. She and Yvonne linked their arms with mine, and we made our way back to the car.

The ride home was quiet. Yvonne and Edgar fell asleep, and Craig drove silently. Fern and I were still awake, but we didn't talk. We were all exhausted.

I sat staring out the window at the night. It was mostly farm pastures and forests, so there weren't many lights, but I watched the dark shadows as we sped past them, trying to absorb everything that had happened at the concert.

My hand was definitely hurting and stiff. I guessed it was swelling up. I hoped I hadn't fractured any of my bones. I thought of the wet, splattering *crunch* of the guy's nose and smiled. I was proud of myself for not being afraid of the blood, and not being afraid to help Fern. I admired my own strength. It was nice to know I had it. Never again would I fear anyone, be it Brandi or some psycho at a concert.

Soon enough we arrived at my house. I didn't want to wake anybody up, so I reluctantly leaned forward to whisper to Craig. Despite the awesome night we'd had, I still didn't like the guy. But I didn't want to be rude.

"Thanks for the ride," I said.

"Yeah, no problem," he replied. "I guess I'll see you at school?"

"Yep," I said and climbed out of the car. As they pulled away from the curb, I pranced up the driveway, feeling like a million bucks.

xXx

When I walked into the kitchen, my mother was sitting at the table in her pyjamas with a cup of chamomile tea in front of her. My boots were broken, my ears were ringing, and I'm sure I smelled terrible, let alone the fact that I looked awful with my smeared makeup and scraggly ponytails. Her stunned facial expression verified all of these things.

"I'm fine," I said before she could say anything. "I just look bad because it was very hot in there and there were a lot of people."

"Okay," she said, nodding. "What happened to your boots?"

"They broke. They were bad quality, I guess."

"How was the drive?"

"Uneventful. We came straight back. Pretty much everyone was asleep on the ride home. Totally safe."

Mom poured me a cup of tea, and I pulled off my boots. Sighing, I plopped heavily into the chair across from her. "It was a pretty fun night, though."

"How was the concert?"

"It was great! This band none of us had heard of opened, and they were only okay. But Surgical Carnage was great! Everyone was freaking out, and there was a mosh pit —"

"What happened to your *hand*?" Mom interrupted.

I looked down. It was really red, and definitely swollen. "Well, I had to help out Fern." I smiled. "Some guy, a real jerk, sort of assaulted her. In the crowd, he started trying to grab her. So I punched him in the face."

"Is it broken?" Mom got up to get me some ice from the freezer. As she wrapped it in a cloth, I moved my fingers. My hand definitely hurt, but my fingers all moved.

"I don't think so."

She handed me the ice and I pressed it to my hand. "So you punched a guy in the face?" She was frowning, and I realized that I should probably try to take some of the glee out of my story.

"Well, I had to. What else could I do? I had to get him away from her."

"But weren't you there with any boys? Didn't they help?"

"There were a lot of people there, but I was the closest." I scowled. "Besides, you can't always wait around for some *guy* to save you."

Mom fumbled for words for a moment. "That's true. But I don't think . . . I don't know if . . . I don't know if that was the best idea . . ."

"Mom, nothing *happened*. It was like self-defence. I hit him good to get him away from Fern, and then we immediately got away from him."

"What did the police say?"

"Nobody called the *police*," I retorted. Mom didn't get it. Why, once again, was I surprised? "I took care of it. The guy was an idiot."

"Was Josephine okay?"

"What does *she* have to do with anything?" It hit me right away that I'd lied and said that Josephine was going to be at the concert with us. Stupidly, I tried to recover. "Of course she was fine. She wasn't there when it happened. She'd gone to the back area of the club, with this other girl, Yvonne."

Mom studied me. I could tell she didn't believe that part of the story. "Well. I guess it was a tough situation, and I'm glad you helped Fern," she said. "But, Rachel, you have to remember, people can be unpredictable. I don't want you to get hurt."

"I can take care of myself," I said.

"Just promise me that you'll do your best to stay away from tricky situations like that."

"I do already. I *promise.*"

We said goodnight and headed to bed. I washed the makeup off my face, got changed, and crawled under the covers. My journal sat on the nightstand. I wrote:

> *Riding through the night on blackened wings*
> *Singed with blood and vengeance, hear the angels sing*
> *The demon crawled inside me when you hurt my friend*
> *Don't get mad at me when I know I must defend*
> *I crack your face and the blood spills out*
> *No one's going to hear you if you scream and shout*
> *Your blood is on my fist and my teeth are bared*
> *This is what you get for trying to make me scared*

FOURTEEN

My hand wasn't hurt too badly, and by the time I went to school on Monday, the swelling had mostly subsided. I was still riding high from the concert, and even though I was back to wearing my old winter boots, I felt unstoppable. As I walked through the halls that morning, I couldn't help but scan for Craig. Part of me hoped I'd see him. I knew he respected me for what I had done, but the first friendly face I saw was Josephine.

As we waited for Mr. Lee to begin art class, she noticed my hand. "What happened?"

"Oh, nothing," I said nonchalantly. "I was at a concert and this guy got out of line. I had to step in. I punched him in the face."

"*What?*"

"It was a Surgical Carnage concert." I muffled a yawn behind my hand. "Metal music. I went with Fern and a few other friends."

"You punched someone?"

"He was groping Fern in the mosh pit. I was right there. Someone had to stop him. I think I probably broke his nose." I smiled.

"You were in a *mosh pit?*" Josephine twisted her lips, confused. "Punching people?"

"Just him."

"Are you okay?"

"I think he's the one you should be asking. There was blood all over his face."

"That's terrible."

"Not really."

Mr. Lee started talking, and we were silent, listening to him outline the day's assignment. Boring — a coloured pencil drawing of an apple. Each table would be given a different variety of apple and we'd have the length of the class to sketch it as accurately as possible. He came by our table and put a bright green Granny Smith in front of us.

Josephine and I worked quietly for a little while. I could tell that Josephine disapproved of what had happened, but she wasn't saying anything. Just like my mother. It was becoming more and more apparent that I had been right all along. No one could truly understand me, unless they *got* me. And it seemed like Fern, and a few of her friends, were the only ones even coming close.

"So how was the concert?" Josephine finally asked. "Other than what happened with that guy?"

"It was a lot of fun," I said. "Really cool people. Great band. It was in St. Charles, so we got home really late. It was definitely after two in the morning."

She was quiet again for a while, and when she spoke, her voice sounded timid. "You know, I would have liked to go."

"No, you wouldn't," I said. "You're not into the music."

"So? It still would have been fun." Her voice was small, and part of me knew that she was nervous to talk to me about this. But at the same time, it really was ridiculous. She would have hated the concert. She didn't even like Fern!

"I don't think you would have liked it. And there wouldn't have been room in Craig's car for you anyway." I lifted my nose a bit, focusing down at my drawing as I shaded.

"Who's Craig?"

"Oh," I waved my hand casually, "he's that guy from last fall with the Bloodvomit shirt. With the long hair. I used to have a crush on him, but we're just friends now."

"Oh." Josephine scribbled at her drawing for a bit, and then abruptly put down her pencil crayon. "Rachel, do you *like* me still?" Her voice wavered as if she was going to cry.

I rolled my eyes. "Of *course* I do. Don't be silly."

"It's just that you don't seem like the same person anymore." She was getting more upset, and she lowered her voice to a whisper. "We used to go shopping all the time, we'd talk about guys, you know. I feel like you're really pushing me away."

"It's just because I've made a few new friends. You're jealous."

"I am not *jealous!*" I glanced at her and saw her eyes shiny with tears. I had to look away. "I just . . . you're my best friend!" She wiped her eyes.

I didn't know what to say. I'd been feeling so great all weekend, and here was Josephine, trying to make me feel like shit. "You have other friends, you know," I muttered. "From Our Lady. Why can't I have other friends too?"

"I . . . I just . . . I try to make an effort to include you and invite you to meet my friends, and you just act like what you do is so *special*, like I could never fit in with your friends or something."

I glanced up at Mr. Lee. He was focusing on some other kid's work and not paying any attention to us. I didn't want a scene. "You already know Fern. You could fit in with her," I said. "It isn't about who my friends are. It's about what we do. You would have hated that concert."

Josephine scowled. "Yeah. Well, you know what I told you about Fern. I wouldn't be so quick to become her best friend."

"Oh, really?" I turned on her, narrowing my eyes. I had to really concentrate to keep my voice low. "Well, I heard some stuff about you too, Josephine."

"What?"

"About your mother's boyfriend," I hissed. "About how you slept with him. And that's why you and your mother moved away."

She stared at me, speechless, her eyes round and wet. Fat tears rolled down her cheeks. "What do you know about that?"

"*Everyone* knows." I was being a jerk. I knew it. But she had to understand what a hypocrite she was, spreading rumours about Fern, when she also had rumours going around about her.

"That's . . . you . . . you don't understand . . ."

I shook my head in disgust, mainly at myself, and tried to soften my voice. "Listen, it's your business. All I'm trying to say is that you should be careful when you're spreading gossip. Because there's gossip about you too. If you don't want people talking about you, don't talk about other people."

Josephine stared at me, her shoulders shuddering as she tried not to burst into tears, then she finally got up and hurried out of the classroom. Mr. Lee watched her and then looked at me. I shrugged and went back to my drawing.

I did feel bad. Josephine had been my first real friend, and I understood why she would be jealous that I was meeting people and having fun without her. She had been catty and immature about the Fern rumours. But still.

When she returned and silently resumed her apple drawing, I leaned closer to her. I was ashamed of myself. I knew I should pity people like Josephine, who weren't strong enough to be happy with themselves and needed to put other people down to make themselves feel less jealous. "Hey," I whispered. "I'm sorry I said that."

She looked at me sideways. "It's none of your business, what happened in that situation."

"I know."

"I won't say anything bad about Fern again. But you have to promise that you will never, never mention that stuff to me ever again."

"I won't."

"I mean it, Rachel."

Obviously Josephine had been through something bad. Yvonne had made it seem like this scandalous, funny thing, with Josephine salaciously stealing her mother's boyfriend, but obviously that hadn't been the situation. I wanted to ask Josephine what happened, but she focused on her drawing for the rest of the class, ignoring me, her cheeks red. I remembered how in the car, it had occurred to me that the guy sounded like a child molester. This seemed like a more accurate scenario, based on the facts I knew and on Josephine's reaction. I should never have brought it up. There was a big difference between these two rumours, one being a friend in a peacock-killing Satanic cult and the other her having been abused by her mother's boyfriend. One was ridiculous. The other, possible, and devastating.

XXX

At lunch Josephine made small talk but avoided looking at me. She was still upset, and that was fine with me. She had other friends if she wanted to talk about what had happened to her, because she obviously wasn't going to confide in me. A small voice inside me suggested that no one would want to confide in someone who would treat her situation so callously.

After school, I shut my locker and slung my book bag over my shoulder. I was about to head down the hall when I felt a tap. It was Craig.

"Hey," he said and grinned.

"How are you?" I asked. He really was cute.

"Not bad. How's the hand?"

"All healed up," I said, opening and closing my fist to show him.

"Great. Well, see you around," he said, then smiled again and headed in the other direction. It was weird. He was handsome and cool, but I hadn't forgotten that underneath it all he was an asshole. He could smile at me all he wanted. And believe me, I was glad that we were now friendly. It was good having someone else at school I could get along with. But I knew I would never like Craig, not in any genuine way. He'd been so shitty to me that first time in the hall. Sure, maybe I had proved myself to him. But he hadn't proved himself to me.

Fern called after dinner that evening and asked me if I wanted to go get a cup of tea downtown. Since I had no homework, my parents agreed, so I met her at this nice little tea shop and we ordered a pot of green tea with sliced lemons. I didn't know much about tea. My parents had always been coffee drinkers, except for chamomile, but Fern was all into different teas.

"So," she said. "Do you really want to start a band?"

"Maybe. I mean, sure. I have a ton of lyrics written."

"Have you tried singing?"

"Not really. I sing along to music in my room. I can kinda growl a bit." I blushed.

"Well, I think we should really try." Fern looked eager. "In class today this idea for a guitar part just struck me out of nowhere. Just this really cool, heavy part. I wrote it down, so when I got home, I tried playing it. It sounded awful without any effects of course, but it's good."

My mind started racing. "So, you'd play guitar. I guess I could try singing. But we'd need bass, drums . . ."

Fern nodded. "Edgar has a bass. His dad used to be in some jazz band or something a long time ago. I think he'd be interested. I have no idea about a drummer, though."

We sat, thoughtful, for a few minutes, sipping our tea. A band! It would be fun. We could play shows. I tried to imagine myself onstage. With a microphone, screaming and growling. In front of a crowd. "I can't think of any heavy metal bands with girl singers," I said.

"I know there are a few, but they aren't very big. Craig had a CD, I forget the band's name. But they had a girl singer. She was okay. But I bet you could do way better." Fern was definitely serious about this. "We'd be awesome. We'd just have to get together a few songs, and we could play shows and stuff."

"What about gear? It's expensive. You'd need an amp and some effects pedals."

She nodded. "Yeah, we'll have to work that stuff out. But what do you think? Do you want to really give it a try? I could talk to Edgar, see if he's into it."

"Yeah," I said, smiling. "Sure. Why not?"

FIFTEEN

The next weekend, Fern and I met up with Edgar at the same tea shop. Fern and I had talked on the phone every evening that week, fantasizing about going on tour and playing live shows. I'd written in my journal a ton, drafting new lyrics. I'd turned up my DED CD really loud and tried to emulate Balthazar Seizure's singing voice. I sounded pretty decent. I could definitely rumble and roar and growl and gurgle like he could, but I felt silly doing it. I knew I'd need to practise more.

We sat at the table with Edgar and laid it out to him. "We want to start a band," Fern said. "A metal band. We'd like you to be in it."

"Really?" Edgar leaned forward, interested. "Doing what?"

"Can you play bass?" I asked.

"A little bit, I guess." He frowned a little. "I mean, my dad has a bass and stuff. I've played around on it. But, I mean, to play metal music? That's difficult."

"We're not saying we're going to play a show next weekend," Fern said. "We all need to practise. I'm going to do guitar, and I need a ton of work. It's more just to see if you're interested, if you want to be in the band. We'll figure the rest out as it comes."

"What about you, Rachel? What are you going to do in the band?" he asked.

"Sing. I can do it. I just need to practise. And I have a ton of lyrics and stuff."

"What about a drummer? Do you guys know anyone?"

"No," Fern said.

He thought for a second. "We could put up a flyer at the record store or something."

"Does this mean you want to do it?" I said.

"Sure," he said. Fern and I exclaimed happily, clasping hands. "But," he said, "I'd want to do it right. We need a drummer. We all need to be damn good. Metal's not easy to play."

"Remember Catastrophic Enzyme?" I said. "They sucked, and they got a show opening for a big band."

We all laughed.

Once a week we would meet at the tea shop and talk. We called them "band meetings," even though it was just the three of us. Most of the time we just chatted about silly fantasy stuff. Travelling the world, getting a tour bus, meeting celebrities. We had no drummer, we had no name, and we had no music — sort of important, right? We couldn't move forward without three things, but the three of us got very passionate about the idea.

I spent all my time after school going through my journals and poems, trying to piece together actual songs. Sometimes during the week Fern and Edgar would get together in Edgar's basement and play guitar and bass. Edgar's dad didn't mind the noise downstairs, but Edgar worried that once we got a drummer and started actual rehearsals that it might be too loud. His dad had some amps and gear left over from his band days, so they were able to use them, but the gear was old. We had no money to get anything new, but what we had seemed to work just fine.

Summer came and we could focus on the band full-time. Josephine and I had remained friends, and since she was going to spend most of the summer visiting relatives I didn't have to worry about trying to politely budget time for her. I would be able to immerse myself spending time with Fern and Edgar.

We realized that without a name for the band, there was only so much we could do. We had ideas but all of them sucked; they either sounded too funny or too clichéd, and we couldn't settle on anything. Most of the time when we'd try to think up ideas we would just end up laughing, unable to take it seriously. Bloodbeard? Vampirate?

One boiling July afternoon, I came into the kitchen from my bedroom to get something to snack on and my mother was on the phone with one of my aunts. One of my great uncles or someone had gotten sick, and they were chatting about his stay in the hospital. As I made myself a bowl of cereal, I half-listened to my mother's side of the conversation.

"Oh, he's still on the oxygen. And they've got him on a colostomy bag as well. To be honest, I'm almost glad he's in the hospital — this heat would have been too much for him. Although I can't understand why he just doesn't buy an air conditioner . . ."

My mother talked on, and I carried my cereal back into my bedroom. What on earth was a *colostomy bag*?

I grabbed my dictionary. *Colostomy bag: a container positioned to collect feces discharged through the opening made by a colostomy.*

A quick scan of the page revealed that a *colostomy* was *a surgical opening in the colon to bypass a diseased portion of colon and allow the passage of intestinal contents.*

Hideous — but interesting. An idea struck me, and I thought it was pretty great.

XXX

At the tea shop when I met Fern and Edgar that week, I smiled triumphantly. "I have an idea for the band name."

Both of them rolled their eyes and grinned. To be honest, I'd said that very thing a few times before, and so had they. And every idea had resulted in gales of laughter. When they'd laughed at my ideas, I'd joined in, but secretly I'd been hurt by it — I thought I'd had some pretty good ideas. But I was sure this time they'd love it.

"All right, so what is it?" Edgar asked.

I paused for dramatic effect. "Colostomy Hag."

"Colostomy Hag?" Edgar sputtered. "What the hell is that?"

"Like, colostomy *bag?*" Fern said. I nodded, grinning.

"What's a colostomy bag?" Edgar asked.

"When the doctors have to drain your crap out of you, because you've had surgery and can't use your intestines, it gets drained into a colostomy bag," I said.

He thought for a second, and nodded. "That's damn gross. And *hag!*"

"Because there's girls in the band," I said.

Fern started laughing. "You know what, I love it! It's disgusting and it's hilarious. I vote for Colostomy Hag."

Edgar smiled, shaking his head. "All right, I agree. It's the best we've come up with."

"All right!" I raised my hands in the air. "We're called Colostomy Hag!"

And so that's what the band would be called. I started sketching out ideas for band logos and artwork. I was definitely getting ahead of myself, but we did need a logo. I brought my sketches to the tea shop and ran them past Edgar and Fern, and they picked out what they liked. Deciding on a name for the band definitely made things feel more official, but we knew that all of this would go nowhere without the music. And we still didn't have a drummer. Without a drummer we couldn't play songs. We couldn't even rehearse until we had the full band, so all our plans were pretty much hollow.

It was early August when Fern and I went downtown to look around at some stores. I'd been doing more around the house so that my parents would help me make some changes to my room, and they had upped my allowance as well, so I had a bit of money. Fern and I looked in a few of the thrift stores and didn't find anything good, so we headed to the music store.

It had become a bit of a habit for us to browse the bulletin board by the cash register. There was rarely anything interesting: flyers for concerts we weren't into, people selling instruments, offering piano lessons, stuff like that. I couldn't think of a time when I'd seen anything on there that even came close to interesting, much less anything to do with heavy metal. None of us had gotten around to advertising on the board ourselves to find a drummer yet.

That day, however, we saw a new flyer. *Drummer Needs Band — influenced by DED, Gurgol, Goreceps, looking for like-minded individuals to rock with.* There was a phone number listed.

"Great!" Fern exclaimed, grabbing a pen out of her purse and writing the number down on the back of her hand.

"'Looking for people to *rock* with'?" I wrinkled my nose. "That sounds dorky."

"Well, it's not like we've got tons of people to choose from. Let's call him and see what he's like," she replied.

She was right. The flyer seemed almost too good to be true, despite its idiotic wording. We went to a pay phone on the street. Fern put in her quarter and dialled.

"Hi, yes," she said shortly, "I'm calling about the flyer in Bee Music. About the drummer." She paused, listening. I watched her face. "Yeah, we've got a band. Vocal, guitar, and bass. Doing original stuff." After another pause she listed off a few bands we liked, mentioning DED and Gurgol. "We have a female vocalist, and I play guitar. So there's two girls in the band."

After chatting for a few more minutes, she set up a meeting with him at the tea shop for that evening. I tried to mentally calculate whether or not Edgar would be available, while she wrapped up the call.

Finally she hung up. "Okay, he sounded nice. His name is Socks."

"Socks?"

"Yeah. He didn't tell me his real name."

"That's not a very cool nickname," I muttered. Pairing that with the *I wanna rock* flyer, I wasn't feeling very hopeful. "He's probably a complete moron."

"Well, there's only one way to find out," Fern said. "I'm going to call Edgar and tell him to meet us tonight."

The two of us met Edgar a half hour before Socks was supposed to show up. Edgar had been playing his bass all afternoon and looked pretty exhausted when he arrived and sat down.

"I'm really glad we found somebody. The songs are shaping up and it would be nice to be able to get together and actually try to play something," he said.

"I don't know," I said. "This guy sounds like kind of a loser to me." I explained to Edgar the way the flyer had been worded.

"So what if he wants to *rock*? He sounded perfectly nice on the phone," Fern said, lightly slapping my hand and giving me a grin. "I mean, when it comes down to it, we want to *rock* too, don't we?"

Edgar laughed. "I wonder why his name is Socks."

"Maybe because he stinks," I said.

After a little while, the bell above the tea shop door jingled, signalling the arrival, presumably, of Socks. We knew right away that it couldn't be anyone but him. He was tall and burly, with long shaggy brown hair and a long goatee. He wore a metal shirt pulled down over his substantial belly and long black shorts. And bright white socks pulled up high on his shins.

"Oh, wow," Fern said.

He scanned the room for a moment and when he caught sight of us, his face lit up and he raised his hand in greeting. "Hiya!" he said brightly, turning the heads of the other tea shop customers as he came to our table.

We all stood up to introduce ourselves and shake his hand, and then he pulled up a chair and we all sat back down.

"So, yeah, it's great to meet you all," he said. "I've been playing metal since I was a kid. I just got out of school and I'm looking for a band to play with, get back into it."

"We're just starting out," Edgar said.

"You must be bass, right? Fern here told me it was two girls on guitar and vox, and a dude on bass."

Vox? I had to prevent myself from shuddering noticeably. I didn't want to offend him. He did seem like a nice guy.

"Yeah," Edgar said, grinning. "Fern's guitar, and Rachel does *vox*."

I smiled, probably showing too much tooth as I tried to make it as genuine as possible. "That's right."

"Can you wail?" Socks said to me, very seriously.

I hesitated as Fern and Edgar both covered their smiles and awaited my answer. "Uh, yeah, sure I can. I can wail."

"Well, that's good then." Socks sat back. "A band's only as good as their singer, you know. And a girl singer in metal, well, that'll be somethin' else. Don't come across that too often."

We asked him some questions about himself. He was a few years older than we were, having just graduated from high school. He was working for his father's construction company and had been playing drums for years.

"Why do they call you 'Socks'?" Fern asked.

"'Cause I always wear nice white ones," he said, lifting his foot and pointing at the socks we had all noticed when he walked in. "Guess it's kinda my trademark."

Socks invited us to his house to hear him play. He lived a short drive from downtown and had a minivan parked outside the tea shop. "You can't have a drummer without a vehicle," he said as we walked to the van. "Gotta have some way to carry your stuff. It's not easy like a guitar case!"

As we drove to his house, he chatted about how he'd been in a few bands while he was in school. "Nothing serious, of course," he said. "Just jamming out on the weekends. Played a few gigs, really small stuff, did a battle of the bands, that kind of thing. I'm definitely looking for some serious players this time around."

"We haven't rehearsed yet, we're still writing," Fern told him. "We have maybe five or six songs, and Rachel's working on lyrics for them. We wanted to get a full band together before we started going through them, even though Edgar and I have been playing together."

"Sounds good," Socks said, turning off the main road onto a tree-lined side street. "I'm pretty intuitive. I'll be able to come up with some beats once we start jamming."

No one was home at Socks's house, and we filed through the side door down into his basement. The ceiling was low, and we walked through the rec room to a smaller darker area. He flipped on the light switch in this smaller room, illuminating a giant drum kit.

"Wow, double kick!" Fern said, gesturing at his two kick drums. "You can play that?"

"I consider it to be a necessity when you're playing metal," he said, smiling. "So you want me to just rock out for a bit? Give you guys a show?"

"Sure," Edgar said.

Socks sat down behind the kit and began to play.

And it was pretty much decided immediately that we wanted him in the band. Any hesitations I had about him being a bit dorky went out the window. He was really, really good. Exactly what we needed. The band was finally coming together. He played complicated fills, pulled back and played steady rhythms, sped up to the point where his hands were a blur across the kit, and all without missing a beat.

After he quit, we hung out on the couches in the rec room and chatted some more. "My parents won't care if we want to rehearse down here on the weekends," Socks said. "I got my van, so we can pick up your stuff and move it all in down here."

"Sounds good." Fern nodded.

"Oh, by the way, the band got a name?"

"Yeah," I said. "Colostomy Hag."

Socks threw back his head and laughed. "That's *good.*"

The sun was setting when we left Socks's place, and since Edgar and Fern lived farther out than I did, I was the last one to be dropped off and ended up by myself with Socks in the van.

"I'm super stoked to hear you sing, I gotta say," he said. "I'm glad you guys gave me a call. You're all real nice people."

"Yeah, hopefully this works out," I replied. "You're a great drummer. I'm excited to rehearse."

"It'll work out. Of course it will. We just gotta jam a bit and see. Get some songs going, play some gigs." Socks turned onto my street, and I saw Mom kneeling in the front yard wearing her floppy brimmed straw hat. I pointed at the house. "That's my place."

"Is that your mom? Awesome!" He smoothly moved the van directly in front of the house, and Mom looked up from her pile of weeds. Her eyes widened as she saw Socks waving frantically at her. To my horror, as I climbed out of the passenger side, he hopped out of the van and extended his hand to my mother.

"Hi, I'm Socks!" he announced.

Immediately my mother's eyes flicked down to his legs, and she nodded vaguely, as if verifying the nickname. She then took off one of her garden gloves and shook his hand, glancing at me. "I'm Rachel's mother, Marilyn," she said.

"Nice to meet ya. I can't wait to hear Rachel sing," he said. "I'm gonna be the drummer in the band if everything works out."

Mom looked at me, and I smiled, lifting my shoulders. "It was nice to meet you today, Socks," I said, hoping to get rid of him.

"Oh, you too, Rachel," he said, shaking my hand as well. "I'll see you next week. Colostomy Hag . . . what a name! Looking forward to it!"

I stood next to my mother as we watched him climb back in the van and pull away, waving at us happily through the window.

"Rachel?" she said.

"Let's go inside and talk about it," I said.

SIXTEEN

They sat across the table from me as if I was at a job interview. My father had no idea what had happened, so Mom filled him in.

"I guess Rachel is starting a band," she said.

He looked at me, and I nodded. "Just for fun. With a few friends. Fern and Edgar, and we just met the drummer today."

"Socks," Mom supplied. "They're called . . . *Colostomy Hag.*"

A loud chuckle erupted from my father, and Mom was grinning too, even though I knew they were both trying hard to be stern and serious. I smiled, and then we all laughed.

"That's a funny name," Dad admitted. "What are you going to do in the band?"

"I'm going to be the singer. I've been writing a lot of lyrics, and Fern and Edgar have been working on music. We're going to rehearse next week."

I was very surprised that they hardly argued with me,

beyond the usual crap about being careful. In fact, after a while of talking about how it wouldn't mess up school in the fall, they were pretty supportive.

"You've always been good with writing, and I think it'll be great for you to have something to channel that into," Mom said.

Dad agreed. "I don't mind this idea at all."

"It'll be a fun hobby," Mom said. All right. So they weren't going to take it seriously, that was fine by me. They could look at it as a silly little project. And if they looked at it as something that I could do that would keep me off the streets and away from the dreaded booze 'n' drugs, even better. It still irritated me that they had such little faith in me, but that was fine. Didn't matter. We had a drummer! We were going to *jam* next week, and I would finally get to show them how I could *wail*. I laughed to myself, thinking of Socks and how ridiculous and good-natured he seemed. We had a *band*. I went to my bedroom and looked up at a poster of Marie-Lise. Sweat poured off her face, makeup smeared, hair flying as she clutched her bass, one booted foot braced on the stage monitor in front of her. Maybe that would be me one day.

I felt rejuvenated, and for the next few days I threw myself into the housework I'd been assigned. As I weeded the back garden I listened to music on my headphones, studying the vocals, noticing what I liked and disliked about different singers, and making mental notes on what to try at rehearsal. As I hung up the winter blankets from the back closet to air out on the clothesline, I fantasized about being onstage, with people screaming and cheering and knocking each other out in the mosh pit. It was fun, trying to imagine what I would wear and how I would style my hair and do my makeup. Of course I envisioned myself as being the ultimate in coolness, flanked by Fern looking gorgeous and Edgar looking tough, bounding around the stage with his dreads flying. And Socks in the back, looking mean, growling behind the drum kit.

It was all good to think about these things, but before rehearsal as I waited for Socks, I actually felt nervous. He'd picked up Fern, Edgar, and their gear first, and I sat on the front lawn with my lyric book in my lap. I knew it was silly to be nervous: it would be our first rehearsal together. None of us knew what we were doing. Fern had expressed my exact worry on the phone the other night: "What if I suck?"

It was reassuring to know she was just as nervous as I was. I mean, I'd sung along with my CDs in my room, with the stereo blasting loud enough that my family couldn't hear me shrieking along, but how would my voice sound by itself? What if they didn't like the lyrics or thought I couldn't sing? I recalled how Socks had said that a band is only as good as its singer. What if they wanted to find someone else?

I shook my head, trying to calm myself. The band was mine and Fern's. If Socks or Edgar didn't like it, well, we would find other people to play with.

The van pulled up, and Fern grinned at me through the passenger window. Edgar pulled open the back door for me and I climbed in beside him.

Everyone was happy and excited, and we chatted the whole way to Socks's house, blasting some DED on the car stereo.

"This is gonna be great," Edgar said to me over the loud music. "I can't wait. Me and Fern have five songs all ready to go, all we need is Socks to get into it with the drums and for you to put your vocals in."

I nodded and smiled, still afraid that I was going to disappoint. Fern turned around in the front seat and stuck her tongue out at me. I grinned and stuck mine out back.

We carried all the stuff we needed into Socks's basement. Edgar had borrowed some amps from his father, and the guys carried those down the stairs while Fern and I carried the guitar cases. "I'm nervous," I said to her while we were alone on the stairs. "I don't want to sound bad."

"I know what you *mean*," she commiserated. "I've been practising every night and Edgar says I sound great, but still."

"I know you'll be awesome," I murmured, squeezing her arm. "I can't wait to hear you play."

"You're going to be amazing too." Fern would have my back, no matter what the guys thought.

While Edgar and Fern set up their amps and pedals, Socks set up a microphone stand for me, also borrowed from Edgar's father, and I plugged in the microphone.

"Hello," I said, and jumped. The others looked up, startled at the loudness of my voice.

"This is going to be *really* loud," Edgar said.

"It has to be, so she can hear herself over the drum kit," Socks said. "You guys are going to have to turn up pretty loud too."

"Won't your parents be pissed?"

"Nah," Socks replied. "They aren't home. And the neighbours are all old people, half deaf anyways. I jam down here all the time, nobody ever said anything."

Socks took his seat behind the drum kit and Fern and Edgar pulled their guitars over their shoulders, checking the amps. Once everything was set up, there was an awkward silence. For some reason Socks was looking at me expectantly, as if I was supposed to get things started. I panicked and fumbled, trying to think of something to say. I glanced at Fern and realized that both she and Edgar were also looking at me, waiting. I felt blood rush to my face and hoped they didn't notice my confusion.

"Okay, so, let's play a song," I said awkwardly.

"Right," Edgar said. "So Fern, why don't we play something and then, Socks and Rachel, you guys can join in when you're ready. We'll just go through it a bunch of times."

"Cool!" Socks replied, raising a fist from behind the drum kit.

"Okay," I said, nodding. Fern gave me a nod and a small smile, which I tried to take strength from. She looked absolutely amazing, with her long white hair contrasting the shiny black of her guitar. I didn't feel ready, but I felt proud.

Facing each other, Edgar and Fern counted themselves in and started playing. Socks and I watched as Fern's fingers moved quickly over the fretboard for the song's intro melody, and Edgar backed her up. I was surprised, to be honest. They both played fast, and it was better than I had expected it would be.

They moved into the first verse, and Socks joined in with a crash of cymbals, proving, indeed, that he could play intuitively. Somehow he was able to estimate where chorus would turn to verse and back again, and when he missed it at one point he immediately corrected himself so it was barely noticeable. I stood and watched Socks's hands moving so fast they seemed to be a blur, throwing in the double kick for the chorus portion as Fern and Edgar thundered along. It was so loud that my stomach felt a bit queasy, and as they relaxed into the song, I was struck with the thought that they all played better than I had thought they would, especially for a first rehearsal, and I felt even queasier at the thought of joining in. Fern launched into a solo, her fingers dancing up and down, and it was a little sloppy but she corrected herself so quickly that it was obvious she was going to be a really good player. Even Socks, hammering away on the drums, watched her and nodded to himself as if acknowledging how amazing she was.

When they finished, the three of them grinned at each other.

"That was great," Socks said. "Sorry I had a couple little screw-ups here and there."

"Nah," Edgar replied. "That was amazing. It'll be even better when we go through it again."

"You're amazing, Fern," Socks said.

She smiled. "Thanks. It was a bit sloppy, but I'll nail it." She looked over to me, and I smiled at her. "What do you think, Rachel?"

"I hope I can do it justice," I said, trying to infuse my voice with confidence.

"Let's run through it again," Edgar said. "Can you join in, Rachel?"

"Yeah." I stepped up to the microphone. I ruffled the papers in my little lyrics book, completely horrified. Not only had I seen how amazing this band was going to be, but I was also about to prove to the three of them that I had no place in it. I felt Fern's eyes on me and I looked up at her. She nodded. I looked away, totally betraying my nervousness.

This time Socks counted them in, and I tried to remember the structure of the song. I opened my mouth during the intro and let out a growling wail, surprised at how loud it sounded coming through the speakers. The three of them looked at me, Edgar breaking into a giant grin, Socks nodding in approval, and I stretched the shriek for as long as I could. Fern smiled and rolled her eyes, as if she had known all along that it would be okay and I was silly to have worried. But as the song rolled uncontrollably towards the first verse, I knew there was still time for me to completely fail at this. My eyes flicked down to the lyrics. It was one thing to roar during an intro, it was another thing altogether to make it through a song in pure growling shrieks. I pictured Balthazar Seizure in my mind, and Marie-Lise, and took a deep breath.

Riding through the night on blackened wings
Singed with blood and vengeance, hear the angels sing

It wasn't perfect, and I missed my cues a few times, and Edgar messed up during the bridge, but Fern nailed her solo perfectly. To this day it's pretty much the exact same song as it was that first time we played it. We played that song over and over again that afternoon, changing things here and there, making suggestions to each other. By the end of rehearsal we pretty much had what ended up being "Blood on My Fist."

SEVENTEEN

We started rehearsing every weekend, and I knew I was impressing them with my vocals. I listened to music non-stop at home, always putting on DED and trying to emulate Balthazar's voice as best I could. He really was the best vocalist of all the bands I listened to, never overdramatic with his growls, never drawing out a roar for too long, knowing when to back off and let the music become the focus, knowing which parts to emphasize, which lyrics to highlight by taking the edge off, and even allowing himself to regress back into a whisper at times.

A lot of other vocalists made mistakes, I thought, and had no dynamic. Some of them would go over the top to the point of sounding ridiculous. Some would draw out a roar until it almost sounded like a burp. Some would add too many random growls and totally dominate the song, which detracted from it. Balthazar never did these things, which made him distinctive, and that's why I tried to work with the same style he did. At rehearsal I relished when the others would smile as I allowed myself to start with a whisper and escalate to a shriek, and as I would accent as opposed to overpower what they were doing musically.

One afternoon at rehearsal, we were sitting on the couches in the rec room. We'd been working on a few new songs and now had four to run through. Socks put on a CD by some band none of us had heard of: there was a guest vocalist on one of the tracks that he wanted me to hear. Her name was Annika. Apparently she was from Norway and did guest gigs on a bunch of different metal albums. I was curious to hear another female metal singer.

The music was mediocre, but I straightened my back and smiled to myself as I listened to the song. She wasn't any good, allowing her voice to get carried away and dominate the song. It was almost as though she was trying to exploit her voice, to emphasize the novelty of having a female vocal in a heavy metal song, and it was annoying. I congratulated myself for not making the same mistake. Yes, it was going to be unusual for a metal band to have a female singer. But I wasn't going to attempt to draw attention to it in the way that this Annika did. Colostomy Hag was going to succeed, or fail, on its true musical and lyrical merits, not because of the presence of females in the group.

We finished listening to the song and were still relaxing on the couches when Socks commented, "We got a pretty unusual band here, don't you think?"

Edgar laughed. "Two girls, a black guy, and *you*. Yeah, I'd say it's pretty unusual."

"And not just that." Socks nodded. "I mean, Rachel, you're so much better than Annika, and she's the most prominent girl singer in metal. You kick her ass. And Fern, you are amazing on guitar. Like, *really* good. And you're going to get better and better."

"That's surprising?"

"Well, yeah," Socks said. "I haven't seen a girl play guitar as good as you, like, ever."

One night when I was on the phone with Fern, I brought up what Socks had said. "Why do you think there aren't more girls in metal? I mean, I can think of Marie-Lise and that Annika, but that's it. It's all guys."

"I don't know," she said. "Maybe it's because guys don't want to give girls a chance or something. Maybe they think girls don't have the aggression to play metal. You see how surprised Socks is by the fact that I can play. Maybe guys just dismiss us, because they think we can't fit the image or something. Or think that we can't play. Or they hear that awful Annika and just assume that girls can't sing metal either."

"I think we have a really good chance to prove them all wrong," I said. "Imagine if we play shows? Get famous? We'll be the only band with girls in it that's done that."

"Except for Marie-Lise and Gurgol," Fern agreed. "Wouldn't it be cool to meet Marie-Lise? Talk to her and ask her what it's been like for her in the band?"

"Yeah," I replied. "I think it'd be pretty cool to meet Balthazar Seizure. He's such a damn amazing singer. I'd totally like to ask him a couple of things."

She laughed. "You *like* him," she teased. "You totally crush on him. You do realize you're always talking about him, right?"

"It's because I find him inspiring," I said. How silly, to have a crush on a musician. So what if he was really talented and also had all that long hair and those gorgeous eyes and was so tall and handsome and . . . it was foolish to have band crushes. I giggled then, even though I knew it was ridiculous, and looked up at my poster of him. He looked back down at me, and I

143

wondered if one day, if our band ever did anything important and got anywhere, whether or not he would be impressed by me. The whole thing was so ridiculous, but I couldn't help it.

As summer waned I made some changes to my room, as promised by my parents and as earned by me by doing extra stupid chores around the house. It wasn't so bad, weeding the backyard or sorting through the basement storage or whatever other pointless idea my parents dreamed up to justify giving me the money to buy black bedding and paint for my furniture. I'd just put on my headphones and focus on Balthazar's voice while I mindlessly worked.

The duck lamp ended up in Melissa's room.

EIGHTEEN

School started again, and the problems I'd had with Josephine at the end of last year seemed to have blown over. We had a few classes together, and she chattered about her summer — her family and going to parties and other crap — as though we hadn't argued at all. It was nice to have a friend there even though I couldn't have cared less about school. I would just drudge through the week, waiting for weekend rehearsals, and spend my nights doing homework, listening to music, and writing.

Edgar got the idea to try recording our rehearsal. Socks rigged up a few microphones around the room, and we ran through our four songs. We sat back on the couches afterwards and played back the recording.

I was happy to hear that my attempts to incorporate Balthazar's techniques were working. I sounded really fucking good. Hearing the songs played back without seeing my friends play them was really weird. Without watching Fern play her solos, for example, I was able to listen to them objectively, and once again acknowledge how good she really was. The recording was pretty crappy, but all of us were really impressed with the way we were starting to sound.

"We *have* to play a show," Socks announced afterwards.

"We can't play a show with only four songs," Fern said. "But I agree, it would be awesome."

Socks burned copies for all of us, and even though it sounded lousy, I listened to the CD over and over. We were a good band. Even the shoddy recording couldn't hide it.

As winter neared, I was finding it very hard to focus on school when all I wanted to do was spend time with Edgar, Socks, and Fern working on music. I was jealous that Fern and Edgar went to the same school and I was stuck at Glen Park with Josephine. Sometimes I would see Craig in the hallways, and we'd wave at each other, but I was finding it increasingly frustrating that I was basically alone at school. During classes I would sit and look out the window, daydreaming, and often writing lyric ideas in my notebooks rather than taking notes on whatever subject I should have been focusing on.

One afternoon I was in the school bathroom, washing my hands, when the door swung open and in walked Brandi. I immediately looked away from her, back to my reflection. My stomach jittered. I was pissed at myself. All of last year I hadn't had any problems with her. In fact, she hadn't spoken to me in such a long time that I felt stupid for reacting to her at all. But I couldn't help it. She paused, and to distract myself I pulled out my lipstick and focused on my reflection, leaning forwards and applying more of it to my lips.

"It doesn't really help," she said.

I rubbed my lips together and didn't look at her.

"The lipstick," she said, in a mock-helpful tone. "It really doesn't help you look any better."

I turned to her. She stood there, with her eyes wide, trying to make herself look innocent, but she had a pleased smirk.

"You don't think so?" I had never had such prolonged eye contact with her, and I was pleased to find that my fear was subsiding. I stared at her, and she boldly met my gaze.

"You're still fucking ugly. No lipstick or hair dye is ever going to help you with that." She grinned, folded her arms, and waited for my response.

I tucked my lipstick back into my skirt pocket. "You know, you haven't spoken to me in a really long time. What's inspired you today?"

"I'm just trying to give you some tips."

I didn't respond to that, just stared at her, and to my pleasure I saw her falter for a second. "Don't you have anything to say for yourself?" she finally said.

"Sure," I said. "I've spent a lot of time thinking about you." I smiled. "Ever since that day after exams, I've thought about you a lot." I took a step towards her, maintaining eye contact. "I've even had some really nice fantasies about you."

"Oh, really?" Brandi was starting to look a little upset, a little uncomfortable, but she managed to retain the smug tone. "What are you, a dyke now too? An ugly dyke?"

"Oh, no. Not those kind of fantasies." I grinned and she swallowed. I felt a rush of joy realizing that I was scaring her. "Very, very different ones. You bitch."

"You're crazy," she fumbled, breaking our eye contact and rolling her eyes. She tried to paste the smirk back on her face.

I took another step towards her, still grinning. "What's wrong, Brandi?" I said. "Don't you want to know what I think about? Don't you want to know what goes through my ugly head?" I was really enjoying this. Her growing discomfort made my heartbeat pick up. I almost felt giddy. "I dare you to push me. I dare you to touch me again," I pressed. "Try it. Just fucking *try it*. Like you did before."

At this, she attempted to rally. Smirk gone, her face turning red, she returned my gaze. "Maybe I will."

I felt like I was dancing, like my body was buzzing. "Then do it, you stupid bitch," I laughed. My face was starting to hurt, but I couldn't stop smiling. I reached my hands out to her as if I was inviting her to hug me. "I'm here right now, Brandi. I *want* you to," I said.

"You're fucking crazy and this isn't worth my time," she said, beginning to turn towards the door. Immediately I darted at her and grabbed her blonde ponytail in my hand. She cried out in shock. I yanked her head back and put my mouth close to her ear.

"Don't fuck with me again," I hissed. "Because I will *kill* you. Get it? I'm not kidding. I will cut your throat."

"Leave me alone," she howled, and I jerked her hair, silencing her.

"No. You leave *me* alone. I don't bother you, do I? I never have. So give me the same respect. Because I will cut your throat, Brandi. I'm sick of you. And watching you die would make me very happy." I was full of shit, of course, but I relished in feeling her body trembling with fear, in the stench of her sweat beginning to show beneath the coconut perfume. "I'll cut your head off and wrap it in a sheet," I said, resisting a very strong urge to lick her earlobe. I imagined how horrified she would be if I did that, out of nowhere.

Brandi twisted and pulled herself away from me, and I let her go. She whirled to face me, one hand rubbing her sore head, cheeks scarlet, a light sheen of sweat glinting on her forehead.

"You're psycho," she stumbled, trying to collect herself. I

was pleased to see no trace of smirk or sarcasm in her tone, and absently nodded in agreement, continuing to smile at her.

"Keep away from me," she said. "From now on. Just leave me alone."

"That was never a problem," I said. "You're the one who leaves *me* alone from now on."

She couldn't disagree, so there was no reply as she left. I turned back to the mirror to examine my reflection, and I wondered two things. Would Brandi *tell on me*? I hadn't had a run-in with Ms. Coates since the poetry incident, and I didn't exactly relish the idea of getting called to her office. I was pretty confident I'd be able to talk my way out of any trouble, but if she called my parents, they'd get all freaked out, and I didn't want anything to interfere with band practice.

The other thing I realized was that Brandi had come into the bathroom and hadn't actually *gone*. Presumably she'd come in here to pee. Of course, how could she calmly go into a stall to use the toilet in front of me after I'd completely terrified her? I pictured her, with my hand gripping her hair, peeing herself in her stupid designer jeans, and I laughed loudly and sharply. It echoed in the tiled room, and I clapped my hand over my mouth to stifle the sound. I caught the reek of her hairspray on my hand, and my stomach turned, jerking me from my happy thoughts. I turned on the faucet, pumping soap from the dispenser into my palm and scrubbing my hands ferociously under the water.

I should probably note that this was the inspiration for our song "Piss Your Pants," the lyrics of which I began to write that very day when I went back to class.

If Brandi told anyone about what had happened, nothing ever came of it. Whenever I'd see her in the halls, she'd avoid my eyes and hurry past. I imagined that she'd kept her mouth shut about it, too embarrassed to tell anyone that I, the ugliest bitch at school, had won against her. I treasured that memory the same way I treasured the memory of the asshole at the Surgical Carnage show. It was like I had some secret knowledge that no one else knew about. I was above the rest. I only had a year and a half left at this stupid school, but in my mind I was already done with it. I knew I was going somewhere very special, and Brandi and Josephine and every nameless asshole I passed in the hall were irrelevant to my future. And in my head I challenged every one of them, daring them to mess with me. I felt unstoppable. A nice feeling, while it lasted.

NINETEEN

I was loading my books into my locker after school when I felt a tap on my shoulder. I turned to see Craig standing behind me.

We hadn't become close or particularly friendly. He still hung out with Fern and Edgar, but I didn't join in — especially since I had no desire to drink, and that's what they'd often do on Saturday nights after practice. I would always opt to go home afterwards, and it wasn't just because of my aversion to drinking and my antisocial feelings about being around strangers. After practice I was usually on such a high that I wanted to be by myself to go through my lyrics and think about how rehearsal had gone.

Craig still made me feel slightly uncomfortable. Even though we'd hung out at the concert last year and now acknowledged each other at school, I couldn't fully erase the humiliation of that moment when I'd asked him about his shirt and he'd shot me down. I hated the fact that I'd had a crush on him and he had rejected me. I harboured a strong dislike for him, even though in an odd way his approval was important to me. I don't know. I guess my feelings about Craig were very mixed, and avoiding him was the best way to avoid thinking about him.

But there he was at my locker. I was annoyed that I did still have a reaction to him. He was attractive. But just because I thought he was a tiny bit cute didn't mean I wouldn't be able to eventually find someone else who I actually *liked*. Because I knew Craig was an asshole.

"How are you doing?" I said.

"I'm good," he said. "How's everything going with the band?"

"Awesome," I said. "We're sounding great."

"Yeah, Edgar played me one of your recordings last week." He grinned. "You sound amazing, I have to say. I was surprised, hearing you sing like that."

"Thanks," I said, lifting my chin slightly.

"What I wanted to ask you was, do you guys want to play a show?"

"We've sort of talked about it."

"Okay, because I know a few guys who have a band. They were thinking of doing a show. Just a small one, you know, in St. Charles. They're looking for a band to play with, you know, to make a night of it."

I paused thoughtfully. "Well, I could ask the guys."

"Yeah, I was going to call Fern and Edgar about it tonight. But I wanted to talk to you about it also."

"What's their band called?"

"Heathenistic Bile," he replied. "They're okay. I haven't seen them play before. They're from St. Charles, I think they've played a few shows. But they're really small. I have a demo CD, I could bring it tomorrow if you want to hear it."

"Sure," I agreed. "I'll check it out. Talk about it with the others."

He nodded. "There's just one thing, ah — the singer, my buddy Paul, well, I guess when I told him about your band he was kind of . . . well, he wasn't too into the fact of there being a girl singer."

I hesitated. "Well, he'll see that I'm really good."

Craig leaned against the locker next to mine. "Yeah, that's what I said. I told him I'd heard you and that you were good. But, I mean, he just thinks that girls shouldn't be in metal."

"Hasn't he heard of Gurgol?" I scoffed. "Marie-Lise?"

"Yeah, of course. But, you know, some people are like that," he shrugged. "So maybe you guys can talk to him and work it out. I don't really know what else to say. Paul's a great guy, he's just not into the idea of it. I'm sure he'll change his mind."

I was absolutely infuriated. This crap friend of Craig's hadn't even heard our band, was looking for a band to play with, but was going to be stupid about us just because of *me* singing? It would be one thing if he heard our music and didn't like it, or if I sounded terrible. But I knew I didn't sound bad, I knew we were a good band, and he was writing me off because he was an asshole. I didn't want to play with a bunch of jerks, but at the same time a show sounded great. I didn't like the concept of *having to hope* Craig's friend would change his mind and decide to give my band a chance. I mean, who the fuck was Heathenistic Bile anyway? Was *heathenistic* even a word? A bunch of illiterate sexists writing *us* off because they don't think girls can be in a heavy metal band? Ridiculous.

I called Fern that evening, fuming mad. "I mean, I don't even want to play with a band like that!"

Fern was quiet for a few moments, thinking. "I don't want

to play with them either. But at the same time, wouldn't it be so satisfying to prove them wrong?"

"No! I don't want to prove anything to people like that."

"Well, I do," she said. "If they think you're not going to be able to sing, and that I won't be able to play guitar, they're dead wrong. We'll show them. And we'll do it because we're coming in pissed. They won't know what hit them, and they'll have to admit that they're wrong."

"But what if we *aren't* any good? I don't want to prove them *right*."

Fern spoke sharply. "Rachel, if you don't believe we are good, then why are we doing this at all?"

She was right. But I trooped on angrily anyway. "I just don't see why we have to go into this having to prove ourselves. It's bullshit."

"Every band has to prove themselves," she said. "Girl or guy singer. No matter what. Some bands fail and some succeed, and it's based on *proving* how good, or bad, they are." She sighed. "And let's be real. There really *aren't* many girls in this type of music. I have a feeling deep down inside me that if we move forward with the band, we're going to see a lot of this type of attitude."

I laughed. "Yeah. For a second I forgot that pretty much everyone on earth is an asshole."

Craig brought me Heathenistic Bile's demo CD the next day, and that weekend after rehearsal the four of us sat down to listen to it. The CD only had two tracks on it, both bad recordings, both songs okay. Nothing about their music sounded very original to us, but it was fine.

"At the very least, I think we should call this Paul guy and talk to him," Edgar said. "It would be great to play live and try out the songs and see how it goes."

I was hesitant. I didn't want to play a show with jerks, but I could understand that playing a show was for the good of our band, even though I would have rejected it had it been my decision alone. We didn't need Heathenistic Bile.

"I'll call him," Socks offered.

And so the show was set up. Three weeks from that weekend we would drive to St. Charles in Socks's van with the gear and play at a club called the Toe. We wouldn't be paid to do the show. Apparently the show's promoter was a DJ on some St. Charles college radio station, and his whole deal was getting metal bands to play to keep the scene moving and help independent bands. I wasn't keen on having to spend money to play — even driving the van to St. Charles would cost us gas money — but I came to understand that this is the way it worked. You can't expect to be paid to play your music, certainly not at your first show. The cover would be five dollars, and that money went to the Toe for hosting the gig.

The natural side effect of this was the stress of hoping that a lot of people came out so that the promoter wouldn't be disappointed in us or Heathenistic Bile. Our band hadn't played before, but Heathenistic Bile had.

"Paul says that they've done two shows before," Socks said one day after we'd rehearsed our eight-song set. "He acts like they're big time, like they're some experienced band." Socks himself, having drummed for several bands in the past, had played about twenty shows. He'd warned us that the turnout to this show wouldn't be very good. "Two shows is hardly enough for Paul's band to have built up a fan base. I mean, I'm sure that their friends will come out, but the way this guy brags about it you'd think that they've toured or something."

I hadn't had any contact at all with Paul, only Socks had, and he'd also spoken to the DJ promoter guy to work out what time we should show up and when the show would start, that kind of stuff. Instead I started working on flyers for the show. Apparently Heathenistic Bile was making flyers for St. Charles, but I knew we had to pull our weight as well. I didn't want this Paul guy or any of his bandmates thinking we were lazy, giving them more reason to dislike us.

I drew a flyer in black and white with all the necessary information on it: the location of the Toe, a nod to the DJ's metal radio show, the ticket price, the door time. I drew the name "Heathenistic Bile" in a jagged font, and beneath theirs, I added "the first ever concert of Colostomy Hag" in a slightly larger font. I couldn't resist making ours larger, even though it was disrespectful to the other band because they were headlining the gig. It galled me that I had to put our name underneath theirs at all, but it would have been rude not to do so.

I filled the centre of the flyer with a stark marker drawing of my old favourite, a violent and bloody rendition of Judith and her maidservant pinning a wretched and mutilated Holofernes to a stained mattress and slicing into his neck. For good measure I couldn't help but try to make Judith resemble me and the maidservant to resemble Fern, with long blonde hair streaming from underneath the ruffled cap on her head. I didn't know what Paul looked like, or else I would have tried to make Holofernes resemble him.

I worked hard on the flyer and everyone loved it. One evening Fern and I went to the copy place and made a big stack of black-and-white photocopies, then I borrowed my mother's staple gun and we proceeded downtown.

We stapled posters to every telephone pole we came across, noting happily when people would stop to read it. We knew none of them would come, of course, but it was a good feeling to be out promoting our band, even if it was just along our hometown's crappy streets.

We stopped to put a poster up on the bulletin board at Bee Music, and the guy working behind the counter came over to check out what we were doing. It was the same long-haired guy who had directed me towards the DED CDs that day long ago.

"I've never heard of either of these bands," he commented, studying the flyer.

"Heathenistic Bile is from St. Charles and Colostomy Hag is our band," Fern told him.

The guy looked at us. "You guys play in the band?"

"Yep," I retorted, hoping I didn't sound defensive. "I sing, and she's on guitar."

"Rad!" the guy exclaimed. "I didn't know there were any metal bands in Keeleford."

"You should come to the show," Fern offered.

"Yeah, I don't know. I don't have any way of getting to St. Charles, but I'll try," he said. "That's cool, two chicks in a metal band. You guys should do a show here. I know a bunch of people who would come."

"Hopefully the next one," I said.

"Cool. Well, good luck with it. If you want to leave a couple of these flyers here in the store, I'll hand them out to people who might be interested."

That was awesome of him, and we left the shop feeling really good. I knew it was on such a small scale, but I was starting to feel important, as though we were making contacts and promoting the band and getting on the road to doing something amazing. It felt like we were somehow rising up and above, as if we were somehow becoming different.

TWENTY

All of us took turns reposting flyers. Ours would get torn down or posted over with different ones. I'd go downtown and see that our flyers had been covered with advertisements for some craft bazaar at some church nearby, and I couldn't help but get pissed off at them. The Wesley Presbyterian Church Craft Bazaar and Free Horror Movie Nights at the Southdale Movie Theatre became our enemies, halfhearted as it was. They probably hated us too, because we'd cover up their flyers in retaliation more thoroughly than they'd covered ours. We'd joke about having violent run-ins with the sweet old grannies from Wesley Presbyterian, with them beating us down with their umbrellas. One Sunday afternoon when I was downtown with Edgar, we actually *saw* a sweet old granny striding efficiently down the street with flyers under one arm and an umbrella in the other, and we erupted into gales of laughter, likely confusing the old dear as we passed her.

We had a half hour to play at the gig, so we had honed eight songs, bringing us in at just under thirty minutes. We rehearsed like mad every Saturday, and sometimes during the week as we got closer to the show day. One of my major motivations was not leaving Paul or his band with a leg to stand on in terms of us being a weak and silly band. It was akin to my feelings about Craig: dislike paired with a guilty desire to impress. I roared, I growled, I wheezed and whispered. I was sounding amazing. Edgar had improved as well, and Socks was consistently great. Fern's guitar playing had become almost flawless, and towards our last rehearsals she was playing her solos perfectly.

We talked a bit about what we wanted to wear onstage. Socks insisted that he could only play in shorts and of course his white socks; at every rehearsal he had taken off his shoes and placed them neatly beside his drum kit, claiming he played better without wearing them. Edgar didn't see anything wrong with just wearing some variation of his usual black T-shirt and black cargo pants.

Fern and I decided to wear matching black tops that laced up the back, and I would wear a blue plaid skirt and she a red one. I secretly loved that blue and red reflected the colours of Judith and her maidservant. The week before the show, Fern bleached her hair again, striving to make it as white as she could, and I dyed my hair black again. I couldn't help but feel that Fern was rather obviously copying Marie-Lise but she looked awesome, so I put it out of my mind. Was how I looked so original? Not at all, so who was I to even think anything about how Fern looked?

My parents were supportive of the gig, even though they politely declined my politely offered invitation to attend. My grades hadn't slipped and, if anything, I was much happier than I had been before the band started, so there was no reason for them to argue with me about it. When that Saturday afternoon arrived, my mother sent me out the door with "break a leg" sentiments.

The van pulled up, Socks and Edgar having loaded the gear the previous night, and I climbed in the back, feeling the buzz of excitement and adventure. Fern was bouncing in her seat and reached over to hug me, Edgar let out a whoop as Socks pulled away from the curb, and we were on the road. Colostomy Hag was on its way to a show.

I pictured being in front of an audience, finally; the cheering and applause, the lights sweeping over us, how amazing we would look and sound. Maybe Paul already had a bias against us and no one had heard of us, but after tonight that would change. We'd win them all over and show them that we were a force to be reckoned with. Their mouths would drop open when they saw how amazing Fern was on guitar, and I would show them what I could do, and it would all begin tonight.

Socks put on our crappy demo CD as we moved onto the highway and turned it up. I opened the window, feeling the cool air blow on my face, and closed my eyes blissfully. I was reminded of going to the Surgical Carnage show — the first time going out with people I could be friends with, feeling that excitement of fitting in, and here it was again, only better this time — I was in a band, I was a vocalist, and I had a bond with the other three people in the van. We were going to do awesome things. Socks roared along with one of my roars on the CD and punched the steering wheel happily.

When we arrived in St. Charles late that afternoon and found the Toe, a heavy, sober feeling came over all of us. The music was off, and we were quiet as we pulled into the parking lot. I saw six guys and a few girls milling around, standing next to a parked van.

"Is that them?" I asked.

"Probably," Socks replied. I studied them through the window as Socks steered the van into a parking space near the other vehicle. They were all looking at us as well, and none of their expressions were particularly friendly. Every single one of them had long black hair, the guys and the girls, and they all wore black, some with wallet chains hanging from their pants, some with spiked wristbands.

"Don't they look like a friendly bunch," Edgar murmured.

"They're probably thinking the same thing about us," Fern said in as bright a voice as she could muster, but I knew by the way she stared out the window that she wasn't getting the best vibe either.

Socks hopped out of the van and approached the group. As the rest of us dawdled in collecting our purses and knapsacks, I watched him shake a few of their hands, talking animatedly. I appreciated him making such a positive effort. They looked like a bunch of assholes to me.

The inevitable couldn't be postponed for very much longer, so I climbed out of the van and forced myself to approach the group. One of the guys walked over to meet me, flanked by two girls.

"Hi, I'm Rachel," I said. "I'm the singer."

"Paul," he replied, making no move to shake my hand. "Singer and guitarist for Heathenistic Bile. These are my girlfriends, Kate and Jennifer."

I smiled at the two girls, receiving only sour-faced responses

161

in reply. They looked at me almost challengingly. *Great.* "Nice to meet you," I attempted.

One of the girls flatly said, "I'm also Paul's hairstylist."

I quickly looked at Paul's rather unremarkable hair and noted that it was long and black and dyed likely out of the same drugstore box as mine. "Girlfriends, huh? Like, you all date each other?"

"Yes," the other girl purred, sliding a possessive arm around Paul and flashing me a dirty look. I resisted the urge to reassure her that I had no intention of hitting on her boyfriend — sorry, *their* boyfriend — and instead asked Paul, "So what's going on?"

"We're just waiting for the owner to get here so we can load in. He should be about ten minutes or so."

I nodded. "Are those other guys in your band?"

"Yeah, drummer and bassist. The other three guys are our crew."

"Crew?"

"Yeah. They load in our gear for us, help us onstage. Our show gets pretty insane. Where's your crew?"

"We don't have one." I was getting pissed off.

"Right, it's your first show. This will be our third," he said. "We're probably going to have a few hundred people tonight. Heathenistic Bile is really starting to take off. A few record labels have already contacted us."

I swallowed and tried to infuse my voice with pleasantness. "That's great. So maybe we should get our gear out of the van so when the owner gets here we're ready to move it inside?"

"Sure. You know, my guys could help you if you need a hand with your gear — if you give them a couple bucks, of course."

"Oh, I think we'll be fine," I said and turned back to the van so he wouldn't see my scowl. There was no reason to make the gig go badly by screaming in his face that he was an idiot.

Fern and Edgar had already opened the back of the van and were gathering the gear. "That guy is a fucking moron," I hissed when I had rejoined them. "Those two girls are his *girlfriends*."

"They've been shooting daggers at me the whole time," Fern muttered.

"The rest of those dudes over there are their *crew*," I said sarcastically. "They're so *big time* after playing two whole shows."

Socks had come back to us in time to hear my last comment. "Well, not really a *crew* — a couple of their friends. They seem like good guys. The band guys, though, well . . . I don't know."

"Apparently their live show is *insane*," I reported.

"What does that mean?" Edgar asked.

"Oh, I'm sure we'll find out," I muttered.

The owner arrived and unlocked the back doors, and as we watched Heathenistic Bile's pals start carrying in guitar cases and rolling in amps, the band stood with their girlfriends, smoking cigarettes and laughing amongst themselves.

"Apparently some record labels have been talking to them," I said.

"Oh, bullshit. It's all bullshit. They're just full of themselves," Socks replied. "Their bass player was telling me that a few hundred people are coming tonight. I don't see how, but I hope he's right. That'd be amazing."

"I wonder what they mean by *insane*," Edgar worried. "We're going to look boring."

We loaded in our gear after them, carrying in the drum cases, guitars, and amps. The guys from the other band stood by and watched us, which I found extremely irritating. Every time I would come back out for another load of stuff I could feel their eyes on me, particularly the girls', sizing up me and Fern. I wanted to scream at them that we were not there to *pick up guys*. We were in a band and we just wanted to play music and have fun.

The Toe was disgusting. It stank like years of old spilled beer, and it didn't make matters any better that right beside the back door was a giant, reeking dumpster. I had to stop myself from gagging a few times as I made my trips past that thing. The stage in the bar was really small and only a few feet off the ground, and there were a few places on it that were apparently unstable and had been marked off with tape so that we would know to be careful if we stepped there. The owner was a tired old guy who Sharpied an X on our hands so that we couldn't drink, which was fine by me. Socks was the only one of us who was of age, and I noticed that the Heathenistic Bile guys were X'd as well.

There was still about two hours until the doors opened, and apparently Heathenistic Bile was using that time to soundcheck. Our gear would sit at the side of the stage until they were finished. So the four of us decided to go eat and come back to the bar later on.

The street in front of the Toe was deserted, not exactly lending credence to Paul's claim of hundreds coming to the show. The area itself was pretty dirty and rundown, and we found a really sketchy restaurant up the street.

"So there's a guy there named Mitchell, he's the Toe's sound guy," Socks reported once we'd ordered our cheap food from the stained menu. "He's going to mix our sound tonight. He's also doing Heathenistic Bile's sound."

"But how can he do our sound if he's never heard our music?" I asked.

"He'll just wing it. I'm sure he's been doing sound there for years, done tons of bands. He seems like a grumpy guy. Tonight is going to suck," Socks warned us. "Make no mistake."

"I'm still worried about what kind of show they put on," Edgar said.

"We saw them load in their gear," Fern reminded him. "I didn't see any crazy props or anything, just instruments. I guess they probably just get really into it."

"I guess," Edgar said.

"Well, we'll get into it too," I said stubbornly. "We'll upstage them." I spoke more confidently than I felt. I'd never *gotten into it* before, but I was hoping that once I was onstage in front of a crowd, something would just sort of kick in instinctively.

"Besides, we have two chicks in our band. That sets us apart from them already. They're just a bunch of boring kids with big egos. What they're doing has all been said and done before," said Socks. "We already have an edge, just going in."

He was trying to motivate us, but it didn't do anything to lessen the feeling of dread at the table. My stomach was starting to feel queasy, and we ate the greasy food in near silence. It was a far cry from how great we'd all been feeling when we left earlier that afternoon.

TWENTY-ONE

The doors were set to open at 7, and our band to take the stage at 8, so we went back to the bar shortly after 7. We showed the guy at the door our wristbands and walked into a dark, pretty much empty room. I was shocked to see less than twenty people sitting at a few of the tables around the room. Loud music played on the overhead speakers, but the room was dead.

We stared at the emptiness in disappointment, and then Socks turned to rally us. "Okay. Let's go get dressed and then get our gear set up. We have less than an hour, right? So let's get ready to *rock*." I appreciated his effort, but all it was doing was depressing me even more. "I'm ready to go, so I'm going to find Mitchell and then I'll meet you guys at the side of the stage in a little while." He smiled and gave us all an inspiring thumbs-up, and then walked off towards the bar.

Fern, Edgar, and I went past the bathrooms towards the little room we had been shown where the bands could relax.

We opened the door and all the guys from the other band were sprawled on the disgusting, torn-up couches. The walls were covered with graffiti and marker scrawling, mostly of sex organs in all manner of stupid mutations, and band stickers posted here and there.

"Hi guys, getting excited?" Paul greeted us. One of his girlfriends was applying black liner to his eyes.

"There aren't too many people here," Fern said.

Paul shrugged. "It's still early. People come later. By the time we get onstage, this place will be packed."

"Right on," the bass player agreed, and everyone in the room except for us laughed.

I wanted to ask them whether or not sitting on those filthy couches was a good idea, considering the amount of piss and bugs that likely festered there, but didn't bother. It was actually a pretty fitting environment for those assholes, as far as I was concerned.

Edgar decided to go find Socks and start getting ready, and Fern and I took our knapsacks into the girls' bathroom so that we could get dressed and do our makeup.

"It's cute how his girlfriend is doing his eyeliner for him," she hissed, struggling to put on her pantyhose without placing her shoeless foot onto the disgusting tile floor.

"Oh, she's his hairstylist too," I said, tugging down on my skirt to straighten it out. I was really starting to feel sick from nerves, and I took deep breaths to try to calm down.

"How helpful," Fern scoffed. "I wouldn't be so pissed about it if they were nice people. Those girls act like we're prostitutes or something."

"Yeah. It's irritating."

Clothes on, we turned to the cracked mirror over the sinks to quickly put on our makeup. "Fern . . . are you nervous?"

"Yeah, a bit. I'm more disappointed that there aren't many people here."

I was almost relieved that there weren't, because in my nervousness I was doubting my own abilities, worrying that we weren't any good. Once ready, we walked through the bar, across the large empty expanse of floor to the side of the stage. I felt the few people who sat there watching us, and it was a pretty lousy feeling. Socks was onstage already, setting up his drums, and even though the music was so loud I couldn't hear, I saw his lips pursed in a merry whistle. I really wished that I knew how to summon up that level of cheerful relaxation.

Edgar was talking to a tall guy at the side of the stage. Leaning in, he introduced us. "Robbie, this is Rachel and Fern. Guys, this is Robbie. He's the DJ and the promoter."

"Great to meet you," Robbie greeted us, smiling. "I'm really excited about your band."

Fern and Edgar went to set up the rest of their gear, leaving me standing with Robbie and now having to make conversation.

"Heathenistic Bile is great, really great," Robbie continued. "There aren't many local metal bands. We're happy you could make it."

"Thanks," I replied. "We're excited for it."

"There aren't many people here," he continued, gesturing needlessly to the dead-empty dance floor in front of the stage, "but you know, word will spread and more and more people will start coming out. You know, the last Heathenistic Bile show, we had about fifty people come out."

"Is *heathenistic* a word?" I said.

"Huh?"

"I was just wondering, is *heathenistic* actually a word?"

"Well, yeah, I guess it means, you know, 'like a heathen.'"

"But wouldn't the proper word just be 'heathen'? It can be used as an adjective as well as a noun. Or *heathenist*?"

"I don't really know." Robbie looked confused as to why I would even care. "You know, I should probably let you get ready."

I felt bad. "Yeah. Hey, you know, thank you very much for this, and helping and everything. I think you're doing a great thing with these shows, and I'm happy we can be part of it."

"No problem," he said and smiled at me before disappearing back into the bar.

I stood and watched the others set up, trying to keep from looking at the people in the bar. I could feel their eyes on me and started to feel even sicker, but I tried to keep a bored, relaxed expression on my face.

Socks seated himself behind the drum kit and Fern and Edgar took their places on either side of the stage. My microphone stand stood alone at the front of the stage between them like a spindly flag that I was going to have to stand behind for the next half hour. I burped and tasted my greasy dinner, and realized that vomiting was an actual possibility.

Fern and Edgar looked over at me. I could see fear in their eyes as well, and I looked at Socks, who grinned and gave me a nod. It was time.

I took a deep breath, lifted my chin, and walked onstage with what I hoped was a purposeful, confident stride. I stopped behind the microphone and stared into the abyss in front of the stage, squinting under the bright lights shining in my eyes, and realized that the overhead music was still blasting loudly.

I didn't know what to do. I stood there like an idiot, jealous of the others for being able to tinker with their instruments, and searched my mind frantically for some way to signal for the music to stop playing. But I didn't know who was in charge of the music, and I couldn't see much because of the stupid lights. My face started to burn with horror.

The music came to a full and abrupt stop and the sudden silence was almost worse. After a hideous pause, I cleared my throat and was horrified to hear the sound amplified through the microphone.

"Hello," I faltered. *Hello!? What the fuck!* "Hi. We are Colostomy Hag." The silence that followed was even worse than my polite, cheesy introduction. I heard hard clapping begin, a single pair of hands, and looked over past Edgar to see Robbie applauding alone at the side of the stage. I knew he was trying to be supportive, and I tried to smile at him, but the lone clapper somehow made it even worse.

Thankfully Socks immediately counted in the first song, and we launched into it. My cheeks were burning with embarrassment in that first minute, especially when I realized that I was not going to be "rocking out" in any way. I stood behind the microphone, squinting through the lights, and tried to bob my head along to the music. I could feel failure coursing through my body. Peripherally, I saw Fern start moving a little bit, but on the other side of me, Edgar remained stock still as well.

When we finished the first song, a smattering of applause went through the room, and I tried to smile with confidence. "Thank you," I said, relieved for a moment until I remembered that we still had seven more songs to play.

We launched into the next song and I did my best to try to act like I was into it. I realized that I was just tapping my toe like some kind of moron, so then I awkwardly stopped doing that and bobbed my head instead, letting my hair cover my face a little bit, hoping that somehow it would look cool. I let out a few roars that hopefully sounded impressive, and the set continued. At one point I looked up and saw a long-haired guy in the middle of the dance floor in front of the stage, headbanging furiously. Excitement flooded me, until I saw the guy hurriedly rejoin his friends at a nearby table, laughing. So he'd just been making fun of us. Great.

The applause between songs lessened after each one, and by the time we had two songs left, there was actually dead silence in that space. Even Robbie was nowhere to be seen, which was probably more of a blessing than anything else. All I could do was wipe my sweaty palms off on my skirt and wait for Socks to count us in. At least we were close to being done. In the rehearsal space, the set always went by quickly. This felt like a sweltering, bright eternity.

Halfway through the second last song, a small group of people formed in the middle of the room. I peered out, squinting, to see who it was. Anger started to build in me as I saw it was Paul and the other guys in Heathenistic Bile. Paul stood with his arms folded and a small grin on his face. He looked ridiculous — with all the black-and-white makeup on — and he had the nerve to stand there, smirking at *us*?

My anger didn't offer me any sense of power. The same feeling that had swept over me when Brandi had confronted me in the schoolyard so long ago began to creep in. I tried to toss my hair back and continue singing with confidence, but the embarrassment and anger was turning into crippling despair. I turned away from the front of the stage and tried to focus on Fern, who was still making a valiant but completely ineffective attempt to move to the music. I couldn't look at Paul and his friends. I was so angry at myself.

When the set finally ended, I walked off the stage to the smattering of disinterested applause. I strode as fast as I could through the club, avoiding eye contact with everyone, towards the girls' bathroom. Once inside, I sat down on the toilet and slouched over, my face in my hands.

TWENTY-TWO

After a little while I heard a small cheer from the crowd, muffled and faraway. I remained seated, rubbing my eyes with my hands, smearing my stupid makeup, not like it mattered. Through the walls I heard Heathenistic Bile begin their set.

The bathroom door squeaked as it swung open, and I heard footfalls on the tiles. Whoever it was walked slowly across the floor and paused.

"Rachel?" It was Fern.

I took a shuddering breath. "Yeah."

"Are you okay?"

"Not really." I cleared my throat and sat up straight. "What's going on?"

"They just went on," she said. "You should come check it out."

"Where's our stuff?"

"We packed it up. It's sitting next to the door. They won't

let us load out until the band is offstage. I guess it's too loud to open the door."

"Sorry I didn't help pack."

"That's okay."

I opened the stall door. Fern was leaning against the sink counter. She looked tired, her makeup smudged as well. She smiled at me. "They suck, if it makes you feel any better."

"Worse than we did?"

"In a different way than we did." Her smile faltered, throwing her face into a lopsided grimace. "Don't feel bad. We *tried*. It was our first show."

"I was terrible," I muttered. "I just stood there."

"It's okay. Next time will be better. We can't expect to have an amazing show right off the bat." She touched my arm, and I appreciated it, but I knew that she had to be pretty disappointed in me. I was supposed to lead onstage, step up and take control of the show, exude confidence and spearhead everything. And I hadn't. All my fantasizing in my room had turned into nothing but a joke. I sucked.

"I don't know if I can go out there," I said. "Are the guys mad at me?"

"Why would they be *mad*? No one's mad."

"What about the crowd?" The thought of walking back out there made me feel sick. A memory of the headbanging guy making fun of us flashed in my mind, and my stomach ached sharply at the image of it.

"No one cares. They're all watching Heathenistic Bile. And I really think you should check them out."

I sniffled and smoothed out my skirt. A glance in the mirror showed my hair was frizzy, my makeup was smeared, and I looked like shit in general. "I look awful."

"You look tough. Now *please* come back out."

I followed Fern back into the club, and Socks and Edgar

173

were standing at the back. There seemed to be a few more people in the place, and everyone was crowded up at the front by the stage. Still, the place was mostly empty — nowhere near the number of people that Paul had smugly predicted.

"Great show!" Socks cried when he saw me, and yanked me into a hug.

"Thanks," I replied and smiled weakly. I knew he was just being his sunshiney self and trying to make me feel better, but I did appreciate it. Edgar hugged me too, and I was relieved. Part of me had seriously worried that they would be angry at me for failing so bad.

"There's no one here, really," I observed, looking around the club.

"Probably mostly their friends," Socks agreed. "Have you checked this out yet?"

I focused my attention on the stage. Heathenistic Bile was headlong into their set by this point, and all of them were wearing white facepaint with black ringed eyes and mouths. Their bass player and Paul, of course, were freaking out, whipping their hair around and leaping. It would have looked cool except for the fact that their two guitar players weren't matching the energy.

Kate and Jennifer, Paul's two girlfriends, were also onstage. They'd changed into shiny black vinyl shorts and fishnet stockings with high boots and halters made of the same cheap material. Both of them had their eyes screwed shut and heads thrown back, expressions of ecstasy on their faces, and they swung their arms and ran their hands through their hair as they tried to gyrate sexily to the fast beat. It completely didn't work, and I couldn't help but grin.

The crowd didn't seem to mind. Everyone was throwing their hair around and tossing their fists in the air, but there were so few people there, the whole thing seemed slightly ridiculous.

"Did you notice the chain?" Fern said into my ear over the music.

One of the stock-still guitar players indeed had a length of metal chain attached to a dog collar around his neck. The other end of the chain fastened to his amp.

"I guess it's so he doesn't get *out of control*," I observed, and Fern and I laughed.

The song ended, and the crowd cheered sparsely. "Thank-fuckin'-*you!*" Paul shouted into his microphone. "You guys are the *fuckin'* best."

"Yeah, all thirty of you," I muttered under my breath.

"Sometimes, when the moon is just right, bad things happen in the night," Paul rhymed, glowering at the crowd. I drew my breath in sharply in surprise as the crowd actually *cheered*. "Killers come out in the moon's dark glow. And the killers are people you sometimes know." His voice sounded thin and melodramatic, like a grade-school kid at a recital, reading off cheesy lines that echoed through the somewhat empty room.

"Are you scared?" Paul demanded of the crowd. They clapped in response.

"I said are you *fucking* scared?" he repeated, his voice rising to an embarrassing shriek. The crowd cheered. "*Fuck yeah!*" someone called.

"This is *awful*," Edgar murmured to me.

"Blackskull!" Paul commanded. *What the hell was he talking about?*

I heard a thin, weak wail, and my eyes flicked to the chained guitarist, who had thrown his head back and apparently roared. But because it was not into a microphone, it sounded flaccid.

"Blackskull — are you ready?" Paul addressed the guitarist, who was, presumably, Blackskull. He walked to the guitarist's amp and unchained him. The crowd cheered weakly again. I noticed that Kate and Jennifer were still gyrating for some

175

reason — even though there was no music.

As Paul unchained the guitarist, he spoke into his microphone. "It is time . . . to *unleash the beast!*" And Blackskull let out another thin howl.

I couldn't help it. A shriek of laughter erupted from my mouth, louder than I had intended it to be — a resounding, echoing honk. Everyone in the room heard it and looked back towards us. Paul and *Blackskull* faltered onstage for a moment, but then Paul glowered. Their next song began. The guitarist moved to front and centre of the stage, bobbing his head a bit more than he had been and letting his tongue loll out of his mouth. Presumably this was the beast . . . *unleashed.*

"I can't believe you laughed like that," Edgar leaned in and said. "They all heard."

"Who gives a shit?" I replied. "This whole thing is a joke. I've seen enough. Can we leave?"

"Not yet," Socks reminded me. "Let's just sit back and enjoy the show."

Eventually the *beast* was chained back up, and the set continued without much more hilarity. I knew Edgar was worried that I had offended them by laughing, but I honestly didn't understand why he would care if we'd hurt their feelings. This whole night was a joke. Sure, maybe the crowd hadn't cared who we were — but they liked *Heathenistic Bile.* I was totally fine if their fans disliked us. If this was what they thought was cool, I wanted to be the exact opposite of it.

And so what if Paul and his moron bandmates had heard me laugh? They were pricks and had been from the get-go. I knew we'd had a lousy performance, but we didn't have ridiculous dancing girls onstage. And we certainly hadn't unleashed any pathetic *beasts.* They were embarrassing.

After their set ended, the crowd filtered out after high-fiving the band, and their "helpers" started tearing down the equipment. I couldn't resist approaching Paul, who was sitting on the edge of the stage with his two girlfriends and a few other girls who'd come to the show and were now fawning over him.

"Hey, Paul! *Great* show," I trilled, ignoring the girls, who glared at me in sync as if someone had pushed a button.

"Thanks," he said casually. I could tell he was surprised by my confidence. I guess he had assumed I would be demoralized after our lousy performance — which, in fairness, I had been — but watching their set had put me in such a great mood. I grinned at him, and I fed off the impression I was gathering that he was slightly intimidated by me. "You guys *rock*," I gushed. And I turned to Kate and Jennifer, smiling. "And *wow*. You girls are so *sexy*." My sarcasm impressed even me, and I knew I was being a bitch, but I wasn't like Edgar. I didn't feel like I needed to get along with everyone we met. This was making me absolutely glow.

Paul tried to rally, raising his nose slightly. "I'm sure you guys will improve. It was a rough show for you, but it was your first, and not bad. It's not easy to be a singer, or a good frontman." At this, his gaggle of girls laughed.

I nodded. "To be honest, part of me wants to stop singing and strip down and just dance onstage, really. Maybe it would be a better role for me."

"Maybe," Paul snarled.

"Well, give my regards to Blackskull," I said, allowing my voice to take on a death-metal growl as I said the name. I smiled brightly and then walked out the side door, past their roadies, and through the parking lot to Socks's van, where I helped Fern, Edgar, and Socks load in our gear.

Fern and I sat together in the backseat on the way home, Socks and Edgar sat up front, all of us quiet and tired. But my body buzzed. I kept replaying my confrontation with Paul and running through different possibilities in my mind. He'd been so cocky, sitting with the girls, and I wished I'd embarrassed him more. I kept imagining punching him in the nose, right in front of them, and then walking haughtily away. I grinned at the thought of him trying to look cool in front of his harem while wiping the blood away. I stared out the window into the darkness of the passing countryside and weighed the pros and cons of this fantasy scenario. Paul didn't strike me as the sort to call the cops. And he sure wouldn't have been able to hit me back. There wouldn't have been any repercussions.

Socks broke the silence from the front seat. "So how do you guys feel about tonight?"

"I thought it was great," I announced. "That band sucked so bad."

"You shouldn't have laughed," Edgar said. "That was totally uncomfortable."

"If you thought that was bad, you should've been there after the show," I bragged. "I went up to Paul and totally told him where to go." I explained to them how sarcastic I had been, unable to keep myself from laughing as I imitated my *Blackskull* closing line.

"Oh, jeez," Edgar grumbled.

"They were terrible," Socks said, "but we could have done way better."

"No one was even thinking about us by the time they went on. I mean, they were so embarrassing, they made us look good," I insisted.

"No, they didn't," Socks corrected me. "I agree that they were

178

embarrassing, but that has nothing to do with how we did. I think we should look at how *we* did, and see how we can improve."

"Yeah," Fern nodded from beside me.

"Oh, we'll do much better next time," I said dismissively. Of course we all had learned from tonight's show. I hadn't forgotten about our performance, but I didn't want to dwell on it.

"I don't know how I feel about what you said to Paul," Edgar said. "I don't think it's a good idea to burn bridges like that."

My face got hot. "*Burn bridges?* What are you talking about?" My voice was rising; I couldn't help it. "Do you really care if we have a good relationship with that band? You want to play with them again? Give me a break."

"Don't get me wrong, I didn't like them," Edgar said. "I just don't want to start going around telling bands to fuck off, you know? I think it's probably important to keep good relations with the other metal bands around here, even if they suck."

"Well, you can give Paul a call tomorrow if you want. Go for a coffee or something," I snapped. "I don't regret what I said. I'd do it again. And I'd probably say something worse. They suck. I never want to play with them again. They are assholes. If you want to go buddy it up with Blackskull, be my guest."

Everyone was silent when I stopped talking, and I started feeling stupid, which made me even angrier. I folded my arms and stared out the window.

Finally Fern spoke. "Rachel, they definitely were assholes. I personally don't care what you said to Paul —"

"Well, you should," Edgar interrupted grumpily.

"But I do think Socks is right, we need to talk about our show," she continued. "Otherwise no bands are going to want to play with us. We're not going to be able to move forward."

Everyone started talking about how we'd sounded versus how we'd looked, and how we needed to really try harder

179

for more energy next time, and out loud I agreed and half-listened. I was still thinking about what Edgar had said. He seemed to think it was a bad move to establish myself as a force to be reckoned with. Why couldn't he understand that it was obviously better to be aggressive? Not to take any shit from anybody? Maybe that was a good reputation to have. After all, this was metal music. What part of it did he not understand?

TWENTY-THREE

I was determined not to have a shitty show ever again. I wasn't naïve enough to think that wouldn't take time and practise, of course, and I wasn't stupid enough to ignore the fact that trying too hard could result in Heathenistic Bile–like stupidity. It was a fine balance.

I spent a bunch of time on the internet, watching live concert videos of my two heroes: Marie-Lise from Gurgol, and Balthazar Seizure from DED. There weren't any female metal singers I could watch for inspiration, but that meant that if I could combine the elements I admired from Marie-Lise and Balthazar, I would be original in a lot of ways.

Marie-Lise, of course, played bass and I couldn't copy her as much as I probably would have tried to if I'd also played an instrument. Fern — as much as I loved her — wasn't being very discreet in her attempt to emulate her. I mean, Fern continually bleached her hair, and she still wasn't able to get it as pure white as Marie-Lise.

What I admired the most about Marie-Lise was her aggression and confidence onstage, and, of course, her style. She somehow managed to leap around stage in giant platform boots, sweat onstage without smearing her makeup, and wear cute dresses and skirts without ever coming across as looking skanky. She would take command of the crowd in front of her side of the stage by just glancing at them. In my opinion it was no small feat that she managed to intimidate all those long-haired guys pressed at the front of the stage, especially since there was a strong possibility that they felt the same way about women as Paul did.

My favourite video was one where Marie-Lise had moved to the front of the stage. It looked like a crazy show. Hundreds of people were crammed up front. Wrenching her bass, she skipped lightly to the front of the stage and placed one foot on a monitor, gazing challengingly into the sea of faces, and a ton of hands reached up through the wall of flying hair and banging heads, stretching towards her frantically.

She stayed just out of their reach and taunted them, banging out the chords, always making eye contact with the crowd and sneering. She was amazing.

But the best part of the video was when some greasy, big-faced asshole lunged at her. I couldn't tell if he was climbing *on* people or what — that part happened out of frame — but he was somehow able to *grab* Marie-Lise, his sweaty arm extending towards her like a hairy, damp snake, his mouth stretched in a wild, ecstatic grimace. His hand gripped her knee and pulled her slightly off-balance, and then moved up her stockinged thigh. It was disgusting.

But Marie-Lise's face betrayed no alarm at all. Her eyes flicked down at him, and then she smoothly swung her other knee forward, neatly smashing the leering ape right in his face. A small smile crept over her face as he reeled backwards into the crowd in a spray of saliva and blood. The music was drowned out on the recording as everyone cheered in support of her. That's where the clip ended.

I wanted to be like that. In command, unstoppable, and ready to deal with bullshit at a minute's notice. Skimming across the stage as light as air, into the music without looking overwrought and melodramatic. God, she was amazing. And she hadn't been afraid to smash that guy. How could Edgar be pissed at me for telling off an asshole, when Marie-Lise could knee a guy like that in the face and be adored? No, Edgar was wrong.

Balthazar Seizure had a different vibe than Marie-Lise, a different sort of confidence and presence. But he had the same command of the crowd and prompted the same frantic response. DED was a bigger band than Gurgol and played to giant crowds of what looked like thousands. Browsing through the video clips, I could find everything from performances in dark bars to middle of the day festivals in Europe and South America.

They had giant props onstage: a huge skull that slowly leaked dark red blood from its eye sockets and jagged nasal cavity, a rack that contained fierce-looking medieval weapons. During one song, Balthazar grabbed a big battle-axe from the rack and swung it around, cleaving into a guitar amp, hacking into it several times before finally slicing its blade into the stage floor as the crowd reached a frenzy. He exuded a dark gloom mixed with a psychotic air, grinning evilly at the audience, letting out frightening roars from behind his curtain of long black hair. The other guys in his band headbanged and bounded around the stage, but Balthazar mostly stood in one place, and his stillness and imposing height were just as effective in making the crowd go insane as any movement could have been. The fact that his face was slim and handsome made him even more appealing.

183

I studied the video clips closely, and even though Colostomy Hag didn't have another show booked, I knew I would be more prepared next time. I kicked myself for having been so weak at our first show. The next one, whenever it was, was going to be completely different.

We all stayed busy. We kept rehearsing once a week, and I focused on writing lyrics and doing more designs, just ideas for posters or whatever else we needed. Socks suggested that we try to record a full album at some point, and so I started designing rough ideas for album art. School continued, life at home continued, but I had sort of stopped paying attention to those things. I was completely immersed in my little world, of being with the band and spending my free time doing creative things in my room and studying videos. I maintained my grades and was agreeable with my family. It was all just an exercise in getting through the parts of my day that were standing between me and the things I actually wanted to do. I became very good at feigning interest in Melissa's grades, my father's stories about his class, and the boring assignments and projects I was given in school. I don't understand why some people argue with their parents or give attitude to teachers. It is so much easier to just smile, nod, and say the expected responses. You don't have to actually care, and no one will flag you as any sort of concern.

Fern called me one night freaking out. "Gurgol is coming."

"Oh my god," I said. "When?"

"St. Charles in two weeks. Do you want to go?"

"Oh, totally," I said. "You know, we should try to meet Marie-Lise."

Fern got a little quiet for a few moments, which she always tended to do when we talked about Marie-Lise. I figured this was because she was always trying to play it cool so that no one would suspect how much she truly admired and idolized her. "Yeah, but I mean, how?"

"If we showed up early I bet we could find her somewhere. I mean you remember how we just hung out for hours before our show. We could have fun with it — try to find her, and if we can't, maybe we could do some shopping or something."

"That'd be cool," Fern agreed.

A huge blow came when Socks made some calls, just to see if Gurgol needed an opening act, and found out that Heathenistic Bile had somehow landed the gig. "I don't understand that at all," he grouched at rehearsal that weekend. "I don't see how they got that gig. They have no fan base, and they're terrible."

"Maybe *we're* wrong?" Edgar fretted. "Maybe they really are wicked awesome and somehow, we just don't get it?"

"Nope," I shook my head. "And you know what's going to make this amazing is that we're going to get to watch a huge crowd laugh at that shitty band. It's going to be awesome."

Socks and Edgar didn't want to come up to St. Charles early with us, so Fern and I took a bus. The guys would meet us there later, and we'd all drive back home in the van. The bus made stops in the small towns along the way to St. Charles, picking up more people and dropping off others, which was aggravating. After a while both of us just fell asleep. We'd gotten up early to catch one of the first buses so we could have the whole afternoon to search for Marie-Lise.

When we got off the bus in downtown St. Charles, we got into a taxi and asked the driver to shoot us off at the club where Gurgol was playing that night. In the cab, Fern fretted, looking into the mirror in her powder compact. "Do I look okay?"

"You look great." We had discussed what to wear so that we would look cool if we met her, but not ridiculously done-up. Fern had opted to wear a black dress and tights, and I'd gone for a black sweater and dark navy jeans. I remembered the girls who'd flocked around Paul after our show, and I didn't want to look like some sort of desperate groupie. We wanted to talk to Marie-Lise to get her insights into being in a band, into what it was like as things moved forward, and about being female in the industry. Not to kiss her ass or be just another face in the crowd.

The cab dropped us off outside a large club. The front doors were bolted and the street was deserted. "So what now?" I was starting to lose my nerve a bit. I totally felt like a stalking, hovering groupie, sniffing around.

"Let's check out behind the club. You know they'll load in through the back doors," Fern suggested.

I felt like a fool as we carefully walked around the building. Even if we did see Marie-Lise, what if she didn't want to talk to us? What if we annoyed her? What if she was a huge bitch? And who did we think we were anyway, trying to force her to talk to us?

It then occurred to me that walking out back might result in an encounter with Heathenistic Bile. What if they were back here too, buddying it up with Gurgol? I didn't want them to see us slithering around like desperate losers. I was starting to think this had been a really stupid idea. But I followed closely behind Fern, who must have started feeling stupid too, because when we reached the corner of the building before the back parking lot, she paused.

"Rachel," she whispered, "what if Paul and those guys are back here?"

"Yeah. Maybe we should turn back," I murmured.

Fern peeked around the corner. "There's a tour bus."

Now afraid that members of either band would come up behind us and catch us doing this pathetic spy routine, I glanced behind me. "Let's just get out of here," I said. "I feel like an idiot."

"Me too. But check out the bus."

I peeked around the corner and saw the big tour bus parked by the back doors. There was no sign of any people around and there were no other vehicles.

"What time is it?" I said.

"It's just after noon."

"They're probably all asleep on the bus," I figured. "Let's go. This is really stupid."

Resigned, we left the parking lot area and walked up the street away from the deserted club towards a small shopping area. My heart sank as I realized we still had hours and hours before the show, and what were we going to do? Go back to the club when they were soundchecking and try to break in? For what purpose? I was annoyed that I'd even made this suggestion.

We decided to go to a coffee shop and sit down for a while. As we walked up to the shop, there were a few people sitting out at the patio tables despite the chilly air. Fern grabbed my arm and hissed, "Look."

Marie-Lise was sitting with a cup of coffee and a magazine. She was wearing big dark sunglasses and was dressed in jeans and a sweater, but it was unmistakably her.

"What do we do?" Fern asked.

"Let's get something to drink," I suggested. We went into the shop and ordered two coffees, then abled onto the patio and chose a table a little ways from her.

I didn't want to stare at her too obviously, and made a conscious effort to keep my eyes on Fern. "We won't get a chance any better than this," I said. "We should go talk to her."

"I don't know. I don't want to bother her," Fern said, her gaze flicking from me to Marie-Lise.

"She's just reading a magazine. Let's go. We'll regret it if we don't," I said. Fern tried to protest, but I picked up my drink and approached the table where Marie-Lise sat.

"Excuse me," I said as politely as I could. "Are you Marie-Lise?"

She looked up from her magazine and gave me a pleasant smile. "Yes, I am."

"Er, are you busy? Mind if we join you?"

She hesitated, and in that moment I truly felt like the rudest person on earth. Quickly, I tried to redeem myself somehow. "I mean, I know you're on tour and you're always around people and stuff. It's gotta be pretty draining. If you'd rather just sit and relax by yourself, no worries. I totally understand. You don't know us, I mean, for all you know we're psychos, right? We don't want to annoy you."

"You're not annoying," she said, continuing to smile. "Sure, why not sit down. I mean, I have to get going in a little while, though."

"I totally understand," I said, putting my drink on the table and pulling up a chair. Fern followed suit. "You gotta load in and soundcheck, all that stuff." I was trying to speak with authority, to relate to her as one band member to another and show her we were on the same page, but I could tell I wasn't impressing her.

She nodded, continuing to smile at us. "So, you know I'm Marie-Lise. What are your names?"

Fern and I introduced ourselves, and she shook our hands across the table. I could tell she was in a "mode" — obviously the mode she would always be in when meeting fans. I wondered if there was any way to get her to feel comfortable with us. It was interesting, seeing her like this, with no makeup on and her pale hair pulled back into a messy ponytail.

"So, how's the tour going?" Fern asked in the softest, most terrified voice I had ever heard come out of her mouth. I wanted to giggle, she was so nervous.

"Oh, it's great," Marie-Lise said. "We're out for five months.

About halfway done now, and everything's going wonderful. Great shows." She sounded so formal, as if this was an interview.

"There's a reason we wanted to meet you and talk to you," I interjected. "See, Fern and I are in a band ourselves."

She nodded. "That's very cool. What do you guys do in the band?"

"I sing, and Fern plays guitar."

"Awesome. What's the band called?"

"Colostomy Hag," I said proudly.

Her frozen smile flashed into a genuine grin for a second. "That's one of the best band names I think I've ever heard," she laughed.

"Thanks!"

Almost immediately, she flipped back into the super-pleasant mode. "If you guys want to give me a demo, I'd be happy to give it a listen."

So that's what it was. She was used to being approached by people who were hoping that she could help out their own projects, use her in some way. Well, luckily for us, we didn't have a demo worth giving her anyway. And if we had brought it and tried to give it to her, all it would have done was solidify in her mind that we were just like everybody else.

"We don't have a demo. Actually, the reason that we wanted to meet you is to let you know that, I guess, you're a bit of a role model to us."

"Oh, that's very sweet of you to say."

"No, seriously. There aren't many women in metal. You're one of the few, and as we're just starting out in a band, I mean, I guess we just wanted to get some of your perspectives on things. I mean, you're amazing onstage. You don't take any crap from anyone."

"And you're a great bass player," Fern added.

Marie-Lise took a sip of her coffee. "That's nice of you guys

189

to say. And I mean . . . yeah. You're right. Things were pretty difficult, especially at the beginning."

She took out a cigarette and lit it. Fern quickly reached into her own purse and took one out, and inwardly I rolled my eyes.

"To be honest with you guys, I mean, I've met girls like you before. Girls who are in bands, just starting things out. And you never hear anything from them again. It's like they lose interest. Or maybe something happens that discourages them, you know? And they don't think they're going to have a place in this business." Marie-Lise blew smoke thoughtfully. "When I got started, I met a lot of assholes. People who just don't think that a girl should be there, you know? More like, the girls should be waiting offstage to boost the guys' egos and stuff."

"I totally know," I said, nodding.

"And even now, I mean, sure. Sometimes I still meet up with someone who wants to disrespect me. Sometimes it's someone in the crowd, sometimes it's someone behind the scenes that's supposed to be there to help me."

"So how do you deal with it?" I asked.

She grinned, relaxing. "Well, I mean, if it's someone in the crowd, I love that. I'll punch him right in the face. You just can't let it get to you, can't let it do anything to affect what you're doing. My whole thing is — what if I got upset onstage? There's one asshole there who wants to disrespect me, and there's five hundred people there who are giving me a chance, and there's another four hundred and ninety-nine who think I'm awesome. This is one person. And if I were to burst into tears, or walk offstage, I would be changing nine hundred and ninety-nine people's opinions of me. Over one jerk."

"That's true," I agreed.

"See, when you're in this business, you need to have a goal. That's what I think. A reason that you're doing it. Something to keep in your mind to focus on and work towards. So when you're at your lowest you can picture whatever it is in your mind, and remind yourself why you're not going to quit." She grinned. "Because you're going to want to quit. And you probably will, in all honesty. Most people do. It's not all glitz and glam like everyone thinks."

"What's it like?" Fern said.

"Work is what it is. Hard work. And it doesn't pay off. If making money is your goal, I'd suggest finding a new one. Only a few bands make it really big and make that money and have that lifestyle. Everyone else struggles. We're still struggling and we've been in the band for seven years now."

I was a little surprised to hear that. Gurgol was in all the magazines, they were very popular. I'd assumed they were doing great. "What's your goal?" I said.

"To make music with my friends and have incredible experiences alongside them. To see the world, which we've done and are still doing. To have a different kind of life than everyone I knew growing up. That kind of thing. An interesting life. Something amazing to look back on. I chose a different path than most people I know. And I'm proud of it, even if it isn't buying me a house." She laughed.

"What's it like being on the tour bus?" Fern said. I tried not to scowl. She sounded like a fan, and here I was, trying to be an equal.

"Work," Marie-Lise repeated. "All of it is work. Definitely. I love the guys. And that's the other thing I should tell you. You're going to run into a lot of assholes who will hate you because you're a woman in metal. Make sure that whoever you are in the band with supports you and believes in you. Make sure they'll have your back, no matter what happens. And have theirs."

I felt like we were being watched and flicked my eyes to the sidewalk. To my surprise, I saw Kate and Jennifer, Paul's stage dancers or girlfriends or whatever the hell they were, walking past the coffee shop. Their eyes were riveted to our table, obviously noticing us having our friendly coffee with Marie-Lise. I tried to suppress my grin and turned my attention back to her as the girls passed, wanting to solidify the impression they were getting of us being friends. "Do you ever get lonely?"

"Sure," Marie-Lise said. "All of us do. Even though you're constantly surrounded by people, I feel alone a lot of the time."

"And that's why you'll get off the tour bus in the morning and come have a coffee by yourself," I said.

She laughed. "Exactly. Being alone for a while makes me feel less alone when I go back."

"That makes sense."

Marie-Lise stood up. "It was great meeting both of you, but I should really get back to the bus."

"Thanks for talking to us," I said, and we shook hands.

After Marie-Lise shook Fern's hand, she reached forward and touched a strand of Fern's hair, gazing at it. "You should try using Pegasus," she said. "That's what I use when I bleach my hair. It's kind of expensive, but it really works to get it nice and pale. You don't end up with that sort of brassy yellow."

"Thanks," Fern said.

"Bye, girls," she said and made her way down the sidewalk.

We sat at the table and watched her walk back towards the club. "That was amazing," Fern said. "I really can't believe we met her, and she was so nice to us."

"Paul's stupid girlfriends saw us here with her too," I said. "They walked by. They'll totally think we're friends with Marie-Lise. Fucking awesome."

"You know, it was weird. I was completely nervous with her. I felt stupid."

"Nah. It was fine," I said. "I liked what she had to say. I fucking can't wait to see the show tonight."

We sat thoughtfully for a few moments, and then Fern said, "Do you have a goal with the band?"

I thought for a second. "I'm sure I do, I just have to think about it for a while," I said. "What about you?"

"Well, I guess part of it has to do with being able to play the guitar well," she said, furrowing her brow. "I mean, I really love it, and I love how far I've come with it. I want to see how good I can get with it."

"And be able to show that off to people," I said, smiling.

"Yeah, I guess that's part of it too," she said. "I mean wouldn't that be part of it for everyone? Wanting attention and to stand out and everything?"

I was mulling over my goal, my reason for wanting to do Colostomy Hag. Was it because I wanted attention? Because I wanted everyone to think I was cool and talented and original? I guess part of it was that. I think I really also wanted to *show* people, the type of people who were going to naysay us, and me, and make fun of us, that they were wrong. I wanted to surprise people. If they thought that a girl couldn't lead a metal band, I wanted to prove to them that they were dead wrong.

TWENTY-FOUR

Socks and Edgar joined us in line. We told them all about meeting Marie-Lise and what we'd talked about. Socks lamented that we hadn't had a demo to give her and reiterated that we needed to get into a studio and record songs, release an album.

We heard a shout and looked back — it was Craig and Yvonne. We invited them to join us.

"How have you been?" Yvonne asked me. "It's been so long. I hear you guys are in a band. I can't wait to come see you. When's your next show?"

"Nothing planned right now."

"Yeah, I couldn't make it. I'm really sorry. But you sing! How cool is that? I seriously can't wait to check the music out. Remember how you punched that guy in the face at Surgical Carnage? I can't think of any chick who'd be better to front a metal band than you, Rachel."

We filed in shortly, telling Craig and Yvonne everything we could about Heathenistic Bile. The concert began — and I was horrified to see that Blackskull had the chain on and everything. "They're totally going to do it again!" I shouted to Edgar, and we laughed.

The place was packed — hundreds of people. Bigger than the Surgical Carnage crowd had been. We found a place along the back of the club where we could all see the stage. Heathenistic Bile definitely upped the ante this time — Kate and Jennifer wiggled wildly, fishnet-clad on each side of the stage, and Paul was even more dramatic, but the crowd didn't seem into it. A few heads moved at the front, but there was no mosh pit or anything, and the cheer that would rise after each song was lukewarm.

When it was time to *unleash the beast*, there was no crowd response at all. Paul and his band steeled themselves and pressed on, Blackskull emitting the same weak howl as before, but no one responded except for a few random shrieks here and there.

"Probably their friends," Socks said. "Same guys from the Toe."

I noticed a few people in the crowd laughing at the proceedings, which made me smile. Morons. They thought they were better than us, and it was vindicating to see that we weren't the only ones who thought they sucked. It would have been nice to land this gig, opening for Gurgol. It would have been a good opportunity for us, especially because of Marie-Lise. If the crowd was into her being in the band, maybe they'd be into our band too.

Heathenistic Bile finished their last few songs, and the crowd halfheartedly cheered them offstage. Immediately the vibe in the room picked up. Gurgol was next.

We all hung out chatting a bit while we waited, and Craig came up beside me. I'd seen him around school, but I hadn't been thinking about him or boyfriends or school — or anything, really, except the band.

"How have you been?" he said.

"Fine. You?"

"Oh, busy with school and shit like that. I totally want to come out to your next show."

The last time I had really talked to Craig was the day he'd given me Heathenistic Bile's CD. "So, those guys are your friends, eh?" I said, gesturing to the stage.

He blushed a little. "Yeah, kinda. I mean, I know they aren't very good, but you know, at least they're nice guys."

"Not really," I corrected him. "In fact, Paul is a complete asshole."

"Well, he's always been pretty cool to me," Craig said, then frowned. "Sorry about that. You know, I mean, sometimes people put on an act, right? I guess Paul's trying to act like a tough guy in his band."

"Paul's band isn't big enough for him to warrant putting on any kind of act," I said. "His twenty fans are his friends. And since when does an 'act' mean treating people in other bands like shit?"

"Whoa, okay. Let's not talk about Paul anymore. I'm not trying to piss you off. Actually I wanted to ask you a question."

I could tell by the way he was gazing at me that it was going to be some kind of soppy, romantic thing. "What question?"

"Just, maybe, did you want to go out to eat or something sometime? Or, like, to a movie?" His eyes searched my face nervously.

In that moment, I felt the power shift between us. When I had met Craig, I'd thought he was cute, and he'd humiliated me. Since then, the few times I'd seen him, he'd either said stupid shit or just faded into the background for me. But still, he'd always had that moment when we'd met. He'd still *won*. And in this moment, it changed. Going out to see some boring movie with Craig was the absolute last thing I wanted to do. And now I was in control.

"No," I replied.

He stood there, staring at me for a minute, waiting for me to continue. When I didn't, he faltered. "Oh, er — do you have a boyfriend or something?"

"Nope. I just don't want to." I stared back at him. It really was that simple. Was he looking for me to offer some sort of excuse? Is that what I was supposed to do?

"Well, don't worry about it, then," he fumbled. "Don't worry about it." He went away from me then, back to stand next to Edgar, and I shrugged. If I hadn't been good enough for Craig last year, he wasn't good enough for me now. And I had far more important things to focus on than *going to a movie* with some guy.

The lights went down, the crowd roared deafeningly, and one by one, the members of Gurgol came out onstage as a garbled music-box melody played. First the drummer, then the guitar player. As each guy emerged, the crowd freaked out even more. Next, Marie-Lise came out — absolutely glowing in a white slip-dress and white boots. She'd curled her hair and it bounced in long ringlets tied on either side of her head with black ribbons. Her mouth was a slash of red lipstick, her eyes hollowed out with black. She looked a far cry from the girl in jeans drinking coffee in the sun that morning. The crowd screamed for her. She smiled prettily and picked up her bass, taking her place on the stage.

Finally, Josh Galligan, the singer, came out and grabbed his guitar. The crowd bellowed. They started to play.

I looked over at Fern. Her eyes were riveted to Marie-Lise. I smiled.

The show was amazing. I admit I really only watched

Marie-Lise. She had her whole deal down perfectly — moving forward to the crowd, twirling away from the outstretched hands. Part of me wanted to try to get to the front of the crowd to be near her, but it was so packed I knew I wouldn't be able to get close. Craig and Socks went to the mosh pit, but I stayed back with the others. It was nice being able to see the whole stage from where we stood.

They played for an hour, and at the end of the last song, Marie-Lise threw herself down on the ground, thumping the last notes of the song out of her bass. She lay close to the front of the stage, and I saw hands reach out and grab her hair, tugging it. She let them, and when she sat back up, they all respectfully let go of it. By this time the black makeup around her eyes had melted in her sweat and streamed down her cheeks like tears. Her lipstick was gone, and her hair had fallen out of its ponytails. She looked insane, and sitting on the stage, she grinned at the crowd one last time.

The lights went out and in the darkness the band left the stage. The crowd screamed, but they weren't coming back out. The house lights came on.

"That was great," Edgar said, and I agreed. Fern's face was shining with excitement. I wondered how long it was going to take before she went shopping for Pegasus bleach.

XXX

"Socks, what's your goal with the band? Why do you want to do it?" Fern asked as we drove home. Craig and Yvonne had gone in Craig's car, and it was the four of us, with Fern and me in the backseat.

"Having fun," he replied immediately. "I like to have a good time. I'd love to go on tour, see the world, all that."

"What about you, Edgar?"

"I don't know," he said, and thought for a moment. "You

know, I guess maybe I'd like to make a difference. Leave something behind, you know? Be remembered."

"All the more reason we gotta get in a studio and record," Socks said.

"Studios are expensive," Fern said. "We don't have any money."

"Yeah, but if we maybe knew someone with a good computer program and a space to record," I said, "couldn't we do it ourselves? We recorded our rehearsal at your place, Socks. Couldn't we do a full CD the same way?"

"You're right. If we had software where we could record each instrument as a separate track, then mix them together at the end of it . . . we could. My computer's crap. I could call a few friends and see what I can come up with. We might be able to do it really cheap. That's a good idea."

TWENTY-FIVE

Socks had a friend named Ken, who played in some local bar band, and they rented a rehearsal studio down by the river. In that rehearsal space, Ken had a recording set-up. He said he'd help us record for pretty cheap, so we all pooled our money. I pitched in my birthday money, as pathetic as the sum was, and as the school year ended we went into the "studio." It was fun — we created a schedule with Ken where each of us would record our parts one at a time, and condense all of it into a few hours a day for a week. Socks was first on the schedule, and we all wanted to be there, of course.

The room was in a small building with five other rehearsal spaces in it. Ken explained to us that most of the rooms were empty at the moment, and when we got our first look into their room, I was so relieved that we used Socks's basement for band practice. The rehearsal space was filthy from years of use. The rug was an undistinguishable colour, the ceiling had water damage stains mushrooming across it, and the walls were covered with spray paint. Ken and his band had brought in some clean furniture and tried to tidy it up, but there was only so much that could be done with such a place. The good part was that it was soundproofed, cheap, and it was nice to go and sit by the river if you felt like taking a break.

Ken seemed like a good guy. He was probably in his early twenties, a bit older than Socks, and I was pleased to see him wearing a DED shirt. Socks had told us he was into good music, even though his band played generic rock covers at their bar gigs.

He had some good mikes and let Socks play on his drum kit, because the kit was in better shape than Socks's. The only thing we did bring along for Socks was the snare drum, because we preferred it to the way Ken's sounded.

Ken sat at his computer while Socks flawlessly played through all twelve of our songs. I was impressed by this — I familiarized myself with my parts by feeding off cues from the music. Socks just knew the rhythm of the songs. I supposed that was his job, but it still impressed me.

Ken suggested that Socks run through each song one more time, to ensure a good take or a different option, and Socks sturdily played through again. Edgar, Fern, and I sat on a couch, watching and trying not to make any noise that could be picked up by the mikes. Socks made a few mistakes this time through, but happily began again when it was required.

The goal was to get one of us done a day, and the next day was Edgar's turn. He listened to Socks's drum parts through headphones and played along, his amp miked. Ken sat riveted to the computer. Multicoloured tracks appeared, scrolling across the screen, representing Edgar's bass lines. He definitely started and stopped a lot and it became clear that his parts were going to take awhile. So Fern and I wandered out to the river, sat in the grass, and I watched her smoke cigarettes.

The next afternoon was Fern's turn, and as the rest of us sat on the couch and watched, it became very clear to me that she had improved a lot. And she'd been really good before. As she launched into the solo in "Blood on My Fist," she absolutely soared and I noticed that it had grown more complicated as well, as if she had slightly reworked it. It was amazing. Even Ken looked over at us on the couch, lifted his eyebrows, and nodded approvingly as she played. I folded my arms. He was impressed because she was a *girl*, and that pissed me off. But at the same time, I also glowed with pride.

When Fern had finished, she took off her headphones and Ken said, "You're a fucking great guitarist." I waited for him to add *for a girl*, but he didn't.

"Thanks," she said. "Shall we go through them again? I have some harmonies I'd like to put down for a few of the parts, and a couple more things to add to broaden the sound. I'm the only guitar onstage, but I figure that it's okay to have the CD sound a bit different."

"Sure it is." Ken nodded. Fern put back on her headphones, and I heard the tracks start over in her ears.

That night I found it hard to sleep. I was excited to get started on my vocals the next day. When Fern had finished and I'd gone home, my parents had asked me if I wanted to get a job for the summer, and I'd done my usual nod, smile, and look concerned routine. I felt like I *had* a job. Our band was in the studio — sort of — and that was work, wasn't it? I knew my parents weren't going to understand, but once our CD was recorded we might actually sell some of them and make some money. Being in a band could be a job, right?

The next afternoon we all got back to the rehearsal space.

I'd brought my little binder with my lyrics in it, and I was relieved to see that Ken had brought out a little music stand for me to set it on.

"Okay, guys, same drill," he said as Socks, Edgar, and Fern sat down on the couch. "Rachel, you'll hear the tracks coming through your headphones. Do your thing. We'll just go through the songs one by one, and if you need to stop, let me know." He seated himself at the computer.

I thought about this for a moment. "So you guys will just hear me singing then?"

"Yep," Ken said.

I didn't like the sound of that very much. "Can't we have the music playing along in the room?"

"No, because the mike will pick that up. We need as clean a vocal take as we can get," Ken said.

My face started to heat up. "I don't know if I can do that."

Ken swivelled around in his chair to look at me thoughtfully. So did the others. I started feeling both very stupid and very angry. My cheeks pounded as I tried to find words to explain without sounding like a moron. "It will be hard for me," I said, "with you guys just *staring* at me, and all you can hear is just *me* sounding bad."

"You don't sound bad," Fern said.

"That's what we all did, anyway. We all went through that," Edgar said.

"It's *different* though, with a voice," I bumbled. "I have to be all *into it*."

"We all had to be into it," Edgar said.

"It's *different*," I said, hearing frustration in my voice. I was annoyed that I couldn't even look at them as I tried to argue my point. The old stereotype, I knew, was that singers are all temperamental, and I didn't want to be that way, but couldn't they understand that this was completely different than recording a guitar part? I thought of my voice ringing cleanly out in this room, thought of the faces I was going to have to make in order to achieve the vibe I wanted, thought of them all watching me silently, and shuddered with embarrassment.

"Okay, okay," Ken said. "Well, the rest of you guys can go outside or something and I can stay in here with Rachel. I *have* to stay here, okay? I will sit with my back to you if it makes you more comfortable, but this is really the only way to get a good vocal take."

"So . . . all singers have to do it this way?" I said, ashamed, feeling like a true novice.

"In a real recording studio, the singer would go into an isolation booth and everyone else sits outside and hears the voice going along with the music. But that's because they're in isolation. We can't have the mike pick up any sound other than your voice, otherwise it's going to sound like shit." Ken didn't sound frustrated, exactly, but he definitely didn't have his usual casual tone.

"Okay then." I looked up at the ceiling, too ashamed of myself to look at my friends. "So do you guys mind waiting outside for a while?"

"Sure," Fern said agreeably, standing up.

"If that's what you need," Edgar said. I could tell he was annoyed.

"We'll pick up some cheeseburgers," Socks said.

As they left the room, I flipped through my lyric sheets on the music stand. After the door closed, I felt like I should say something.

"Ken, er — I'm sorry. I'm not trying to be a hassle."

"No, it's okay," he replied. "You know, it's a common thing. I'm not a singer, so I don't know what it's like. But, I mean — that's why the isolation booth exists, right? People don't like having to sing in a quiet room with everybody watching."

I didn't even like the idea of him staying in the room, but he'd promised not to *look* — god, I felt so stupid, like a little kid. He asked me if I was ready to start, and I told him I was. I put on my headphones. "Blood on My Fist" began. I tried to use the music to empower myself. I couldn't let a little thing like *someone hearing me sing* ruin this CD, right? I closed my eyes, took a deep breath, and roared as best I could into the first verse, trying to pretend that there was no one else in the room, that I wasn't in this room at all, that I was somewhere else completely.

It was a very long and irritating process, to be honest. I knew I could do better on some of the songs and wanted to re-record them. Sometimes I'd screw up, my voice breaking at the wrong part. At one point in the middle of a great take of "Needles and Eyes," the others came back and knocked loudly on the door. Ken stopped the recording, talked to them quietly at the door, sent them away, and then we had to restart. I felt like the hours were slipping by. It was taking much longer than it had for the others. And my voice was starting to wear out — a totally natural thing that, naively, I had not anticipated. It was so damn hard trying to get into the mood, trying to sound *into it*. I wasn't onstage, I was in a small, smelly room. My friends were annoyed at me. I wasn't completely comfortable with Ken. I kept my eyes closed and tried to project myself somewhere cool, like onstage in front of thousands or in some music video or something, but it was really difficult. After three hours we only had half the songs done, and our time was up. Ken worked evenings, so we always had to wrap up towards late afternoon. I sat down wearily on the couch as he went and got the others, and we all convened in the room.

"We'll have to come back again tomorrow afternoon," Ken

said, yawning and stretching his arms above his head. "We didn't get everything done."

"How's it sounding?" Edgar asked.

"It's sounding good," he replied. "Great. Rachel's a great singer. I'm honestly sort of surprised," he grinned. "There aren't many good female metal voices."

Normally I would have scowled at such a comment, but I was too tired. Fern, sitting next to me, put her arm around me. "Yeah. She's awesome."

"So we'll just need tomorrow afternoon. Rachel, if you want, just come by yourself tomorrow and we can finish it off." I nodded in reply. "Then, once I get all her stuff recorded, I can send you guys the files and you can mix it or whatever."

In Socks's van on the way home, I tried to explain to them that it had been difficult for me to capture any sort of vibe, and I grudgingly apologized for needing them to leave. Everyone was nice about it. Socks reiterated what Ken had said about it being a common thing, but I still felt lousy. I didn't want to be some spoiled singer, you know? If I was going to have a reputation I wanted it to be something else. Not spoiled. Not a princess who had to have things her way.

My voice was hoarse and shot. Was I even going to be able to do the recordings tomorrow? How long would it take to get my voice back to good shape? I felt an irritation creeping over me. My role here *was* different from everyone else's. And if the band moved forward, I couldn't see it becoming any less difficult.

XXX

That night in my room I started drawing. I drew a skeleton hanging from a noose, dangling in front of a crowd of people, a background of shadowy faces, all watching, some of them disinterested, some of the faces mocking and laughing. I gave

206

her long black hair, like mine. I remembered our show with Heathenistic Bile, I remembered that afternoon in the studio. The skeleton was exposed and humiliated, and the faces around her were enjoying it. I remembered Fern trying to be positive and supportive of me. I drew another skeleton beneath the hanging one, this one with long white hair — the white I knew Fern wanted her hair to be — grabbing the dangling legs as if trying to support the weight of the body, to stop the skeleton from hanging. For good measure I added in a severed head, wrapped in blood-soaked cloth with only the wild eyes visible from within. The head of Holofernes. It was on the ground beside the white-haired skeleton. After I had finished sketching this out, I sat back and looked at it. You sort of couldn't tell whether or not the Fern-skeleton was trying to help the me-skeleton by lifting her legs, supporting her weight, or if she was pulling on them, trying to speed up the process. Oh well. I sort of liked that double meaning, that confusion.

I took my markers and started colouring.

Scream into This, I scrawled along the bottom. Yeah, Rachel — scream into the microphone like it's not a big deal, while we all sit here judging you. Just scream. Dance like a little monkey for everyone.

TWENTY-SIX

That night I could barely sleep because I was so angry. I don't even really know who or what I was angry at. The whole situation, and everyone in it, I guess. Angry at the band for not understanding I had a different job than they did. At Edgar, who always seemed like he was going to be contrary with me, no matter if it was getting pissed that I made fun of the Heathenistic Bile guys, or if I insisted that singing was different from playing bass. I was angry at Fern too, for no good reason, and Socks as well, even if it was just for being so damn cheerful all the time. I was angry with my parents for suggesting I get a summer job. I felt very disconnected from them — they were a blur to me. And I was definitely angry that I had to go back into that stupid room again and do the rest of the songs. I have never liked going into the studio. There is a hollowness and dishonesty to the whole thing.

Ironically, even though my voice was still wrecked, the next day with Ken went pretty smoothly. I did my best to sound good and get through it all. No one was there except me and him, and he faithfully did not look at me during the whole thing, and we finished off the rest of the songs within a few hours. I was relieved when it was over.

"So let Socks know I will upload all these files to his server within the next few days," Ken said when we had finished. "If you guys need some help mixing the tracks, I'm happy to give a hand."

"I'll tell him," I said, leaning back on the couch. Now that we were finished, I was completely exhausted. "Thanks for doing this for us."

"It's not a problem." He smiled at me. "You guys are actually pretty awesome. I think this CD is going to be amazing. You're going to release it on your own?"

"Once we save up enough money to get them printed," I said.

"Cool." He nodded, and paused for a second. "I hope you don't take offence to this, but I think people are going to be pretty impressed that you're a girl, and that your guitar player is a girl. The music is awesome."

I prickled. "Is that because it doesn't suck? You're surprised that it doesn't suck?"

"No, no, not like that," he said. "It's just that it seems like you guys are really committed to it. You have to admit that there aren't a lot of girls in this whole thing, this kind of music. There isn't much to compare it to, to even begin to make a lousy statement like 'girls in metal suck.' The only other female singer I can even think of is Annika, and you're way better than her."

"I guess."

"She doesn't suck. And your music, girls in the band or not, doesn't suck. To be honest, I think you guys are going to actually be able to do something with it. You're original. People are going to be interested."

I nodded. *I know all of this.* "If they can get past the fact that we're girls."

"Fuck anybody who feels that way," Ken said dismissively. "Use your band to show them how wrong they are."

I know that too.

xxx

About a week later Socks called to say that he'd received the recorded tracks from Ken, and that everyone was going to get together at his place to start listening through them and choosing the best takes. I was excited about getting started on this, but my parents had to throw a wrench into everything.

"So you're all finished with the music recording?" my father asked me that very night as we were having dinner.

"Yes."

"Have you started looking for a part-time job?"

"Yes." I was lying. "I've been looking on the internet."

"Well, I have some good news for you," Mom said. "A friend of mine owns a coffee shop downtown, and she's looking for some extra help for the summer. I mentioned that you're looking for work, and she said she'd be happy to hire you until school starts!"

Both of them beamed as if this was the best possible news, and I immediately matched their smiles. "That's great, thank you for doing that for me," I said. "But I would kinda prefer to find my own job. I'd feel bad if I messed up or something. I wouldn't want your friend to get mad at you for suggesting me."

"You won't mess up. How could you mess up?" Mom said.

"You're not supposed to mix business with friendship, right?" I said.

"You'll take the job and do just fine," my father said.

"You start tomorrow morning," Mom trilled.

Weak adolescent that I was, my smile vanished and I immediately started complaining. "I can't start tomorrow. I have things to do," I said. They were surprised by my sudden anger, which I could understand. I had tried to keep that stupid smile on my face as long as I could.

"You're talking about the band, I'm sure," Dad said. "And you know by now that Mom and I support your creative projects. But you're going to be starting your last year of high school in the fall. It's very important that you learn responsibility and work ethic. I see this happen all the time, you know. Kids just slacking off all through school. Their parents don't teach them any sort of structure and where do they end up? Flipping burgers their entire lives."

"What's wrong with flipping burgers?"

"Nothing, of course," Mom said, "as long as that's what a person *wants* to do. You have some big decisions coming up in the next year. Decisions about college. You're not going to be a kid anymore. It's a good time to start experiencing the world."

How was I going to get any sort of world experience working in some crappy coffee shop? Of course there was no way to express this to them. I realized that this was not a conversation, which implies interaction and communication. I was being *told*. So, fine. I would work the stupid job. Whatever would shut my parents up. I didn't even bother telling them that Fern didn't have to work, and neither did Edgar, and that they would have the summer to work on our CD, the important thing, and I would be left out of it. I knew my parents wouldn't care about any of those things, despite their supposed support for my *creative projects*.

XXX

The next morning I dutifully walked down to the Rosewood Café at 9 a.m. My mother's friend, *Mrs. Spangler* — no first name basis here — did not seem very impressed by me. I smiled happily as her eyes scanned my dyed hair and my inappropriate makeup.

"You'll have to wear your hair in a ponytail for hygienic reasons," she said pleasantly, "and I'm afraid you'll also have to wash off your eye makeup. We get a lot of senior citizens in here, and they don't like that sort of thing."

"Sure," I said, rather disappointed. I had hoped she might dismiss me on the spot. Instead, she handed me a yellow apron.

"Put this on once you're done washing, and we'll get started."

Mrs. Spangler showed me how to make coffee, where the tea bags were, and explained the selection of sandwiches and muffins. She walked me through using the cash register. It was all so useless. My band was mixing our first CD and here I was, serving huckleberry muffins and tea to old people, wearing a stupid yellow apron. I loathed my parents and I loathed Mrs. Spangler.

But at least it wasn't gruelling and only took up half of each day. I was able to go to Socks's house after my shifts, walking over every afternoon, to listen to the songs as they came together and help the others out. And when I got my first paycheque, I have to say that was pretty amazing. My own money. And I could do whatever I wanted with it.

My parents were off my back about everything, happy that I had settled into the job. It sucked getting up that early, but Mrs. Spangler seemed to like me more and more, and I felt productive. I was making money, I was working on music, and I could afford to buy some new clothes and stuff. Even the customers were pretty nice. We had some regulars who would come in, some old ladies who started calling me "dear." It sounds lame, but it sort of made me happy.

One particularly hot afternoon, an older man came in. He took a seat at a table by the window and scowled at me. "Can I get some service?" he said.

"You have to order at the counter," I called back, trying to maintain my customer-service pleasantness.

"Well, I don't feel like getting up," he said.

"Well, when you do, I'll be happy to take your order." I didn't like the guy. When rude people came in, Mrs. Spangler had always dealt with them, poised and pleasant. But this time she wasn't in the shop — it was only the second time she'd left me there alone for a while, as she went to the supermarket — and it was my first time dealing with a rude customer on my own.

Which, of course, wasn't sitting well with me.

The man stared at me for a while, and I stared right back, expressionless. The silent confrontation should have made me feel awkward, but instead it made me feel excited. The man finally looked away, uncomfortable. "Get me a coffee, black, and a chocolate muffin."

"You'll have to come up and pay first," I called back, too happily and too loudly.

"You can come here and get my money," he said.

"No can do."

The man sat for a few more moments and then gave in. He came up to the counter, took a five dollar bill out of his pocket, and literally threw it at me. I calmly picked it up, rung in the sale, and gave the man his change. "I'll bring it *aaaaall* to your table for you, sir," I said, smiling brightly and sarcastically. He glared at me and went back to his table, sitting down.

I decided to take my sweet time getting his coffee and muffin. I wanted him to get angrier; I was anticipating the conflict, wondering what his reaction would be. I wasn't afraid of him. This was exciting to me.

After several long minutes, I finally carried his coffee and muffin to his table. "I really, really, really hope you enjoy this."

The man exploded. "How dare you talk to me like that? The *customer is always right*! You have absolutely no business giving me such attitude!"

As he ranted, I continued smiling brightly and placed the coffee mug in front of him. Infuriated, he grabbed the mug and actually threw it down onto the floor, splashing hot coffee on his chest. As the mug shattered on the floor, he cried out in anger and surprise.

I knelt down to pick up the pieces and cut myself on one of the jagged edges. I gasped as I saw blood ooze from three of my fingers, dark and red.

I stared at the blood as the man freaked out. "Now I've burned myself! You bitch!" he shouted, clutching at his coffee-soaked shirt. I knew the coffee had to have burned him, and I stood back up again.

"Oh, no!" I cried. I reached out towards him to "help" and his eyes locked onto the blood dripping from my fingers.

"What the hell!" He tried to pull away, but I began to pluck at the wet areas of his shirt, wiping my blood on it, all the while staring into his horrified eyes. I really, really tried not to smile.

"Get away from me!" he screamed.

"I'm so sorry!" I cried, unable to resist grinning at him, wiping blood all over the shirt.

At that moment Mrs. Spangler returned. "What is going on?"

Immediately I fixed my expression back to concern. "He spilled coffee on himself!" I cried, continuing to clutch at his shirt.

"You're bleeding, come away from him!" Mrs. Spangler pulled me back from the table and grabbed a handful of napkins. She began to dab at the man's shirt, but he finally sprang out of his seat. "She is *crazy!*" he shouted, pointing at me. "She was completely rude to me, and then she started wiping her *blood* all over me!"

I couldn't help it — the looks on their faces were so hilarious, I started laughing. I doubled over, unable to stop myself. I heard Mrs. Spangler say my name a few times, trying to get my attention, but I just laughed and laughed.

So that was the end of my time at the Rosewood Café.

TWENTY-SEVEN

As July became August, it seemed like my parents were avoiding conversation with me. I could tell they were worried, and I figured it was probably because Mrs. Spangler had told them what had happened. I wondered what she had said to them, what words had come to her mind to explain it. *Insane? Unbalanced?* She had to have told them about the blood, and the way I had laughed. I guess my parents didn't know what to say to me about it, how to ask me anything. I had told them that I'd had an argument with a customer and that's why I had been fired. Then that evening the phone had rung. And then they had talked in low voices. And then we didn't speak of it again.

Which was fine by me. I hadn't wanted a summer job anyway. It pleased me that they didn't confront me about it, but it was another reminder that I really had to keep that sort of thing under wraps. I didn't want to draw any attention to myself. It would only end up limiting me and flagging me to people. It was a mistake to have laughed. I should have played it all off like an accident, and that way, only the asshole would have been weirded out by me.

XXX

Fern, Edgar, Socks, and I finally had the twelve final mixes. I showed them the drawing I had done the night of the vocal recording, and though they didn't see the deeper meaning I had put into it, they loved it. Fern wanted to use it for the CD cover, and everyone agreed. They even liked *Scream into This* for the album name. I was proud. We scanned it into the computer. One weekend we all dressed up and Yvonne took a picture of us standing against a brick wall, looking appropriately sullen and evil, for the inside of the CD jacket.

Now all we had to do was get the damn thing manufactured. Which was going to be costly. Edgar's parents loaned us the money, which we assured them we would pay back as quickly as we could. We decided to only get two hundred printed up, which seemed like a small amount, but of course no one even knew who we were, so who knew if it would end up being too many?

XXX

Fern called me one evening towards the end of the summer. "So I just got off the phone with Socks," she said excitedly. "Check it out. Ken has some friends in a band, they're metal. They're called Torn Bowel, apparently nice guys. They're from ...."

"Okay," I said.

"Well, they're going on a tour the week before school starts. Just a short thing, four shows around the province. They were going to go with some other band, but one of those guys broke his leg so they had to cancel."

217

"Okay?"

"So I guess Ken recommended us to them. And they'd like us to go on the tour."

"Shit, *really*? A *tour*?"

"Well, only four shows," Fern said, but I could hear the excitement in her voice too.

The four of us met the next afternoon at the tea shop. Socks told us the details. He figured we could take the van with the gear and all of us share a hotel room each night. We could sell some of our CDs, hopefully, and make a bit of money to pay for gas and the hotels. We weren't going to be paid to do the shows, but that was okay because apparently Torn Bowel was getting pretty popular, so it would be good exposure for us.

"They're not a big band, but I guess people are starting to like them," he said. "I think it would be a good idea to go with them. Ken says they're nice guys too, so it should be fun."

"Do you guys feel like we're ready to play four shows in a row?" Edgar asked. I figured he was probably reminiscing about the only other show we'd done and how badly it had gone.

"I feel like we can definitely do it," Fern said confidently.

"We just have to remember to keep the energy up," I added. "I feel like all of us probably learned from last time. I know I totally did."

"All right then. You guys talk to your parents tonight and make sure they're cool with it," Socks said. "Once you find out, call me, and I'll call these guys and let them know we're in."

"You are too young to go on a *tour*," my father said with a tone of finality in his voice. "You are still in high school. This whole thing is ridiculous."

"I'm not a little kid," I whined lamely, hating the sound of my voice. Melissa kept her eyes on her dinner plate.

"You can't be serious about this. Do you know what happens on *rock tours?*"

"Dad, it isn't like that. It's just four shows, everyone's nice, nobody does drugs, nothing like that. It's just a chance to play our music for people. Everyone's going to be super careful and it's less than a week anyways!"

"The answer is an *absolute no*," Dad said and started eating again.

"I think it would be fun," Melissa offered. "I think she should go."

"Well, you are not in charge of making decisions in this family," Dad said. "Mom and I are. And that is our decision."

We lapsed into silence, and I seethed with anger. I knew everyone else's parents would be fine with it. Why did I have to have the stupid parents? I was going to be the one to ruin it for the band. I was going to have to disappoint everyone. But my parents wouldn't care about any of that. I had to think of an approach that they would understand. I tried to calm myself down.

"The thing is," I began, steadying my voice, "I only have one year of high school left, and then college. I'll have to give up the band. We all will. I just think this is probably going to be the only chance I will ever have to do something like this. Even though it really is on such a small scale."

My mother looked up at me. "So you are thinking about college?"

"Of course," I said earnestly. "I know this whole music thing is temporary. I have to grow up. I just wish that I could do this one thing, just to have some fun and play some shows before I really *buckle down* and think about my future."

My mother and father looked at each other across the table. "What have you thought about taking in college?" Mom asked.

"Well," I said brightly, "I think I'd like to take my interest in writing and instead of doing lyrics, maybe get into journalism or something. When school starts, I'm definitely going to make an appointment with the career counsellor and talk about a plan."

My father nodded. "That's a good idea."

"Writing lyrics is my passion, but I know it isn't practical."

"So you are going to stop this whole band thing and look at things more practically?"

"Of *course*. But I would like to do just this one thing, just for the experience. It's only four days. Will you guys please think about it?"

Their eyes met across the table once again. "We'll talk about it after dinner," Dad said. I smiled gratefully, glad they had bought it. There was no way I was going to give up the band, of course. College was the last thing on my mind. But I was proud of myself for having come up with that stuff, and having conveyed it so convincingly.

A few hours later my mother came into my room and sat down at the end of my bed. "So your dad and I talked about this whole idea, and we've decided that you can go."

"Awesome! Thank you!" I said. Now I needed to call Socks and tell him I was in, but of course my mother had more to say.

"We have to talk about a few things first, though, Rachel."

I nodded and widened my eyes, looking at her with what I hoped was a concerned and attentive expression. She started talking about how my future was important, my grades were important, and they had always been proud of me, and blah blah blah. She gave me some useless warnings about the dangers of drugs, of drinking and driving. I nodded the whole time, agreeing with everything. And then she started talking about what had happened at the Rosewood Café.

"Mrs. Spangler told me that you were laughing because you had gotten blood on the customer," she said worriedly, studying my face. "Do you want to tell me what that was all about?"

"It was horrible. I was so embarrassed and uncomfortable."

"Why were you laughing?"

"It was a horrible, totally terrible reaction to feeling so embarrassed. I couldn't help it. And of course, I made it worse," I said sadly. "I'm sure Mrs. Spangler thought I was crazy."

My mother shrugged and nodded. "She said it was very odd."

"That's what I thought would happen," I said. "It was so awful. I felt like a moron." I stared down at my hands, clasping and unclasping them in my lap. I could feel my mother studying my face.

Finally she said, "Mrs. Spangler was very disturbed, I think. I don't think she understood that you were laughing because you were uncomfortable, or nervous, or whatever it was."

I looked up, startled. "Why else would a person laugh about that? It was *horrible*! Does she think I'm a psycho or something?"

My mother touched my hand. "Mrs. Spangler doesn't matter. Of course you're not a psycho," she said, smiling. "I just wanted to talk to you about that. Your dad and I weren't sure if we should say anything about it."

"You should have talked to me about it earlier!" I said. "All summer you guys have been walking around here thinking I'm insane?"

"Not quite," she said, laughing. "Okay. But I feel better about it now, and you're right, we should have asked you sooner. Now go ahead and call your friends."

I wonder how Mom would have reacted if I had told her how exciting the whole thing had been. How I had thought about it since and laughed even more. Or about how I secretly had a fantasy, deep in a dark place inside myself, where I imagined showering someone with my own blood. The way they would fear it, the disgust and horror, the way they would scream as I poured and smeared and slathered my unknown, alien blood all over them. This was so exciting I could barely even admit it to myself, and the thought of communicating it to my mother almost made me start laughing all over again. Luckily, I managed to hold it in.

I suppose it was around this time that I started nurturing my desire to be feared. I wanted to surprise people who underestimated me, and rather than simply impress them, I wanted them to *regret* having felt that way. I became fixated on that moment of realization — whether it was the look on the guy's face from that concert after I had punched him, when his eyes widened and his hands caught his own blood, when he realized that *I* had done it to him, or the way the coffee shop customer's eyes had registered that same fear as I wiped blood on him, or even Brandi staring at me in horror. I wanted to inspire fear and revulsion in people who tried to undermine me. I wanted to watch their opinion of me change, read it in their eyes. The fantasy of covering some judgmental asshole with a bucket of my blood was definitely appealing to me. I wanted disgust and fear and for them to know that I was in control. I had no outlet for any of this, of course, and I had a tour to plan for.

At that point we had barely two weeks to get ready. We rehearsed a bunch of times, of course, even though we all knew the songs. Every time I saw Fern, whether it was at rehearsal or to go shopping or have tea, her hair was another shade lighter. She had obviously tracked down Pegasus hair bleach. I redyed mine, as well, and carefully picked out four different outfits that would all look awesome. This was going to go well. It had to. We were going to be killer onstage.

The tour started in Torn Bowel's hometown, Port Claim, which was about four hours north of us, so we were going to leave pretty early on the Thursday morning of the first show. Through these conversations with everyone, I started learning more about planning tours: obviously the nights when most people would come out were weekends, and since the Port Claim show would likely be the busiest, it made sense to have booked it on a Thursday. The other three cities would be smaller shows, and all but the Sunday night one would be weekend nights. This meant that our second-ever show would be a busy one, which was a bit nerve-racking, but all of us were feeling confident.

Four boxes of *Scream into This* arrived, fifty in each, and they looked great. Totally professional. We decided we'd sell them for fifteen bucks each, which was probably a little high, but we had to pay our expenses on the road and we also had to start repaying Edgar's parents. Who was to say that anyone would even want to buy one, right? We could lose a ton of money and be that much further behind on the loan. But there was no point in worrying about that. We could also sell out and come back with three thousand dollars.

Thursday morning, as I waited for the van to arrive, I'd dressed in pure Marie-Lise-on-tour style. I wore jeans, a T-shirt, and a big pair of black sunglasses. The only one who'd be able to call me out on ripping her off would be Fern, and when the van pulled up, I saw she had the same idea as me. We grinned awkwardly at each other, acknowledging it quietly, and as I climbed into the backseat beside her, dragging my suitcase, I was at least able to have the satisfaction that my hair wasn't pure white and hers was.

"You guys both look like rock stars," Socks said.

TWENTY-EIGHT

We arrived in Port Claim after five irritating hours of traffic. At this point we were late for load-in, but there was nothing we could do about it.

We pulled into the parking lot of the idiotically named Klub Klang, and as we swung the van around to the back, I saw another van with a few guys standing around outside it. I was immediately reminded of the assholes from Heathenistic Bile, and felt my guard rise.

But they turned towards us and smiled as we pulled in, raising their hands in greeting. I didn't see any cheap, shiny leather or dangling wallet chains. Just a bunch of long-haired guys in jeans, all grinning.

We hopped out, and the guys all came over to meet us. There were five of them — Jamie, Billy, Kevin, Phil, and PJ. No extra crew, no glaring girlfriends. Everybody shook each other's hand, introducing themselves, and immediately their singer, Billy, started a friendly conversation with me.

"So Ken says you guys are fucking amazing," he said, smiling. "I can't wait to check you guys out."

"Yeah, same," I said, easing into the whole thing, feeling more comfortable. "We're really excited to be along. Thanks for having us."

"Oh, it's going to be fun," he said. "It sucks my buddy's band had to cancel, but we're happy you guys could come out with us."

"Do you guys tour much?"

"Sometimes. Just a week here and there, mostly. We all finished school last spring, which is gonna make it easier for us to focus on doing the band, you know?"

"Not going to college?"

"Maybe. We want to take a year and try to get the band going, you know? We can always go to college if it doesn't work out."

Torn Bowel had already loaded in their stuff, and so we loaded in our gear as well. We were happy to find out that we would get a soundcheck as well, after theirs, so we sat down and watched them set up their equipment.

This club was about the same size as the Toe, but a bit cleaner. It still smelled like shit though. I was starting to figure out that every bar and club has the exact same smell of old beer and piss. On the wall behind the stage, *KLUB KLANG* was written in huge red letters, but to my relief one of the Torn Bowel guys busied himself hanging their band banner up to cover it. For some reason that name really rubbed me the wrong way.

The house guy at the sound desk gave them the signal, Torn Bowel jumped into a fast song when they were ready to go. They were really good. Billy was an amazing singer, casually moving in and out of roars and growls. All of them played very comfortably, obviously treating this like a not-a-big-deal soundcheck. I made a mental note to also pretend it was no big deal for us to have a soundcheck.

When they finished their song, Billy called out to us. "How's it sounding out on the floor there?"

"Great," Edgar said.

They ran through another song, sounding amazing, and then they were done. It was our turn. They moved their gear to the back of the stage, making room for us to set up in front of them, and as Socks and Edgar began lifting our amps up to the stage, I found myself standing next to Jamie, one of the guitarists.

"How was your drive up?" he said, grinning at me.

I smiled back. "Not bad. Took awhile. Are you guys going for food now or anything?"

"I think we're gonna wait for you guys. Check out your soundcheck, and we can all go grab food if you guys feel like it," he said. He pushed his blond hair behind his ears in what seemed like a nervous gesture.

"That sounds good," I said. He was still smiling at me, and I couldn't help but smile back, but now there was going to be an awkward silence. I could feel us careening towards it. "Well, I guess I should get up there," I said, and climbed onstage.

Turning back, I saw Billy whisper something to Jamie, who then punched him good-naturedly in the arm, and they both looked back at me and smiled, then walked to join the others at one of the tables. For some reason that filled me with a stupid good feeling, and I smiled to myself. Jamie *was* pretty cute.

We started our soundcheck and launched confidently into "Skinner," one of our newer songs that we hadn't performed at the last show. Everything seemed to go smoothly for us, and after we'd finished, the Torn Bowel guys clapped and whistled. The sound guy seemed happy with it, and so were we. Because we were going on first we left our gear set up.

We all went to a sushi place a few blocks away and got a big table together. It was a really good atmosphere, everyone talking happily. I got a seat next to Fern, and Jamie sat on the other side of me.

I hadn't had sushi before, and Fern helped me pick something from the menu that didn't sound too scary. As the dishes started arriving, I eyed everyone else's choices of weird, nasty-looking slimy fish slices and was glad I'd chosen my cucumber and rice rolls.

"So you guys are from Keeleford. I've never been there. What's it like?" Jamie asked, lifting a wet-looking piece of raw salmon to his mouth.

I told him about our city, how small it was, how dull. It had been okay when I was a kid, with the river downtown and the trails on the outskirts. He'd grown up here in Port Claim and told me about how he'd enjoyed living by the lake, how he and his friends camped in the forests beside it, and about how the city had grown and good clubs were starting to crop up. A better place than Keeleford to start a band, I guess.

At the other end of the table, PJ, their drummer, started telling a story about how last winter over the holidays they'd booked a two-week tour across the country, had driven in their van through the snow, almost froze to death, didn't spend the holidays with their families, and barely anyone had shown up to any of the shows so they'd lost all their money. It sounded pretty depressing to me, but they were all laughing about it, so I joined in too.

Socks was completely in his element, goofing off and telling stories of his own about bands he'd been in. Even Edgar, who was usually pretty quiet, was happy and chatting. I mainly sat and listened without offering much, but it was great. Such a far cry from the attitude we'd gotten from Heathenistic Bile. I wondered which was more common: snobby assholes or friendly people, when it came to musicians. I wanted to talk about Paul and his cronies, figuring that was a pretty funny story I could bring up, but at the same time I wasn't sure if Torn Bowel knew them or were friends or something, and I didn't want to look like a jerk.

xxx

Klub Klang had three small rooms upstairs where the bands could get dressed and hang out. They were totally gross, but everyone sat down on the couches anyway. When we'd come back in, the doors had opened and there was a bunch of people on the floor. Already the night was shaping up to be much better than the last show.

Fern and I went to the private bathroom to get dressed. We'd bought matching skirts, mine was red and hers was blue, and we did our makeup as dark as we could. She looked amazing with her hair as pale as it was now, and because she was wearing black and blue, the Marie-Lise look was somewhat lessened.

This club had a stage entrance that led right to the stage from upstairs. When it was time for us to go on, the four of us crowded at the side.

Edgar peeked around the corner and looked back at us, grinning. "There's a ton of people here."

"Awesome," Fern said. "Let's have a good one, guys."

We all grinned at each other, and the three of them walked up onstage. To my surprise there was a general cheer that went up from the crowd.

When they'd all settled themselves with their instruments, the house music went down and I took a deep breath and walked up onto the stage.

The floor at the front of the stage was packed, and I felt eyes on me as I walked across and grabbed my microphone.

"We're Colostomy Hag," I announced as strongly as I could, and immediately Socks counted in the first song.

On either side of me, Fern and Edgar started moving, she in a wash of white hair and he with his dreads flying. Awkwardness hit me for a moment, but instead of freezing up, I took a deep breath, planted my hands on my hips, and hoped that my stillness looked like a deliberate attempt to contrast their movement. I scanned the front row of people, making eye contact with all of them.

Their heads were moving, and I was pleased to see some girls in the crowd as well, mainly looking at me and Fern. I didn't get a sense of boredom or mocking from anyone. They all seemed into it.

I began singing and moving to the music, trying very hard to win them over by throwing myself into the song as roughly as possible. I moved up close to the crowd, and while no hands reached up to me, the guys there definitely got more into it. As they started moving and headbanging, it fuelled me as well. I threw my hair around, I let it lay in front of my face and roared through it.

At the end of the song, the crowd cheered loudly. I could feel all of us onstage swell with relief and pride.

Towards the end of the set, with the crowd clearly enjoying it, I noticed a guy who had pushed his way to the front. Throughout the last song he placed his elbows on the stage and leaned on them in an obvious sign of boredom, and every time I made eye contact with him he mimed a very dramatic yawn at me. I did my best to ignore him, not sure of how to deal with him, and tried to focus instead on the other people who were having a good time. He was a like a scab or a zit that you try to ignore but is a constant nag.

When we paused before our second-last song, the crowd cheered, and the guy cupped his hands around his mouth.

"Hey, bitch," he shouted at me. "Why don't you get off the stage and let a *good* band play?"

Fury boiled inside me. "Hey, *prick*," I shouted back into the microphone. "Why don't you come on up here and *kiss my ass*?"

The crowd shrieked in approval and support. I grinned at all of them as the next song began. I'd won, not only the confrontation with the guy, but also the crowd's full respect. I moved to the other side of the stage where a few guys were throwing their hair around and knelt down by them. Glancing to the side of stage I saw Jamie and a few of the other Torn Bowel guys watching. When they saw me looking at them, all of them grinned and pointed at me. I bristled with pride.

I moved back to the centre of the stage and started singing, but when I looked down at the crowd again I saw the asshole smiling at me. He curled one of his hands into a loose fist, brought it up to his mouth, moved it away, then brought it forward again, smiling at me the whole time as he offensively pantomimed what, apparently, I could do to him.

I raised my middle finger with my free hand, continued to sing, moved up to the front of the stage, pressed it directly onto his forehead and shoved. He stepped back. Everyone around us cheered. The guy kept grinning at me and moved his hand down between his legs, grabbed himself, and leered at me.

I snapped.

I threw my microphone to the ground, where it landed with a loud bang and started feeding back. I guess the guy at the sound desk caught this and shut it off immediately. Fern, Edgar, and Socks kept playing, but I felt their eyes on me as I launched myself off the stage, landing directly on the asshole.

He fell backwards and the crowd parted to accommodate us. I landed on top of him but one of my knees smashed on the floor. I barely felt the pain. My eyes were riveted to his face. He clearly hadn't expected me to leap onto him and he'd hit his head when he fell, stunning him. When his eyes focused on me again, I made sure he saw me hock a huge glob of spit into my palm, and I then slapped his face with it.

I could hear the band continuing to play and I knew we were surrounded by people watching and cheering, but I felt detached from it all. He lay beneath me, trying to wipe the spit off his face, looking up at me in confusion. I wanted him to be disgusted, I wanted that *reaction*. That *regret*. The spit hadn't done it. I was vaguely aware of flashes going off around us. People were taking pictures.

Inspired, I raised my middle finger again, made sure he could see it, and then shoved it into my mouth, as far as I could into the back of my throat. My stomach heaved a little. A scream went up from the crowd around us, but he was still confused. Not afraid.

I shoved my finger down my throat again, and this time I retched a little bit. My eyes started to water. The asshole finally realized what I was going to do and started kicking and flailing, trying to buck me off him. I slapped him again with my free hand, again shoving my finger down my throat.

Finally I vomited a stream of half-digested rice and cucumber sushi all over the guy's face. Stupidly, he had opened his mouth to cry out, and as I retched, his mouth filled with it. It splattered into his eyes and poured down his cheeks, blinding him. He started to splutter and choke. Everyone around us was going absolutely wild, but again, I was only half-aware of it. Once I had finished puking, I reached to his face with both hands and started rubbing it in, grinding it into his eyes, poking my puke-covered fingers into his mouth to get more of it in. He was blubbering, crying beneath the deafening roar of the crowd and the band playing. I wiped my hands off on his shirt and stood up, leaving him a mess on the floor. I felt hands patting me on the back, and on the head, congratulating me. I climbed back onstage as the song finished. I was glad they'd kept playing.

The crowd went wild when the song was done. "Thanks,

guys," I said, smiling cutely and curtseying as if nothing had happened. I was happy the mike was back on again. It would have been very awkward if it hadn't been. "We're Colostomy Hag. Please, please don't fuck with us."

TWENTY-NINE

"Holy shit, that was insane," Jamie said. All the Torn Bowel guys crowded around me, patting my back and talking excitedly. "You fucking puked on that guy, holy shit. That was nuts."

"Fucking asshole deserved it."

"Fuck that guy. Rachel, you're fucking amazing."

I grinned and made my way towards the stairs. On the way I passed one of the club employees carrying a case of beer. He grinned and nodded at me. I had totally won respect, and all I had done was treat an asshole the way he deserved to be treated.

In the bathroom upstairs, I did truly look awful when I saw myself in the mirror. My eye makeup had streaked down my face in rivulets to my chin, and my lipstick had somehow smeared up my cheek to my forehead. But I loved it. I looked like a fighter, like a fucking warrior.

Fern burst into the bathroom at a full run, her face beaming, and grabbed me, throwing her arms around me. "Rachel . . . that was *amazing.*"

"Thanks," I said.

"Are you okay? Do you feel all right?"

"Yeah, I'm fine. I didn't throw up because I was sick or anything."

"I know, I know. Just wanted to make sure." She looked me up and down. "God, you look tough right now."

I laughed.

"Sorry I didn't jump down there and help you. I didn't really know what to do," she said.

"It was fine. I was okay by myself. I'm glad you guys kept playing. It made it even more awesome, like it was no big deal. If you'd stopped playing, that totally would have ruined it."

"Rachel, you're crazy," she grinned. "I love it."

I rinsed my mouth and wiped my eyes, but I didn't bother fixing my makeup. Fern and I went to join Edgar and Socks at the back of the club. The plan had been that once our gear was loaded off, we'd try to sell some of our CDs. We found Edgar and Socks sitting at a table with the box of CDs and a few people milling around. Torn Bowel had just gone on, and I couldn't help but gaze a little bit at Jamie as we made our way over to the guys.

People were buying CDs, handing their money to Socks, and Edgar smiled at me as I sat down beside him.

"Are you all right?"

"Yeah, I am."

"That was pretty gross," he said. "I'm glad you did it though. For a second I wondered if I was going to have to jump down there and break it up."

"Nah, it was fine."

Socks turned to us. "We've sold a bunch of CDs," he said. "I think everyone liked the show a lot. People asking about the band and stuff. And definitely asking about *you*," he said to me.

As if to punctuate this, I looked up to see two girls standing by the table, smiling at me.

"Hi," I said.

"You were awesome," one of the girls said. "When's your next show?"

"We're on tour right now," I said proudly. "Tomorrow we're playing in Bridgeford."

"Oh, well, that's too far away for us, but if you ever come back to Port Claim, we'll be here," she said. "I'm going to buy one of your CDs."

"Thanks," I said, and as she moved over to talk to Socks, her friend stepped forward.

"I just want to say I think it's awesome what you did," the girl said shyly, looking from me to the floor nervously.

"We can't let people push us around," I agreed.

"I know. That guy was a jerk. I think you're awesome." She gave me a tiny smile.

I couldn't help but lean across the table to hug the girl. "Thank you so much," I said. I felt like a damn celebrity or something. She bought a CD as well. Socks grinned, flashing me the small stack of bills we'd made, and my face started to hurt from smiling so big.

Billy announced from the stage, "This next song is for our friends in Colostomy Hag. Usually it's called 'Fingernailed,' but tonight we're going to call it 'Suck My Puke.'" Everyone cheered and we laughed.

I leaned back in my seat beside Edgar. "I wonder what happened to that asshole."

"He got thrown out," Edgar reported. "I guess the security guy at the door didn't see what happened onstage, so when he saw the guy, he thought he was too drunk and had puked all over himself."

"Oh, man! Are you serious?" I giggled.

"Yeah. I mean, the other security guy knew what happened, but the guy was a prick anyway so nobody bothered to help him out or explain it, you know?"

"Really."

"Yeah, totally." Edgar nodded. "Everybody seems to think you're pretty amazing, Rachel."

"If more people treated assholes like assholes, then anyone could be a hero."

XXX

At the end of the night, after everyone had cleared out and the house lights had come back up, both bands started the loading-out process. Fern and I had changed back into our jeans. We were all pretty tired. I couldn't wait to get to the hotel, have a shower, and get into a bed. We'd sold a bunch of CDs and made about two hundred bucks, which totally surprised us. After the gear was in both vans, we hung out with the other guys for a while in the parking lot.

"So, who wants to go grab some drinks?" Billy asked.

"I'm the only one who's of age," Socks said. "And the only driver."

"Ah, okay. What time are you guys gonna pull out in the morning?"

"Probably around 10."

"Okay. Well, we'll see you guys tomorrow at the club then." The guys started climbing into their van. I tried to catch Jamie's eye, and when I did, he gave me a friendly smile and a wave. I wondered if I had only imagined that we'd sort of had a feeling between us earlier, because it seemed to be gone now. As we drove to our hotel by the highway, I kept thinking about that while the others chatted. Had the whole puking thing changed how Jamie looked at me? How could that be?

I would have thought that my strength would have made me more appealing. I scowled at myself for even caring. So what if he didn't think I was attractive anymore. I guess he was the sort of guy who wanted to date some precious wilting violet. Well, that wasn't me.

THIRTY

The next shows were a definite introduction to what touring is really like. On the second night, I realized that I'd forgotten to pack more than one pair of knee socks, even though I'd brought four outfits. I was sort of grossed out realizing that I was going to have to wear the same pair for the rest of the shows. Socks, on the other hand, embraced that sort of thing — the rest of us were confused when we realized that he hadn't brought any luggage, and then horrified when he said he planned to wear the *exact same clothes* the whole time. "It's only four shows," was his defence. Edgar tried to argue that at least some extra underwear might have been warranted, but Socks apparently didn't see that to be the case.

It turned out that when I'd jumped onto the guy in Port Claim and bashed my knee, I had actually hurt myself. On the second morning a dark purple bruise had appeared, and it hurt to bend my knee. That was just something I was going to have to deal with. Every hotel we had booked had two beds in it — one for me and Fern, one for Edgar and Socks — so at least we could get pretty decent sleep.

That first night had definitely been the biggest crowd. We were well received at each show, and no one else messed with me — even though I was steeled for it. I met everyone's eyes confrontationally, almost daring people to be assholes, but no one was. Most people were out to see Torn Bowel, but no one was flat-out rude. We sold enough CDs to pay for our hotel rooms, with a little leftover for Edgar's parents' loan.

Everyone in the other band was great, but I couldn't help but fuss a little bit about Jamie's demeanour. He was super friendly to me, as they all were, but it had definitely changed, and I wondered if I had imagined something more that first day than had actually been there. At the end of it, everyone exchanged phone numbers and email addresses and there was a lot of talk about touring again, playing more shows, and everyone was hugging each other goodbye. It was nice to feel as though we'd made friends with another band.

It was only four days, but I was completely exhausted. I felt like I could have slept for a week. My parents were relieved that I was home in one piece, and of course they and Melissa wanted to hear everything about my *rock tour*. I told them everything as PG as I could. There hadn't been any "debauchery" or craziness at all, so there wasn't much to omit. I did, however, leave out the part about the puke.

Which, apparently, had been extremely important.

Socks emailed Fern, Edgar, and me a link. "This is a music magazine from Port Claim," he wrote. "They have an online version. PJ's going to mail me a hard copy. Thought you guys would want to check this out."

I clicked on the link. *Stunner Magazine: Port Claim's Alternative Music Magazine*. Stunner, huh? Laaaaame. But I scrolled down and found a review of our show with Torn Bowel.

METAL AND VOMIT AT KLUB KLANG

Thursday night in Port Claim doesn't offer much for people looking to go out and have a good time. But last Thursday there was a lineup outside of Klub Klang on Royal Winter Avenue, one of the city's oldest metal bars. Newer clubs opening in the city have resulted in touring bands and events taking a pass on Klang, preferring instead to play at what could be described as trendier and more contemporary venues, but some of us remember when Klub Klang was the only place in the Port to go for a guaranteed good night of music and headbanging.

Local favourites Torn Bowel have played here a few times over the last year, amassing a larger and larger fan base, and Thursday night was no exception. When I arrived, a good-sized line had formed outside, larger than their last gig here four months ago, proving what we all already know: Torn Bowel is destined for greatness.

Along for the ride was a band I had not heard of before, Keeleford's Colostomy Hag. This band is comprised of four very talented musicians and performers, and much to my surprise, two of them are female. I hate to say it, but when I saw these two girls onstage I could not help but roll my eyes. I did not know what to expect, and neither did the crowd at Klang that night, but we were all in for a surprise. I admit that I had dismissed them when

I saw them, and almost immediately was force-fed my words.

I have not heard a female voice in metal that sounds quite like raven-haired vocalist Rachel's. Her uniqueness and power onstage paired with her small stature and cutesy outfit is a combination to be admired. The pale-haired guitarist puts many others to shame with her talent. The entire venue was impressed with the band's skill, and their songs are not another uninspired rehash of greats like DED and Bloodvomit. There is a melody and uniqueness present that must be heard, and thankfully I picked myself up a copy of their debut CD, Scream into This.

When petite growler Rachel sent a heckler sprawling and actually proceeded to vomit all over him in front of two hundred cheering supporters, she transformed herself into somewhat of a new hero in the Port's metal scene. The band must be seen to be believed, and Thursday night proved the unpredictable and talented nature of Colostomy Hag. Another legendary moment at Klang, and Torn Bowel had not even taken the stage yet . . .

We'd gotten press. And more than a brief mention as an opening band. We'd made close to five hundred dollars in CD sales. If we could sell five hundred dollars' worth of CDs in four days, imagine if we went on a real tour? For a few months? My mind reeled.

School was starting in a few days. My last year of high school. Craig had already graduated, and I figured I would just eat lunch with Josephine, as usual, and do my own thing. Get through it as fast as possible, agree with everything my parents said, and figure out how to tell them that I was going to take a year off before college. I wanted to talk to Fern and Edgar, see how they felt, if they wanted to plan a tour again, maybe for next summer even though that was a year away, see if their parents wanted them to go to college and how they were going to deal with that. There was a lot to think about.

And the whole thing with Jamie still bothered me. No, there hadn't been anything between us and I had probably imagined anything I had felt, but I had *liked* him. I guess. Sort of. As much as you can like a person for having known them for ten minutes. The only other person I'd ever liked was Craig, and that had been a complete waste of time, and so long ago now that it made no sense at all. And he'd asked me out, but I'd said no. Was there something wrong with me for not having a boyfriend? Was this something I should be worrying about as well? Entering my last year of high school without ever having kissed a guy, or even really having *wanted* to kiss a guy?

XXX

Good news came the night before school started. Fern called me, freaking out. "Guess who is playing in St. Charles in October? Oh, you won't ever guess."

"Heathenistic Bile?" I shrieked in excitement.

"No, you idiot," she laughed. "Oh god. It's awesome!"

"Who?"

"DED. They're coming. They're finally coming! I'm going to pick up tickets tomorrow after school if you want to come."

And so, with all the giddy, blind enthusiasm of a little child chasing something shiny across the street and running into the path of a speeding truck, I set my course towards the worst possible thing that could ever happen to a person.

It's the type of thing where you look back on all the choices you made that led you to the horrible moment and wish that you could go back. Just change it. The kind of thing where your stomach gets queasy when you remember how stupid you were, and you want to pull out clumps of your own hair and slap yourself in the face to somehow get rid of the regret you feel at your own past ignorance.

And there were so many omens too, now that I look at them. Socks and Edgar couldn't make it that weekend. So it would just be me and Fern. Craig, who was still pals with everyone, had moved to college and couldn't afford the tickets. Even Yvonne bailed. It was just me and Fern, picking out our outfits for weeks, giggling on the phone. Sitting in my bedroom, listening to *Punish and Kill* on repeat, staring up at my poster of Balthazar Seizure, saturating myself in it, *inviting* it.

It was going to be the biggest concert, the most exciting event in the last few years for us, and no one else we knew was going. Yeah — Fern and me, standing together in idiot silhouettes against the fucking mushroom cloud.

THIRTY-ONE

That fall, our band got offers to play a few more shows. I guess word had spread about our show, and not only did a few places in Port Claim offer us gigs, but a few bands from other cities wanted us to open for them. All the offers were pretty lousy. Yeah, we'd had a good show, but no one was offering us money. The places in Port Claim couldn't pay us enough to compensate for the gas money it would cost to get there. There was no way to gauge how many people would come. And besides, with school being in and me trying to keep the band quiet from my parents, it wasn't likely at all that I'd be able to go away for a possible weekend show. The others were understanding about it; it wasn't like we were giving up some great opportunities.

And besides, Fern and I had enough to look forward to with DED coming.

As the day of the concert drew nearer, we laid out our plans. Of course we were going to try to meet the band. Fern had already packed up a few of our CDs to give them, even though Edgar worried that we shouldn't be giving them away. He was right, we needed every cent of the money, but this was a good opportunity.

"Maybe they've heard of us already after the whole puking thing," Fern said.

Maybe. I didn't want to get ahead of ourselves, but the night before the show as I gazed at my outfit in the mirror, I definitely felt like Fern and I were going into this as more than *fans*. It was the same vibe I'd tried to inspire when we'd met Marie-Lise, but this time with more experience. We'd *toured!* Kind of. Surely that put us up on the same level as DED. I shook my head, laughing at my own stupidity.

I thought my outfit looked great, black and blue striped knee socks and a black skirt and top. I'd match the light blue in the socks with the same shade of eyeshadow, which I thought would look very striking. My eyes moved from my reflection in the mirror up to my poster of Balthazar Seizure.

"Tomorrow," I said.

Our plan was pretty lame. We were going to take the same early bus to St. Charles, exactly the way we had done for Gurgol. The difference was that last time, Socks and Edgar had met us at the show and we'd all driven back in the van. This time, we'd purchased return tickets in hopes that the show would end in time for us to catch the last bus back to Kuolofowd. If we missed that bus, well, we'd just have to figure something out. Nice, right? See? Another damn sign. I don't know what the hell we were thinking.

But at the time, it just seemed like details. We'd work it all out later. The important thing was getting to St. Charles and trying to meet DED.

I sat in the window seat with Fern beside me. "Fern, have you ever had a boyfriend?"

"Yeah. Last year. That guy Steve, remember?"

"Oh, right." I remembered Fern talking to me on the phone about him. At the time I had been disinterested in the whole thing and had barely paid attention when she'd talked about him. "That was for a few months, right?"

"Yeah, like three months." She rolled her eyes. "He was a jerk."

"Right." I'd never met the guy, but I recalled something about him dumping her for some other girl. "He was a jerk."

"Guys are a waste of time," she said firmly, settling back in her seat. "I don't want to think about that stuff."

"I've never had a boyfriend," I said.

"You're just saving yourself a lot of grief." She smiled. "What about that Jamie guy, from Torn Bowel? He liked you, didn't he?"

I was surprised. I guess I hadn't imagined that. "Not really. I think he did for a few minutes for, like, one day. But then after that first show, I think it went away."

"Maybe he was grossed out after you puked."

"I don't even care. I don't want a boyfriend," I said, lifting my chin. "I have other things to think about."

"I feel the same way. But you know what, after you meet Balthazar Seizure, and he falls *madly in love with you* . . . you might change your mind." She reached over and dug her finger into my ribs, grinning.

"Oh, right!"

Fern and I got off at the station in St. Charles. The DED show was at a place called Terminal 66. As we had last time, we got into a taxi and had the driver take us there. It was across town

246

from the bus station, and traffic in the city was annoying, so the cab ended up costing us more than we'd planned. But finally we pulled up in front of the big building — much bigger than Gurgol's gig — and climbed out of the cab.

"Oh, no," Fern said. We were beside the driveway that would lead us to the back parking lot, but it was closed up with a big chain-link fence, and the gate was padlocked. Part of me was relieved. If we had been able to get back to the buses, what would we have done? Knocked on the door?

"Do you think they're in there?" I asked.

"I'm sure they are," she said. "But we aren't getting in."

"What do you think the chances are that they'll be hanging out in some coffee shop nearby?"

"We can go look."

Fern and I walked around the area. We had time to kill. Any patio we saw had no one resembling anyone in a band sitting on it. It seemed like we were out of luck. I was sort of feeling like a stalker anyway.

We chose one of the coffee shops and ordered ourselves some drinks and sandwiches. It would be too bad if we didn't get to meet DED today, but at the same time, I mean, how many people get to meet bands anyway? We were lucky that we'd managed to run into Marie Lise.

Fern and I spent the afternoon walking around. We went to a department store where we tried on some expensive makeup samples, a bookstore where we spent a few hours browsing and reading, and finally a small restaurant where we had dinner and got changed into our outfits for the show. Fern and I had always managed to have fun even back home walking around the downtown for hours, so wasting a full afternoon together in St. Charles was no problem.

It was early evening when we wandered back to Terminal 66, and there was a giant lineup out front. The sun was going down and it was getting chilly. I was glad I'd brought my sweater, pulling it on as we joined the end of the line.

When the line finally started moving and we got up to the doors, the security guy hollered at us, "No backpacks inside. You have to check them," grabbing our tickets and ushering us inside. The lobby of the place was packed with people, some filing into the main room and some crowding around the coat-check area. Fern and I took our purses out of our bags and eventually managed to get up to the counter, where we had to pay five bucks each to check our backpacks.

"The CDs are in there," Fern lamented.

"Yeah, so are our clothes." But we had no choice, so we checked them, and then entered the main room.

The place was packed. Fern and I tried to find a place along the side of the room where we would be able to see the stage without getting pushed around. We finally found a decent spot, and as I surveyed the crowd, I thought I saw a few of the Torn Bowel guys on the floor. Before I could point them out to Fern, they were swallowed up into the mass of people. At least people-watching, and trying to see if I could find them again, was a way to pass the time before the show began.

There were two opening bands, both well received by the crowd but completely mediocre as far as I was concerned. I wished that we'd gotten this gig, but Fern explained that the two bands were on the same record label as DED and so they were probably on the tour with them to try to get them famous as well. It was more money for the record label that way. Well, I didn't see them getting famous. They weren't very good.

When the second band had finished, the room started to buzz. DED was next, and we watched some crew guys bring off the second band's gear. DED's stuff was set up behind it. The guys worked quickly, carrying the giant rack of weapons I'd seen on the internet videos. They pulled away a sheet to reveal the giant skull. The best part happened when the last band's banner was pulled down, and DED's giant banner was revealed beneath it. *DIE EVERY DEATH* was scrawled in giant letters, and the crowd cheered.

The room went completely dark. The cheer was deafening. There must've been a thousand people there, maybe more. Fern and I yelled too, adding our voices to the roar. Giant flames shot into the air from either side of the stage, revealing the five band members standing stock-still, each at their instruments, Balthazar centre stage.

When the flames went down, everything launched into blackness again.

"Die every death. Die every death." The low voice came through the dark, whispering into the microphone, and we all screamed. The crowd began to chant along with him. *Die every death. Die every death.*

The flames shot high again as the band launched into "I Ignore Your Screams." Fern and I started freaking out, along with every other person in the room.

The band played incredibly, with Balthazar looming tall and angry above the crowd. He swung around his battle-axe, he growled and paced, he stalked across the stage. The skull began bubbling the dark red blood from its eyes, and Balthazar filled his hands with it and threw it at the crowd. They played every single song I could possibly have wanted to hear. Sometimes people would climb up onto the stage to dive and crowd-surf, and Balthazar would go up behind them and shove them roughly back into the crowd, glowering and snarling.

It was absolutely amazing.

THIRTY-TWO

We should have left after the show, along with everyone else who started filing out. We should have gotten in a taxi and gone back to the bus station to wait for the late bus home.

"Let's try to meet them," I said instead. The house lights had come on, and the crowd pressed towards the back of the room and the exit doors. The room stank of sweat and smoke, and the crew guys were beginning to leisurely tear down DED's equipment.

"How?" Fern asked.

"We'll ask them." I gestured at the guys onstage.

"What about the CDs?"

"Forget them. If we meet them we can tell them about the band. They probably won't care anyway. But we can ask them how to get a record deal and stuff like that. Get some advice."

"That's a good idea." Fern and I walked up to the stage.

"Hey," I called up to one of the guys. He looked down at me.

"We want to meet the band."

The guy grinned at me. "You want to talk to that dude over there," he said, pointing. There was a door beside the stage. In front of it stood a large, fat guy with long hair. In front of him stood a group of girls, all in short skirts and dresses.

"Great," I muttered. "There's a bunch of skanks and they'll think we're no better than they are."

"We can try," Fern said. She took my arm and we went to the back of the group of girls.

"C'mon, Jerry. Pleeeeease?" One of the girls was flirting with the fat guy. "Last time I came through I hung with the band. Sid will want to see me again."

The big guy grinned at her, obviously enjoying this whole thing. I was disgusted to see his teeth were brown and rotten. "Sid won't remember you, sweetheart," he said, moving his eyes across each of the girls.

"Sure he will."

The girls started to talk all at once, each of them insisting they knew someone in the band, and all of them were being so flirtatious with this toad. I was completely confused by it.

"Jerry, if you get us backstage, we'll make it worth your while," purred one of the girls, sliding her arm around her friend. Both of them smiled at him seductively.

"That's what I like to hear." Jerry laughed. "C'mon back."

The other girls wailed in disappointment as he allowed the two girls past him and through the door. The group began to disperse.

"I'm not going to blow that disgusting guy just to meet a bunch of assholes," I heard one of them say to her friend in disgust as they walked past us.

"I don't like this," Fern said.

I really didn't either, but I felt a familiar feeling come over me, and it was almost comforting. My eyes locked to Jerry as he paused in the doorway, obviously to see if there were any more *takers*. He made eye contact with me, and I immediately smiled at him. His eyes narrowed lasciviously. He figured he could take advantage of us. I imagined my fist pounding into the soft folds of his fat face, his snotty nose exploding into blood. He would pay for misjudging us.

"Nobody's going to blow anybody, and we're going to meet the band," I said to Fern through my smile, never taking my eyes away from Jerry's, linking my arm through hers and stepping towards him.

I felt her hesitation, but she fell into step beside me and we approached the door.

"Can I help you?" Jerry asked us, grinning.

"We'd like to meet the band," I said, continuing to smile.

"Oh, would you?" he teased. "Well, there's a toll."

"We aren't going to pay any toll," I said. "See, we're in a band ourselves."

"*Are* you?" he replied, widening his eyes in mock surprise.

"Yes. We'd like to ask the guys some questions."

Jerry's eyes moved past me, losing interest, obviously seeing if there were any other girls behind us that he could hit up. Apparently there weren't. "Well, you may as well come on back," he said, settling his gaze on us once again. "I need a few more back here anyway."

He stepped back, and Fern followed me through the door. It closed behind us, swallowing us inside. We were directly next to the two girls who Jerry had allowed in before us. They still had their arms around each other and were giggling frantically. They sounded like a damn aviary, so fluttery, light, and brainless. Thankfully the two of them still had the presence of mind to give Fern and I dirty looks. *Of course.*

"Follow me," Jerry said and headed up a flight of stairs. The four of us proceeded up behind him. It was dark, and Fern took my hand as we climbed. "This is pretty weird," she whispered.

I squeezed her hand. "Don't worry about it. Once we meet the band it'll be okay. Fuck this Jerry guy."

At the top of the stairs, we turned down a hallway and Jerry knocked on a closed door. He paused, and then opened it. Then he stepped backwards and swept into a low bow, obnoxiously motioning for us to walk past him.

Fern and I followed the two twittering girls into the room.

"Guys, I've brought some ladies to hang out," Jerry said.

"This ain't no place for a lady!" came the reply, followed by a chorus of laughter.

The room was small, with two leather couches. Between them was a table covered with wine and beer bottles, as well as a half eaten vegetable tray and a messy ashtray. Sitting on the couches were the members of DED. I scanned all their faces, seeing Ed, Sid, Victor, and Chaos, but there was no sign of Balthazar. Chaos and Sid had their shirts off and towels around their necks. The room stank of cigarette smoke and sweat, with the constant club reek of old booze, and a touch of urine. I wrinkled my nose.

The guys all grinned at us, raising their hands in greeting, which set the two girls off into more gales of laughter.

"Hi," I said assertively, stepping around them. "I'm Rachel, this is Fern."

"What's up, girls?" Ed said, grinning at us. "Come sit down, have a drink."

There wasn't any room on the couches to sit so I hesitated, unsure of where to go. The other two girls moved forward immediately and made as if to sit down on two of the guys' laps.

"Not so fast," Jerry said. "You two have some unfinished business to take care of. Don't worry, I'll have them back here in no time."

The guys started hooting. "Of course you will, man. Two

minutes? Thirty seconds?" Everyone laughed. The girls followed Jerry back out into the hallway, and the door closed behind them. Fern and I stood facing the four of them.

"Sit down," Ed said to us again.

"I'm okay," Fern said. I didn't reply. There was no way we were going to sit on their laps for god's sake.

"Want some wine?" Victor gestured at the bottles on the table.

"No thanks." I cleared my throat and smiled at them. "We're really excited to meet you guys."

"What is this, an interview or something?" Chaos piped up. "Yeah, we're happy to be here, blah, blah. Come on, relax, sit down, have a fucking drink, let's just chill and have some fun."

The door opened and my heart stopped as Balthazar walked in. He was taller than I thought he would be, totally looming over Fern and me, and his hair was wet. He smelled like soap. I gazed up at his handsome face, unable to really grasp that I was standing here, right in front of him.

"I think she likes you, Bal," one of the guys joked.

Balthazar looked down at me and smiled. I smiled back. "The shower's free if anyone wants to use it," he said, and then moved to the table and poured himself some wine. He took a sip, turned back, and surveyed us. I fumbled for something cool to say as they all stared at us.

"Well, this is boring as shit," Balthazar said to his bandmates.

What did they want us to do? I didn't understand. Would they prefer the company of the giggling idiot girls? There was a bad atmosphere, a tension.

"We have a band," Fern said, taking a cigarette out of her purse and lighting it.

"Oh, do you *really*." Balthazar yawned. "Why don't you tell us *all* about it?" There was a round of chuckles that followed this comment, and my stomach slowly started to freeze up. They were *assholes*.

"We kinda don't want to hear about your band," someone else said. "We kinda just want to get laid. You know?"

I had no idea what to say. I felt stupid as hell. Me and Fern standing there in our stupid outfits, thinking they'd actually care we were in a band too. To them we were no better than the other girls, willing to twitter and fawn and fool around with their fat roadie.

"We'll go then," Fern said. There was an urgency in her tone that I didn't understand. I felt like I was missing something.

Balthazar sighed loudly and slammed down his glass. "No, you'll *sit down and have a drink.*"

The next thing I knew, he had taken Fern by the shoulders and shoved her down on the couch between Ed and Sid. Her face registered surprise and fright, and I moved forward towards her. "We'll leave," I said, reaching for her. But someone grabbed me. The room spun and something jolted me, hitting me hard in the back of the head. When my eyes cleared I was looking at Balthazar's fist, clenched around the front of my shirt. I was against the wall. He'd slammed me up against it. "Have a drink," he said again.

My lips moved as if to talk, but my brain couldn't find anything to say. I didn't understand what was happening. I heard laughter coming from somewhere in the room, but I didn't know from where. I couldn't see around Balthazar and I couldn't move.

"We get very tired of boring girls," he told me. I had no idea what he meant. He kept talking to me in this low tone but I couldn't understand what he was saying. I heard a shriek and I knew it was Fern. *What was happening to Fern?* I tried to pull away from the wall, but Balthazar's fist still gripped my shirt. He tossed me against the wall again, bouncing my head off it, and I blacked out for a second. The next thing I knew I was down on the floor on that disgusting carpet. I lay there.

Balthazar was standing over me, laughing about something, and I couldn't get up. I was too stunned, trying to understand what was happening.

I heard another shriek — Fern again. I looked up to the couch where it came from. I was behind the couch and I saw her hand fly up, and a big fist wrapped itself around her wrist.

Were they *raping* her?

One look at one of the guys standing over the couch answered that question for me. He was watching whatever was happening there and fiddling with his belt.

They *were*.

I opened my mouth and let out the loudest scream I could, screwing my eyes shut and throwing everything I had into that scream.

A huge rough hand slapped down over my mouth, cutting it short, and I opened my eyes to see Balthazar's face directly over mine. "Shut the fuck up," he hissed.

I can't get into what happened after he put his hand over my mouth. I really can't. But I can tell you how I felt about it. A few minutes after Balthazar climbed on top of me I was fully lucid again. I heard them joke to him about being careful not to get any "diseases" from me. I didn't know what was going to happen after he was done with me. I was too afraid of them to think about anything other than the fact that they might kill us. I mean, I'd like to say I was running through plans in my mind to get away, to attack him, to summon up all the rage I usually have and break free, to crawl out from underneath Balthazar and escape. But honestly, I thought he would kill me. Have you ever been afraid that someone is going to kill you? I didn't have any sort of adrenaline rush or anything. It was just pure, simpering fear. I didn't look at him. I kept my eyes closed.

I didn't want to see. My hands were free and I brought them up to my eyes, as if trying to protect my face. I didn't know what else he was going to do. I was aware of sounds — I heard them talking and sometimes laughing. I heard Fern crying. I didn't see anything. I could smell his rank, rotten breath as it blew over my neck and hands in warm, erratic waves.

Finally he climbed off me and moved away, and I felt a scratchy cloth hit me. "Clean yourself up," he laughed, and when I peeked down I saw he'd thrown an old towel onto me. I heard him joke with the other guys that I was "free" if they wanted a "go," and I felt myself ready to throw up, ready to scream again. I heard other voices joke back that I was "too ugly" and relief filled me for a moment, until I remembered that they might kill us and I covered my face again.

"Grow the fuck up," Balthazar said, grabbing one of my hands and jerking me up to my feet. I saw Fern standing by the wall, stick-still, her hair covering her face.

"Look at this," Sid said. "Get them out of here."

"Get out," Balthazar said in disgust. Fern stayed completely still by the wall, and I tried as best as I could to snap myself out of it and grabbed her hand.

I pulled the door open, and almost slammed into Jerry, who was returning with the two giggling girls. Would this *never* end?

Jerry paused and looked at us. I violently pushed my way through the door past him, pulling Fern behind me, and as we burst into the hallway and ran, laughter echoed around us. "I guess it's 1997 all over again, guys?"

THIRTY-THREE

Fern acted as though she'd been hypnotized, but for some reason, my mind was clear and mechanical. Okay, get back downstairs. Done. Go back into the venue, done. Go to the coat check, hope the girl is still there. She was, cleaning up and looking at us as if we were crazy. Get our backpacks. Done. Get the fuck out. Done.

Don't think about what just happened. Just get the fuck out.

Fern followed me onto the street, and I put my arm around her. It was chilly. I started walking. I didn't even know where I was going. I just had to get us away from that place. Away from them right away. My eyes were so wide I felt like a lunatic. My mind raced. Get us out of here.

I found a park, a small long one that followed a path between two buildings. It was dark and there were benches. I led Fern to one. We sat down. She stared straight ahead, and I put my head in my hands. I had a thousand thoughts, a million thoughts, all of them running, racing around, and I couldn't grab any of them to focus on. I closed my eyes and let them run through me.

"Rachel," Fern said after a little while.

"Yes."

"We have to go to the police."

Yes, we should. That was the first step. "No. We're not going to the police."

"Rachel, we have to."

"Do you think they'll believe us? DED gets tons of girls, whenever they want. Why would they bother doing this? No one would ever believe what they've done to us. The cops won't do anything. We went back there ourselves, I mean . . . we came to the show and went backstage, all dressed up." My head pounded.

Fern was silent for a few moments. "But we have to do *something*," she said, her voice rising to a wail.

"I know we do."

A thought was taking shape in my mind, something concrete, something exciting, but I couldn't put my finger on it. I couldn't focus on it. Not yet. But I could feel it there, slowly forming. We had to do *something*.

The first thing to do was to go to the bus station. I focused on every step, every action that would take us forward. I couldn't bear to look backwards. I *knew* what had happened but I did not want to envision it. I knew there would be plenty of time, the rest of my life, to think about it, to relive every horrible detail. But right now I had tasks, and I focused on them. We were two hours away from home, and we had to get back. We had to figure out what to do right now.

I held Fern's hand and set out to find a taxi. I began to steer us into the general direction I thought the bus station was so we could walk and collect ourselves before getting into a cab. She knelt on the sidewalk and threw up, punctuating it with sobs, and I knelt beside her and rubbed her shaking shoulders. Again, I felt my eyes were wider than they normally were, absorbing more than usual, in greater detail: the way the streetlights cast patterns on the sidewalk through the tree branches, the small glittery hair clip on Fern's head, the dry grass and the crushed juice box in the gutter.

When she said she felt well enough to get in a taxi, I hailed one. As we drove through the streets, she laid her head on my shoulder. I felt frozen, too aware, too sensitive. My skin felt as though stick-legged bugs were crawling over it. I pressed my arm tighter against Fern, screwing my eyes closed, noticed I was trembling, realized I wasn't — it was Fern, huddled against me. I felt some sort of hollow, failed protectiveness for her.

We got out of the taxi at the bus station, which was still open, thankfully. The attendant said that there would be a bus leaving in two hours that made a stop in Keeleford on its way someplace else. She flicked her eyes between Fern and me, noticeably weirded out by us, so I tried to smile as calmly as I could and then led Fern towards a row of plastic chairs to wait. I didn't want the woman to call the police, because if the police came it would spoil everything. My mind was working on some idea that would show itself to me eventually. I needed time.

I got Fern a can of Coke and she sipped it, wiping her eyes. "Rachel, we have to go to the doctor," she finally said in a wet, wavering voice that sounded as if it could escalate to a shriek very quickly.

"They used condoms."

"Yeah, well, we have to go to the doctor." Her voice took on a keening tone and her breath started coming in short gasps.

260

"If we aren't going to the police, we should at least be going to the doctor."

An image entered my mind of poking, prodding doctors and I slammed it away, swallowing hard, actually stamping my foot to distract from the coiling nausea inside me. "Let's just worry about getting home right now."

Fern pulled her sweater around herself and closed her eyes. I wasn't sure if she had fallen asleep.

We had two hours before the bus home. That was enough time to head back to the club. I was struck with the urge. I could go back. They would probably be on their tour bus, all of them. I could find some way to block the door, prevent it from opening, and set the bus on fire. Fern had a cigarette lighter, I could take that with me. Block the door, somehow set the bus on fire, and they'd roast inside it like hot dogs in a tin can. The bus would get so hot that their skin would stick to it, the tires would melt, the smoke would smell like burning rubber and bacon. Especially that fat fucker Jerry, his skin would split open and all that fat would come drooling out of him like melted butter, and it would smell exactly like bacon. And it would make the bus floor slippery, so while they were running around, all on fire, trying to escape, they would slip in puddles of bloody fat. They'd all be on fire and their long hair would be on fire too. They'd get all charred, their skin black and flaky and their teeth would be so white.

The next thing I knew they were announcing the bus over the loudspeaker and Fern was shaking me awake. "You fell asleep," she said. "Come on."

It was jarring to go from the brightly lit bus station into the cramped dark of the coach bus, but there were only a few other passengers so Fern and I got a quiet spot together at the back. She sat next to the window, pulled her sweater hood over her head, and promptly fell asleep. As the bus pulled away from the curb, I stared out into the dark street and lamented that I hadn't actually gone back to light the bus on fire.

When we got back to Keeleford the sun was starting to rise, and as Fern and I walked on the street leading uptown, everything had a sort of misty surreal quality to it. Not dark but not light, no cars in the streets, just a few faraway birds beginning to chirp, the sky hovering between dark blue and pale orange.

We'd slept the whole bus ride home, but sitting unconscious in a lousy bus seat doesn't count as sleep and I felt bone tired. My makeup had smeared into my eyes and they burned dryly. The air felt damp, and as we walked both of us folded our arms close to ourselves to keep out the chill. Fern looked rumpled, stained, and exhausted. I knew I looked the same. "How do you feel?" I said.

"Tired," she said. "I want to go home and sleep."

We walked through the familiar neighbourhoods as the sun rose and cars started appearing on the streets. We went our separate ways at the usual corner, and I walked the rest of the way home alone, feeling strangely calm. The image of those guys burning to death with their hair alight like birthday candles gave me a strange sense of amused hope, and I tried to hold on to that feeling as I walked up the driveway in the early morning light and realized my parents would probably be waiting up for me.

I think they were prepared for something very different. I was not defensive, I was not defiant. I quietly agreed that I should have been home earlier. I agreed that I should have called. I agreed that I was *definitely not going to any more concerts; not while I lived under this roof.* They asked me what Fern's mother would think of this. I told them she was probably angry as well, and justifiably so.

I didn't like sitting in the kitchen. I felt like I had something wrong with me, a cloud or an aura of what had happened, some evil that I didn't want in the house where I grew up, around my parents, sitting in the same kitchen chair my little sister sat in, permeating the air. I needed to wash myself, get the layer of sick off me, become myself again.

The whole time they yelled, I could also feel that they were concerned, and they hadn't expected to feel that way. I sat there, my hair a mess, my face smeared, holding my arms tightly around my body, staring at the floor. I could feel their eyes on me and despite the fact that they tried to sound angry, they were horrified at how I looked. I could tell they both wanted to ask me if I was all right, and were torn between that and their desire to punish their rebellious teenage daughter.

I guess it's hard to be compassionate when you've sat up all night planning to be pissed. I can totally get that. I didn't want to talk to them about it anyway, obviously. I would've had to make something up, which I didn't really have the energy for.

When they had finally stopped talking to me, I went into the bathroom and got out of those clothes. Taking them off felt incredible, as if I was stepping farther away from what had happened. That only lasted a second though. I saw blood. I couldn't pretend anymore. I couldn't be strong anymore. I was home, I was alone, and now I was going to have to feel every second of what happened. I was glad I had turned on the shower before I started crying and throwing up, so my parents couldn't hear.

THIRTY-FOUR

I started walking in the woods out past Clyde Road, which is on the edge of town and pretty remote. It took me about an hour to walk there from my house, but the walk was good. Walking and just being quiet had been very helpful to me in the days since it had happened. The weather was getting a bit colder, and the leaves had started changing. It was my favourite time of year, walking down sidewalks covered with dry leaves, watching blackbirds flocked against the white sky, smelling smoke in the air. It always brought clarity to me, and everything that had happened left me with more of a need for clarity than I'd ever had.

I'd torn down all my DED posters, wadded them up, and shoved them into the same plastic bag with my clothes from that night, which I'd wrapped in another bag and shoved beneath the back porch of our house. I didn't want the stuff in the house, but for some reason I wanted to save it. I'd been having trouble focusing on anything, which was why I was walking a lot.

I went to school and stayed away from my parents as much as I could. I was quiet in my bedroom, not listening to music, not causing any trouble. I could hear them talking in those concerned, low voices all the time and I knew they were talking about me.

The phone would ring, and it would be Socks or Edgar, wanting to know how the show had gone and if we were going to have a rehearsal or anything, and I basically just told them that I was busy with school, which after a few days didn't cut it, but they didn't push me on it. I didn't hear from Fern at all, but that was okay. I knew what was going on.

Basically all I can really say about what was going on in my mind was that I was working very, very hard to keep any flashes of that night from coming into my head. I was doing everything I could to keep my mind busy and moving, because if I stayed in one place for too long, or got lazy, the images would flood in, and my stomach would knot and my teeth would clench and my eyes would sting with tears. It would make me feel very physically sick and I would try to drive it out of me, to the point of actually pinching myself or knocking my head into the wall. It sounds crazy, I know. But I had to do something.

And so I started walking, mostly at night, and I began to find a certain peace coming over me, even though I refused to allow my mind to go back and settle the score with the memories. I felt peace, and I felt an almost gleeful desire to hit and stomp and kick and destroy that was so strong it would make my palms sweat out.

I called Fern, and we met in the woods in the late afternoon after school. I hadn't spoken to her until earlier that day, and we agreed it was time to meet. She looked tired, her eyes sunken and her hair dull, and she wore dirty jeans.

We hugged each other and she tried to smile at me, and I could see how destroyed she was, how much this was affecting her. I felt tears threaten at seeing her suffering, but, as I was now so used to doing, I steeled myself against them and swallowed them back, shifting the focus onto what I wanted to tell her.

"I have a plan."

"What's that?"

"We get our revenge."

She studied me with those exhausted blue eyes, leaning against the tree at her back. "How do we do that, Rachel?"

"It won't be anytime soon. But it's possible." I could feel myself about to jabber uncontrollably, and I was aware that I was clasping and unclasping my hands spastically, but being around Fern again and being able to articulate what I had been formulating for the last few weeks was overwhelming me. "We have to get close to DED again. We just have to get near them. And then we kill them."

"Kill them, huh?" A small, amused grin appeared.

"I'm serious," I said, looking into her eyes, feeling almost ready to plead with her to understand. "Fern, we kill them."

She stared for a few moments. "How?"

"It doesn't matter. However. Poison them or light their bus on fire. However we can. But we work hard, Fern." Tears were streaming from my eyes, pouring down my face, and splattering onto my chest in giant drops. "We work hard at the band and we get famous. We get on a tour with DED. We get close to them again and we fucking kill them."

She was silent, and I mopped at my eyes with my sweater sleeve. "I know it sounds crazy, but they have to pay for what they've done to us." My breath came in gasps; I was losing control, and I struggled with myself, heaving air into my lungs, grappling for poise. "You know they've done it before and they'll do it again, and no one else is going to stop them. And I don't give a fuck, I want to stop them. I want to show them. Make them sorry they ever messed with us."

I sat down in the leaves and covered my face with my hands, rubbing my eyes and breathing deeply to calm down. When I looked at Fern again, she was smoking a cigarette and studying me.

"Do you really think you could do it?" I was pleased to hear a lack of sarcasm in her tone. She was taking the idea seriously.

"Yes," I said. "Definitely."

"Why not just go to another show, get backstage again," she swallowed hard, "and do it then?"

"Because no one would care if some psychotic faceless slut did it." Anger built up in me. "I want to *show* them. I want to be someone, Fern, not just a random groupie in the back room. I want people to listen to us and ask us why we did it. I want *everyone* to know."

She puffed on her cigarette, looking off into the distance. "I don't know if I can kill anyone, Rachel."

"I know I can," I said. "I'll do it. I don't care. I don't care what happens to me." Tears threatened once again, and I dug my fingernails into the palm of my hand, pushing them away. "I want them to pay. I don't care. I just need us to work together on this, Fern. You're the only one who knows what happened."

She smiled sadly. "You know we'll do this together."

I smiled back and felt wetness in my palm. My fingernails had drawn blood, I had dug them in so hard. I raised my eyes back to Fern, who was still smiling, and saw no joy in her eyes despite that big smile. I don't think I've seen much in her eyes since that whole thing happened, to be honest.

THIRTY-FIVE

I finished school — the three of us did. School had been pretty much irrelevant to me since I'd started the band. I got good grades, but I didn't care. Every free minute I had I tried to spend working on the band. I applied but I wasn't going to go to college and I didn't worry about telling my parents my decision. They stayed away from me, and I gave them nothing to worry about. I kept to myself and finished school, I wasn't loud, and I wasn't going out to parties or coming home late. They couldn't complain, right? Besides, Melissa was starting to enter some annoying rebellious phase, and Mom and Dad had to focus on her messes instead of mine.

The only places I went at all, really, were band practices and to see Edgar, Socks, and Fern. Socks was looking forward to the summer — he wanted to book a tour and just hit the road for a few months. Edgar was balking at that idea, Fern and I were all for it, so we ended up talking about money a lot, which wasn't what I was interested in at all. Edgar always was pretty sensible, wanting to make sure everything would work out. Socks was maybe too easygoing. I don't know what was going on in Fern's mind those days, but all I wanted to do was get on the road and get things going. I had energy and nowhere to channel it except at rehearsals and into my artwork.

Socks and Edgar noticed that something was different with me and Fern, but after asking us once what was wrong, they dropped it. I tried to cover it up with enthusiasm, but I'm pretty sure it was all overwrought and seemed weird. Fern, on the other hand, had become very quiet and more observational, nodding instead of discussing. It disturbed me. I hoped that she would regain more of her old self. In practice, instead of being aggressive and confident, she seemed timid and weak. I had no idea what was going on in her mind, but I could see myself trying to channel everything into my plans, to turn everything into drive and energy. Mad is more productive than sad, right?

I'd lie awake in bed and imagine glorious ways to destroy that band. The concept of lighting the bus on fire was always a good standby; the image of that fat asshole's swollen, split flesh and the crackle of their hair blazing always calmed me. I entertained myself with images of poisoning them, putting something into their drinks and watching bloody foam stream from their lips. Even something as simple as driving a plain old stick from the backyard into Balthazar's eye could often do it. When an image of his face would pop into my mind unbidden, I would immediately imagine driving my thumb into his eye, relishing the warmth of the spasm and clench around my thumb, the eye bursting beneath my thumbnail and all that weird congealed jelly stuff squirting out and down his cheek.

I also developed a pretty bad habit of digging my nails into the palm of my left hand, causing cuts that would bleed, as I had that day in the woods with Fern. I'd pull off the scabs when the wounds tried to heal, and after a while my palm was a mess and only got worse. I ended up getting a bunch of blood on my bed sheets because I tore off the scabs before bed or unknowingly in my sleep. The skin around the scabs would harden into dry ridges and I would tear those off too, stripping them along as far as they could go into the healthy areas of my palm and causing more blood to well up. I would wad up a white sock and clench it in my palm whenever I picked at it during the day. I kept all the bloody socks in a bag under my bed.

The whole throwing-up thing in Port Claim had definitely worked in our favour. Word had started getting around about the band in the months since that had happened, and there was a small but present demand for our crappy CD. Socks put together a cheap little website to sell them, and mail and money started trickling in. People wanted to know when we were playing in their city, if we wanted to play with their band, all kinds of stuff. We hadn't played any shows in a long time, and it was pretty awesome that people really, really wanted us to.

And then we got a really amazing-sounding offer. We all knew Goreceps — I'd really gotten into their album *Excrement from Birth*. They were from the U.K., and we got an email from their manager offering us a tour with them. A week and a half touring across England, and two shows in Ireland and Scotland.

Of course there was the money issue. We'd have to cover our own flights, and four round-trip tickets to the U.K. were pretty expensive. But Goreceps's manager assured us that the crowds there would be quite large, and they would pay us a small sum for each show. We could also sell our own merchandise and CDs. We had a few hundred dollars from the CDs we'd sold already, and we could put that towards doing a run of T-shirts. So all we had to do was somehow scrounge up enough money for the flights — everything else would be taken care of.

I made the design for the T-shirt. Two blood-spattered women pressed against one another, dresses torn, faces skeletal, and eyes hollow beneath their long ratted hair. One was dark haired, the other pale. They pressed their bony hands together, the fingers entwined, gripping a hank of black hair. Dangling from their grasp was a severed head, several teeth wrenched from its dry gums, dark blood oozing from its scooped-out eye sockets. I pressed my pencil hard into the drawing, adding the best smirks I could to the girls' exposed bone faces, willing their happiness to reflect in the dark hollows of their eyes. It was Judith and her maidservant and the head of Holofernes, but of course, it was me and Fern and the head of Balthazar. That legend, that myth, was going to be our reality. I pored over the drawing for hours and hours. I dreamed that my teeth had been sharpened down to pointy nubs, and I used them to bite through stomachs, chewing at spongy entrails while my mouth filled with blood over and over again.

Edgar's parents agreed to loan us money for the flights. My parents agreed I could go. I hadn't caused any tension in the house since that horrible night, and I think they were worried about me being *depressed* or something. The T-shirt was printed. We packed our bags for tour. Fern and Edgar would bring their guitars, Socks would share a drum kit with Goreceps. We filled our remaining suitcases with CDs, shirts to sell, and stage clothes, and went to the U.K.

THIRTY-
SIX

It was called the Flesh for Lunch Tour and right when we got
off the plane things felt very organized. We were met at the
airport by Richard, who shook our hands, gave us laminated
cards with a picture of Goreceps and our name on the front,
and the tour dates on the back, and brought us to a van. We
were exhausted and hoping we'd be able to sleep — it was early
afternoon in London, but our body clocks were telling us it
was 8 a.m. and we hadn't been to sleep. Sleeping on planes is
impossible. It's such a horrible feeling sitting in the fake night
they give you, where they dim the lights and everyone closes
their eyes, and it seems like you're the only one still awake,
you're the only one who didn't plan ahead and stay up the
night before so you'd actually be tired during fake night. You
feel lonely and isolated, and you also get to panic because you
know you're going to land in a few hours and be just exhausted,
destroyed, and expected to face a whole new day. And that's

what happened to us. Richard said we were going straight to the first venue, as there was a show that night. And so we did.

We'd landed in London but the first show was in Manchester, a few hours' drive northwest. At least we could try to sleep in the van as Richard drove. I sat next to the window with Fern beside me. She stared out the window and I stared at her. Her cheeks were hollowed, and I realized how much weight she had lost. Socks and Edgar were excited about being in England, chatting with Richard about how the buildings looked different and laughing about different shops' names. I was dimly aware that we were in another country and it was totally interesting and different and exciting, but for some reason I couldn't stop staring at the sharp jut of Fern's cheekbone. My stomach lurched at the thought of how unfair it was, at how she couldn't enjoy what was happening as much as she should have been able to. So I closed my eyes and tried to calm my racing heart by thinking instead about how every mile that passed, every step forward, was taking us closer to our new goal. We would get a tour with DED. It would happen.

A few things became clear as the tour began: one was that the guys in Goreceps were pretty nice, which was a relief. Two was that some people in the U.K. knew our music, and the only explanation was that they'd heard it on the internet. This pissed Socks off especially — we hadn't mailed many CDs over here, and he was frustrated that we'd lost potential sales. It was a weird double-edged sword — people liked our band over here and it was surreal to see people singing along in a foreign country, but they clearly hadn't bought the CD.

The third thing was that our reputation had preceded us. A lot of people at the shows had the perception that we were "insane." Certainly most of the people at the shows were impatient for our act to finish so Goreceps could take the stage, which made sense, and a lot of those people were guys who had no interest in our band, especially with two girls onstage. But the story of my vomiting had gotten around, and to my dismay it seemed I was expected to provide some sort of shocking performance.

I was already prepared to steel myself against aggressive metal guys at the front of the stage and was becoming pretty good at ignoring taunts and jeers and bullshit sexual gestures. But over here it seemed to take on a new intensity.

At one of the first shows, there were about four guys pressed against the stage as we played, and they openly tried to intimidate me. "Try puking on me, *bitch*," one of them kept jeering. I tried to ignore them, and Edgar positioned himself in front of them in hopes of shutting them up, but between songs they'd spread their arms wide, calling to me, daring me to do something. I hoped they'd get bored, but they seemed determined, and despite the overall positive reaction from the crowd, I was having trouble ignoring them. I could feel their eyes on me and it unsettled me, which in turn made me furious at myself for allowing them to intimidate me.

When we had only two songs left, they finally cut it out. I was relieved, but then I saw that they had turned their attention to Fern. She was focused entirely on her guitar and her fingers moved quickly, gliding up and down its neck. Sweat dripped from her face, and her mascara had melted into dark circles under her eyes. Above her, a red spotlight glowed, bathing her in scarlet light, making her white hair appear pink. She looked so beautiful in that moment.

And I saw one of the guys had pushed his way to position himself in front of her, and his arm reached up towards her. It reminded me of the video I had seen of Marie-Lise so long ago, where the asshole in the crowd reaches up and is thrown back by her violent kick. I watched this guy's hand grab the hem of her skirt and tug her forward. She stumbled, catching herself before she fell, but raising her hands from the guitar.

I froze as I watched the panic strike her face, her hands immediately flying to clutch her skirt protectively. I dropped the microphone as the guy continued to yank on her, his lips drawn back from his teeth as he laughed. His gums looked purple and diseased in the red light.

Socks and Edgar continued to play and the microphone began squealing, feeding back, cutting through my stupor and causing the people in the crowd to recoil with its piercing shriek. I grabbed the microphone back up, stopping the noise, and leaped towards the guy, raising it above my head like a baseball bat.

There was a loud, intense thump as I brought the microphone down on the guy's head. Immediately it began to feed back again, but I ignored the grating sound. I don't know if Socks and Edgar stopped playing. I was unaware of any noise except the shriek of the microphone and the booming as I brought it down against this creep's head again and again. It sounded like a giant, overwhelming heartbeat, thudding and soul shaking, and I was dimly aware that the guy's yells of pain were also amplified by the microphone.

I felt hands on my shoulders and snapped my head up to see Edgar had come to stop me. I realized my eyes were burning and I wondered when I had last blinked. All I had been aware of was the pounding heartbeat of the microphone, the squealing as it fed back.

"Cut it out," Edgar yelled at the guy in the crowd in front of us, and I felt an electric thrill run through me as I realized that I was *right*, my friend was siding with me.

I pulled myself together and looked at the crowd. All was quiet, and every face I could see was looking at us, aghast. I

275

could tell they were waiting for direction, unsure what to think about what I had done. I realized I was in control here. They would listen to what *I* said.

The prick stood there, rubbing his sore head like a little kid would have, a mix of fury and confusion on his face.

"Say you're sorry," I ordered him in my most patronizing tone, chastising him like the child he looked like. My voice echoed in the silence. The crowd seemed to hold its breath.

"No way, *you stupid whore*," the guy said, but he was far away enough from the mike that he sounded hollow, thin and pathetic. His voice broke on the word *whore*, making him sound even more idiotic and weak.

I brought the microphone down again, hard, onto his head, and the sound boomed hollowly through the room. The crowd began to cheer.

"Listen here, *you fucking insect*," I said, raising my voice to be heard over the cheers. "You don't touch girls like that. Do you *get it*? Now, I know this isn't my show. It's a Goreceps show. But if it was my show, I'd kick your ass the *fuck out*."

The crowd roar was deafening, and I looked back to see that the guys from Goreceps had come out on stage and were applauding. I realized that they were applauding *me*. Their singer, Jacob, made a gesture. Security moved in and dragged the asshole away through the crowd.

I stood there beside Fern, who seemed oblivious to it all and was wringing her hands, and wondered why the fuck security hadn't done anything to stop the guy *in the first place*.

THIRTY-SEVEN

"You're breaking new ground," the interviewer said. "There's been a rallying of girls in metal. How does it feel to be a role model?"

The tape recorder was sitting on the table between us. I'd never done an interview before, and this woman worked for *Blood Sledge*, so I was sort of nervous. One of the biggest metal magazines in Europe, and here I was, sitting backstage, on a tour with a great band, being asked what it feels like to be a *role model*? It was surreal.

"I don't think I'm a role model," I said,

"Three nights ago in Leeds you beat a guy over the head with your microphone because he was grabbing your guitarist. A lot of girls look up to that."

"I think a lot of girls should beat guys over the head if they're going to be assaulted like that, because what that guy did was *assault*," I said, feeling my pulse quicken. I took a deep breath. "I don't get why people act like that. Why they think they're *entitled* to treat girls that way."

"Do you see a lot of this sort of thing while you're touring? Do you think there's an element of sexism in the music industry?"

I frowned, wondering if she was joking or if this was a serious question. "Definitely. I think a lot of guys have a sense of ego and over-confidence in this industry. Particularly . . ." An image of Balthazar flashed in my mind. I quickly dismissed it, clenching my fists. "Er, particularly musicians."

The interviewer giggled. "Well, some might say that girls rather enjoy the attention of musicians."

I swallowed my urge to reach across the table and slap her. I took a deep breath and replied calmly, "Not all girls. I think it's a good lesson for some of these . . . *assholes* to remember that. Not every girl is going to fall at your feet and do nothing but *giggle*. I don't understand that perspective."

The interviewer had stopped smiling and now seemed nervous, as though she knew she had offended me and wanted to clarify her point. "But there really are so many groupies —"

"Not every girl is a fucking *groupie*," I snapped. Her eyes widened in the silence that followed, and I was aware of the soft whirring of the tape recorder. The faces of the two girls who had been backstage with me and Fern, the ones who had to deal with the disgusting roadie, flashed in my mind. What had that night been like for them? What had happened to them after we had fled? I didn't want to come off as a bitch here, so when I spoke next, I softened my tone. "And groupies don't deserve to be treated badly either. It seems like some guys at shows just have a problem with women. It makes me so angry. I mean, Fern is onstage, playing guitar, and some guy thinks he has the *right* to just grope her, and no one does anything. I don't understand that."

"Yes, you're right," the interviewer said quickly, smiling back, glad that our conversation had gotten back onto a positive note. "There has always been violence against women at concerts, and I'm glad you're addressing it."

"Well, everyone should be damn well addressing it," I said. "There are enough girls at these shows that we should be looking after each other."

The Flesh for Lunch tour seemed to end before it even began, really. A week and a half isn't a long time at all, especially when you're playing really cool shows every night. By the last night, though, I have to admit I was a bit relieved. We hadn't bothered doing laundry, so all the clothes we'd brought were getting raunchy. The food provided each night by the different clubs pretty much sucked — usually just a plate of greasy sandwich meat and, for some reason, a huge variety of buns and bread, and cheese that looked off the minute it hit the table. Not eating well paired with the huge amount of physical energy it took to perform each night proved to be very draining. And I don't even want to get started on the mystery bruises and bumps on my body.

The final night in England, we got to our hotel and I sank into bed, shocked by how exhausted I felt. It seemed like I had been running on some sort of high, knowing we had shows each night, and now that I knew all we had to do was get up and get on a plane the next day to go home, I was ready to collapse.

"It was a good tour," Fern said from the next bed over.

My eyes were closed, and through my haze of exhaustion I heard the flick of her lighter. "Yeah, it was. Some really good shows."

"Definitely." She blew smoke audibly.

279

"The Goreceps guys were really cool," I murmured. "I hope they're glad they brought us along. It seemed like we brought our fair share of fans to the shows, even though I don't really get how that's possible. Can you believe people over here know us?"

"They seemed nice," Fern said stiffly, referring to the guys from the other band. "They didn't seem like they were doing anything shitty to anyone."

I lay quietly, listening to her smoke.

"Rachel, do you think we'll get near those . . . assholes again?" she finally asked.

"I promise we will."

"Because . . . sometimes I just don't know how to make the shit feeling go away, and I really don't know . . . I just don't know what to do." Her voice lowered, strained. "I don't know how to deal with this. I mean, here we are in England, you know, we just did a tour, we played some great shows, and it's like none of it even *matters*. I feel like I'm watching everyone around me, and none of them are paying attention or something. Like I can't understand what they have to be so happy about." I heard the light ringing of glass as she ground out her cigarette in the ashtray.

"We'll get close to them," I said.

Then she was silent, and I waited to hear the slow, heavy sound of her sleep breathing. Part of me wanted to speak again, to reassure her again, but I didn't know what more I could tell her. I had no plan, just a goal. I rolled on my back, and in the dim light filtering through the window blinds, I watched the remnants of a wave of her smoke drift silently through the room like a storm cloud moving through the night sky. I dug my fingernails into my palm and felt the relief of the warm trickle of blood.

THIRTY-EIGHT

We landed in a rainstorm. We piled our gear and ourselves into a van cab, putting together the last of our money to afford it. We were silent during the ride back into the city, and I became very self-conscious of the fact that we totally reeked. From the instruments, which stank like cigarettes and old beer from the dirty venues we'd played, to the bags of our filthy, sweaty clothes, to just plain us, I'm sure the cab driver was pretty unimpressed with us.

"It was a good tour," Socks said from the front seat, turning around to look at us. I was sitting next to Edgar in the middle, and Fern had curled up in the back next to a pile of our backpacks. I stared at Socks, feeling as though I was half asleep. His long hair looked greasy, and he was clearly exhausted. I'm sure I looked no better. "We had some good shows and some good press. Good job!" He grinned and gave us all the thumbs-up.

From beside me, Edgar laughed and I smiled tiredly back, and there was no sound from behind us at all. I wondered if Fern was asleep.

"We have to focus on money," Socks continued, and I wondered if he'd spent the flight home brainstorming. "Next time we tour we have to ask for more money. And we almost sold out of shirts, so we need to print more. Which we have no money to do."

"My parents aren't in a rush to get their money back," Edgar said, referring to the flight money they'd loaned us.

"Nevertheless, we need to focus on making money," Socks said. "But great tour!"

The cab pulled up to Fern's house first, and she gathered her things and smiled wanly at us. "Call me soon," she said, standing outside Socks's rolled-down window, and waved as the cab backed out of her driveway and drove away. She stood motionless, watching the van as we drove away, a sad figure in rumpled jeans, with a wool cap pulled over her tangled white hair.

"Okay," Edgar said immediately. "What happened?"

Socks looked at me intently, and I hesitated. "What do you mean?"

"Something is wrong with Fern," Socks said. "Since before the tour. For the last few months she hasn't been herself. At all."

My mind raced. I was painfully aware of the cab driver, sitting there listening. "I don't know what you mean."

"She barely *talks* anymore," Edgar said. "I tried to ask her what was wrong one night on the tour and she just stared at me, like she didn't understand what I had asked. Like I was speaking another language or something."

"I don't think anything is wrong," I said. "She seems fine to me. She talks all the time."

Socks frowned. "She's not like she was before and you know it. What are you hiding?"

I glared at him. "Nothing. If Fern is going through something maybe she just wants to be left alone. Did you ever consider that?"

Edgar touched my arm. "You know it's just because we care about her. Look, is she okay?"

I guess I really hadn't considered that Socks or Edgar would notice anything wrong, even though I knew Fern was visibly withdrawn and had been for months. I wasn't sure if I was even acting like myself anymore. I don't know why I was so surprised that our *friends would care*. Of course they would. I had no idea what to say. After a few seconds of fumbling for words, I finally spoke. "You're right, Fern is in a bad place right now. It's sort of private, so I don't want to speak for her."

"Is she okay?" Socks said.

"Yes. I think the best thing for her is for the band to move forward. To keep her mind off things, and to have something to look forward to. Like a big tour." *With DED.*

They both nodded. Then there was quiet for a few moments. I stared out the window at the rain as we neared my neighbourhood.

"Are *you* okay?" Edgar said after a minute.

I felt both their eyes on me, watching closely. "I'm totally fine."

XXX

I don't know if they believed me or not, but as I climbed out of the cab and waved goodbye I tried to give my most convincing smile.

I walked up the driveway and through the side door of the house. Immediately I heard two kitchen chairs scrape back as my parents jumped to their feet. Mom and Dad were both wide-eyed, exhausted-looking, totally freaked out. I froze. "What's wrong?"

They stared at me and relief swept over their faces. "Rachel," Mom said. "You're home!"

I couldn't tell if I was in trouble or not. They'd been agreeable when I had asked them if I could go on the tour. I had told them everything about it, and they had been okay with it, especially once I'd shown them the plane ticket and they realized the whole thing was legit.

"Yes," I said. Their eyes followed my movements as I put my dirty, reeking shoulder bag and backpack down. "I'm home. Is everything okay?"

"Are *you* okay?" Mom said.

They both looked pretty stunned. I fumbled to grasp what was going on. "Yes, I'm totally fine."

Dad sank down into his chair, rubbing his temples with his fingers. "When we agreed to let you go to England, I don't think we'd really thought it through. I visited Germany the summer after I graduated from high school. Saw the sights, visited, and travelled. Backpacked from hostel to hostel. Berlin, Frankfurt, Ingolstadt. Met so many incredible people."

I had heard *Dad's Trip to Germany* story many times. When I'd told them about going to England, Melissa and I had sat though another memory lane diatribe. "Yes, Dad, I know."

"So when you wanted to go to England, I guess I thought it would be similar to my trip. And a great experience for you."

"We figured if the group of you were there together, you would be safe," Mom said. "Your dad had such a great time."

"But then as the reality of it sunk in — touring, bands, being around alcohol and drugs — we started to worry maybe we had made a mistake in allowing you to go."

"Okay, but remember, I don't drink or do drugs," I said. "We were on a schedule. We weren't just goofing off or whatever. We were paid to be there." I did my best to be patient. Of course they couldn't understand. Of course it wasn't like Dad's stupid backpacking hostel trip.

Mom took the passport and had a look. "This is pretty neat."

"Yes." I unzipped a pocket on my shoulder bag and pulled out a laminated card on a lanyard. "Here's the tour laminate," I said, showing them the list of the dates and cities of the tour. "I wore this the whole time."

"You visited so many cities," Mom said, looking over at Dad. "That's really something, isn't it?"

They both studied me. I knew I was a mess, totally smelly and dishevelled. But I had been on tour overseas, with the laminate and passport stamps and a hideous bag of dirty clothes to prove it. And I wasn't drunk or stoned or sick. It made me feel good to see them at a loss for words.

"So," Dad said, "your band is doing really well? Making money?"

"Well, we opened for Goreceps," I explained. "It wasn't *our* tour, technically." I started feeling resentful again. I had already explained this to them weeks before. They hadn't listened. "Like I *told you*, they invited us. Edgar's parents paid for the tickets, and we sold CDs and shirts that we had made ourselves."

"I've always wanted to go to England," Mom said, smiling. "Rachel, I almost can't believe it. You toured and travelled, made your own CDs and shirts."

"I did the shirt designs myself. And our CD cover." I couldn't help it. I started to feel proud, and wanted to share that with Mom and Dad. I'd spent so many hours in my room alone, working on designs, working on lyrics, so many hours at rehearsals, singing and working on my voice, and here my parents were, talking about it with me. It felt damn good to see their interest.

"And you write all the song lyrics," Dad said.

"Yeah." I smiled. It was a goofy smile, probably. Like, a genuine one.

285

"You really have achieved so much," Mom said.

"Mom and I were worried the whole time you were gone."

"Why did you let me go then?" I said. "If you honestly thought I was just going to go party or something? For *a week and a half*? You were fine just letting me go?"

"This was going to be it," Dad admitted. "Once you got back, no more band. It was going to be college or a full-time job."

"And now?" I asked. "Now that you can see this band moving forward? That I can make money at it? That I'm not a drug addict?"

They were quiet. They didn't know what to say. I shrugged and took my bags to my room. My sister wasn't even home. As I unpacked wads of still-damp clothes from my backpack, I realized how much it must suck to be a parent. You devote everything to your kids, who just end up growing up and disliking you. I felt bad for them briefly, but at least they had each other. In that moment I decided I wouldn't have kids. I don't think I could handle the level of betrayal I'd feel once I realized that they weren't interested in me anymore.

THIRTY-NINE

Socks's voice was urgent and excited on the other end of the phone. "The owner is coming out. The *owner* of Recordead is flying here!"

"I *hate* that name," I said.

"I know. It's terrible. But who gives a shit? It's *Recordead Records*. Do you know how many wicked bands they have?"

"Yes." Pretty much all the bands we listened to were on Recordead Records: Surgical Carnage, Gurgol, DED. I'd always hated the name. Such a shitty pun. Why would you go to so much trouble and be so passionate about the music and have just the worst possible fucking name!

"Well, I just wanted to make sure you know that the guy who runs the label is coming here, on an airplane, in two weeks. To see us."

"So are we going to put on a show?"

"Yes, if you're up for it," Socks said, and I heard the crumpling noises of paper as he pulled out his notes. He cleared his throat. "I was thinking we could play the Toe. I was talking to Robbie — the promoter with the radio show?"

"Right." I remembered two things about Robbie — one was that he was the only one who had clapped after our first song during that first show with Heathenistic Bile. The second was that I had felt bad for him, having heard all the stories of the money he'd lost booking metal shows.

"Well, he was saying he'd help us out. He says he'll rent out the Toe for us, and give us an interview on his show."

"Cool."

"Totally!" Socks continued. "I was thinking we could get Torn Bowel to play with us. I've kept in touch with PJ — he said they'd love to do another show with us."

"Okay," I agreed. I remembered their guitarist, Jamie, and how he'd totally stopped flirting with me after I puked on that asshole.

"So we'll have the guy from Recordead come out to that show. Robbie thinks we can get something awesome together. He thinks it'll be a great night." I was quiet, grateful for Socks. The guy was basically managing us. "He says he's had a lot of interest in the band on his radio show. People calling in, talking about the U.K. tour, the interview you did in *Blood Sledge*. He gets a lot of requests."

I agreed to do a telephone interview with Robbie that Saturday night in anticipation of a show at the Toe in St. Charles the following Friday night. Socks confirmed that Torn Bowel would do the show. I didn't hear anything from Fern — which wasn't unusual nowadays — but Edgar had spoken to her, and we decided to have a rehearsal in Socks's basement the night before the show.

XXX

"So we're live on air right now with Rachel from Colostomy Hag," Robbie said over the phone. I wasn't allowed to have the radio on, so this didn't feel like a broadcast of any sort to me. Of course, I wasn't even sure anyone would be listening in the first place — Robbie's show was on at 1 a.m. once a week for an hour on Saturday nights. This just felt like a silly phone call.

"How are you tonight, Rachel?"

"I'm good, thanks."

"Just back from your U.K. tour with Goreceps, right?"

"A few weeks back, yes."

"Awesome. I have to say it's sort of an honour to have you on the line right now. Colostomy Hag is getting an amazing reputation," he said.

"Er, that's nice of you."

"So how was the tour?"

I talked for a minute or so about the Flesh for Lunch tour, how cool Goreceps had been to us, despite our limited amount of socializing with them, and what an interesting experience it had been to go overseas and have people know our music. "That was really cool. I'm still not sure what to think of that, it seems so impossible."

"Do you find that the pressure is on you now, somewhat? You've had a few incidents at your shows — notably, of course, when you threw up on that guy in Port Claim, and now having humiliated a heckler and having had him thrown out of the venue. Do people expect some kind of crazy behaviour from you?"

"Maybe a little."

"Do you find it difficult to be a woman in a metal band?"

"Sometimes it's frustrating. Me and Fern, who plays guitar, get shit sometimes when we're playing. There are a lot of guys who aren't into respecting girls in bands. Or just generally."

"Before this interview we were playing some DED," Robbie

said. "I'm sure it goes without saying that you guys are fans. Did you get a chance to catch their show when they came through a while back?"

It felt like a giant tennis ball had appeared in my throat. My head started pounding and I fought to remain calm. "Oh yes, it goes without saying, huge fans."

"They put on a great show," Robbie said.

"Amazing," I said. My vision blurred and went black, even though my eyes were wide open and unblinking.

"And what nice guys, too. I didn't have a chance to get them on the show, but they're great to their fans. Have you had the chance to meet them?"

"Unfortunately, no."

"Well, I'm sure one day you'll be sharing the stage with them," Robbie said.

"That would just be a *dream come true*. There's nothing I'd like more."

"Well, until that day comes, you can catch Colostomy Hag next Friday night at the Toe, right here in St. Charles. They're playing with their old tour friends Torn Bowel. Doors are at 9, ten bucks at the door. This is *not* a show to miss."

FORTY

I knew I had to do something big. Or something awesome had to happen. I was terrified that no one would come, despite Socks's reassurances that Robbie had had a ton of interest come in through the radio program.

Fern and I had started spending more time together. I'd go to her place and we'd just hang out. Most of the time we wouldn't even really talk. I'd bring along my sketchbook, lie on her bed, and draw or draft lyrics. She'd sit on the floor and play her guitar. It was nice to be alone with her again, even if our relationship felt like it had changed. In a way, it was as though we had never been apart.

As the show drew near, I took Fern downtown to go shopping. We picked out two matching navy blue-and-black plaid jumpers and matching collared white blouses. It was a pleasant afternoon, reminiscent of the first times we'd hung out together. She laughed at jokes, she talked and seemed excited about the show, but still there was always something missing.

I decided I'd wear a pair of the white knee socks I'd been keeping wadded under my bed, the ones I'd been using to soak up the blood from my scabby palm. By this point I'd gotten into the habit of keeping my left hand clenched in a fist so no one could notice the raw skin. Sometimes I'd wear a black fingerless glove on it, which made me look tough and hid the scabbing.

The socks were nasty, there was no way around it, with a mildewed scent and a sour undertone. But no one would notice that.

When the four of us pulled up to the Toe, there was a large group of people clustered around the building. The chain-link fence leading to the back of the venue was closed.

"What the fuck! How are we supposed to soundcheck if there's some stupid shit going on here already?" I said as Socks slowed the van. "Did Robbie say what else was happening here today?"

Edgar peered out the window. "Are they here for *us*?"

The four of us stared as Socks stopped the van in the middle of the street. There were about a hundred people on the sidewalk, from a large group in front of the venue leading into a line up that was beginning to snake around the block. From the group, we saw Robbie emerge, waving his hands at us, signalling to turn the van towards the back gate, which he went over to unlock. Heads turned towards us from the crowd of people, hands pointed.

"But it's only *noon*," Fern said.

Robbie opened the gate, then Socks pulled through, and I felt eyes on me as we drove past the crowd. My cheeks flushed. It was extraordinarily unpleasant being on display the way I was. And I'll tell you, it's a very different thing from being onstage, when you are somewhat in control of things. It's like having someone study you while you're eating your morning cereal in your Garfield T-shirt and ripped pyjama pants. It's weird.

Robbie closed the gate behind us and Socks navigated the van to the alcove by the back door. Faces pressed against the fence, trying to catch a glimpse of us.

"There were a few kids here who *slept* in the line last night, if you can believe that," Robbie said as we got out of the van. "This show is going to be incredible."

He went on and on, and we started loading our gear in. I was thankful for the dark, cold, smelly interior of the club. It was nice to have the chilling, crawling feeling of being watched dissipate. Piss soaked as it was, this place was our refuge.

Torn Bowel arrived a little while after we did, and it was a pretty pleasant reunion. They'd just come back from a tour, and they'd been on the road for a few months. All of them sported *tour moustaches* and had the same look in their eyes, the look a band starts to get when they've been away from home for too long. They laugh really hard at jokes that no one else can understand, and there is both panic and exhaustion. The panic feeling seems to hit when you know you're getting close to going home.

Jamie extended his arms to me and we embraced. I caught the stink of his black T-shirt, stiff with dried sweat, and felt the rank greasiness of unwashed blond hair against my cheek. I didn't really understand the ferocity of his happiness to see me, but on both sides of me the others were all hugging, so I went with it. Besides, after four months on tour, it was understandable that he would be a little overwrought. I'd felt those twinges myself, even after our short tours. Jamie's eyes were wide, his smile desperate, his breath heavy with night after night of alcohol and who-knew-what-else as, for some unknown reason, he leaned in to kiss me.

"Whoa, there," I said, turning my face so his lips landed clumsily on my cheek.

"Sorry, Rachel. You just look *great*," he said, smiling at me.

"You look good too. How was tour?"

"It was fucking *great*," he said. "But I have to say, I'm glad to be almost done. Tonight is going to be amazing. The best. It's so good to see you again."

Things were bustling around us, gear being moved and set up, but Jamie stayed with me. I could feel Fern's eyes on me from across the room, could almost feel her disapproval physically, burning into my face. I stood stiffly as Jamie ran one hand up my arm to my shoulder, tried to keep from jerking back as he put his fingers in my hair. I didn't understand where this was coming from — the last I had seen of Jamie, we had parted as polite acquaintances. I hadn't really cared then, and I certainly didn't care now.

"You guys are doing really well," Jamie said. "You went to England, I hear. I saw a few magazines with you guys while we were on the road."

I nodded, swallowing the lump in my throat as he casually ran both hands down my arms, past my wrists, and twined our fingers together, as though we were a comfy, intimately involved couple. I fought the urge to push him away and shriek until my eyes poured blood.

"The last time we saw each other, on that little tour, you know, I didn't get a chance to say goodbye the way I wanted to," he said. "I'm glad we get to see each other again today. So I can make that up to you."

"You didn't say goodbye to me because you thought it was gross that I puked," I reminded him.

"That's not true. It was so cool. I didn't think it was gross at all."

"Yes, you did," I said. "Remember the first day? We were pretty much flirting with each other."

He laughed and seemed to blush. "You're pretty blunt!"

294

I ignored him. "We were talking, all that. I sort of liked you, I mean, as much as you can like a person that you've only known for half a day, or whatever. You were asking me about where I grew up, all that stuff. But then I puked on that guy, and you didn't really seem interested after that."

"No, I — I thought it was . . . pretty cool that you did that."

I began slowly untangling my fingers from his. "I know you did, totally. But you have to admit, it wasn't very . . . *hot*."

Jamie laughed. "Fuck, okay fine. You're right. I didn't think it was hot."

I felt a lot better now that we were no longer holding hands, so I grinned at him. "Right. So I just don't get it. Why are you holding my hand and touching me right now? Tell me it's because you're tired and crazy from tour. Otherwise I might think it's because you saw a picture of me in a magazine so now you think it would be cool to be with me. Because really, dude, why else would you be trying to hit on me today?"

Jamie studied my face. I could tell he was put off by my forthrightness. I could almost hear his mind racing to figure out what the answer should be. I stared back at him, still grinning, and shortly he grinned back, his face relaxing, and he nervously tucked a strand of greasy hair behind his ear. "I'm just tired. And you know, it *is* good to see you. I'm stoked about this show."

I still don't know what his real reason was, but with that out of the way we were free to be just friends, and this time when we hugged it was nice, friendly, harmless. As we embraced, I saw Fern, sitting on the stage, half turning her action, half smiling at us, her expression frozen.

XXX

The last time we'd played here with that shitty Heathenistic Bile, we'd used the girls' public washroom to get changed. This

295

time, Robbie had the owner unlock a small shower-room backstage that we could use. The small, tiled room was filthy and stank like burnt hair and old beer, but it was nice to know we'd moved up in the world.

"I wonder what happened to Heathenistic Bile," I mused to Fern as we got dressed. I was wearing my white bloody socks and sneakers, and she wore black fishnet tights with black boots, but the matching plaid dresses and blouses looked great. Fern was looking in her compact mirror, applying dark lipstick.

"Who knows," she muttered. "Remember how that guy kept going on about how they had all this label interest or whatever? Maybe they're rich and famous by now."

"Oh, I bet." Muffled through the club walls, we heard a tremendous cheer as Torn Bowel evidently took the stage. I sighed as they launched into their first song. "How cool is it to be back here at this club? Robbie was saying it sold out. Remember there were twenty people here last year?"

Fern nodded. "I know. And it's weird having Torn Bowel open for *us*." We were quiet for a while, and then she asked carefully, "So what's going on with you and Jamie?"

I scoffed. "Nothing. I think he's just a little confused."

"I saw him touching you," she said, her growl betraying her disgust. "What was up with that?"

"Nothing."

"He just got off tour," she said. "Probably used to girls doing whatever he wants."

I considered this. "When we toured with them, they didn't really hang out with girls after the shows. They always just played video games. I don't think they're *that* type of band."

After a few moments, Fern swallowed hard and seemed to calm. "I guess you're right. I just didn't like seeing him touching you like that, is all. It just seemed like he was really forward, really arrogant about it."

296

"I think Jamie's a nice guy." I stood beside Fern and leaned my head on her shoulder. "Don't worry about me. If Jamie had tried anything, I would have smashed his face in. Seriously."

"I would've been two steps ahead of you," Fern said.

FORTY-ONE

Fern and I joined Socks and Edgar in the main dressing room at the Toe. The same destroyed, filthy couches were there, but we'd chosen to put our bags on them. Socks was drumming on one arm of the couch with his drumsticks, and Fern crouched on the floor to tune her guitar. Edgar squinted, leaning towards my legs.

"What the fuck is that on your socks?" he asked. "Is that *blood*?"

I gazed down at the white knee socks. The rusty brownish smears looked particularly awful in the harsh fluorescent lighting. My left hand clenched instinctively, and I felt the familiar sting of raw flesh on my palm. "Looks real, doesn't it?"

"*Is* it?" Edgar asked, raising his dark eyes to scrutinize my face.

There was a knock on the door, and Robbie poked his head inside. "Guys — I want you to meet someone."

A tall man followed him into the room, and I disliked him on sight. He was probably in his fifties, with a small pointed nose and half-lidded eyes that indicated to me he was drunk, and likely had been for most of his life. His hair stood up in bleached-blond clumps, giving him a sort of aging surfer look. He wore what was clearly an expensive grey suit, but the black shirt underneath was unbuttoned low, to reveal cobwebby white chest hair.

"This is Tom Manic. He's the owner of Recordead Records," Robbie announced.

"Love your band," Tom said in a sleepy-sounding voice, holding a hand out towards me. All of us took a turn shaking it. We introduced ourselves. He continued. "Glad to be here tonight. You got a great turnout."

"Thanks for coming out," Socks said. "The show tonight's going to be great."

"Yes," Tom agreed. His gaze moved to Fern, and then to me. "You know, I've never been a fan of girls in bands."

My smile froze.

"Well, look at her!" he laughed to the others, widening his eyes with amusement. "Relax, darling! You've proved me wrong. Honestly when I heard that story about you throwing up all over that poor kid, I thought, 'I have to meet this girl.'"

For some reason everyone laughed at his comment, so with effort I turned up the sides of my mouth. I understood we were supposed to try to impress this guy, but really. *Tom Manic* with his pointy weasel nose? *Really?* This was the guy who owned one of the biggest record labels? This sleepy-looking bastard!

"It's nice of you to come all this way," I said, with some effort.

"Oh, I absolutely love coming out to these smaller cities," he said, waving his hand dismissively. "It's so rare I get the chance to really get into these *salt of the earth* communities. Los Angeles can be so *tiring*. And some of the biggest bands really do come from these sort of nowhere cities, you know?"

We heard the crowd roar as Torn Bowel finished their last song, and then the house music came back up again.

"We're up," Edgar said.

"Great. Right. Well, *break a leg*, you know?" Tom chuckled lazily, as though he'd just made a witty comment, and then he gazed at me for a moment. "It'll be interesting to see the performance. We'll talk after, right?"

He left the room, and Robbie trailed him, pausing before he closed the door to wiggle his eyebrows and give us a thumbs-up.

"He seemed nice," Socks said.

"He seemed like a sleazeball," I said.

"We can talk about it later," Edgar said. "Right now, we have a sold-out crowd waiting for us."

Socks and Edgar left the room, and Fern picked up her guitar. "Planning anything insane?" she asked.

I shook my head shortly, following her out into the dark hallway. I didn't have any idea. I was angry, knowing that everyone and this Tom guy, even Fern, expected something from me.

And nothing happened. Well, no one in the crowd harassed me to the point where I wanted recourse, anyway. When we walked onstage I was shocked to see how many people were there, crowded up against the stage and as far back as I could see. I felt all eyes on me, a feeling that I was starting to enjoy at this point, just a little bit. I also noticed how many *girls* were in the audience. Girls with their hands up in the air, mouths open in shrieks I couldn't single out because it seemed like *everyone* in the room was cheering — and we hadn't started to play.

Even if I thought Tom Manic was a douche, my chest swelled with pride that he was witnessing *this* show. It was impressive.

I looked back at Socks, who'd sat down behind the drums and was giving me a giant grin. Edgar on my right stared out across the crowd, thumping his fist on his bass. I looked over at Fern, who had thrown her head forward. Her white hair fell over her face like a wedding veil. Hands reached out towards her from the crowd. She lifted one hand, pointing a delicate finger to the girls in front of her. It was going to be awesome.

And it *was*.

I didn't even have to throw up on anyone.

There's a famous photo that was taken of us after this show. We're all sweaty and dishevelled of course, because we'd just gotten offstage, but I love the photo anyway. Socks is giving the most insane leer — showing all his teeth, and his hair looks like a bunch of wet straw. Edgar has his arms folded and his chin up, like he's all snobby or tough or something, which is hilarious. He's glaring. Fern's hair is half-covering her face and she's grasping my hand in one of hers, holding the neck of her guitar off the floor with her other one. The one eye you can see looks dark and wet, like she's been crying, but it's only sweaty eyeliner running down her cheek. I'm staring directly at the camera, my eyes ringed with melted black makeup, my lipstick smeared across my chin. It looks like smeared blood coming out of my mouth. I remember I felt such a sense of accomplishment when this photo was taken. I remember that I was worried my hand was going to bleed onto Fern's — I was sure the scabs on my palm had opened up during the show, and I couldn't tell if my glove was wet with blood or with sweat or both.

This was the night following our signing a record deal with good ol' Tom Manic, even though I disliked him. I guess I should add that it would be fair to say, as Edgar pointed out, that I pretty much disliked everyone we met, so my opinions couldn't really be trusted.

FORTY-TWO

Everyone knows the horror stories of disappointment and swindling that come with the two words *record deal*. Some people get pissed when a band they like signs a deal, because it means they've *sold out*. And I guess there's still some residual imagery that comes with it as well — rock stars wearing sunglasses, on inflatable mattresses floating in pools, drinking out of coconuts, getting wasted in hotel rooms, smashing glass tables, and the old stuffies at the record label chuckling and shaking their heads as they foot the bill — *oh, those crazy rock stars*.

Well, it isn't like that anymore, at least as far as I know. You can't trash a hotel room, because nobody wants to pay for your ass, because bands don't really sell billions of albums anymore. This doesn't mean that musicians are down-to-earth, humble folks who are just happy to play music. Oh, no, there's plenty of ego and entitlement. It's paired with a weird, panicky feeling, though. I think some of these clowns who get on labels

302

end up confused — they really do believe that the poolside lifestyle still exists somewhere for them. They'd do better to stick to their basement cocaine parties, where they can *truly feel they're partying like rock stars.* The whole "why be a small fish in a big pond when you can be the biggest douche in your neighbourhood" syndrome.

And of *course* you can do all the drugs you want and go to greasy parties and end up with a nosebleed, eating Vicodin, and depressed about your syphilis. But nobody's going to spoon you till you feel better, because there's someone better-looking than you who wants to party.

Is my bitterness showing? All of the things we saw with other bands were, of course, just background noise to the fact that getting on Recordead Records got us one step closer to being in the same room with DED. Who, I am willing to wager, were at one point the biggest douches in their neighbourhoods.

And I have to digress about Tom Manic too. Chest hair and woodpecker nose aside, he really did believe in Colostomy Hag and, from everything I can tell, we got a decent and fair deal from him. We didn't have a manager. It was always Socks who stood at the helm of our business decision-making. But he never led us wrong, so we signed with Recordead for a three-album contract.

Scream into This ended up being released with all the songs we'd been playing for over a year. We'd already released it ourselves, of course, but Tom had us re-record it at a better studio. I scorned the whole thing — especially when the guy in the studio asked me if I wanted the kick bump on — but the recordings do sound a hell of a lot better than our demos.

In case you don't know — whatever a band does, the record label advances them the money. And then they *recoup* it. So when a band gets a chunk of money to do an album — paying for things like studio time, or a producer, et cetera — the label

303

will get every penny back from record sales. Same with touring. It can get really complex, but let me just say that the band gets paid *last*. The label recoups, the sound guy gets paid, the bus driver gets paid, the merch person gets paid, everybody gets paid, and then whatever scraps are left, the band gets. That's because it's our *investment*. Besides, *why should an* artist *need money for doing something they love doing?*

We did some awesome photo shoots, and there were some just of me (one that made the cover of *Smasher* magazine of me holding a sword) and some of me and Fern, naturally. One photographer guy wanted both of us to wear these weird metal bikini things. Fern was pretty into the idea for some reason. It weirded me out. One minute she wasn't talking, the next she was dolling up in that crap. I definitely wasn't into it. There was nothing else for me to wear, so I ended up yanking this white sheer curtain off the window and wrapping myself in it like a shroud. Fern looked pretty good in that bikini, which is probably why she started showing up in all that "*sexy women in rock*" stuff. It's weird though, because I'd get mentioned in that garbage too. I guess all you have to do, really, is be female and show up.

One photographer who contacted us was particularly cool. She had a lot of ideas for band pictures, and all of them were pretty awesome, but naturally I love the one that I had suggested the most: us doing a reenactment of Judith slaying Holofernes. It was amazing getting to physically act out those parts for the shots — Fern holding Socks down on a bed, me bringing up the knife, and Edgar holding a candle, looking on, like some sort of guard. Of course there is no guard in the original painting, and Socks isn't anything like the Holofernes I've imagined, but I wore blue and Fern wore red and the image is dimly lit and the bed has long white curtains and the pictures are amazing.

So what if so many of these pictures end up being used now to illustrate the crimes Fern and I have committed? *PROPHETIC*, the headlines read, but in all honesty I don't know how realistic killing anyone was to me at that time. I don't know what was going on in Fern's mind. I'd definitely had my share of fantasies, and there was a hate burning inside me that would creep up at night, crawl up my throat like bile, almost burning. And then I would turn around and pour it into another Colostomy Hag design or another song idea.

I guess I was walking a thin line then, between trying to forget what had happened — quash it and compress it into a tiny little box — and then giving in to that sick fury. I'd let myself feel it a little sometimes, and my vision would go blurry, and my chest would tighten, and I'd press my lips together hard to keep myself from screaming till I was hoarse. And, of course, I would dig my fingernails into my palm and focus on the sting, and that would bring everything back around into focus again.

FORTY-THREE

I woke up in the vibrating coffin, and panic overtook me for a moment. It was dark. Absolutely dark. My hands jerked up from under the blanket and slammed into the ceiling right above my face, but the noise was absorbed by the rhythmic thrumming that accompanied the vibrating and jerking.

I'm on the tour bus.

Reaching to my right, I pulled aside the black plastic curtain that ran along the side of my bunk and peered out into the unlit corridor. My eyes adjusted, partially helped by a thin strip of light that shone beneath the door that led to the front lounge. Across the aisle from me was Fern's bunk, her curtain closed. Above her was Timmy — our tech, which is basically a fancy word for roadie — and his curtain was closed too. Beneath her was Edgar's bunk, with the curtain open. I could make out the wadded mounds of his sheets. Beneath me was Socks, and above me was our tour manager, Toad, who also did our live sound.

Toad was squat and chubby, with a belly so formidable that it always peeped out from beneath whatever black band shirt he wore. His hair was long and his face was bloated, with a crooked nose that had clearly been broken for him a few times. His face was actually froggy — to the point that when he said that he'd earned the nickname *Toad* for his prowess at *Super Mario Kart*, I'd actually opened my mouth to tell him what I considered to be the more likely truth. Luckily, I guess, I'd immediately received warning looks from all three of my wonderful bandmates.

It had become sort of a morning routine, this peeking out of my bunk to see who was up and who was still asleep. This was only the beginning of the second week of tour, but a few times the first week it had only been me and Timmy awake for a while in the front lounge. Roger, our grey-haired and grandfatherly bus driver, was pretty decent at making conversation while he drove, but I didn't really like being around Timmy. He was a quiet guy and just way too into gear and instruments. He and Edgar could talk for hours, but it was awkward with just the two of us.

I lay lazily in my bunk, staring into that corridor, listening to the engine, somewhat lulled by the motion. The first few nights on the bus had been horrible I'd alternated between lying awake, paralyzed with fear that we were either currently or about to be driving directly off a cliff, and being woken up every few minutes by the rocking and lurching and noise. I was becoming accustomed to it, but that was probably just out of exhaustion.

After the re-release of the album on Recordead Records, we'd done a few more shows around the area, a lot of promotion and interviews, and after a few weeks, the label wanted us to go out and promote the album. We were on tour with Gurgol — which was insane — and the headliner, Ripsawdomy. We were the third band on the bill, but it was an incredible tour to be on. We'd gotten the bus — paid for by good ol' Tom — and, with our laminates coolly worn on our hips, we tried to look like we knew what we were doing. We had toured before, of course, in the U.K., but the first morning of this tour, when I'd looked out the window into the parking lot of the venue at all the rough-looking, long-haired dudes milling around smoking, I had felt like the most incredible novice.

Ripsawdomy was not a band I was very familiar with. I'd heard of them, but I'd never gotten into them. They were four immense guys — one of them had to be almost seven feet tall — all with long hair and very dour expressions. They mainly stayed on their bus, from what I could tell, which was fine by me. The singer looked old and grizzled, and the younger guys didn't appear to have any interest in us at all.

But being with Gurgol — now that was fucking exciting. We hadn't *really* talked to them, but because we were coming offstage when they were going on, we'd had a few small interactions. It was amazing to be on tour with Marie-Lise and see her every day. I'd watch her in the mornings, when the three tour buses were all parked at the venue. She came off her tour bus with a little white dog and she'd walk it around the parking lot, sometimes drinking coffee from a travel mug. Once or twice I'd seen their singer, Josh, take the dog out in the mornings, or one of the other guys. I would watch from the front lounge windows, grateful that they were tinted so no one would know what a creepy fucker I was being.

At the side of stage in between sets, I'd passed Marie-Lise a few times and she always smiled politely, clearly distracted, but looking so damn gorgeous and put together. When Fern and I had met her at that café she'd looked so cute and casual in her jeans, but to see her before a show, in her stage clothes, was just awesome. I'd seen her so many times in videos and photographs, but it was nothing compared to the real thing, and close up. Her hair was still white, without a trace of the yellowy orange that so often haunts people who bleach their hair — Fern included. Her makeup was perfect, her skin powdered as pale as her hair, her false eyelashes with little gems on them, her perfect red lips, and her amazing outfits. She was alternating between three dresses on this tour — three identical dresses in different colours, and black stockings. It was all I could do not to stare at her every time I saw her, to just walk past all casual.

Fern had curled her hair and put bright red streaks into it. I was sure it was so that she would not look so obviously like she was trying to copy Marie-Lise. I liked the look. It was as if she'd grabbed clumps of her hair with bloody hands and just wrenched her fingers through the strands.

I don't know if I'd expected Marie-Lise to recognize us from that day in the café, but it didn't seem like she did. On the first day of tour, she and the other guys from Gurgol had said hello to us briefly, which was clearly their attempt to be nice and friendly. On tour people tend to only care about their own band. Well, I guess that's true in *life*, as well. At least they'd made the gesture. Here we were at the beginning of the second week and no one from Ripsawdomy had said anything to us yet. But, I mean, it wasn't like we were going out of our way either.

The shows had been good so far. We were easily playing in front of a thousand people a night, which were the biggest crowds for us yet. I'd seen a few of our T-shirts here and there, but based on the fact that pretty much everyone in the crowd was tall, long haired, scowling, and basically looked exactly like the guys from Ripsawdomy — it was a Ripsawdomy crowd. Some nights I'd noticed people watching us from the side of stage: some of the guys from Gurgol, maybe one or two of the Ripsawdomy guys, but I didn't want to gawk, so I wasn't sure. None of them watched the whole set, but I have to admit that when I knew they were watching, I tried to look *extra awesome*. We all felt like pros. Timmy would run onstage if any problems came up, we got a soundcheck every day (it was Gurgol who didn't — our gear was set up last, as we were first to play) and when we were done, we'd go relax on our *tour bus*, for god's sake. Timmy, Toad, and the guys would go have a drink or something, or we'd stand side of stage and watch the other bands. When the night was over, we'd get on the bus and sleep or watch a movie or whatever. If the next venue was really far, Roger would drive through the night with the other two buses, like a fleet. If it wasn't so bad, he'd stay at the hotel and arrive early in the morning for the drive. It was starting to feel like a real tour.

I walked out into the front lounge, blinded for a moment by the sun. Edgar and Toad were on one of the couches. The countryside swept past the windows; I could hear Roger whistling up in the driver's seat.

"Where are we?" I said, squinty.

"Washington State," Toad said around a mouthful of cereal, balancing the bowl against his chest so as not to spill. "Not far from the club."

"Maybe about twenty minutes out," Roger offered in a jolly voice.

I plunked down next to Edgar on the couch and gazed out the window.

"Nice to see you too, *Little Miss Sunshine*," Toad said.

"Whatever, *Toad*," I said, glad that the name was also an insult. I didn't really like Toad, and mornings on the bus did nothing good for my mood. I looked like shit, I felt like shit, and it was impossible to fix it. Bus water is kind of gross, so you brush your teeth with bottled water. And you always wait till you get to the venue or a gas station so you can use their toilets and wash your face and whatever else, with what is hopefully clean water. But let's be frank. Venue bathrooms are horrible.

Some backstage dressing rooms are nice, some have showers, and even laundry. But most of the time you're washing your face in a sink where some kid probably threw up a bunch of beer a few hours earlier.

The bus pulled up to the venue, Bennys — I found the missing apostrophe irritating. It had a huge parking lot and there were some buildings on either side of it, but otherwise we were in the middle of nowhere. I saw that Ripsawdomy's bus was already parked; Roger pulled up alongside it, grinning out the window at the other driver, who was smoking in the lot. Gurgol's bus was nowhere to be seen.

"This place seems weird," I commented. "Sort of isolated."

"They've been having big metal shows here for years. This place is a *classic!*" Toad said, and from next to me I heard Edgar suck in a quick breath of annoyance. We both knew was what going to happen next. Toad launched into some long-winded story about some band he'd toured with a few years ago, and how they'd played at Bennys, and how *those were the days* when the club could serve booze past 2 a.m. and the Hells Angels would show up and whatever else. I had a bowl of cereal and gazed out the window.

I'd picked up the somewhat revolting habit of smoking, but only because it afforded me the chance to gracefully exit a situation and buy myself ten minutes alone outside. When I was done my cereal, I tiptoed through the bunk area to the empty back lounge, found my clothing bag, took off my stupid flannel pyjama pants and pulled on the dirty jeans I'd been wearing every day. Then I changed into a T-shirt, grabbed the hoody with the cigarettes in the pocket, went through the bunk area, noted that Fern's curtain was still closed, walked back up past Edgar, Toad, and now Timmy and Socks — who were all talking about guitar strings or something — and left the bus.

It was a little bit chilly, being the end of September, and I

311

walked down the thin space between the two buses towards the open lot behind them and lit my cigarette.

When I cleared the two buses, I hesitated. The very tall Ripsawdomy guy stood there by himself, slouched in his hoody, also smoking. We made eye contact and I froze, intimidated.

"Sorry," I said, as if he owned the parking lot and I was a bothersome insect.

"No, no, it's okay," he said, waving his hand at me for some reason. "You're in the opening band, right?"

"Yeah. I'm Rachel," I said, walking closer and extending my hand to him, immediately feeling like a fool. He reached to shake it, looking down at me, and though his hood was up the long light brown hair tumbled forward from it and his eyes were really blue, like-the-fucking-spring-sky blue, and his face looked smooth, really nice skin, he was handsome, no — he was *cute*, even despite the stupid chin-beard, and I swallowed hard. As we shook hands, his brow furrowed and a frown spread over his face. "I'm Chris."

"Yes, you're in Ripsawdomy," I said brightly, trying to make sense of what was happening. I figured that my head would only come halfway up his chest if we were standing closer. I tried to calculate exactly where it would reach without looking anywhere but at his face.

"Yep." He puffed on his cigarette, studying me, and his frown deepened. I felt awkward, wondering if he disliked me, wishing I had at least brushed my hair this morning, wondering why the fuck I cared. I recognized him as the guitar player, but not the singer, who also played guitar. I didn't want to make too much eye contact with him, even as he stared at me, knowing somehow that he would easily read my nervous turmoil. The cigarette was starting to make me feel sick, but I guess it wasn't really the cigarette.

I fumbled for something to say, and as my mind raced, a

hideous stench reached my nostrils, wafting in the cool morning breeze. It stank worse than anything I'd ever smelled, like shit and blood and something even worse, and it hit me like a rock to the face. I yelped, "What the fuck?"

Chris didn't even react. He gestured with his hand. "There's a slaughterhouse next door."

"That's *brutal!*" I clapped my sleeve over my lower face.

"I've played here six times," he said, unfazed. "Stinks every time."

I didn't want him to associate me with bad hair, lame conversation, and that horrible abattoir reek, but I didn't want to leave either. "You've played here six times?"

"Yep."

"I understand it's a really, uh, *classic* venue or whatever."

He stared at me. "Yeah, I guess it is sort of . . . *classic.*"

Immediately I was back in high school, in the hallway with Craig, and my idiotic *grapevine* comment. I realized I couldn't see Craig's face in my mind. I couldn't remember anything except he had long light brown hair, as did the giant in front of me. Odd how things can change, yet stay the same: here I was standing in front of a real metal musician, on tour, beside my own tour bus, and yet I still sounded like a bungling idiot.

I puffed on my cigarette to buy myself time, aware of his scrutinizing frown. I met his eyes for a split second and all I saw on his face was disapproval, and I felt my cheeks flush with embarrassment. "Well, sorry," I said, throwing the butt into the gravel. "I didn't mean to bother you."

"No bother," he said.

"Heh, well, okay. Have a good day," I managed to get out, then turned and made my way back between the buses as gracefully as I could in case he was still watching. My cheeks pounded with blood. I didn't give a shit what he thought, right? It galled me that I just couldn't manage to sound cool, no matter how hard I tried. I looked like a fool in front of that guy, and now he'd think our band sucked even worse than he probably did yesterday. Well done, Rachel.

FORTY-FOUR

Bennys' parking lot filled up quickly, a definite sign that it would be a great show. We had a small dressing room decorated with the requisite penis graffiti. I pulled on a pair of my bloodstained white knee socks. Fern had stayed in her bunk all afternoon until our soundcheck, and emerged looking worn and withdrawn. She put on her makeup quietly, and I watched her in the mirror. Our eyes met and I smiled at her, and she smiled back, but it was a tired smile. The sound of Timmy checking the gear onstage and the chattering of Toad and the guys faded to a wash as we looked at each other.

We were halfway through the set and it was a good one. Despite Fern's melancholy, she was absolutely savage, kicking the audience in front of her into a frenzy. For some reason Edgar was on top of his game too, a wash of flying hair, and I figured it was because we'd done six shows in a row and were starting to get into a good physical and mental place to be for the tour. I was in pretty fine form as well — I'd torn a scab off my palm accidentally, leaped in the air, and when I landed, I smeared some of the blood down the side of my face. I whipped around to the left and saw Chris's towering figure watching at side of stage next to Timmy.

I whirled away, pretending I hadn't seen him. I *wished* I hadn't — I was now hyper conscious of every step I took, every gesture, every shriek. I felt clownish and juvenile with the blood on my face.

He remained there for the entire set, and when I left the stage there he stood, talking with some of the guys from Gurgol. I glanced at him, and he was looking at me with the same grouchy expression. I hurried past into the dressing room, my clothes soaked, out of breath.

I buried my face in a towel, appreciating having our small dressing room to myself for a few moments while the others and Timmy got the gear offstage. I turned to the mirror, examining my flushed face and sweaty, scraggly hair, and then I saw him appear in the doorway behind me.

"Is that real blood on your socks?" he asked.

"Yes," I said, looking at myself again, very conscious of my shiny red Rudolph nose and smeared makeup. I looked truly horrible and was a bit irritated that he would just follow me here immediately after our performance without giving me five minutes to chill out and comb my damn hair or whatever.

Edgar appeared in the doorway beside him. "Oh, hey man!"

"Great show, dude," Chris said to him, and they did one of those stupid finger-snapping handshakes that a lot of guys just seem to instinctively know how to do.

"Oh, cool, thanks for watching," Edgar said, clearly elated

that Chris had watched the set. "It's a great crowd, they're really excited for you guys."

While they chatted I took the opportunity to put some powder on my face and fix up my hair a little bit, and then Socks and Fern came in. Toad followed them, and one of the other guys from Ripsawdomy walked past and must've seen Chris so he stopped in, and they all started talking loudly and drinking beer. We heard Gurgol go onstage, and I stood next to Fern and smiled and talked, and all the while I just felt Chris's eyes on me. Even though I didn't look at him once, I couldn't stop smiling this stupid little smile. I'm pretty sure I was batting my eyelashes.

So things continued like that for a few days, which on a tour feels like an eternity. Chris stood by the side of the stage and watched our set every night, and sometimes guys from his band or Gurgol would watch too. And I'd watch Gurgol and sometimes I'd watch Ripsawdomy, but I refused to stand at the side of the stage like that. I didn't want him to see me there, so I'd stand just out of his line of vision, aligned with an amp or something, so I could just stare at him as he played. The band was pretty good. Their singer, Chick, had a pretty unfriendly air about him, and he didn't really bother with us or with anyone else, but it seemed like for the most part the bands were starting to warm up to each other. At first, things on the tour were all about being efficient and everyone stayed out of each other's way, but gradually we were all making friends.

The nights had a chill, but none of us were complaining. We were slowly making our way south, and soon enough the air would be heavy and humid and we'd be sweating, and we'd give anything for a chilly night in the parking lot after the venue had closed, snug in a hoody, smoking in the dark. It was one such night when I was outside, around the side of our bus. I could hear a group of tech guys and band guys smoking and laughing across the lot, but I felt awkward joining them, so I just sat in my spot and listened to the crickets in the long grass that lined the parking lot behind me. The others in my band were on the bus watching a movie.

As I sat smoking, I heard the telltale gravel crunch that someone was approaching. I already knew who it would be, and when Chris appeared, I smiled at him.

"I was hoping I'd find you out here," he said. "Thought I'd take a walk over and see. Is there room on that curb?"

"Sure," I said, sliding over. He lowered himself down beside me, sighing, and lit up his own cigarette.

"Getting warmer," he commented.

"It is."

"Soon, it'll be too hot to breathe. Man, I *love* the heat." He stretched his arms over his head, yawning. "Fuck, I'm tired."

"It was a great crowd tonight," I remarked.

"Fucking rad." He nodded. "You guys were killer."

"Thanks."

"You're a great fucking singer. Really take charge of the crowd."

"Thanks."

"I really like watching you." He swayed sideways, playfully bumping my shoulder with his.

I fumbled for words. "Well, uh — I'm glad that you do."

I looked sideways at him, and he was looking at me, and when our eyes met, he smiled, and I realized that I hadn't seen him smile before. He'd always just been wearing that grouchy, scrutinizing scowl. His teeth were straight and the smile lifted his face, almost illuminated it. I smiled back.

"Look, Rachel, I was just wondering, I mean, maybe one of

these nights, after the show —"

He was cut off by the sudden appearance of Fern and Toad coming around the side of the bus. Toad took one look at us and then fixed me with a leering smirk. "Oh, are we *interrupting* anything?"

Chris got up and the two of them did another one of those handshake things, and for some reason I couldn't bring myself to look at Fern as she lit her cigarette.

"Nah, man, it's all good," Chris said. "Just smokin' with Rachel here." He took a last drag of his cigarette and flicked the butt into the darkness. "Well, have a good night, guys," he said, and left.

"What was that all about?" Toad asked, lighting his own smoke.

"Nothing. He likes the band," I said, aware that I was trying to pacify Fern as well. I had this impression that she would feel betrayed by me hanging out with Chris, though when I did finally look at her, she didn't look perturbed. She just stood, placidly smoking and listening to our conversation while covering a yawn.

"That guy's one lucky dude — he gets *so* many chicks," Toad grinned. "You know who his ex is, right? That model, the fetish chick, Sophie Cleaver."

Images flashed in my mind of a black-haired, corseted, '40s-styled girl with pin curls in a bathtub wearing stockings and stilettos. I'd seen pictures of Sophie Cleaver. I swallowed hard, and Toad laughed, obviously noticing my discomfort. "She's hot," he pointed out needlessly.

"Why'd they break up?" I said.

"Ah, who knows? Maybe because he was getting so much action on the road," he chuckled. Fern shot him a withering look, which I doubled. Toad had this way of talking like he was always surrounded by a group of really douchey guys.

319

"You barely even know him. That shit's a rumour. He seems like a nice guy," Fern said defensively, and I raised my chin.

"Yep," Toad said. "He's an awesome guy. I guess I'd just be careful, is all, if you're getting *involved* with him or whatever, Rachel."

I followed the two of them back onto the bus and went to my bunk, my mind spinning. He'd dated a famous and gorgeous pin-up fetish model with a great body, and here I was, short and not famous and wearing filthy stage clothes. I pictured my sweaty, blotchy post-show face, and my dirty, matted hair, and compared it to the perfect makeup, the smooth skin, the pouty perfection of Sophie Cleaver. I winced, burying my face in the pillow. And was it true about the girls on the road? In the short while we'd been on tour I hadn't seen Chris with any girls backstage. He was the quiet one in his band — the others would yell and party and get all rowdy, and he always just seemed to be the quiet observer. But I barely knew him. I felt like an idiot. And what was I going to do? *Ask* him? Look like a jealous weirdo? And why *was* I jealous?

Lying there, processing these thoughts in the dark, I heard the bus engine start and felt the gentle vibration that was starting to become soothing. The bus pulled out of the parking lot, beginning our drive through the night. As I drifted off to sleep I heard the Velcro tear of another bunk curtain open and close.

FORTY-FIVE

The next day I woke up with some inane resolve to ignore Chris, or something — some juvenile plan to pull away from him and thus cause him to worry what was bothering me. I could put on this self-righteous disgust at him for *all of his many affairs* or whatever, and it would result in him having compassion for me and wanting to impress me or something. The plan was stupid and didn't end up happening anyway. I didn't really see Chris at all that day — his band had somewhere to go, a radio interview, maybe. I don't know. They weren't at the venue all day, their crew soundchecked for them.

We were somewhere in Florida, in a horrible part of town. There were dumpsters everywhere and it *stank*. Our buses were parked in the back lot very close together. There were creepy crackheads wandering around through the alleys. Toad warned us not to go far from the venue, basically not to leave the parking lot, so we hung out on the bus. Edgar was taking pictures of some of these derelicts through the bus window. I remember Toad, Timmy, and Socks had a magazine with Sophie Cleaver on the cover and were drooling over her. I was all quiet and grumpy because I was insecure. It was stupid.

I don't really remember the show — it was one in a line of many — but I do remember feeling bad for the kids at this show because they'd had to line up outside the club and it was just such a shitty neighbourhood to have to be in. I don't think Chris watched the show that night; I don't remember — fuck, I guess it's all just eclipsed by what happened after.

I was sitting on the bus after midnight, Toad and Socks playing some video game, Edgar and Timmy watching a movie in the back lounge. Fern wasn't on the bus — she'd stayed back in the venue to use the phone or wash up or something, and Roger wasn't going to be there until around 4 a.m. because it was only a few hours' drive to the next venue. He was at his hotel room.

So everything seemed pretty normal. I had changed into shorts and a black T-shirt and was watching Toad and Socks's game, then I decided to go for a cigarette. Toad, hammering controller buttons, didn't take his eyes off the screen as I put on my hoody. "Don't leave the lighted areas of the parking lot," he warned. "And go into the venue, tell Fern to get her ass on this bus. I don't want to have to spend my night chasing after any of you."

Yeah, you look real *worried.* "Whatever," I said. I stepped off the bus, my eyes sweeping the dark parking lot. I noted with irritation that Ripsawdomy's bus was already gone, and I'd had no interaction with Chris the whole day. Gurgol's bus was parked next to ours, shades drawn. Light flickered from within — it looked like the band was watching TV or something.

I walked behind our bus, my eyes scanning the dark lot. We'd parked beneath the one light in the lot, which in my opinion

322

sort of made us sitting ducks. I sat on a curb just beyond the light with my back to a brick wall and lit my cigarette.

To my left was the back of the venue and a short alley that led to a street. To my right about fifteen feet away was another dark building and a dark alley that I couldn't see the end of — it loomed like a long dark mouth. I stared at that alley for a few moments, trying to see farther inside of it, but I couldn't make anything out. My skin crawled, goosebumps rising on my arms despite the hot night air. I reassured myself that I would have plenty of time to run onto the bus if anyone came loping out of that alleyway towards me.

I resolved to smoke faster than I would normally, and as I puffed, I gazed at the back of the venue. I noticed that all the lights were dark — the back door was closed. Wasn't Fern still in there? The finality of that closed door, the stillness of the lot, gave the impression that the venue had been closed for a while.

Where the fuck was Fern?

Fear knotted my stomach. I actually felt it wrench and contort hideously as my mind tried to figure out where she could be. I felt my whole body break into a sweat, soaking my shirt, and my eyes darted around the shadows of the parking lot. My growing panic was only compounded by the noise that I heard next, the sound that floated gently from the dark chasm to my right.

"Hey."

I was on my feet, frozen, my every sense attuned directly to that alleyway, my breath ragged, my eyes unblinking and straining into that dark gap, feeling like they could burst out of my skull.

"Rachel? Come here."

I swallowed, my mouth dry. It was Fern. I had no idea what she was doing in that alley. She didn't sound hurt, she sounded excited somehow, like she'd found something. I took a tentative

323

step towards her voice.

"Hurry."

My eyes adjusted as I got into the darkness, and I could make out a few overflowing trash cans and a figure that I guessed was Fern. She was standing over a pile of garbage. The whole alley smelled horrible, like old booze and rotten food, and I smelled sweat, probably mine.

"What's going on?"

"*Shhhhh.*" She leaned in and continued in a low voice. "I need your help."

"Okay." I waited for her to continue, my eyes wide and dry, trying to absorb everything they could in the darkness. She was still wearing her show clothes, and she had an excited energy to her and seemed jumpy and fidgety.

"Look." She gestured down to the pile of trash she was standing above.

Confused, I looked down and realized that it wasn't a pile of garbage at all — Fern was standing above a *guy*. He was lying on his back and I noticed he was shaking slightly, his eyes bulging as wide as mine felt, glaring up at us.

"*Whore,*" he croaked, and Fern pulled back and kicked him — in the side of the head — *hard*. His head snapped to the side and he groaned.

"Shut the fuck up," she said, hissing down at him.

"Fern, what's going on?" I whispered, feeling a jumpiness of my own beginning, clenching and unclenching my fists.

"I'm not sure. I'm not really sure, Rachel."

"Okay. Okay. Who is this guy?"

"I was coming out of the venue," she said. "I heard a girl, she screamed. It was some druggie chick, some homeless girl."

"*A stupid bitch like you,*" the guy said, and Fern kicked him again, this time connecting the toe of her boot to his jaw, and my mouth filled with saliva as I saw his face tilt to the side to spit out a tooth in a drool of blood.

"He grabbed her," Fern said. "He was touching her and he *hit* her, Rachel, and he dragged her into this alley. And I just followed him in. He had her down on the ground. He was pulling off her clothes, and she was crying, Rachel. She sounded like a little girl."

"I bet you bitches'd *love* to know what I was gonna do to 'er," the guy slurred.

"What did you do, Fern?"

"There's a bunch of old liquor bottles lying around." Fern gestured absently. "I grabbed one and I just hit him in the head with it. A couple times. He sort of rolled off her. She ran away."

We stood silently. The only sounds were his ragged breathing and spitting. I felt blood race through my veins, making them feel icy, cold, snaking through my body. I knew where this was going. I was stunned by her violence. Her excitement was contagious, and I wanted it to continue, but I wanted it to stop. I didn't want to get caught here. I dimly thought about Toad, about the guys, if they came off the bus. They would come looking for us.

"What do you want to do?" I said.

She didn't say anything, her hair hanging in her face, her eyes locked to mine. "He's a dirty son of a bitch rapist."

We stared at each other, trapped in this weird purgatory, and I swallowed hard, not sure what to say or do to tip the scales and cause whatever was going to happen to happen. I knew at any moment someone could find us, and my ears were alert, almost aching to catch and decipher any sound.

Fern looked around, and I watched as she bent and picked up a dark piece of cinderblock or brick. She turned her full attention down to the man on the ground, who, for some reason, was making a repetitive, low, raspy chuckle like a skipping record. Fern stepped over him, paused for a moment, and then raised the brick over her head.

I have a snapshot in my mind's eye of Fern in this moment, her hair blocking her face from my vision, her long, lean arms stretched high. To be honest I don't know if I could have done it — been the one to change things forever the way she did, been the one to raise the brick. As she brought it down, I felt the way you feel when you go down that first hill on a roller coaster. That relief, but at the same time, that twinge of regret. *Here we go, too late to stop it now — do I want to stop it? Is this terrifying or fucking amazing —*

I don't know what sound was made when she slammed that brick into the guy's face because a shriek of laughter erupted out of me at the same time it impacted.

You know, I wish I could say that all the fantasies I'd had, the weird convoluted images of Judith and the maidservant and putting me and Fern into those roles, came to life for a moment. I wish there had been this sort of mysterious, mythological, candlelit romance to it all — but there wasn't. She brought that brick down onto that guy's chuckling face a few times, and I just *couldn't stop laughing.* And I was trying to keep quiet, trying to keep that laugh in, with my hands over my mouth, gasping. It was really weird. And she ended up falling, I think she was crying — and by this time it was pretty horrible, the guy on the ground didn't have much of a face. It was too dark for me to really tell, and I didn't want to see, really. But he was making this weird whistling noise, this wheeze, so he wasn't dead, it was like air was still moving in and out somewhere. And she was just sitting there and she was crying and told me to finish it, to finish him.

And I was still laughing. Fuck, I don't know why. I reached down for the brick, I tried to carefully avoid the wet end of it. It was heavier than I'd expected and my arms felt rubbery and weak — for a second I wasn't sure if I was going to drop it. But I grasped it in both hands and I brought it down on the mashed dark blur where it seemed his face used to be. I raised it and brought it down again, trying to ignore the warm splashes on my arms and face. I mean, this really was disgusting. I shut my mouth pretty quick — I didn't want any of that shit going in my mouth and giving me diseases or whatever — but I still managed to laugh through my nose, like a true maniac. At least Fern cried.

The whistling noise stopped and I paused with the brick, listening. I could hear Fern's ragged, short breaths. The man was still. The alley was still and heavy. I stood like a statue. A heavy, meaty stench began to drift, moist and hot, from the pile of body beneath me. My stomach lurched.

"Don't puke," Fern ordered, standing up beside me. She took the brick from my hands. "We have to go. We have to clean off and we have to bring this brick with us."

"*Okay.*" My voice sounded slow and stupid. Fern took off her dark, pleated skirt, and started wiping her face, her arms. As I watched her, I heard the familiar rumble of the bus engine from the parking lot at the end of the alley. Roger was back on the bus. *How long had we been back here?*

"We have to go," Fern said urgently, tossing me her skirt. I hastily wiped off my face, my arms. I gave her the skirt back, and she began to walk down the alley, hopping back into it.

"They're going to know," I mumbled, walking behind her, tucking my hair behind my ears. It was stiff and clumped — probably a real nice mixture of days' worth of show sweat and blood.

"Just go fast. It's too dark, no one will see," she replied, tucking in her blouse. I saw she was carrying the brick. *The murder weapon.*

We emerged back into the parking lot, and in its orangey light I looked down at the palms of my hands. There were some smears on my arms, some brown streaks, and thank god I'd worn black. The front of Fern's white blouse was spattered. There was nothing to be done. The Gurgol bus was gone. I hadn't heard it leave, which seemed odd. I'd been paying such attention to every sound, I thought I'd been so *aware* back there.

Fern yanked the bus door open, and I climbed up behind her. Roger was sitting in the driver's seat, which, thankfully, was pretty dark. "Almost left you girls behind!" he joked, not even looking up from his map book. We laughed in unison, high and feminine, and pulled back the curtain to enter the front lounge.

Socks and Toad were still playing their game. Fern pushed immediately to go through to the bunk area, and I was right behind her.

"Not so fast," Toad said. We stopped and looked at him. His eyes remained locked to the television screen. "I don't know what you girls were doing out there, but this is a *bad city.*" He finally took his eyes off the screen to look at us. "You look like shit! Jesus!" We didn't answer. "Anyways, for fuck's sake, we all need a shower. It's a day off tomorrow, and I want everyone fucking washed up and doing their goddamn laundry." He said it as though there were more people here than just me, Fern, and Socks. "This bus is starting to smell like shit."

"Yes, it is," Roger confirmed in a good-natured voice from up front through the curtain.

I glanced at Socks, and he was staring at me. I looked away, then wondered if that was a suspicious thing to do. Fern held the brick behind her back. I didn't dare look at it. She murmured some affirmative to Toad, then went into the bunk area, closing the door behind her. I opened the door to the tiny bathroom in the lounge and flicked on the light.

The bus started moving, and I instinctively grabbed the counter to brace myself until I could adapt to the motion. It was becoming second nature at this point — I'd got my *sea legs* from standing, walking, and sleeping on a moving bus. Looking in the mirror, I was relieved to see my face was clear of blood. It had dried in my hair, though, and there'd be no way to wash it until we were at a hotel shower — or at least a proper-sized sink. I grabbed some paper towels, wet them in the pathetic drinking-fountain sized bus sink, and began to towel off my arms.

Socks's massive frame appeared in the bathroom door. "Can we talk?"

"Of course," I smiled at him. It wasn't unusual for any of us to towel off in a sink, and I went quickly, wiping the areas where I'd spotted the worst streaks while I retained eye contact with Socks.

"Where'd you guys go tonight?"

"We were just in the venue, then we walked around a bit."

"Shit, Rachel! Don't do that! I was too scared to go anyplace in this city. You could've been fucking killed."

I laughed sharply. "You worry too much."

"Look, promise me you won't do anything like that again. Me and Edgar worry about the two of you, you know." He lowered his voice. "Fern's just not right anymore, and I get that you and she are really close and need time to yourselves. I know that. But please just don't take any dumb risks."

"Okay," I said.

"What the fuck is that shit on your shirt?" he asked, eyes flicking down.

I looked down and saw dark splatter on the black fabric. It was so obviously blood. I looked up at Socks, met his wide blue eyes, and didn't know what to say.

He sighed, clutching at his own shirt. "I totally puked on this shirt three days ago and tried to wash it out at the venue with that pink fluorescent pump soap," he confided. "It still smells. All our shit's so dirty. You want to hit a Laundromat tomorrow?"

"After I wash my hair," I grinned, holding up a matted, blood-crusted handful off my head.

"I hear you. I puked in my hair too," he said, "and it's *still* stiff."

We smiled at each other and he retreated back to his seat beside Toad. I finished rinsing all visible areas of my arms and face, then brushed my teeth with bottled water. Fern then appeared in the doorway. She'd changed into a black shirt and cut off sweatpants.

"My clothes are in a plastic bag in the back lounge. I had to get changed in the bunk area cause the others are back there, but they didn't ask any questions." She talked in a quiet voice, but with a casual lilt to it. I stepped out of the bathroom so she could get in, and I watched her hold some paper towels under the tap.

"You okay?" she asked me.

"Yes," I nodded. "You?"

"I'm great," she said and smiled at me. "I think it's going to be okay."

I left her in the bathroom and went into the long, dark corridor of the bunk area. The door to the back lounge was closed. I went to my bunk and in the darkness, quickly took off my soiled T-shirt and jeans. I wadded them up in a ball and put them at the foot of my bunk. Then, just in my underwear, I pulled the covers over me.

After the sticky heat, the rush of air conditioning made my skin erupt into goosebumps, crawling over me unpleasantly. I pulled the blanket up to my nose, loving the soft feel of the pillow, relieved we would have a day off tomorrow, that I would step under the clean spray of a shower. My eyes drifted closed, and my thoughts turned to Chris. It seemed I hadn't thought of him for so long, as if days had passed. I wondered where he was going to be spending his day off tomorrow.

FORTY-SIX

We stopped halfway to the next show at a Florida hotel. Socks, Fern, and I stepped off our frigid bus into that humid soup. The sky was blue, the sun blazing. Fern was chatty, and that dank alley felt the hundreds of miles away that it was. I hadn't had time to process last night. Part of me felt like it hadn't actually happened, but then I would catch Fern's eye and she'd smile, and I knew it was real. Her smile was bigger than it had been for a long time, and her positive mood was infectious. As the three of us made our way towards the hotel, she linked arms with Socks and joked around — I hadn't seen her like this in forever.

The three of us carried backpacks full of dirty clothes to the laundry room, and there was Edgar, grinning smugly at us as he pulled his clean clothes out of a dryer. He was always up before the rest of us.

"Anyone want to hit the beach?" Fern said brightly. Edgar

immediately looked at Socks and me for an explanation for her good mood. I shrugged.

"I'll join you," Edgar said, smiling at Fern. It felt good. When the band was first forming, Edgar and Fern had spent so much time working out parts together. Her withdrawal had caused a lot of confusion for Edgar, and he'd become quieter and less outgoing as well. He was a quiet guy to begin with — and Fern had brought him out of his shell.

"Awesome! I want to get some cheeseburgers. I feel like I haven't eaten in fucking forever."

While Edgar, Socks, and Fern talked about how to spend the day off, I crammed wadded handfuls of my wretched laundry into a washing machine. The clothes smelled sweaty, wet, and musty. I quickly shoved in last night's clothes.

Once the laundry was set, Edgar and Fern took off to check out the restaurant next door while Socks and I headed up to the room. Toad, who'd left us card keys and a note with the room number, was lying on the bed in a clean shirt and shorts, his long hair wrapped in a white towel.

"Timmy should be out soon — once he's done jacking off," Toad said, flicking channels; I could hear the shower running through the closed bathroom door. He looked at us. "You guys look like shit. Rachel, your hair looks like a wig made out of dog shit." I glared. He laughed.

Once Timmy came out of the bathroom it was my turn — and my god, that shower felt good. I washed my hair, horrified by the dirty water that rinsed out, and then shampooed twice more. It sucks how gross touring can be. We'd had thirteen shows in a row — and nothing but a sink shower on any of those days. Girls who want to sleep with rock stars should remember that. The guy you're making out with may not even have brushed his *teeth*, let alone washed his ass, for days.

I put on a clean sundress and left the bathroom. Timmy and Toad were both lying on one bed, Socks on the other, all staring at the TV. I took Socks's place when he got up to shower.

I'd like to say that I felt some overwhelming need to meditate on the events of the night before, that it was haunting me, that I felt the urge to confess to the others what we had done. But honestly, the only thing that had really followed me into that morning was the grossness. The blood and the whistling noise. The sweat and the darkness. The smell. The worry of getting caught. As Toad flipped channels, I wondered if anything would be on the news about the dead guy. But I wasn't very worried about it. I felt cool, clean, and comfortable lying on that big bed.

The telephone rang in our room. Toad answered. "Hello? . . . yeah. Oh, hey man. Good, good. You?"

He chatted for a few minutes. I tuned him out until he held the phone out to me. "Rachel, it's for you."

"What? Who is it?"

"Just answer it and find out," he said, so I took the phone and held it to my ear.

"Hello?"

"Rachel?" a male voice asked.

"Yes . . . Who is this?"

"Uh, this is Chris, from Ripsawdomy," he said. "Is this a bad time?"

"No," I said, immediately breaking into a nervous sweat.

"I got your tour manager's room number from ours," he said. "I hope that's okay."

"Yeah! It's fine."

"So you guys stopped in the same city we did," he said. "Toad said you're staying at the Cherrywood Inn."

"I guess so."

"Do you want to do something today?" I could tell he was nervous too, and I found myself grinning. He said he would come by the hotel and look for our bus in the parking lot in about two hours. We hung up.

"So?" Toad asked as Socks came back into the room.

"I'm going to meet him, we're going to hang out or something."

"A *date*!"

"Shut up," I said, glaring at Toad. I fixed Timmy with a glare as well. Even though Timmy and I barely spoke, he seemed to be Toad's little follower, so I figured I may as well treat him the same way.

"With who?" Socks said.

"With *Chris*," Toad tattled.

Socks looked at me. "Really?"

"It isn't a date," I said.

"Go, Rachel!" Socks laughed. "Marry him and get us famous."

"Rachel doesn't exactly strike me as the guy's *type*," Toad said. "I mean, he dated *Sophie Cleaver*."

"Yeah, totally," I said. "Normally he likes *hot chicks*. What a step down, eh, Toad?"

"I'm just kidding, don't be so sensitive!" Toad said.

"I think Sophie Cleaver's ugly," Timmy said.

"Well, it isn't a date anyway. And I don't care who he used to date, or currently is dating, or whatever."

"Yes, it is," Toad said. "And you *totally do*."

"She's so *skinny*," Fern commented. She and I were on the bus. I'd decided to get ready for my outing with Chris there, to avoid Toad's remarks from his bed-throne. Fern and Edgar had brought back a bag of tacos, and once we'd eaten, Fern had

334

followed me back to the bus. Now she was reading one of Toad's tattoo magazines with a feature on Sophie Cleaver.

"It's because that stupid corset she's wearing is yanked so tight," I muttered, trying not to overdo my eyeliner. A few weeks of putting on show makeup had kind of ruined my gauge for what looked pretty and what looked garish.

Fern turned the page. "She's got her own clothing line. Shit, this girl must be rich."

"Please stop talking about it."

"Oh, here we go: *Sophie and heavy metal guitarist Chris Egerton called it quits in July after three years together.* Three years! Shit."

"I don't know what the hell he could possibly want with me," I said.

"You're awesome. Much prettier than Sophie Cleaver," Fern said. "She's all airbrushed in these photos. You look great without all that. Plus you have talent. You're interesting. I mean, any one of us can pose and look sexy. Fuck, remember all that stupid *Women of Metal* shit I did? The photos don't even *look* like me. It doesn't take talent to stick out your chest and remove any hint of intelligence from your expression." She laughed. I laughed too. This really, truly, was the most engaging, most fun, most *herself* Fern I had seen in so, so long. It was like a switch had been thrown within her.

"So are you and Edgar going to the beach?"

"I think all of us might go, except for you."

"Oh shit. I'll have to forego the pleasure of seeing Toad in a bathing suit."

"I might have to loan him one of my bikini tops," Fern said, and we howled.

"You feel better, huh," I said.

"I do. Much. I feel like last night was a step for me. You know?"

"I think so."

It was sort of funny — we were talking about a murder as if it was a self-help exercise, like meditation or making a collage or something. I have to admit, I felt lighter too. I don't know how to describe this, really. Maybe it was like we'd taken back some small level of control, or somehow expressed an aspect of how we'd felt inside since all that horrible shit happened with DED. Like we were letting out some of the anger. And let's be real. No one was going to miss that guy from that Florida parking lot. You show me one news segment, one missing persons report, one bereaved family member, *anyone* who gave a shit. Yeah, they identified the guy's body when his fingerprints came up in the system because he'd already been to prison for *rape* and *child molestation*. And it didn't even make the news until everything came out about Fern and me and someone connected the dots. So — my friend and I not only started feeling better about ourselves and our lives by smashing that guy's face in with a brick, but we *helped*. We did a *good thing*. But, sure, I get it — not everyone sees it that way.

FORTY-SEVEN

Chris came lumbering across the parking lot wearing the same perplexed frown he always seemed to wear around me, his hair obviously washed and dried — it hadn't looked so *soft* since I'd met him, I adolescently thought. I tried to keep myself from puffing too heavily on my cigarette as I rose from my seat on the curb.

"Hi," he said in his deep voice as he neared.

"Hi," I said, and froze as he leaned down to stiffly hug me. I hugged back. For some reason I patted his shoulder blade as we embraced, the true sign of an awkward, platonic hug — the way one hugs an estranged family member. It sucked. But he was so tall, and he smelled clean, and that soft hair brushed my cheek.

"So," he said, clearing his throat. "There's, er, a carnival thing going on up the road a little ways. Did you want to go check it out?"

"Sure," I replied, and we fell into stride beside each other. Well, that's putting it gracefully. Since his legs seemed about twice as long as mine, I broke into a coltish trot beside him to keep up. He slowed his pace. Eventually we found a common ground. God, it really was uncomfortable. I wanted him to think I was cool, and it just wasn't going to happen. Images of slinky, sexy Sophie Cleaver kept appearing in my mind. She wouldn't have galloped along beside him.

"I have to ask you about your girlfriend."

"Girlfriend?"

"Yes. Ah — do you have one?"

He was quiet for a moment. "No. Not anymore. I was with the same girl for a few years and we broke up a few months ago."

"Oh."

"I was really sad about it," he said. "Guess I still am, in some ways. I really loved her, you know?"

I was touched by the level of emotion in his voice. He lapsed into thoughtful silence again. I didn't want to press the issue. We walked quietly along the road, which was lined with fast-food joints and gas stations and strip malls.

"What about you?" he finally said. "You have a boyfriend?"

I don't know why I was so startled by his question. I hesitated for a moment. "No. I don't really have boyfriends. I'm not — I don't know."

He nodded. "It's hard to keep things going when you're always on the road."

"Yes," I said. I was glad he'd given me a reason.

"Me and my ex — it was hard, and she had her own things going on. It still hurts."

"I understand."

We changed the subject, talking casually about the tour and our bands. I explained how we'd gotten our band started, and hc told me some stuff about his. Cars whizzed past us. He was quiet and attentive. I remembered how Toad had laughed about how much *action* Chris would be getting on the road. It didn't seem to make sense. He was such a quiet, thoughtful guy — not the outgoing party moron type. I reminded myself that I barely knew him, but still. He just seemed too *nice*.

We arrived at the fairground, which was a short walk from the ocean. The warm breeze blew across us as we walked, smelling like popcorn and cotton candy and fried food, and the atmosphere was fun and festive with the spinning rides and music and people. The sun was just starting to lower in the sky, bathing everything in a pink glow. I felt great, walking beside Chris. People kept looking at us, probably marvelling at how tall he was, how menacing he looked. I felt a sort of stupid, puffed-up pride. I wanted to take his hand, but I didn't.

"Do you want to go on the ferris wheel?" he asked.

"Sure," I said, picturing us gazing across the ocean, the sparkling sunset in its reflection, totally cute and sweet. It would be a beautiful moment, something we would remember forever. I really did get ahead of myself in this stupid dreamy way. It was all too great. In Florida, in the sun, at the fair, with this giant famous metal guy beside me, wanting to take a ride on the ferris wheel. You know the type of dumb-ass giddy thing I mean. It really did feel nice.

The ferris wheel was quite big, and there was some horrible rock music playing as Chris gave the tickets to the weirdo running it. We climbed into the car, and it swayed. The guy clanged the safety rail to lock us into the seat, and we jerked into motion.

As the car began its ascent, the wind swept over us, catching the ends of Chris's hair and lifting it, stealing the breath from my throat and making me instinctively reach for the lap rail. I gripped it in my hands, which were sweating, and focused on ignoring the fact that the ground was falling farther away from us with each passing second. To my horror, the wheel groaned as we reached the top — a sound that signalled either something needed oiling on the damn thing, or something was full-stop wrong with it. Either way I was ready to get off the ride, and we were only making our way around for the first time.

I tried to breathe deeply as we flew over the highest point and began to descend. I glanced sideways at Chris. His eyes were fixed over the hand rail, his brow furrowed, his lips pursed in the usual tight frown.

We fell through the air and were back at the bottom. My stomach felt like it was full of helium. I was concerned I might cry out. As we moved along to ascend once more, the shitty radio music blasted in our ears for a quick second, and I braced myself. I was not going to look like a fool. The wheel groaned again, and I didn't know if it was my imagination or not but I felt the whole thing shudder slightly. I moaned.

"This is horrible," Chris said in a tense monotone. "This really sucks. I don't like this."

"Me neither."

"Fuck." We fell silent again as the ferris wheel swept us down and around, up again, and over. Chris was dead silent and stiff beside me. We finished the ride without speaking, and when our seat stopped at the bottom, I rose and almost collapsed. My legs felt like jelly and my mouth hurt from frowning.

"Hey, aren't you from Ripsawdomy?" the guy running the ride asked as we climbed off.

Chris scowled. "Yeah. Thanks for the ride, bro."

"*Rock on!*" the guy said, flashing the horns as we passed him. Chris buried his hands in his pockets, striding away, and I broke into my little trot to keep up. Romantic, right?

Chris won me an orange sea horse that felt like it was stuffed with tin foil at the water-pistol-balloon game, and we got some cotton candy and hot dogs. It was fun, but Chris was really quiet. I wondered if it was because the ride had bothered him, or if he was thinking about his ex, or what.

When we were finished at the fair, it was twilight, and Chris suggested we walk along the beach. We took off our shoes and walked along the shore, the water lapping at our toes.

"I've never been to a beach like this before," I said.

"Really?"

"Yeah, never. Florida's just a place you read about in a magazine, or see on TV," I said. "Back where I'm from, right now, it's cold. It's autumn. The leaves are changing colour, people are wearing sweaters."

"Weird," he said.

I felt like I was talking too much, so we walked on in silence. He seemed so pensive. I wasn't sure if I should keep talking or be quiet or what. He seemed perfectly comfortable with the silence, so I decided just to enjoy the moment and the ocean and the sunset, and listen to the gentle wash of the waves and the cry of the seagulls and leave him to his quiet thoughts.

"I'd *love* to get some weed," he said.

"Oh," I said.

"You smoke weed?"

"Uh, not really. Not really my thing."

"I love to get high, play my acoustic, and just really feel music," he said softly.

I looked up at him sideways to see if he was joking. He very clearly wasn't, and I tried to put aside my cynical mind and just accept what he'd said. All of a sudden he stopped and turned to face me. I looked up at him and he looked down at me with

341

that gentle, slightly perplexed expression and those beautiful blue eyes.

"I really like you, Rachel," he said softly.

Because he was so tall, it took him a long time to slowly lean down to my face and I had time to decide I would dismiss what he'd said about the weed and the acoustic. He kissed me on the lips, and I was so nervous and not sure how I felt about it, but I tried to kiss him back and hoped I came across as being calm and cool instead of the bag of fluttering nerves I felt like. He straightened back up again and took my hands. "I think you should come back to my hotel tonight," he said.

"No," I said immediately, and then cleared my throat and started again. "Chris, I mean, I really like you too. I just, I don't think that would be a good idea. I mean not right now. Not yet. I'm just, ah, I guess I'm just not ready for that." I was babbling, and the fact that we'd kissed was giving me this weird, overwhelming feeling of intimacy with him and I felt myself yearning to tell him what had happened, what had happened to me and Fern, because he would understand, and he would care, and he would hate it, and he would want revenge — he would understand everything. Hot tears prickled in my eyes; I was desperate to tell him what they had done to us.

"I understand," he said, gazing at me, not noticing that I was almost crying. "I respect that. I hope I didn't offend you by asking."

"No," I whispered.

He looked out over the ocean, his hair gently blowing. I wanted to reach up and touch it, but he was too tall. It would've been awkward. "You're really special, Rachel. Really beautiful. I want us to get to know each other. And we can take things as slow as you want."

I didn't point out that we lived on opposite sides of the continent and that our tour would end in just a few more weeks. I was content to just stand there, holding his hand, looking out over the ocean. It really was a nice moment, one of those ones you don't forget.

FORTY-EIGHT

Fern was *back*. She was always smiling, she stayed up and watched movies on the bus and laughed and ate a lot. I hadn't noticed how fucking *skeletal* she'd become until she started eating normally again, wanting to share ice cream with me. Onstage she was totally psychotic, playing with more energy than ever, taking on this amazing persona and leaping and darting around, almost manic. She was close with Edgar again as well, and suggested that we start working on new music. She became the life of the party on our bus, and more than once I caught that little moron Timmy staring at her with a stupid grin on his face.

As the next two weeks passed, things with Chris sort of developed into a routine. We'd smoke together outside the buses, we'd watch each other perform (I still tried to do it discreetly), and sometimes we'd go for a short walk after the show and hold hands. The guys in his band started being friendly to me, except for the grizzly old grey-haired Chick, who just seemed completely disinterested in everything to do with our band and breezed around backstage as if he had important places to be.

We even kissed a few more times. He seemed happy with the little routine, and I have to admit I was sort of keeping an eye out to see if he was going to mess around with anyone. Often I'd see Chick in the company of some (much younger) girls backstage, or some of the other guys with their arms around girls, but never Chris. He was always just in the background or joking with his bandmates or drunk or whatever. He didn't talk much when we hung out, and I didn't feel as though I was getting to know him any better, but I figured time would tell. We'd have to figure something out when the tour ended, anyway.

And so we continued. I'd watch Marie-Lise walk her little dog — she'd started smiling more at me and Fern, but she and the Gurgol guys stayed on their bus, whereas the Ripsawdomy guys were usually backstage, ready to have drinks and chill out. Socks and Edgar hung out with them a bunch. I gathered that Gurgol were all vegan and into meditation and didn't drink. They'd hang out with Ripsawdomy sometimes, as they were all old friends, and everyone respected the fact that they were doing this tour their own way. I was bummed out that it didn't seem like Marie-Lise was interested in being friends. I'd envisioned somehow that we'd bond. She was still absolutely amazing onstage, but she really would disappear at the end of the night.

I guess some bands want to party all night, some bands want to keep to themselves, some bands want to do drugs, some bands want to avoid meat and dairy. Colostomy Hag was always right in the middle. We were social, but not insane. We liked to get our sleep, but we'd hang out. Socks, Edgar, and lately Fern were always up to having a few beers and joking around in the dressing rooms. Toad was definitely up for partying. I was a bit more withdrawn than all of them. I wasn't into drinking, and besides, I would usually go off with Chris to hold hands.

The tour moved into Louisiana, and we had a day off in New Orleans. Ripsawdomy had gone on to Baton Rouge for the off day, because their drummer had family there, so I wasn't going to see Chris. Which was fine. Our bus was parked behind a hotel near downtown. Toad, Socks, Edgar, and Timmy decided to walk down Bourbon Street to find cheap alcohol, and Fern and I wanted to explore the less booze-soaked parts of the city.

"Now look — and I mean it — *don't go anywhere stupid,*" Toad said. "You stay on the main streets. There are some really ugly parts of this city, you know what I mean? You stay where there's people, on the main streets. You don't take chances."

It sounded pretty melodramatic, but as Fern and I walked away from the downtown area, I could see what he meant. Some of the area was scarily vacant and creepy. Buildings sat empty; giant abandoned houses were overgrown with weeds and tall grass, their windows smashed out. As we walked past, I thought I could feel eyes following us, and my skin crawled.

There were some beautiful buildings. Fern took a lot of pictures, both of destroyed and preserved architecture. We'd look down side roads as we wandered, seeing shady characters hanging around, so we kept moving. The sun beat down hard on our shoulders.

We found the large, walled-in graveyard where the Voodoo Queen, Marie Laveau, was buried. We opened the rusty gate, and it screeched loudly, making us pause, but we entered. It was like a miniature city, with rows of small cobbled walkways leading along blocks of vaults and crypts. There were beautiful statues, crumbling angels, crosses, and obelisks. We walked slowly, reading names and dates. A lot of them were illegible. We walked in silence, looking for the Voodoo Queen's grave.

"I have to pee," Fern said.

"Okay, let's go."

"No, I want to find the grave. I'll just go back around the corner into those bushes and we'll keep moving."

"Fern!" I was shocked. "You can't pee in a *graveyard!*"

"It's not like I'm going to just piss on someone's *grave*," she said, and laughed. "I'll just go in the bushes. Don't worry. No one here will mind anyway. They're dead, right?"

"I guess."

"Wait here." She started moving back along the path. "Keep your eyes open in case someone comes along."

She disappeared into a thicket of bushes beside one of the nearby vaults, and I looked around. It hadn't occurred to me that there might be someone else in the graveyard. We hadn't encountered anyone, but there could easily be someone else wandering through this stone maze. The stones and crypts were too tall to see over. I shivered.

The bushes where Fern had disappeared rustled violently, and I heard her voice, muffled at first, then rising to a shout. I threw myself towards the sound, scratching myself on the thorny branches to reach her.

In the seclusion of the little thicket, the sun twinkled through the leaves to dapple Fern in moving light. It was cool and shady here, quite nice, really, but sweat prickled my skin. She stared down at a guy.

He looked a bit older than us, and he was dirty. There were leaves in his dark, greasy hair, and he wore a filthy plaid shirt and torn brown pants. He was sitting cross-legged, hands spread in front of him as if under arrest, his eyes huge and unblinking, staring up at Fern.

I absorbed the situation and saw a fucking big knife in her hand, the kind with a curved blade that folds back neatly into the handle. She brandished it in her right hand, pointing it at the guy. Her eyes were wide and wild.

"He attacked me," she said in a high voice.

"I did not," the guy said, slurring. He was drunk or wasted on something, and he flicked his eyes to me and then back to her. "I did not. I did not."

"He did," Fern said. She said the words quickly, never taking her eyes off him.

"Where'd you get the knife?" I asked lamely.

"I bought it in Florida," she replied.

"I did not. I did not," the guy repeated. "I did not."

"Oh god, stop that," I said.

Then it was quiet. None of us spoke. It was kind of funny, this weird tableau of the guy holding his hands out in surrender, Fern standing there pointing the knife at him, and me, just sort of *there*. A light breeze rustled the leaves around us. I felt a giggle coming on.

"I'm sorry," the guy said, startling me.

"I came back here and he grabbed me out of the bushes," Fern explained.

"I did not. I did not. I did not. I did —"

"Shut *up*," I said. I knew where this was going, but somehow it was worse. It was like the polar opposite of the night in Florida. It was bright, it didn't smell like shit, and I could see this guy's face. I could look into his eyes. He gave me a pleading look, his brown eyes sad and frantic. This horrible rush of pity climbed right up my throat. I threw up all down my front and my hands. Fern was unmoved.

The guy started to laugh, pointing at me like a little kid. "Fuck, sorry," I mumbled, wiping my hands on my shorts.

Then, out of nowhere, the guy lunged at Fern. I leaped at

him and she swiped with the knife, connecting with his hand. There was a flash of blood and the guy screamed, pulling his hands to his face. She'd cut his fingers — his pinkie looked pretty bad. I didn't think she'd severed anything. I was right behind him now, and I grabbed him, putting my arms around his neck in a pathetic chokehold.

"Don't do that again," Fern hissed.

"I did *not*! I did *not*," he bawled, beginning to cry. I could smell the stink of booze on him.

"Shut up." Fern stepped forward and punched him in the stomach. The guy let out a gasping grunt, and when she pulled her fist away from him, I saw the knife dripping. It took me a second to realize she'd stabbed him.

As I held him, she took a deep breath and punched him again with the blade. The guy coughed and I let him go. He slumped over into the grass, moving his hands to his belly. I watched his fingers turn slick and scarlet. Blood seeped into the grass. He lay there, gasping.

"There," she said, as if she'd just finished planting a garden or something, *mission accomplished*. His breath moved in and out slowly. He held his hands pressed to his stomach, and blood poured over them. Every now and then he would cough, a wet, bubbling sound.

I didn't like the feeling. I didn't like standing here covered in my own vomit, watching him die. It was too sunny for a scene like this, too peaceful, with the wind and the silence of the graves around us. I didn't like the way it was making me feel about Fern. I squashed that feeling, crushed it, buried it. This was *not* Fern's fault.

I was jarred from my thoughts by the pressure of a hard object on my hand. Fern was giving me the knife, pushing the handle into my palm. "Do it," she breathed. "I can't watch him bleed to death."

I felt like I was in a trance. *Do it.* Do what? I knelt down beside him, holding the knife. This was different from smashing a dark blur with a dark brick. Thankfully he was lying on his side, facing away from me, so I didn't have to see his eyes again. I saw his neck shaking, trembling as he breathed in and out, in and out, faster than he should've been breathing.

"Kill him, do it," Fern's voice came from behind me. I turned the knife so that the blade faced downwards. I didn't know how to kill him.

"This isn't our fault," I said to no one. I began to cry. It was better than laughing. I stabbed the blade down into the side of his neck, yanked it out, then shoved it in again.

It was very rare that I would allow myself to visualize Balthazar Seizure. Since it had happened I barely allowed myself to think of his band's name, let alone the image of his horrible face, because I was afraid that if I did, something inside me would cave in and all the pain and the tears and the fucking fury would come out and I would collapse in some way, just collapse into something that I couldn't come back from. But that night, in my bunk, I let that face materialize behind my eyelids. That skinny face, that leering horrible smile . . . Because it was *his fault.* It was his fault that that guy died. Maybe he had attacked Fern. Maybe he hadn't. Fern needed to kill him. She needed it to heal. And we both needed it to prepare ourselves for what we now knew we would be absolutely, definitely capable of doing. This shit was his fault. Him, and his horrible friends.

I could hear laughter coming from the front lounge. Everyone was drunk. Even Fern was drunk. I could hear her laughter mingling with theirs. I just lay in my bunk staring into the darkness. I needed to think.

I'd killed two people. I mean, I guess it was me. Fern

might've bashed the one guy's skull and stabbed the second guy in the stomach, and both of them might have died from that. Who knows? But I was the one responsible for the end result. The *finishing touches*. It was me: I'd killed those guys.

I wondered how many people in the world have killed someone and never gotten caught. How many people go on to have families and careers and get elected to important government positions and they're secretly murderers. I mean, no one on this bus, or on the tour, knew that they were travelling with two girls who'd killed people. Maybe it was a super common thing. I thought of Chris, I thought of my stupid fantasy life with him, and I wondered if it was possible to just take this with me, just *compartmentalize* it, or whatever melodramatic psychological term could be used to describe keeping this to myself forever and having a nice normal life.

I wanted to feel sorry for that guy in the cemetery, but the whole thing was so confusing. He was a weirdo and he'd probably tried to hurt Fern and the only person who needed to feel guilty for this was Balthazar fucking Seizure. I listened to her laughing in the front lounge and I thought about how light she'd been lately, how happy and enthusiastic about everything, and I figured she was probably insane. I was probably a little insane too. Maybe she had lied about the guy in the cemetery. But I'd stabbed his throat and ripped all those weird tendons with the knife. I'd dug right in.

One thing was for sure. I wasn't going to be able to compart-mentalize *shit*. A long time ago, I'd promised Fern that we would get avenged. We'd come a long way since then, and Fern had turned it into reality. If I could smash a stranger's face in, if I could rip out some guy's throat, I could kill Balthazar Seizure.

FORTY-NINE

We carried on. Fern was crazily happy, and I think Edgar and everyone started getting creeped out by her. She was always smiling, always giddy. She was acting weird. I knew why. I kept waiting for another situation, another night, another call from a shadowy alley, another whispered prompt from my friend to *do it, finish it*. I felt sick when I thought about it. I wondered what my mother would think of me. My little sister. I never called home much anyway.

One night we were in Ripsawdomy's dressing room after a show. Everyone was drinking. Socks and Edgar were there, even a few of the guys from Gurgol were hanging out. Fern was there. She was talking animatedly. I was next to Chris on the dirty couch. I was desperate to have fun as well. It was hard for me to feel social. All I wanted to do was go lie down in my bunk. But it was nice to be with Chris, despite the fact that we didn't seem to be going anywhere. We were still taking our walks, but his silence was starting to bother me. I didn't watch his shows anymore, and if he was watching ours, I wasn't really noticing.

Chick came into the dressing room with some girl. He was wearing his show clothes, but he'd changed into flip-flops. They sat down on the couch, the girl beside me, Chick on the other side of her.

"Hi," she said to me blearily. She smiled at me, eyes half-lidded.

"Hi."

"You were in the band," she said. "You were so awesome."

"Thanks."

Chick put his feet up on the coffee table in front of the couch, and I stared at his toes. The skin was dry and his toenails were long and yellow. I wrinkled my nose in disgust, irritated.

"His toes are fucking disgusting," I said to the girl.

"Huh?"

"His toenails." I pointed. "That's sick."

She just looked confused, so I turned back to Chris. He was chatting with one of the Gurgol guys, but when he saw me looking at him, he smiled and put his arm around me.

"You're beautiful," he said.

"Thanks," I said. "Chris, what am I doing here?"

"What do you mean?" He took a swig of beer.

"What am I doing here?"

He stared at me blankly, then frowned. "Getting wasted?"

"Chris, I'm not even drinking."

He studied my face. "You mean, what am I doing here, like, for your life?"

"I guess."

"I believe we're here for love. Just to chill out and absorb everything. Like music."

"Smoke some weed, play some acoustic?"

His face lit up. "Yes. Exactly. We should do that sometime."

"I was just kidding," I said.

He hesitated, then laughed awkwardly. "I know."

We stared at each other, and that's when I realized that his silences and his frowns and his furrowed brow stares, all of which I'd thought hid some level of deep thought, of quiet intelligence, were really just *nothing*. Chris was kind of an idiot. A nice idiot, but an idiot nonetheless. And we had nothing in common.

"I have to go to bed," I said.

"Okay," he replied, and I wondered if he'd been hit with a feeling similar to the one I'd just had. We looked at each other for another moment, and I felt myself wishing hard that this was different. Just for a second. I wished I was different or he was. I held my breath, admiring his long hair, his smooth skin, his blue eyes fixed on me, holding each other's gaze for longer than we ever would again, because you can't make eye contact for any real length of time with someone you don't have stupid romantic feelings for. But then we looked away. He resumed his conversation with the other guy, and I got up and went to the bus. I felt a burning in my eyes as I crossed the parking lot. There was a little lump in my throat. When I swallowed, it turned into a quiet ache in my stomach. And that was the end of the closest thing to romance I've ever had.

FIFTY

I isolated myself as Fern came out of her shell. She'd go out with the other bands, truly making an effort to become the *belle of the ball*. I'd slump in my jammies, peeking out through the bus's blinds to watch her cavort in the parking lot, arm-in-arm with Edgar, with Socks; somehow even making that douchebag Chick laugh, and a few times I saw her approach Marie-Lise, with a nice result. It probably sounds creepy or crazy, or like I was jealous or something, doing this, watching her, but you have to understand just how *happy* she was. She had been so *off*, so disconnected, so far gone from who she had ~~been, but now... These two unknown guys~~ were dead, and as a result, she was becoming creative, happy, *alive* again. It was so jarring, but nobody really seemed eager to question what was behind it.

Chris basically stayed on his bus as well. With only a few weeks left, a feeling seemed to overtake the tour — that anxiety of being almost done, being close to finished. I'd play the show, go back to my bunk, try to sleep. So did Edgar. A lot of people did — it seemed like a split: you either wanted to party more and make the most of the last weeks, or withdraw early.

I was afraid of going home. I hadn't talked to my parents in a long time, and the thought of going back to that little house — with Mom's paintings on the walls and Dad's books and Melissa's sweet face and my little bedroom — scared me. I didn't feel like I should be there anymore. Like I wasn't the same person. They wouldn't know me anymore — but I guess they hadn't for a long time, anyway.

I toyed with the idea of asking Fern if she wanted to get a place together, or maybe I could move into Socks's basement and sleep on the couch or something. I didn't have a lot of money. I know Socks was looking ahead, into more touring. I just didn't want to go back to the room where I had slept when I was a little kid after everything that had happened. I didn't want to go home.

When you're growing up, you have this sort of vague idea in your mind of what's going to happen, right? I'll go to college, I'll get married to some handsome dude, we'll have some kids . . . And then your life starts to take shape a little bit — for me, it was like, *Okay, I'll be in a band with my friends.* And I didn't know what was going to happen past that, other than some sort of half-assed backup, like, when the band stops, I'll have to get a job. Maybe I'll go to college or something. It's a bit of a void, looking ahead to that. And then a weird flash of *maybe* meeting some guy, *maybe* having a kid? I don't know if I ever seriously entertained either of those ideas. So it was all about the band, and then the weird purgatory afterwards when I guessed I'd have to transition into something else. But then I killed two people. That wasn't one of the milestones I'd envisioned.

I had definitely anticipated some sort of consequence. That

maybe one morning there'd be a knock on the bus door and Fern and I would be dragged, bleary-eyed and pyjama-panted, off to prison. I mean, yeah, we were travelling miles every day and moving along fast, and the dead guys weren't exactly the beautiful *missing persons* girls that you'd see on the top news stories, but I expected *something*.

And there was nothing.

And Fern and I never discussed it. Whenever we were alone on the tour, it wasn't like *Oh, hey, how are you feeling about the murders* or anything. I knew she'd kept that brick from the alley in Florida, but I wasn't going to ask her to see it. So thinking about what had happened was something I did alone, at night, in my bunk.

By now the shows were mechanical. My voice was starting to get tired, I said the same things every night onstage, I did the same moves at the same parts of the same songs. None of us were doing laundry anymore, either, realizing the ultimate redundancy of it. I'm sure the bus reeked, but all of us were beyond noticing. At least Fern's renewed zest for life kept the focus off how disinterested I'd become in the live performances — let the people focus on her and her wonderful energy. I just wanted to go to bed.

Sometimes I dreamed about that broken face in the alley, about the screeching, desperate voice, that hideous repetition, *I did not, I did not, I did not!* until I would have to get out of my bunk and go up to the front lounge and watch the sun come up as Roger drove us along whatever highway in whatever state. I would sit, quiet as a mouse, so he wouldn't know I was awake and sitting there, because I didn't want to talk to him. I just wanted the sunshine to burn my eyes, bleach out the fucking disgusting images. I had no regret over who I had removed from this earth. But does killing someone have to be so bloody, so pathetic, so sweaty, so intense? Like you end up

357

having this horrible, way-too-intimate connection with this vile creature in all of its bleeding, whining, whistling death throes. Why does it have to be so *gross*?

FIFTY-
ONE

We had three or four shows left on the tour when I got back from getting dinner with Edgar one evening. We'd just grabbed some burritos from this restaurant down the street from the venue. It was chilly. We'd started moving north — the tour finished in New York State.

We climbed on the bus. Toad, Socks, and Timmy were listening to music. Fern was still off getting dinner, probably with someone from Gurgol. As I set down the bag of food, I couldn't put my finger on what was making me feel so nauseated.

"Big, big news," Socks said.

I felt like I was going to faint. My head started spinning. In confusion, I sat down on the couch, unable to figure out why I was shaking. I couldn't get control of it. Everyone in the lounge was looking at me.

"What is it, Rach?" Socks leaned in to touch my shoulder. "You okay?"

"What is this music?" I said, but it came out as a shriek. Horrified, I realized it was fucking DED; it was "I Ignore Your Screams." I had shut out their music for so long, I had refused to listen to it, I had torn and burned and destroyed their posters and albums, I had never wanted to hear his voice again, and here it was, an old familiar song, one I had loved, and I knew every word, and I was going to throw up.

"It's —"

"Shut it off, shut it off," I bellowed, interrupting Edgar, waving my arms like a freak. Bewildered, Timmy got up and snapped off the stereo.

"What the fuck is wrong with you?" Toad asked.

I closed my eyes, tried to take a deep breath to clear my head. Shut out that song, remove its residue from my brain. I actually entertained the idea, for a split second, to go and wash my ears.

"I have a headache, the music was just driving me crazy. I don't know what came over me. Can we leave it off?"

"Yeah, sure," Toad agreed, giving me a dirty look. "Sure we can."

"Are you in the mood for some news?" Socks said.

"What is it?" I steeled myself, shutting off the part of my brain that kept whispering to me that I should go to my bunk, hide there, never come out.

"I got a call just now from Tom Manic," Socks said. "We have an offer to play at the Donner Blitzkrieg Festival."

"Where's that?" I asked.

"It's in England. Big, big festival. Big metal crowd," replied Toad.

"Donner Blitzkrieg?" I said. "That's a stupid name for a festival. Sounds like a Christmas thing. Santa's reindeer?"

Toad stared at me. "Right, Rachel. Or it could be referencing the Donner Party. You know, the pioneer cannibals?"

Socks went on to outline the pay and the travel accommodations. "The thing is, we'd be leaving the day this tour finishes. Straight from JFK. The festival is two days after the last day of this tour."

Edgar was concerned about that, but Socks assured him that after the festival gig, we'd be going right home.

"What other bands are playing?" I asked.

"A bunch of U.K. bands, a few Euro bands. A few from here," Socks said. "The headliner is DED."

XXX

Fern seemed thrilled by the news. Everyone in the band was stoked. I tried my best to be enthusiastic as well, but I needed to talk to her. We didn't have a chance to be alone until after the show that night, when I essentially dragged her off the bus to have a cigarette with me.

"I can't do it," I whispered. "I don't think I can be around them. I'll be sick."

She puffed on her cigarette, her eyes wide and white. "You can do it. We'll be close to them. We can get them, Rachel. Don't you see, it's what we've been waiting for!"

I kept shaking my head, feeling myself trembling, my stomach in a vice of knots that hadn't dissipated since I had heard that fucking song before dinner. "How? We can't get them, Fern. How are we going to get them? There'll be so many people around."

Fern didn't reply. She stared at me, studying my face. "I don't care about jail," she finally said. "I don't care about prison. I don't give a shit." She blew smoke out of her mouth. "It's worth it to me. And after everything we've already done — we've already done it, Rachel. We can't go back. There's only one place this is going to go."

She was right. But this was different than a dopehead in

361

an alley. I couldn't imagine how we would do it. Fern seemed determined — even excited. I figured she'd find a way. She had twice before. I would leave it to her to figure it out.

Finally, the tour ended. All three bands had that weird, mostly bullshit camaraderie with one another on the last day that always exists when you're saying goodbye to a bunch of people you could've been close with, could've made friends with, but didn't. Marie-Lise had the same put-on, polite smile she'd had when we said hello as we said goodbye. Everyone was nice on that last night and had a drink together out by the buses, talking about the tour and the shows as merrily as if we had all hung out the whole time and shared something really *special*. Shit, maybe some of them had. I guess I had, in some ways. I glanced at Chris, who was glancing at me. Everyone congratulated us on getting onto the Donner Blitzkrieg Festival bill. They were all heading home — Ripsawdomy was going back into the studio before a European tour, and Gurgol was just going home to relax for the next few months.

Then the bus drivers arrived, and it was time for everyone to say goodbye. Chris and I hugged, and that annoying lump in my throat came back and he stared at me, frowning, perplexed, in the parking lot, and I could tell he wanted to say something, but he didn't. So we just left it at goodbye. I watched the Ripsawdomy bus pull out of the lot and drive away, as Gurgol and my band said their goodbyes. I watched it drive into the darkness. I could have cried.

FIFTY-TWO

We drove right to the airport, we said goodbye to Roger and Timmy, and the bus sped off, leaving us outside the terminal at 2 a.m. with a pile of guitar cases and stinking knapsacks, stiff with the sweat of unwashed clothes. It was hideous. Our show clothes actually had *salt* stains on them from the amount of perspiration soaked into them, which was totally gross. I didn't know that could happen.

We checked in for our flight, Toad leading the way. I was somewhat irritated that he was coming with us, but it was better having him lead the way and taking care of things than to just literally fly blindly into some unknown situation. Having a tour manager was pretty awesome. Once our bags were checked, we went to our gate to rest. The flight was the next morning, so we hunkered down to get some sleep despite the fluorescent lighting. Socks pulled his hat down over his eyes and slumped in a plastic chair. Edgar full-on lay down on the floor, using his backpack as a pillow. Toad busied himself with his laptop, and I slouched my own ass down, ready to try to sleep.

Fern was buzzing with energy. Her knee bounced up and down, her eyes darting around. I could tell there was no way she would be sleeping. I don't know why I was so tired. I was afraid of what was going to happen in England. I closed my eyes and tried to rest, eventually falling into a terrible sleep — the kind where you wake up with a throbbing headache and your back is killing you.

We were like zombies at the gate the next morning. I felt like pure shit. It didn't look like anyone else felt much better. Socks and Edgar went miserably to find any semblance of reasonably priced coffee and food. Toad sat with his arms folded, his hood pulled up. Only Fern appeared unfazed, the same look of jittery anticipation still on her face.

Socks and Edgar returned with a greasy bag of breakfast sandwiches, the kind on a soggy croissant with bacon and cheese and egg and butter. The coffee tasted horrible. The five of us silently ate, not even bothering with chit chat.

We still had an hour or so till the flight once we'd finished eating, and I wandered to the ladies' room to brush my teeth and splash some water on my face. I looked in the mirror, acknowledging that I looked like shit. My hair didn't even look real. It looked like someone had pasted dirty dull black string in clumps on my head. I still had the streaks of makeup from last night's show on my face. The harsh light in the bathroom only made it worse.

But that's the good thing about airports, any time of day. Most people look like bags of shit. People are sleeping on the floor no matter what time of day it is. People barf on planes.

They have long flights. They're hungry and tired. The most put-together, rich, professional people just go into survival mode. You're dragging around heavy bags on your aching back. You're sweating. Plus — you're confused. Who the hell knows where they're going in an airport? So at least no one stared at me too much.

Once done in the bathroom, I wandered a little and came upon a row of payphones. I dialled a collect call to my family's house. My father accepted the charges, and I felt a tightness in my chest crawl up my throat.

"Rachel! How are you!" he cried, and I heard him call to my mother. "Marilyn, grab the other phone. It's Rachel!"

There was a click as she picked up the other extension. Melissa was obviously beside her, and then I was lost in their voices, exclaiming happily they'd seen the band on the music channel on TV a few weeks ago, we were doing so well, they were so proud.

"How was the tour?" Mom asked.

"Fine," I whispered in a thick voice, the lump in my throat swelling even larger, filling it up. It was difficult to breathe.

"We are so proud of you," Dad agreed. "So! You must be on your way home now!"

My throat was dry, and I cleared it. "No," I said hoarsely. "We're actually going to England right now. We're at the airport."

"When are you coming home?" Melissa asked.

My eyes filled with tears, and I closed them, leaning my forehead against the phone. "In a few days."

"Congratulations on everything that's happening for you," Mom said. "We miss you."

"We love you," Dad added.

"I love you too," I said, tears rolling down my face in hot, wet tracks. Yes — premeditated murder is a really positive experience.

365

XXX

"Is that chick on crack?" Toad grumbled as we filed onto the plane. Fern was talking brightly to the attendants, to other passengers, just animated and sunny. I had a seat alone, thankfully — well, not alone, but not with Toad or any of the guys. I had an aisle seat, and to my right was an old couple who immediately put sleep masks on and would likely remain silent and stiff the whole ride. I pulled up my hood, put the scratchy airline blanket over me, and tried to fall asleep as well.

Once we were airborne, I unlatched my food tray and tried to rest my head on it. The white noise of the engine was nice, the gentle normal chatter I could barely hear around me was actually sort of soothing as well. I had the blanket over my head like a cheap ghost costume, minus the eyeholes. I saw leaves, orange and yellow and red — bright autumn leaves, spinning slowly and coasting along gently. I rose from the ground to take in more, and I saw that the leaves were moving along a gutter, a white cement curb, clear and cold-looking rainwater moving along the gutter, carrying the coloured leaves in it, slowly spinning and coasting. And my stomach sank as I saw the sewer coming up, ready to swallow the leaves. I tasted panic in my mouth as I reached forward to save them, to pluck them from the stream before they were lost forever, swallowed into that black cavernous abyss, but I *had no hands*, I reached out but saw nothing, I couldn't see anything except those leaves, helpless and doomed, spinning and coasting to be lost forever, until the harsh, sharp shriek of someone's baby jarred me awake, the blanket falling away from my face.

FIFTY-THREE

We took off from JFK feeling like shit and landed at Heathrow far worse. Socks, Toad, and Edgar looked grim as we all climbed into a taxi outside the terminal. Even Fern's jittery grin was gone. It didn't help that rain was pissing down, hammering on the roof of the taxi as we joined the stream of traffic. I was next to Fern in the backseat, and she put her head on my shoulder. Her big woollen cap was soaking wet from the downpour. It made my cheek itchy, but I didn't push her away.

I stared out the window, first at the narrow buildings and the bright umbrellas, blurry through the glass, and then out at green soaking wet countryside. Here we were in England again and, once again, I didn't feel too much like enjoying it.

After a long, silent ride, we arrived at the hotel. Toad explained that all the bands playing the festival were staying here and we had one room reserved for us that we'd all share. Toad went to check us in, and we stood in the front lobby in our damp jackets, swaying with exhaustion. Next to the lobby was the hotel bar. Music and laughter drifted out, and I noticed a bunch of musician-types hanging out in there. A few of them were also in the lobby, sprawled in the big stuffed chairs. Cigarette smoke lent a haze to everything. Or maybe I was just really tired.

It occurred to me that the DED guys must be at this hotel. Maybe even in the hotel bar. I looked a little closer at the people I could see through the doorway. Lots of black hair, lots of black clothes. Nobody recognizable. I looked over at Fern to see if she'd had the same thought, and our eyes met. She smiled at me brightly, looking angelic in her white cap. I smiled back wearily, unable to fathom where she was getting this energy from. Maybe she'd slept in the taxi.

We headed up to our room, which had two double beds and a cot. Toad griped as he set his shit up on the cot. I collapsed onto the bed and turned on the TV. Edgar and Socks sprawled on the other bed, and Fern headed into the shower.

She emerged a little while later, looking clean and gorgeous. She'd pulled on a tight black sweater and dark blue jeans, even put on some makeup. I could smell her vanilla perfume.

"Who wants to go have a drink?" she asked.

"Me," Socks said, immediately perking up and jumping off the bed. There were no other replies — Edgar and Toad were both passed out.

The two of them left, and I fell asleep almost immediately.

I awoke in the dark room with Fern shaking my shoulder lightly. In the time I'd slept, it had gotten dark. My mind reeled — I needed more sleep.

"Wake up," Fern whispered. "Rachel."

"What's wrong?"

368

"Come have a smoke with me."

"Okay."

I forced myself to sit up. I could see the dark shapes of the guys sleeping, could hear Edgar's light snoring. Fern pulled open the curtains and opened the sliding door that led out to the small balcony.

I followed her out there. It was so cold, I pulled up my hood. My gaze swept over the dark front lawn of the hotel below, along the driveway, lined with glowing streetlamps. Fern lit a cigarette and held it out for me. Then she lit one for herself.

"What's going on?" I asked.

"I saw them," she said, her eyes wide and unblinking. "Sid. And Ed. And the drummer. Downstairs, in the bar."

I swallowed. An image flashed into my mind, a memory of Fern pressed into a couch, the big hand moving to pin hers down. I slammed that door shut fast. "You saw them?"

"Yes," she breathed, puffing on her cigarette. "They were drunk."

"Did they see you?"

"Yes." She laughed. "They bought me a few drinks."

My mouth moved, my lips forming words, but I said nothing. I tried to process what she was telling me. Her eyes had a strange light in them.

"They had no idea who I was," she said, and giggled, a high note of hysteria in her tone. "I talked to them. They like our band. They know who our band is."

I took a few deep drags of my cigarette, staring at her. "They do?"

"Yeah. And they didn't recognize me. Can you believe it?" She was babbling, smiling, gushing like an excited fan, *Can you believe it?* I didn't understand how she could talk to them. I didn't understand why she was so happy now. I breathed in smoke, trying to understand. I tried to imagine being in the same room with Balthazar. Talking to him. Having a damn drink with him.

"Balthazar wasn't there," she said, as if I had spoken the thought aloud. I didn't know what to say. I didn't know what questions to ask. I just stood there, listening to her. She prattled on about how Socks had been all excited to meet them and to talk to the drummer, and how she thought the one guy, Sid, had been hitting on her, and how they'd all *gotten along like old friends*.

"I don't understand how they could have forgotten," I finally said. "I don't understand why they wouldn't remember. I can't forget it. I will never —"

"It is *nothing* to them," Fern said. "They've done it a million times. Why would they remember me? Remember us? It was *nothing*."

I felt tears sting my eyes, and Fern scowled, gripping my arm tightly. "They don't remember, and that's good. I was beside them tonight. We can get close to them." She let me go and rested her elbows on the railing, looking out into the dark, blowing a stream of white smoke into the cold air. "I want this to be amazing, Rachel."

"Amazing?"

She turned her face back to me, giving me a dark, humourless smile. I'd never seen that look on her face before, and it chilled me. I shuddered. "Yes, amazing. I want to kill them *in front of the crowd*."

FIFTY-FOUR

We had to be up early the next morning, which was fine, because after my conversation with Fern, we'd gone back inside and slept hard through the night. None of us were jet-lagged by the time we went out front. There were a bunch of school buses to ferry the bands to the venue from the hotel.

The previous day's rain had given way to a clear, sunny morning. The Donner Blitzkrieg Festival was taking place on a fairground — the main stage was in a large auditorium, the second stage was in a smaller one on the grounds, and the field was going to be filled with vendors. There was a third building for the bands' dressing rooms. There were twenty bands total on the bill — ten on the main stage, and ten on the second, and they would alternate throughout the day. While one band played, the other stage would be changing over for the next band. We were scheduled to play on the main stage, halfway through the day. Toad said we should be grateful the

371

stages were indoors — I had to agree. We'd be playing while it was still daylight, and I imagined it would have been pretty disconcerting to play outside in the sun and cold.

We found out quickly that the day was going to be busy. We were shown to the little cubicle in the bands' building that would be our dressing room. On the wall was our day's schedule — meal times, interviews, and, of course, our stage time. A large area in this building was sectioned off for catering, so we all ate cafeteria-style, filling our trays and sitting at long tables with a huge assortment of people. Another area was sectioned off for media.

I'm sad to say that my last day of *freedom* was so anticlimactic — I ate bacon and eggs and did some really awkward interviews with U.K. press. We did a group photo of the four of us that day as well. I think Fern looks insane in it, but I've only seen it the once.

I had just finished our last interview — they had wanted to talk to all of us, but our set time was approaching, so I did the interview while the other three and Toad set up our gear on the stage. I was hurrying back to our small dressing room to touch up my makeup and wait for Toad to come get me. I was nervous, of course. I'd been flustered all day. I weaved around the people milling in the hallways, rounded a corner, and slammed into someone.

"I'm sorry," I immediately spluttered, backing up and looking right up into the slender ivory face of Balthazar Seizure.

I had blocked his true image from my mind, demonizing him, remembering a twisted, monstrous face. His good looks stunned me. Our eyes locked. I remembered that eye contact, the blue eyes, the black hair. The leering, the lips stretching into a nasty, mocking grin. I remembered the dirty towel. I remembered the feeling of his breath on me. I could not tear my eyes away from his, even as my stomach churned, filled with ice.

"I know you from somewhere," he said in that deep voice. I physically reacted to the sound, unable to keep a sob from bursting out of my throat, feeling every nerve ending, every muscle in my body react, feeling everything in me ready to take flight, to propel myself back and away from him, around the corner, out into that muddy field, to get the fuck away. *Stop it. Keep it together, don't give it away, don't let him know, don't let him remember.* I tried to take control. I somehow managed to turn the sob into a wrenching, horrible chuckle, forcing my face to smile, my hands curling into atrophied, painful fists, my nails digging into my palms.

"What's wrong? Did our collision hurt you?" He smiled, friendly, and reached out for me. I recoiled immediately but tried to cover it up with a casual laugh.

"Oh, no, I'm fine. Just in a rush," I replied, wondering if I was shouting, knowing I looked insane, not caring, just wanting to get away from him. "My band is going on in a few minutes."

He stared down at me for a moment, thoughtful. I didn't understand how he could have forgotten me. This eye contact had happened before, it's just that I'd been crying and he'd been drunk, but it hung in the air between us, heavy like an old dirty towel.

"I know!" His face lit up. "Of course. You're Rachel from Colostomy Hag." He gave me a smile. "I have to say — I'm a huge fan!"

I smiled.

"I'm actually going to watch your show from the side of the stage," he continued. "I haven't been able to see you guys live yet, so I'm definitely looking forward to it."

"I have to go," I said happily. I raised my hand in a friendly farewell and watched as his eyes took in my scabbed, bloody palm. I bolted then, running past him, running harried through the halls, bumping into people and not caring. I threw the door to our cubicle open and flung myself into it as though the walls would protect me. I turned and slammed the door, pressed my forehead against it, taking heaving, shuddering gasps.

"Rachel! What the *fuck*?"

Startled, I turned and saw Toad in the room. I tried to compose myself, tried to grin, but he stepped forward and grabbed me by the shoulders, scowling darkly.

"I don't know what your deal is. And, you know, I don't really care." I met his gaze, holding eye contact with him, and allowed my dislike for him to show. It was met with a matching dislike. *Good to know.* "Just get through today's show. And then go fuck off, go have your little meltdown or whatever you have to do." He released my shoulders, but not before giving me a small shove backwards. It wasn't hard, but it was enough to express that he did not like me and that he could — and probably would have loved to — shove me harder.

"You're a real gentleman," I said.

So I walked onstage for our first big festival show with fury at Toad coursing through me. Horror followed when I saw that Balthazar was, indeed, watching us from the side of stage. I couldn't enjoy it — I couldn't enjoy how beautiful Fern looked, how great Edgar's performance was, how the crowd screamed appreciatively, how their hands reached towards me. I did the best I could, going through the songs, making the faces, smiling and baring my teeth and snarling, but all the while I was hideously aware of him, standing in the darkness, lurking in the shadows, like a thin black spider, waiting to pounce. I came very close to vomiting on that stage. The crowd would have loved it, but I didn't want to show weakness.

Our set was short — only a half-hour — and as I went to announce our last song, the microphone slipped wetly out of my hand. My palm was bleeding, one large scab hanging half off. Shrugging, I raised my hand to my mouth, grasped the scab with my teeth, ripped it off, and spat it onto the floor. Blood dripped from my hand. I raised it and dragged it across my face, smearing blood over my flushed, sweaty skin. The crowd roared. I felt like I was in a frenzy. My eyes stung. I wanted to make Balthazar sick. I wanted to make Toad hate me.

Toad said nothing as he bandaged my hand once we were offstage and back in our little dressing room. I knew he thought I was crazy. It was obvious that the wounds on my hand were nothing new. I'd seen him glance at them sometimes but he'd never asked and he had nothing to say to me now. I can't really blame him. I hated him, and anyway, I was insane, right? It made me smile, sitting there while he pressed gauze onto my bloody palm, imagining how he'd feel if he knew I'd killed two people. Smashed someone's head in.

Doesn't being self-aware negate any sort of insanity? I can rationalize, of course, that the things I had done up to that point were insane, but I also remember acknowledging *I am insane*. Which maybe means I actually wasn't. One thing's for sure — Fern was in the room while Toad was wrapping my hand, looking in the mirror that had been hastily nailed to the wall, fixing her powder and lipstick, brushing her long hair, and humming to herself like a lunatic. To me, she was the picture of madness. But that's probably because I knew she was plotting mass murder while she smiled prettily at her reflection. To Toad, I'm sure she just looked *fuckin' hot*.

Then she and I went to go smoke outside, and as we walked through the building, we passed a wall lined with DED's stage props. That same old rig, the rack of medieval weapons that they always had onstage. The battle-axe, the swords. Fern whirled to

375

me. Our eyes met, and our faces lit up. I swear: it's like the universe *wanted* this to happen. I mean, how many bands bring real, functioning, deadly weapons onstage?

"*They're asking for it,*" I said to Fern, and her shriek of laughter startled the people beside us.

FIFTY-FIVE

I remember everything that happened that night. I can even play it back in slow motion, every detail crystal clear. Maybe because it was my last night free? Or maybe because I was so damn nervous. I felt so completely *aware*. I could feel something moving through my veins — adrenaline, fear. I felt like my whole body was tingling.

As the afternoon progressed into evening, the musicians in the band building started getting drunk. Especially after dinner. The voices echoing and calling got louder. We'd hung out after our show in the dressing room for a while, gone out to the autograph tent shortly after that, and then we were free to do whatever we wanted for the rest of the day. I'd gone onto the fairground for a while, wandering through the rows of vendors. It was cold outside, but there were thousands of people out there. There was booth after booth of rock shirts, boots, jewellery, belts, candy, all kinds of crap. The ground was muddy, and with so many people walking around, it was getting pretty torn up. Everyone's feet were covered with mud, so the floors in the stage buildings were a mess.

Just before DED was scheduled to go on, I was in the dressing room with Fern and Edgar. Socks and Toad had disappeared, probably to go drink beer on the fairground. I couldn't sit still, and I had smoked so many cigarettes that I felt light-headed and sick.

But that didn't stop me from lighting another. My insides churned. My knee jerked up and down as I sat at the little table, staring into the overflowing ashtray. Fern placidly brushed her hair, a serene and wistful smile on her face. Edgar sat across from me, frowning. I could tell he was weirded out by the both of us.

"So," he said. "You guys want to watch DED from the side of the stage?"

My knee stopped bouncing, and Fern smiled. "That's a great idea, let's do it," she said. They both looked at me, and I nodded my head stiffly, butting out my cigarette.

There are walks you never forget. You know, the walk you do down the hallway at the dentist's office, the walk into the hospital for some terrifying procedure. It's a walk full of dread, a walk you want to turn away from. A walk where you can't believe your own legs are carrying you, when every fibre of your being is telling you to stop. You entertain fantasies of some helpful person in white dragging you, while you kick and scream and refuse to take another step. I imagine walking down death row towards execution feels the same.

That's how I felt as we hurried through the dark towards the back entrance of the building where DED had just taken the stage. Fern and Edgar walked ahead, their breath rising in gasping dark clouds from their silhouettes. I couldn't believe it was time. I guess part of me thought that it honestly wasn't going to happen.

I mean, it's one thing to beat the brains out of someone in a dark alley. It's quite another to kill an entire band on a stage in front of thousands of people. Do you hear how crazy that sounds? But that's what was going through my head as I walked behind my friends.

We entered the back of the building, showing our all-access laminates to the security guards. They let us in and I followed Edgar and Fern up the dark staircase that led to the side of the stage. There were several people standing there, watching the show: a few people from other bands, a few scantily clad gigglers, and a bunch of security. DED was onstage. They'd just launched into "This Sad Earth." I looked beyond them to the crowd. It was packed — a sea of faces, everyone headbanging, undulating, raising their fingers and fists, packed in tight. Lips moving along with the lyrics. Eyes locked to Balthazar as he writhed and gestured. The others in the band flanked him, their long hair flying. The lights flashed, bathing everything in scarlet.

They finished the song and began another. I felt a body press in beside me. Fern was breathing heavily, staring at the stage. Her hand curled around mine. It was sweaty. I looked past her to the five security guards on this side of the stage. I couldn't see any on the other side, but I was at a bad angle.

"We're going to get caught," I said. I don't know why I bothered. *Of course* we were going to get caught. She didn't reply, just stared at the stage, eyes wide, her chest heaving with her deep breaths. I started to feel sick. Prickly and sick. Like I might throw up. I grasped her hand tightly. "Let's go," I said. "Let's leave."

She didn't reply. Her eyes looked glazed. "Fern," I said sharply. "Fern."

I'd caught her attention, and she turned her face towards me. I tried to plead with her with my eyes. "We can't. Let's go."

She smiled at me, a sad smile. The strange gleam was gone

from her eyes, and she just looked like my exhausted friend. My tired, sweet friend.

"I'm sorry, Rachel," she said. "I have to."

She squeezed my hand again, and my eyes filled with tears. She let go, and I tensed myself, ready to move with her. I had to do it with her. Beside her.

Beyond Fern I saw Edgar, and when our eyes met, he gave me a big, happy smile. "This is great," he said, but then Fern moved forward, and I fell into step beside her. Just before I looked away, I saw Edgar's smile vanish.

It all happened very quickly. Fern walked onto the stage, smiling. She moved fast, like a cat, towards the weapons rack. I followed. As I watched, she lifted a really big sword with a curved blade. I glanced back. The security guards were just standing there watching. I was confused by that. I dared a glance at Balthazar. He was grinning. I guess he thought this was cute or something.

I spun back to Fern just in time to see her swing the sword, burying it deep into Sid's shoulder. It sliced through his guitar strap on its way, causing the instrument to crash to the floor. The band abruptly stopped playing. I panicked. I lifted the battle-axe out of the rack. It was heavier than I had expected, and I brandished it with both hands, spinning back around.

Sid had fallen to his knees, his black shirt soaking wet with blood. Fern was now on her way to the other side of the stage, raising the sword over her head, towards the other guitarist, Ed. I couldn't believe that the security guards weren't reacting. The crowd, meanwhile, was roaring. I was stunned. *They think it's part of the show.*

Fern had driven the sword into Ed's stomach, letting out a scream as she did, and everything erupted into chaos. I saw Edgar's horrified expression, his mouth wide open in a shriek, and then the guards leapt into action. We were running out of time. I whirled, charging right at Balthazar.

"I'll cut your fucking arm off," I heard Fern scream hoarsely behind me at the guards. "Come onto this stage and I swear to god I will."

I faced Balthazar. Beneath us I heard a loud shuddering — the crowd was pushing at the barricade. There was a feeling rising in the air, a coppery taste in my mouth. I guess it was blood lust. I stared into his blue eyes. I saw fear in them, and it made me laugh out loud.

"Wait," he said, holding his hands out. "Put that down."

"Grow the fuck up," I said, the same words he'd spat at me back when this whole mess got started. "I thought you were sick of *boring girls*."

Something clicked into place for him, registering in his eyes. But it wasn't about me. It was a phrase he used often. Because even though he didn't remember that night, he knew exactly what I was talking about.

"I'm sorry," he said.

"Me too," I replied, and swung the axe as hard as I could.

Balthazar's head flew into the air. And then everything went insane.

My face hit the stage floor. Two security guards had tackled me. Their weight kept me pressed down. I was able to lift my head far enough to see Fern. She'd dropped the sword and was climbing the scaffolding on the front of the stage, her long white hair soaked with blood.

I screamed her name.

People speculate about what Fern intended to do on that scaffolding, why she jumped into the crowd. A lot of people seem to think that she was trying to escape. Crowd surf to freedom, or something ridiculous. But I knew what that crowd would do to her. And so did she. And when our eyes locked, me on the floor, her in the air, she smiled.

A word passed between us.

Goodbye.

I watched her fall. Watched the crowd swarm, bloodthirsty, ruthless. I heard Edgar's strangled scream. And I cried.

FIFTY-SIX

I ended up in a small room, staring at my blood-streaked reflection in the mirror that covered one wall, with a cop trying to talk to me, me crying all over my cigarettes because I couldn't believe what Fern had done to herself.

So now, here I am. My parents won't talk to me right now, and Melissa won't either. I'm hoping it's just because my parents won't let her, and not because she hates me. Socks and Edgar haven't spoken to me. The only people I really talk to are my ~~~~~~ We don't have much in common, but we get along okay, I guess.

I think back over the events of that night, you know, and I do that whole thing where I'm re-thinking everything I said. Like, when Balthazar said, "I'm sorry," I wish I'd said something witty. It's like when you're in an argument, or someone says something shitty to you in the street or something, your brain works overtime after the fact to give you something awesome you wish you'd said. I hadn't walked myself through the events before they happened, I hadn't given myself time to plan. I think that right up until Fern walked onstage, I didn't really believe we were going to go through with it.

It's a bummer. Colostomy Hag got to the point where things were picking up, and we'd all worked so hard to get there, and now it's nothing. The whole thing is spoiled. I'm sorry for Edgar. I'm sorry for Socks. The point was never to ruin anyone's life or waste anyone's time. The point was just revenge.

Sometimes I wish that I could have somehow stopped Fern from jumping into that crowd, even though I know there was no way back for her. But why did I feel there was a way back for me? Should I have jumped? Why do I feel like I can happily live with what I've done? Why do I feel such peace?

None of these questions are really meant to have answers. It's just the stuff that cycles around in my mind. I don't have that much else to do.

ACKNOWLEDGEMENTS

I'd like to thank Crissy, Michael, Erin, Jenna, Rachel, and everyone at ECW Press for thinking this was a good story, and for helping me get it into the best possible form; Nathaniel Radmacher for holding my heart and my hand; Jesse Grimaldi for being my number one and for catching a breeze with me; my father, Alex, and my mother, Louise, for supporting this and all my other ridiculous endeavours; my sister, Emily, who also sings and writes, inspires and supports me; Aimee Echo, Michelle Cosco, Ashley Costello, Ryann Donnelly, Kathleen Binder, Chelsea Davis, Dolores Lokas, Angela Jekums, and all the other women I have shared the stage and road with and learned so much from; everyone at Sonic for putting up with my insanity and always giving me a place to escape to; Rainbow, Mike, Jim, and Owen for filling me with both rage and love and redefining "family"; and Lance, because I wouldn't have written this without him. Thank you.

Published by ECW Press
665 Gerrard Street East, Toronto, Ontario, Canada M4M 1Y2
416-694-3348 / info@ecwpress.com

LIBRARY AND ARCHIVES CANADA CATALOGUING IN PUBLICATION

Taylor, Sara (Sara E.), author
        Boring girls / Sara Taylor.

Issued in print and electronic formats.
ISBN 978-1-77041-016-9 (pbk); ISBN 978-1-77090-685-3 (pdf)
ISBN 978-1-77090-686-0 (ePub)

        I. Title.

PS8639.A957B67 2015   C813'.6   C2014-907614-2
                                               C2014-907615-0

Editors for the press: Crissy Calhoun and Michael Holmes
Cover design: David Gee
Cover image: © Vizerskaya/iStockphoto
Author photo: GRANT MCRUER
Type: Rachel Ironstone
Printed and bound in Canada by Marquis Imprimeur   5   4   3   2   1

RECYCLED
Paper made from
recycled material
FSC
www.fsc.org   FSC® C103567

The publication of *Boring Girls* has been generously supported by the Canada Council
for the Arts, which last year invested $157 million to bring the arts to Canadians throughout
the country. We acknowledge the support of the Ontario Arts Council (OAC), an agency
of the Government of Ontario, which last year funded 1,793 individual artists and
and 1,076 organizations in 232 communities across Ontario for a total of $52.1 million.
We also acknowledge the financial support of the Government of Canada through the
Canada Book Fund for our publishing activities, and the contribution of the Government
of Ontario through the Ontario Book Publishing Tax Credit and the Ontario Media
Development Corporation.

GET THE EBOOK FREE!

At ECW Press, we want you to enjoy this book in whatever format you like, whenever you like. Leave your print book at home and take the eBook to go! Purchase the print edition and receive the eBook free. Just send an email to ebook@ecwpress.com and include:

- the book title
- the name of the store where you purchased it
- your receipt number
- your preference of file type:
  PDF or ePub?

A real person will respond to your email with your eBook attached. Thank you for supporting an independently owned Canadian publisher with your purchase!

31901056283775